A powerful and sweeping historical novel of love, loss, and hope, set against Australia's vast sugarcane fields in the turbulent days after World War II.

1948: Change has come to every corner of the globe—and Rosie Stanton, returning home to northern Queensland after serving the war effort in Brisbane, plans to rescue her family's foundering sugarcane farm with her unstoppable can-do spirit. Coming up against her father's old-world views, a farm worker undermining her success, and constant reminders of Rosie's brothers lost in the war, Rosie realizes she wants more from life and love—but at what cost?

Italian immigrant Tomas Conti arrives at a neighboring farm, and sparks fly as Rosie draws close to this enigmatic newcomer. When an enemy appears with evidence of Tomas's shocking past, long-held wartime hatreds rekindle . . . and an astounding family secret sets Rosie's world ablaze. At the dawn of a new era, Rosie must make her own destiny amid the ashes of yesterday—by following her heart.

Visit us at www.kensingtonbooks.com

Books by Alli Sinclair

Midnight Serenade
Under the Spanish Stars
Under the Parisian Sky
Burning Fields

Novella
Dreaming of Spain

Published by Kensington Publishing Corporation

Burning Fields

Alli Sinclair

LYRICAL PRESS
Kensington Publishing Corp.
www.kensingtonbooks.com

Lyrical Press books are published by
Kensington Publishing Corp. 119 West 40th Street New York, NY 10018

First Electronic Edition: November 2018
eISBN-13: 978-1-5161-0916-6
eISBN-10: 1-5161-0916-3

First Print Edition: November 2018
ISBN-13: 978-1-5161-0917-3
ISBN-10: 1-5161-0917-1

Printed in the United States of America

For my mum, Judy
Thank you for introducing me to the joy of reading and your unwavering
support in all that I do

Chapter 1

Rosie Stanton leant her forehead against the bus window and tried to convince herself she wasn't making the biggest mistake of her life. For twenty-five hours she'd bumped in and out of potholes on the bus ride from Brisbane to Piri River, the lush Queensland countryside keeping her company as doubt persisted in muscling in on her. Nineteen forty-eight should have been a year full of possibilities for Rosie, but now, after the unexpected collapse of her life in Brisbane, this post-war world was one of uncertainty. And now she was returning home to the town she'd avoided for three years.

Outside the window, sugarcane danced with the light breeze and fields stretched under an endless sky. The verdant landscape reminded her of an innocent childhood spent running through the fields, arms out wide, her brothers laughing and chasing. Time frayed memories but compounded heartache. Right now, all she could hope for was acceptance and understanding.

"Oh!" A male voice from the back of the bus made her turn around. A tall fellow with broad shoulders and beautiful olive skin stood in the aisle, wiping his navy-blue suit with a handkerchief. He directed a gentle smile at a young blonde mother who apologized profusely as she cradled her tiny baby. Judging by their polite interaction, they didn't know each other well.

"You can't sit there again." The distraught mother pointed at the seat next to her. "It will ruin your suit."

"It will wash, yes?" His thick accent made Rosie pay more attention.

"I'm so sorry," the mother said, "but the smell of baby vomit won't go away easily." The child started crying and she held him close, making shushing noises, however her heightened state of agitation made the baby cry louder.

"Please." He took the baby in his arms and sang quietly. Rosie couldn't make out the words, but they were possibly Italian, a language she often heard in Piri River when workers came into town. The baby stopped fussing and gazed at the man, fascinated.

The mother reached for a small blanket and quickly wiped herself and the seat beside her. She stopped to take a few deep breaths and pushed a chunk of hair out of her eyes. "Thank you."

The man gave a quick nod before passing the dozing baby back to her. He glanced at the seat. "Perhaps I should move."

"It might be a good idea. And again, I'm so sorry."

The man smiled, tipped his hat and grabbed a battered leather bag from the overhead rack. He looked around the crowded bus, his eyes finally resting on the only spare seat—next to Rosie.

She motioned for him to sit next to her. He made his way down the aisle, apologizing every time the bus went over a bump and he accidently hit someone with his bag. A trail of people were left rubbing their arms or heads, but no one seemed to mind.

The fellow, who appeared to be around thirty, reached Rosie, and went to place his bag in the jam-packed overhead rack. So, he sat down, cumbersome bag on his lap, and positioned himself so half his body was in the aisle and not encroaching on her territory. Despite his efforts, the stench of baby vomit assailed her nostrils.

Rosie turned to face him and noticed the verandah of black lashes accentuating the gold flecks in his brown eyes. His dark, wavy hair framed a handsome face with a strong jawline and an intriguing scar under his eye. "That was very nice what you did back there."

"It is what any decent person would do."

"Perhaps." Her time in Brisbane had proven that people were capable of many things, and not always good.

They fell into silence and Rosie returned to staring out the window, surprised at how much she'd missed the familiar houses, the smooth bark of the gum trees, the sun dancing on Piri River as it snaked through the valleys and mountains.

The rhythm of the bumping bus coupled with the warmth of the setting sun caused Rosie's eyelids to close. She fought for them to stay open, but bus fumes, the smell of baby vomit and the stifling air inside the vehicle had a numbing effect.

Brakes screeched and Rosie was propelled forward. An arm shot across her body but it didn't stop her head from smashing against the metal frame of the seat in front. The bus driver let fly with expletives that would make a sailor blush.

Rosie jerked back with a thud against the seat.

"Jeez." She rubbed her skull and cursed the ache that now pulsed.

"You are all right?"

"I…" A sharp pain shot behind her eyes but disappeared quickly. "I'll be fine. What happened? Why did we brake?"

He shrugged. "An animal? Maybe a kangaroo? Emu? Crocodile? Kookaburra?"

She let out a friendly laugh. "It's good to see you know Australian animals. Did we hit it?"

"No."

"That's lucky." Now fully awake, her inquisitive side surfaced. "You're not from around here, are you?"

"I will be."

The driver crunched the gears and the bus took off again, spewing more fumes into the cabin. She screwed her nose up and shook her head.

The man broke into a gentle smile and held out his hand to shake hers. When she touched his skin, the softness surprised her—no callouses or cuts like the men who worked the fields. "I am Tomas of Palermo by way of Roma, and soon to be of Piri River."

"Piri River?" Her voice came out an octave higher.

"You know of this place?"

"Uh…yes. It's where I live. Lived."

"It is not your home anymore?" he asked.

"It is. Kind of." Frankly, she had no idea.

"Oh?"

"I grew up in Piri River but I moved away a few years ago." Rosie didn't mention the reason she originally left was because of her post with the Australian Women's Army Service as it was not a topic she felt comfortable discussing with someone of European heritage. During the war, Italians in Australia had been sent to internment camps and even though Italy had changed sides and became an ally, it was still a contentious subject for many people.

"You have not decided if you are staying or going? Do you not like the country?" he asked.

"I love it, but…" His eyes locked on hers while she tried to formulate an answer. "But things with my family are complicated."

"All families are complicated, no? We are, after all, many personalities thrown together."

"True."

"May I ask your name?" He leant forward then quickly moved back. "I am sorry for the smell."

"It's fine, really." Though her churning stomach told her otherwise. "I'm Rosie Stanton."

"Is Rosie short for something? I hear Australians like to shorten names."

"I'm Rosalie, but everyone calls me Rosie."

When he smiled, it went all the way to his eyes. "To me, you look like Rosalie."

"I do?" She laughed. "I won't argue if you wish to call me Rosalie."

Rosie had never liked the long version of her name, though there was something magical about the way it rolled off Tomas's tongue.

"Piri River is a long way from Palermo and Rome," she said. "What on earth brings you here?"

"Family." His lips kicked up at the corners.

"How long have they been there?"

"Four hundred and ninety-eight days."

"But you're not counting," she joked, then wondered if her humor might get lost with the cultural difference.

"I have missed my family very much," Tomas said. The fading light fell on the small half-moon scar under his eye. Was it from the war? "I have heard Piri River is beautiful. My nonna always tells me about the fresh fruit, the blue skies, the smell of the rain after a long hot day…" Tomas gazed out the window, his fingers drumming against his bag.

The driver turned on the headlights as they entered Piri River proper. Reg's Pub had closed for the evening, the dark green weatherboard and black shiny doors a welcome sight. Next to the pub, O'Reilly's Service Station remained eerily quiet, the familiar red and yellow of the Golden Fleece logo still visible in the darkness. Across the road, a faint light could be seen burning at the back of Mitchell's Bakery, where her old school friend Laney was no doubt toiling over the hot ovens preparing fresh bread for the next morning.

The bus bumped as it drove over the train line that led to the sugarcane mill, then the vehicle came to a shuddering stop. The doors swung open and Tomas stood and reached for the rack overhead. "May I assist with your baggage?"

She pointed at her new suitcase. He handed it to her and she quietly said, "Thank you."

As she exited the bus she quickly looked back to make sure she hadn't forgotten anything. Tomas alighted just after her.

Clutching her suitcase, Rosie suddenly felt self-conscious in her fashionable floral dress, hat and gloves. In Brisbane, she'd felt perfectly at home in this attire, but now, returning to the town where fashion was a luxury and practicality a must, Rosie felt like a fish out of water.

The bus sputtered into life and left a trail of dust as it continued its journey north. Rosie rested her bag on the ground as she stretched her arms, legs and back. She hadn't realized how much she'd missed the humidity of northern Queensland. There was something comforting in the way the warm, damp air wrapped around her, like an extra layer, keeping her safe.

"Well, I'd best be off," she said, mentally preparing herself for the long traipse to the farm.

"There is no one here to meet you?"

"No, and I'm absolutely fine with that." She picked up her bag and adjusted it to distribute the weight more evenly.

Tomas wore a slightly puzzled expression as his gaze shifted in various directions.

"Do you know where you're headed?" she asked.

"East?" He looked up and down the dark street.

"It's that way," she pointed in the direction of the cinema owned by the Fitzpatricks.

Tomas's eyes stayed fixed on the art deco cinema painted in blue and yellow, sporting rounded corners. "It is beautiful."

"It sure is. It was designed by a female architect in the 1920s. People travel for miles to watch movies here. It's quite the experience."

"It does not look like the cinema of a small town."

"Which is what makes it so special."

Bringing his focus back to Rosie, Tomas asked, "Which direction are you walking?"

"East." Rosie smiled at Tomas, who looked so out of place in this small, rural town. "I guess we're stuck with each other a bit longer."

"I do not mind this predicament," he said, a cheeky glint in his eye.

"You might not be saying that when you realize how far we have to walk. Come on, we might as well get started." She nudged him playfully with her elbow, then chastised herself for the familiarity. He didn't seem to mind, though, because he lightly nudged her back as they set off down the deserted road.

Tomas reached for her suitcase. She shook her head. "It's fine, thank you. I can carry it."

"I have no doubt you can, but please, let me do this. It is my way to say *grazie*."

"*Grazie*." She let it roll off her tongue. "So, is Sicily an Italian province?"

"It is, but in Sicily we have our own language. Other Italians find us difficult to understand, though we have no problem understanding them." Tomas smiled, apparently happy to take on the role of educator.

"I had no idea," she said, feeling less worldly than she wanted. She'd always taken an interest in other cultures, but hadn't quite made it to studying the nuances of Italy and its provinces. Growing up on her farm, Tulpil, she'd been surrounded by an array of nationalities—Pacific Islanders, South Africans, Polish and Czech—and her ear for languages meant she had a wide vocabulary that made conversing with the workers easy and enjoyable. Often, her father would ask her to translate. At least he had trusted her with that.

"Please." He motioned for the suitcase once more, and she reluctantly handed it over.

"Thank you."

Tomas slowed his pace to match Rosie's. She couldn't help sneaking furtive glances at her companion.

When they neared Mrs. Daw's house, Rosie's ears rang with a familiar, piercing sound.

"What is that?" Tomas furrowed his brows and looked skyward.

"Fruit bats." She pointed at the mango tree in the front yard. "They're sucking nectar from the fruit."

"They are very noisy."

"That's how they see."

Tomas stopped and placed the cases on either side of his feet. "How?"

"Bats see by echolocation." She took in his blank stare. "They use high-frequency noises to locate objects around them as the sound bounces off the object."

"They sound like children arguing," said Tomas.

Rosie laughed. "Yes, they do." She cocked her head in the direction of east. "We should get going."

They left the screeching bats and the scent of mangos behind as they travelled farther into the night.

"What's the name of the farm you're going to?" Rosie asked. "Do all your family work there?"

Tomas gave a small, kind laugh. "In a way."

"Huh?" It felt good to walk, but now that they'd left the town and bitumen road behind them, her high heels found it hard going on the slippery gravel.

"My family own a property."

"Is that why you're here now, to help them run it?"

"Yes." He adjusted the suitcases in each hand.

"I can carry mine, really."

"No, no. I can do this. However, I am not sure where I am carrying this to."

"Good point," she said. "My family's farm is called Tulpil."

"I like this name. What does it mean?"

"The Yirrganydji people." She glanced over and saw the blank look in his eyes. "Aboriginal—"

"Ah, yes."

"Yirrganydji is the name of the people originally from this region. When my great-great-grandfather bought land to set up his sugarcane farm, it was overrun by wallabies. And the Yirrganydji name for wallabies is…" She waited for him to answer.

"Tulpil!"

"Spot on," she said. "Piri is also an Aboriginal name."

"This means?"

"Fire."

"Fire river?" He arched an eyebrow, his delight for learning more about his adopted home shining through.

"We need the river to irrigate the sugarcane and we need to burn the cane to get rid of the debris and prepare the fields for the next season. Fire and water play a huge role in farming sugarcane."

"Ah." He nodded. "So, the name of the town relates to fire *and* water."

"Exactly."

He tilted his head to the side. "Your hair is the color of fire."

"Yes." She self-consciously patted it into place. Clearing her throat, she said, "I'm guessing you've not had any experience in sugarcane farming."

He grinned. "This is correct."

"How did your family end up here?"

Tomas hesitated, as if debating whether he should impart the information. Was she being too nosy?

After a while, he said, "My cousins moved to Australia many years ago. They make wine in New South Wales and they told us the sugarcane industry is strong. So, my family came to Australia and bought the property." Tomas tilted his head to the side. "You like to ask many questions. Maybe you are part Sicilian." He laughed and she joined in.

"Nope, I'm Aussie, one hundred percent. Well, my mother's family are French and my father's are from good Ol' Blighty."

Again, with the questioning eyebrow.

"Blighty—England."

He let out a long breath. "It appears I have much to learn."

Her lips twitched. "It appears so."

The town was now far behind. A wisp of clouds drifted across the blue-black sky, obscuring the stars, though the moon retained its brilliance, lighting the way along the rocky road.

Now that she'd started talking, she didn't feel like stopping and the self-conscious feeling began to fade. "You don't need to worry about learning everything about sugarcane in your first five minutes here, I'm sure your family have plenty of knowledge they'll share with you."

"My family are not unaccustomed to working the land. They farmed olives and oranges."

Images of lush green trees with bright orange orbs filled Rosie's mind and she imagined a zesty citrus scent surrounding her.

"My great-grandparents did the farming; my parents and grandparents are people of the city."

She remembered being surprised at Tomas's smooth skin when they'd first shaken hands. "You're not a farmer, either, are you?"

He shook his head. "No, but it is now my future."

"What did you used to do?"

"I am an engineer by schooling, then I…" He drew his lips into a tight line. "I am an engineer."

She desperately wanted to ask more questions, but she suspected Tomas didn't like to be rushed or pressured. *Slowly, slowly, Rosie.*

The clouds now obscured the moon and she stepped around a large pothole and motioned for Tomas to do the same in case he hadn't seen it. His feet hit a loose patch of stones on the downhill descent and he lost balance but regained it quickly.

"Are you all right?"

"I am good," he said, holding his composure.

They walked for a while longer and, once more, she couldn't help herself. "What's the name of the property your family own?"

"Il Sunnu. It means The Dream."

"Oh." She stopped in her tracks. Why hadn't she figured this out earlier?

"What is wrong?" Tomas stopped. The bags swung against his legs.

"Nothing," she said quickly. "Nothing at all."

"It does not appear to be nothing."

Rosie searched the darkness. For what, she wasn't sure. "I'm just surprised."

"Surprised immigrants have enough money to buy a farm?" His voice held an edge.

"No." She kept her tone even. "I'm just saying I didn't get the connection. So, your surname must be Conti."

"It is."

Trying to ease the strange tension that seemed to appear out of nowhere, she said, "I used to play at your property a lot when I was little. The owners had children the same age as me and my…" She let it trail away.

"Your?"

"It doesn't matter," she said quickly.

"You have met my family?" Tomas sounded like he, too, was grappling to steady their conversation.

"No, I've been away."

"Oh, yes, of course."

From her mother's letters, Rosie knew her parents hadn't made any effort in getting to know the Contis, which frustrated Rosie immensely. She'd never been able to comprehend her father's peculiar attitude toward Italians. Then again, she hadn't understood much about her father these past few years.

They continued down the road, their steps in perfect sync.

"I am sorry for my sensitive reaction to your question about my family. Because I am from Sicily, I have found some of your countrymen think I am uneducated and poor and of no value."

"That's horrible."

Tomas shrugged. "This is a new world for me and, in time, I will adjust."

"I have no doubt you will. People can be strange and dreadfully racist. I'm sorry you've experienced it." She took a deep breath, inhaling the scent of eucalyptus trees. It smelt like…home.

"Do not worry, it takes all kinds to make the world spin, yes? Besides, a little bit of the racism is nothing compared to…" He shook his head as if to dispel a painful memory.

"Compared to?" she asked, taking small comfort that she wasn't the only one who started sentences then changed her mind.

"Nothing, compared to nothing." Tomas quickened his pace, as if trying to escape whatever memory pursued him.

Rosie struggled to keep up, her heels making the going precarious.

"Life must have been very hard in Italy," she said, then immediately regretted it. Obviously, life had been hard. Italy not only had to contend with the world war, but it had to endure its own civil war at the same time. "Sorry."

"For?"

"Sorry for prying," she said.

"I believe there are some topics that are better left alone."

His firm tone unsettled her, but his response was justified. War was a subject fraught with heavy emotions that often catapulted people into memories they'd rather forget.

"You're right." Keen to change the topic, she said, "Your English is very good."

This time, Tomas met her comment with a smile. "Thank you. My nonna taught me. She loves languages. She knows English, Spanish and French. And, of course, Sicilian and Italian."

Rosie could make out the lights of the Russell house in the distance. *Not far now.* A sliver of disappointment and apprehension ran through her.

"Like the Spanish and Portuguese," Tomas brought her back into the moment, "the Italian language changes depending on the region. Sicily is my home..." He coughed. "My *old* home and I adapted to Italian when I lived in Rome... I am a chameleon, one might say."

As he spoke, Rosie concentrated on the way his face lit up when he spoke of his home country. Why would he leave Italy, a country he clearly loved with all his heart?

"Where did your nonna learn all these languages?" she asked.

"Textbooks. Speaking with people who had moved to our country. She would speak with Señor Alves from Spain for many hours, asking him different Spanish words and phrases. Nonna would do the same with Mademoiselle Eloise to learn French. My grandmother believed our city was a classroom."

"Oh, I love that. She sounds like a good egg."

"Good egg?" He raised a questioning eyebrow.

Her light laughter danced through the warm evening. "A good egg means the person is special."

He nodded slowly, as if giving this new knowledge time to sink in. "Australians like to make up these sayings, yes?"

"We do, indeed."

"My nonna would enjoy this. Me too." He paused. "I hope one day you meet her."

Rosie hesitated ever-so-slightly and reminded herself that her parents should not force their opinions on her. "I would like that very much."

They climbed the last hill and her calves burned, even though she wasn't the one lugging two large bags.

They reached the crest and Rosie stopped and looked up at the sky. The clouds had floated past the moon, and, once more, a pale glow embraced the sugarcane fields. Directly in front of her was Tomas's place and farther away, Tulpil. An empty feeling grew in the pit of her stomach about the hard conversations to come, while shivers of excitement danced across her skin as she realized how happy she was to see her childhood home.

Rosie pointed at the newly renovated white Queenslander set far back from the road. "That's your place."

"Wow." Tomas placed the bags gently next to him.

"It's rather spectacular, huh?" The previous owners had always taken pride in the old house, but it had descended into disrepair when the patriarch had fallen ill a few years ago. By the looks of the fresh paintwork, Tomas's family had injected some much-needed love into the place. "Welcome to your new home."

Tomas took in the view before him. "It is nothing like I imagined."

"Better or worse?"

"I...I am not sure." He kept his eyes trained on the house. "It is very different to my place in Palermo. Back there, we only had a courtyard. This is a whole new world. So many possibilities."

Tomas locked eyes with her, and, for a precious moment in time, all her worries slipped away as they stood under a star-studded sky.

"I must go." Tomas took a deep breath, picked up his bag and asked, "Would you like me to accompany you to your house?"

She shook her head. "That's very sweet of you, but I'm a big girl. Go see your family, I'm sure they will be happy to see you."

His grin was wide. "I will tell you a secret."

"All right."

"I did not tell them of my arrival."

"They're going to be shocked when they see you!"

"I think they will, yes." He held out his hand, leant forward and kissed her on the cheek. Her face and neck flooded with heat and he pulled away. "I am sorry! Now I am in Australia, maybe I should forget this custom."

Rosie tried to catch her breath, surprised by how much she liked him being near. "Don't ever lose that custom, Tomas. It's who you are."

"*Grazie.*" He wrapped his hands around hers and gave them a gentle squeeze. Tomas held on longer than was necessary. "*Ciao*, Rosalie Stanton."

"*Ciao*, Tomas Conti." Her cheeks ached from smiling.

He slowly let go of her hand, grabbed his bag and took off in the direction of Il Sunnu.

Picking up her suitcase, Rosie headed toward home and traipsed up the long gravel driveway. Visions of playing chasey with her younger brothers pulled at her heartstrings, weighing her down with sadness. She missed

Alex, with his gangly limbs, wicked sense of humor and rebelliousness, just as much as she missed Geoffrey's reserved nature and his passion for the family farm and business.

Rosie looked up at the light shining through the living room window. Across the hall, her brothers' bedroom remained in darkness. What she wouldn't give to once more be in that room, snuggled with her brothers and telling scary stories by candlelight.

Inhaling deeply, she took the last few steps up to the front door and gripped the handle.

Chapter 2

Rosie used her hip to nudge open the heavy wooden door of her father's office. After arriving so late the night before, she'd been tired and had lost the nerve to start the conversation they needed to have. Her mother, and even her father, had been so happy to see her that she didn't have the heart to burst their bubble—yet. Instead, she'd gone to bed and spent the night tossing and turning, wondering how the events of the next day would play out. There was no doubt she'd be met with resistance, but Rosie had dealt with that for many years.

Interspersed between the building anxiety, Rosie had allowed her mind to replay her meeting with Tomas. He intrigued her immensely; she loved that Tomas Conti felt like a welcome sea breeze on a stifling hot day.

Stepping into the room, Rosie balanced the tray in her hands as she struggled to keep the crockery and steaming pot of tea upright. Her father didn't acknowledge her presence until she laid the tray on the battered desk that had sat in this room for three generations.

"I thought this might help." She poured the tea in his favorite china cup—the exact one her great-grandfather used to drink from.

"Not even a stiff drink…" He leant forward and rubbed his forehead.

"A stiff drink?"

"What?" He looked up at her, as if finally registering she was there.

"You said, 'Not even a stiff drink…'"

"It doesn't matter." He shook his head and returned to the pile of paperwork that now sat on his desk instead of in the wooden crates where they'd been stashed for the past year. "This never ends."

Rosie stood on tiptoe and studied the calculations scribbled on a scrap piece of paper. A few figures were way off.

"I could do them for you." She offered a small plate of Anzac biscuits fresh from the oven. The aroma overshadowed the faint musty smell of the papers.

"Thanks, Rosie, but it's complicated. Why don't you go help your mother make lunch?"

"But I…" Her father, John, stared at her over the rim of his glasses and she pursed her lips. Arguing would not get her anywhere. Instead, Rosie picked up the tray and moved toward the door, her heels clacking against the wooden floorboards. An unfamiliar ripple of annoyance travelled through her and before she could stop herself, she turned and faced her father, who was once again hunched over the tower of paperwork. "Is the co-op payment up to date? Because if it is then it's not going to cover July. But if you move the excess from June and take the earnings from May then it all should balance nicely."

Her father drew his brows together and mumbled, his eyes fixed on the numbers in front of him. She closed the door quietly, satisfied she'd had a say, even if it irritated him. Heaviness wrapped around her heart as images of herself as a child with her father flashed before her. It had been so easy when she was a young girl, cocooned in love as they'd sat at the kitchen table, solving mathematics problems for entertainment. In the past he'd encouraged her ability, offered her praise, but when she'd grown into a teenager and showed interest in doing the farm's books, he'd backed off as if she had the plague.

Rosie held the tray as she stood in the hall and studied her most treasured family photo. She'd been eleven at the time and her brothers considerably younger. A photographer had been travelling from town to town, and, as the family didn't possess a camera, Rosie's mother had insisted on taking advantage of the opportunity. She'd used the extra money she'd saved from the household budget and the family had spent a day preparing, with Rosie's mother fussing over everything from a crooked collar on one of the boys' shirts to a stray curl of Rosie's. The photo had been taken in a heartbeat, but the memory stayed forever. She missed those days when her family had felt safe, when war hadn't ripped them apart.

Cecile, Rosie's mother, looked up from the wooden bench, a streak of flour running from her face and into her strawberry-blonde hair. Her mother's grace seemed better suited to American glamour magazines than the harshness of the Australian landscape.

"What's wrong?" asked her mother.

Rosie pointed toward the office down the hallway. "He's struggling. I could do it in a quarter of the time and with way less stress."

"I know." Her mother rubbed her hands on the towel and placed it on the counter. The sun streamed through the open window, highlighting small clouds of flour floating above the dough. "He's as pig headed as your grandfather and just like your brothers are...were..." Her mother bit her lip.

Rosie wrapped an arm around her mother's bony shoulders and pulled her close. Seeing her struggling only reinforced Rosie's decision to return to Tulpil. Although she couldn't pinpoint exactly what it was, Rosie had sensed something in her mother's letters that implied life at Tulpil was still very difficult, and when Rosie had arrived, she could feel a heavy melancholy permeating the house. But, as expected, her father and mother pretended all was fine in their world.

"Mum, we don't know if Alex is really gone."

"He's been missing too long." Her mother sniffed. "We've already lost Geoffrey."

"You believe in miracles, right?" Rosie gently moved back, placed her hands on her mother's shoulders and looked directly into her eyes.

Her mother gave a reluctant nod.

"Then let's not give up hope for Alex."

"I just..." Her mother choked on a sob.

"I know." As time passed, the likelihood of finding out what had happened to her brother dwindled to nothing more than a sliver of hope. All they knew was that as a member of the Royal Australian Air Force, he'd been flying with Britain's Royal Air Force bombers when they liberated parts of western Europe. He'd been involved in the bombing of Dresden in Germany in 1945. The authorities had said he'd returned safely and no one had seen or heard from him since. Rosie refused to think the RAAF had made a mistake, but as time slipped by, hope faded. If he had survived, why wasn't he at Tulpil right now, teasing Rosie and making her laugh?

Rosie hugged her mother tighter, then gestured for her to take a seat at the kitchen table. "I'll make you a cuppa, then I'll finish making lunch."

"But—"

"No arguments." She followed this with a smile.

"Thank you, my sweet girl. I'm so glad you've come to visit. How long will you be staying?"

"There's...uh...something I need to talk to you about."

Rosie's mother clutched her fist over her heart. "Oh no. I thought you looked pale. And you've lost weight."

Rosie sat on the chair opposite and held her mother's hands. "Mum, I'm fine. I just want to stay at Tulpil for a while."

"What have you done?"

"I haven't done anything!" Straight to it being Rosie's fault. No surprises there. "As much as I love Brisbane, I've missed the country. I've missed you and Dad."

Her mother narrowed her eyes, shoved her hand in her apron pocket and clutched something small. "You haven't been at your job long enough to take leave."

Rosie got up and returned to making tea, hoping her mother wouldn't pry any further. Although it wouldn't last long as eventually Rosie would have to come clean, though if she could avoid the subject for as long as possible…. Maybe now was the time to mention the other reason for her unannounced arrival at Tulpil.

Rosie poured the steaming water into the pot and let it steep. She took a deep breath. "Mum, I'm concerned."

"About?"

"About Dad. He's not getting any younger. Neither of you are." She paused, waiting for her mother to object, but instead she was met with silence. "I love you both dearly and I worry. So, I was thinking that I should stay here—indefinitely. I can help Dad with the books, go into the field if we need more hands on deck—"

"Rosie, you know what the answer is."

"From what you've mentioned in the letters, it's been a hard couple of years and I've been away so long, it would be nice to help out. Besides, you told me he'd been to the doctor a few times, and Dad never goes to the doctor."

"Just regular checkups, sweetheart," her mother said quickly.

"He wouldn't go unless something was serious."

Her mother stared out the window where the eucalyptus trees rustled in the light breeze, sending a magnificent, fresh scent into the kitchen. "You have no reason to worry."

Heavy footfalls down the hallway signaled the arrival of her father. He stood in the doorway, his large frame filling most of the space. Clearing his throat, he glanced at the papers in his hand then at Rosie. "You were right."

"About?" She knew exactly what he meant.

"About the accounting." His cheeks flushed red. "I am sorry for not listening."

Rosie didn't dare look at her mother as she suspected she was thinking the same—hell had frozen over.

"Thank you, Dad." She twisted her lips and debated whether to push the envelope further. "Let me do the accounts for you. There are so many other things you need to do and as numbers are my strong point—"

"No, Rosie."

"Dad, please. You can go over it when I'm done to ease your mind." She wiped her hands on the tea towel.

Her father opened his mouth then closed it quickly. Frowning, he ran a weathered hand across the back of his neck.

"Thank you, but no." His chest rose and fell as he took a deep breath. "Bartel has already been helping me with keeping on top of the men's tallies and paying suppliers."

Bartel, the South African foreman, had been her father's right-hand man for almost a decade. Rosie's father had always kept the finances to himself, stating he didn't want anyone to know the family's financial business. The fact her father was willing to hand over the accounts to Bartel told her what she'd already suspected—her father wasn't coping with the workload any more.

"Why Bartel?" she asked.

"I trust him." Her father held up his hand, "It's not that I don't trust you, Rosie, it's just that this is not the work of women."

Determination set Rosie's jaw hard as she willed the tide of rising anger to wash away.

It was no use.

"This 'women's work' and 'men's work' is ridiculous. If someone is capable of doing a job, it shouldn't matter what gender they are."

"Rosie—"

"The government was more than happy to employ women—for less wages—during the war to do 'men's work,' yet as soon as the war was over we were expected to go back to our kitchens and secretarial pools."

She glanced at her mother, whose lips were drawn into a thin line. "You know this isn't a reflection on you, Mum."

"I'm happy doing what I'm doing. I know you don't want the same. You've lived a different life to me, Rosie. And yours is only just beginning."

Her father tilted his head back and stared at the ceiling. Finally, he looked directly at Rosie. "The farm is no place for you. I love having you here, but your life is in Brisbane."

"Why are you both pushing me away?"

"Why do you want to stay here when you've made your life elsewhere?" he asked. "Farm life is not for everyone."

Ever since she could remember, her father had told anyone who'd listen how farming kept this country going, that city folk would starve without farmers. Her father had trained his children—including Rosie—in working on the cane farm. Why would he turn his back on her now?

She straightened her spine. "I have skills—really good mechanical skills—that I could use around here. Times are changing, Dad. Society's expectations are changing."

"Look"—her father stepped forward, his expression soft once more— "I want you to be happy, Rosie, but there is no reason for you to get involved with the business. You're already twenty-seven and no man wants a woman who—"

"Uses her mind? Knows how to fix a tractor?"

"Rosie…" He let out a long-suffering sigh.

"Seriously, Dad, What's the problem?"

He ran his fingers through his thinning hair and closed his eyes briefly. The late afternoon sun shining through the kitchen window highlighted his ruddy complexion where the lines had multiplied and grown deeper over the past few years. "I'm not saying no to upset you. I am the first person to admit you have a talent with numbers. It's just that you'd be surrounded by men all day and—"

"Why would it be any different? I've known a lot of the workers since I was a kid."

"But you'd be working with people outside Tulpil who don't treat women with respect. This world is not as cheery as you believe it to be, and I don't want your heart broken because of it."

"I am not naïve, Dad," she said quietly. "If it was Geoffrey or Alex who wanted…" She let the words trail off, appalled at bringing her brothers into the argument. Rosie looked at her parents, a cloud of sadness gathering in the kitchen. "I'm sorry, I shouldn't have…"

"We all miss them," said her mother.

"I'm going to the office." Rosie's father turned on his heels and strode out the room, his heavy boots echoing down the hallway. When he slammed the door, the plates on the kitchen wall rattled.

Rosie stared at her mother, who cradled her teacup in her hands.

"You have nothing to say?" Rosie asked.

"I wish you wouldn't push him like you do." Her mother took a sip from the porcelain cup.

"Why are you so afraid to stand up to him?"

"I'm not, honey." She placed the cup on the saucer. "I just know how to play my cards. It would serve you well to learn the same."

Exhausted, Rosie went over to the bench and started shelling the peas, angrily tossing the tiny green balls into the bowl. Perhaps if she told her parents why she was so keen to put distance between her and Brisbane…. No. She could barely admit it to herself, let alone her parents.

Rosie needed to find a way to stay at Tulpil—somehow. As her beloved grandmother had always been fond of saying, "Work hard, love honestly, and trust the world will steer you in the direction you need to go."

Rosie now knew the direction she was headed, and hoped she could break through the obstacles.

Chapter 3

Tomas Conti strode up the narrow cobblestoned street of Sicily's capital, Palermo, under the cover of darkness. It had been eight hours since notification of the meeting and every single minute since then had dragged by as if he had a ball and chain around his ankle. This had been his normal state since the war had started. For a country that was once prosperous, it had tumbled into tragic ruin with too many countrymen witnessing suffering and death—more than anyone should experience in five lifetimes.

Mussolini and his fascist government now held the good people of Italy hostage. Since the creation of the Axis Powers, Mussolini's control had generated class discrimination, politics divided friends, obliterated trust, and left a trail of starving families in its wake. Informants, bullying fascists, and the deaths of innocent people created a chaotic world where hope didn't exist and the future was darker than the night sky.

Today, though, Tomas planned to do something about it.

Up ahead, he noticed two of Mussolini's soldiers talking with a couple of Germans on the street corner. They smoked cigarettes, guns casually draped over their shoulders—like no one would dare challenge them—despite Palermo being a city crippled by rising tensions. Tomas kept his head down and walked past the men.

"Where are you going?" barked the Italian soldier.

Tomas's heart bashed against his chest and he tried to remain composed. There was no possible way they could know his plans, but it wouldn't stop them harassing him. "I am visiting my friend who is ill."

"Papers." The soldier held out his hand.

Tomas obediently reached for his identification papers and gave them to the soldier, who scrutinized them then gave them to his colleague, who did the same. A thin layer of sweat coated Tomas's body and he prayed they didn't look at him too closely. Tomas had been stopped countless times since Mussolini's men had taken up residence and he'd gotten used to it, but today was very different and he didn't trust his body not to give him away.

"Address," said the soldier.

"It is on there." Tomas pointed to the papers.

"Where you are going, you imbecile," spat out the other Italian soldier. The Germans looked on, amusement in their eyes.

"Via Napoli, 39." The lie fell from his mouth with ease. Panic set in a moment later. What if they escorted him to make sure? He'd just given them the address of his dentist.

The two Italian soldiers commenced a hushed discussion, casting furtive glances at Tomas, whose body was in flight mode. Only last week he'd lost his friend, Antonio Rosso, who'd been shot for lying to a soldier.

Tomas studied the men. Although there were four of them and they were armed, he was a few inches taller. His long legs would give him a distinct advantage should he need to run, as long as he made the break before they drew weapons.

The soldier shoved the papers at Tomas, who took them and stuffed them back in his jacket pocket.

"On your way."

Without hesitation, he took off down the street, turned a corner and headed for Via Napoli, 39. He ducked in the doorway and surreptitiously looked for anyone following. Convinced he hadn't been tailed, Tomas set off and quickly walked the eight blocks to his original destination. He turned left into an alley, the stench of stale pee and rotting rubbish assailing his nostrils. The once-pristine streets had become rubbish dumps as the lives of people crumbled and terror ruled.

Arriving at a bottle-green door at the end of a dead-end alley, Tomas halted.

Taking a deep breath, he raised his hand and rapped out the series of knocks he'd been given. Paint peeled away from the door and stuck to his knuckles.

Silence.

Should he wait longer before knocking again? Or had he gotten the place wrong?

Raising his hand to knock once more, he stopped when a piece of wood slid to the side, revealing a square hole in the middle of the door. A pair of unblinking eyes stared back.

Tomas gave a nervous cough. "It is an honor—"

The mystery person held up his hand. A moment later the lock clicked and the door opened wide enough for Tomas to slip through. The octogenarian motioned for Tomas to follow. They travelled dark halls, the old man hunched over and leaning heavily on his walking stick. Tomas shortened his steps so he didn't overtake his shuffling guide. They took a series of twists and turns and Tomas marveled at how a seemingly unobtrusive structure now housed a band of individuals willing to put their lives on the line to change the fate of their country.

The old man stopped outside one of the many closed doors and quietly pushed it open, signaling Tomas to step through. Tomas did so and waited impatiently for his eyes to adjust to the muted light of the candles. Before him stood Bruno Abato. Aside from the bushy eyebrows and receding hairline, he still looked very much like he did when he and Tomas were friends in their teens: small and thin, with an oval face and a penetrating gaze. After Abato and his family suddenly left Palermo years ago, Tomas had often thought of his friend, his worry increasing after he'd heard the Abato family had lost money from poor investments in Milan. For the first few years Tomas had tried to find him but, until now, Abato had proved elusive. The nervous teen who used to rely on Tomas as protector had long gone. Before Tomas stood a man feared by many and sought by others because of the hefty price on his head.

Tomas stepped forward to shake his hand. Instead, Abato enveloped him in an embrace and slapped him on the back.

"It is good to see you," said Abato, his voice deeper than Tomas recalled. The tailored clothes that Abato once wore—just like Tomas and the rest of the moneyed folks of Palermo—had been replaced by a khaki shirt and trousers. The material was faded but immaculately pressed.

"It is good to see you, too." Tomas's eyes drifted to the spare chair in front of Abato's desk. Though his legs ached after the long trek on foot across the city, he didn't have the gall to ask for a seat. Abato's greeting may have been warm, however too much time had passed to rest on the affections of a friendship from the past. Besides, he'd heard about Abato's penchant for fighting doggedly and being tough on his men. Sitting because of tired legs would not help Tomas's convince Abato he needed him.

Abato sat, rested his feet on the desk and lit a cigarette.

"I can't believe it's been over fifteen years—"

"Let's not get into reminiscing, Conti. What I want to know is why you want to join the cause. You've never been political."

"Neither have you." Tomas instantly regretted saying it. Just because they were once familiar didn't mean they could be now. He cleared his throat. "War changes everyone. The pain and suffering caused by this dictatorial regime will continue if we don't do something to end it."

Abato took a long drag. Acrid smoke wafted in tufts above his head. "That's a fair point."

Tomas relaxed his shoulders ever so slightly.

"Just because you want to join us doesn't mean we'll have you."

"I have skills you need. Remember my grandfather was an expert marksman? He taught me everything I know."

Abato butted the cigarette on the edge of the battered desk. He lit another, but didn't offer one to Tomas. Once they'd shared apples, pastries and milk during afternoon snacks at each other's houses. Hell, they'd even stolen sweets from the corner shop together. If truth be told, though, Abato did the stealing and Tomas participated in the eating.

"Listen, Conti, there are many farmers we've recruited for our cause who are excellent shots, even if they don't have formal training. Besides, there's a massive difference between shooting at leisure and shooting in war. These country folk are outstanding at both. Also, the weaponry we have is not familiar to you."

"I realize I'll be experiencing a lot of things that are new to me. However, it doesn't lessen my resolve to fight for what is right—no matter the cost."

"I don't want some rich kid sticking his nose in our business just because he's bored. We might be underground at the moment, but we are growing. People have had enough of Mussolini being in bed with Hitler. Our country isn't better for it, we're lapdogs, which is why soldiers who desert Mussolini are joining our ranks. And as our countrymen's discontent grows, so does our strength."

Tomas let the remark about being a rich kid slide. Although fully grown men, their relationship still held strong ties to when they were teenagers. Besides, their lives had changed so dramatically over the years that it was only right that Abato questioned Tomas's motives. "I promise you, I have good reason to want to join."

"I'd heard, and that is the only reason I said yes to this meeting." When Abato looked at Tomas this time, his eyes held an inkling of sympathy. "I'm sorry about your grandfather's passing. He was a good man."

"Thank you." Although it had been five years since his grandfather's death, Tomas had never moved past the emotional trauma of losing the man he'd most admired. Politics had ripped away his grandfather's life and, even though Tomas had promised his family he wouldn't get involved, he couldn't watch his people suffer any longer. When he'd heard about Abato on the underground grapevine, Tomas had to put himself forward.

"Normally I would suspect someone like you to be a spy, however my men have done their work and you check out." Abato pointed to the empty chair. Tomas sat, trying not to get his hopes up. Abato tapped the desk rhythmically with a pencil. "This is not a stroll along the promenade. There is a very good chance you will die."

"I fully understand this." He'd contemplated this decision long and hard, but risking his life was worth it if Mussolini's men could be defeated. He had no idea how, but it had to happen. There just couldn't be more unnecessary deaths. Only recently, Tomas had visited his cousin in a small village south of Palermo. He'd unwittingly borne witness to the German's decree that for every German killed, ten Italians would be shot or hanged; their innocence was of no consequence. The bodies of the school teacher and farmers had been left swinging for twelve hours in the piazza and later buried without ceremony or a priest. The experience had left an indelible mark on Tomas and, coupled with the untimely death of his innocent grandfather, Tomas had vowed to do whatever he could to rescue his people from murderous hands.

Bruno threw the pencil on the table. "You'll be just like everyone else. No special treatment."

"Of course."

"And you'll endure harsh conditions—uneven terrain, starvation, storms, days without sleep."

"I am committed to the cause."

"We could use your engineering skills." Abato lit yet another cigarette, the haze in the room growing thicker. "But I am not convinced I should take you."

Tomas reached into his canvas bag. His shaking fingers clutched the wad of cash wrapped in a few layers of newspaper. Placing it on the desk he edged it toward Abato, who did a cruddy job of hiding his eagerness. He unwrapped the paper, stared at the lira and coughed. He laid a steady gaze on Tomas.

"I will take the money, but that does not instantly buy you a place with us. You have to earn it."

* * * *

The rain had barely let up for three days as Abato's men traipsed through the mountains. Tomas had grown accustomed to his feet squelching in boots and clothes clinging to his body. A constant headache plagued him, and he had no idea if it was from dehydration or a lack of salt—the commodity so precious that people would steal to obtain it.

They sheltered in caves and ravines when they needed sleep, using blankets and eating food they'd bought from villagers sympathetic to their cause. Tomas's injection of cash into the group now meant they didn't have to write promissory notes for the villagers to convert into money at a later date.

As they made their way up a narrow, slippery slope, Tomas's mind wandered back to the first conversation he'd had with Abato. It made sense for Abato to question Tomas's motives. Hell, Tomas had questioned them himself. Was it to assert his independence away from the family? He loved them, though their refusal to get caught up in the war being waged on their doorstep drove him crazy and pushed him to the point where he'd fought with them so intensely that communication had ground to a halt. Tomas had thought, given the circumstances of his grandfather's death, his family would have done everything they could to see Mussolini and his supporters fail. Instead, they had retreated behind their thick double doors in their grief while the world outside spun out of control.

It dismayed him that Nonna, the one person who was always outspoken and renowned for doing the right thing, had shied away from her usual loud political rants. Instead, she'd withdrawn, choosing to sit in her favorite reading chair with a faraway look in her eyes. Since losing her husband, the fire in her belly had burned down to a few glowing embers.

Tomas reached the crest and started the descent on the trail snaking through the valley. They continued for another hour, the heavy, unrelenting rain smashing against his weary body. Eventually, Abato signaled they should take refuge in a cave hidden in a rocky outcrop. Tomas ate the last of the stale bread and observed Abato speaking quietly on the radio, his eyes darting around at the bedraggled band of men. It was a short, sharp, indecipherable conversation, and as soon as Abato signed off, he beckoned Tomas. Abato shoved a wad of chewing tobacco in his mouth and drew his brows together. He chewed for some time while Tomas waited. Eventually, Abato spat a wad of tobacco against the rock. The black clump squelched and made a slow descent against the brown, uneven surface. Abato leant in close, the sour stench of tobacco permeating the cool air. "I need you to look after someone."

"Who?"

"Someone important."

"You want me to be a babysitter?" asked Tomas.

Abato raised an eyebrow. "There is a very fine line, Conti. You *do not* want to cross it."

Even though he shared the same desire as these men to create ways for Mussolini's soldiers to fail, Tomas did not fit in with this unruly group of men from impoverished backgrounds. Tomas wasn't so naïve to think his life of privilege hadn't skewed his view on the world. Sometimes he felt a sense of entitlement creeping in and he had to force it aside. Tomas needed to shut his trap.

Giving a curt nod, Tomas said, "Of course I will do as you ask."

Abato leant in. "You need to look after my sister."

"What?"

This request didn't make any sense. He'd been with Abato for almost a week and not once did he mention family. Abato had made it clear that even though they shared history, Tomas was not to discuss their childhood—ever.

"Rachel?" Tomas whispered. Images of Abato's pig-tailed sibling flashed before him. All he could recall was a smiling, freckled, fresh-faced kid who annoyed the heck out of Abato and Tomas at every opportunity. She'd have to be at least twenty-two by now.

"Yes, Rachel. How many sisters do you think I have?" Abato grumbled.

"It's been so long..." Tomas couldn't fathom Rachel as a young woman now. "How do you want me to help?"

"She's been working on the ground, gathering information on the movements of the Germans and Mussolini's men through her informants. She's also done courier runs. It's easy for her to move through the countryside without being detected."

"I would have thought it would be dangerous for a lone woman out here."

"She's changed since last you saw her. She's now more stubborn than ten of your nonnas put together."

"Now that's a feat." Tomas smiled, but it quickly fell away.

"It's no laughing matter." Abato didn't hide his irritation. "She's been injured and is now holed up not far from here. I need you to get her back to Palermo."

"But I'm not a medical—"

"You're the only one she knows, apart from me. I'm changing plans so we can meet her in the next valley." Abato lifted his chin in the direction of north.

Tomas nodded solemnly, somewhat disappointed he wouldn't be continuing with the men on their mission to create a stronger underground swell. In a way, he felt like he was deserting them.

Abato motioned with his hand for the men to fall behind as they cautiously exited the cave and made their way into the fading daylight. The scent from the peonies followed Tomas as he fell in step.

Up ahead, he noticed Nino, the youngest recruit, and Sabato, the eldest, deeply involved in a whispered conversation. Tomas strained his ears to hear what was said, but he couldn't make out full sentences. Words like "weak," "rich," "untrustworthy" and "green" spun in the air, and it didn't take long for Tomas to realize he was, once more, a topic of conversation.

At the back of the pack, Tomas slowed his pace and put more distance between him and the men. He tuned his eyes and ears to his surrounds, trying to pick up on the slightest hint of something out of the ordinary. His calves ached. Lungs burned. His breath came out in short, sharp bursts.

Leaves rustled in a bush between two large boulders.

Tomas stopped.

Another rustle. Almost undetectable.

He aimed the rifle at the bush, his shoulders tense, fingers clammy.

"Argh!" A scrawny body lunged at Tomas, who doubled over, hoping the attacker would lose control and fly over the top. Bony fingers clawed at Tomas's shirt. Tomas crooked his arm and reached for the aggressor, yanking the strong, wiry body from his and throwing him to the ground. The figure jumped up and launched himself once more, but this time Tomas was ready—he blocked the attack with the rifle, using the butt to lay a bone-cracking blow to the attacker's forehead. The assailant yowled, reeled back and placed a hand on his head. Even in the darkness Tomas could see blood oozing from the kid's skull.

Jesus.

Kid.

He couldn't have been more than seventeen.

Tomas pointed his gun at the teenager, whose hands were held up in surrender. Tomas then motioned for the kid to stand and he did so with difficulty, his emaciated body trembling in the Italian uniform that hung off him.

Tomas looked over to see Abato beside him, gun aimed between the kid's eyes.

"What are you doing?" asked Tomas.

"What do you think? They're sewer rats. If there's one, there are others."
He cocked his head in the direction of the men who had fanned out and
were now scouring the boulders and foliage alongside the track.

"Let's just take him with us."

"For what?" Abato waved the gun menacingly.

"Please, don't kill me." The teenager's high-pitched voice was
laced with panic.

Abato cocked the gun. "In this war, we take no prisoners."

Tomas said, "Maybe he can tell us where the others are. He could—"

"If you won't kill him, I will." Abato spat a wad of phlegm at the kid's feet.

"Please, I will tell you where my unit is stationed. I—"

"I'm not stupid. You'll put us directly in the line of fire."

"I promise you, I won't." His hands shook and his voice cracked.

Tomas had every reason to hate Mussolini and his army, but watching
this young kid who had probably joined to save himself from starving…

"Abato, maybe—"

"Whose fucking side are you on, Conti?"

"Ours." What kind of question was that?

"Look, I'm not wasting what little food we have on him. If we let him
go, he'll reveal our position and I don't need to tell you what happens when
he does." Abato lifted the gun higher and aimed it directly at the center of
the kid's forehead. "One shot and this problem is gone."

"One gunshot will bring their attention to us. These walls echo."

"Jesus fucking Christ." Abato put on the safety and shoved the gun at
Nino, who wasn't much older than the soldier.

The young soldier's wide eyes travelled from Tomas to Abato and back
again. With one deft movement, Abato reached into his pocket, pulled out
a knife, yanked the kid's head back and slit his throat. Blood spurted across
Abato's bare arm as he let the kid fall to the ground, a sick, gurgling sound
punctuating the darkness.

Bile rose at the back of Tomas's throat. His limbs froze.

Abato ripped the canteen from the dead kid's belt and washed his hands
and arms. "There's always a solution to a problem."

The men filtered back empty-handed. Some stared at the prone body
blocking the pathway, while others stepped over the teenager, as if he
didn't exist. What the hell was he doing here? Wasn't the whole point of
this cause to join Italians together in an uprising against Mussolini? How
could they do that when they slaughtered their own countrymen without
an afterthought? The kid would probably have joined their cause in a

heartbeat. Did this make Tomas and Abato and his men just as bad as Mussolini's army?

Maybe Nonna was right. Perhaps he had no business in this war. Then he was bombarded by visions of suffering children and stories of women who had been raped and tortured by the forces. He owed it to the innocents, and his grandfather, to find the backbone to fight for what was right. Enough was enough.

Abato gave orders for the men to move the body and dump it in a nearby gully. They laid a bunch of dried branches over the top while Tomas used the rest of the water from the young soldier's canteen to wash away the telltale blood.

"Move it!" Abato yelled and forged ahead while the men silently fell into line behind him.

Before Tomas took off up the trail, he snuck one last look at the makeshift burial of the young kid. War had many faces, none which were pretty. It forced people to turn against their fellow humans, take risks and fight in bloody battles where no one ever truly won. What kind of existence was this?

Chapter 4

Rosie shoved the wash stick into the copper and gave the sheets one more stir before depositing them into the concrete tub. Her best friend, Kitty, pushed back her blonde locks then rubbed her pregnant belly. Steam from the boiling water raised the temperature in the laundry under the verandah and sweat pooled at the base of Rosie's spine. She turned on the tap, thankful there was still water in the tank, and let the water soak the washing. Kitty added soap flakes and together they started scrubbing the sheets against the corrugated board. Rosie's hands stung, but she continued, regardless.

"You really don't have to help. You could just rest." Rosie wrung out the last of the sheets.

"Who else is going to make sure you do a decent job?" Kitty nudged Rosie, almost knocking her off-balance.

"Very funny." With the back of her hand, Rosie wiped away perspiration and grabbed the heavy basket. They left the dark recesses under the verandah and walked into the blinding sun toward the clothesline. She dropped the basket with a thud that sent small clouds of dust upward.

"You better watch out or Cecile will make you do them again." Kitty nodded at the sheets now streaked with red dirt.

"It'll blow off when it dries." Rosie grabbed the bucket of dolly pegs and started the tedious task of hanging the laundry. Kitty moved to hang the clothes but Rosie said, "No, no. Go and sit in the shade and I'll be with you in a minute."

"Come on, Rosie! I'm totally fine!" To prove her point, Kitty grabbed some pegs and the nearest sheet. She gently slid the taut line to the left and the clothes moved along. "This pulley system is fantastic. I don't have to move a foot!"

Rosie dropped a peg in the dirt, picked it up and rubbed it against her trousers. She reached for the sheet and it slid from her fingers and landed in the dust again. "Bother!"

Kitty laughed. "That's not what you were thinking."

"You know me too well." Rosie picked up a sheet that now had burrs all over it. She shook it, but the prickly balls had well and truly embedded themselves on the thin cotton. "Argh! Stupid, dumb, household chores."

Kitty smiled and reached for the sheet. With a few stylized flicks of the wrist the burrs flew off. "I'm impressed it only took you a day to create this pulley system. You have such a great head for maths and mechanics."

Rosie sighed and handed the pegs to Kitty. "I can't stand by and watch the world pass before me because I wasn't born with a...you know."

"Yes, yes, I know." Kitty slid the line across and hung the last sheet then wiped her hands on her apron. "Done."

They sauntered over to the shade of the gum tree and sat on the bench Rosie and her dad had made when she was ten. Rosie picked up a leaf from the ground, held it to her nose and inhaled deeply. The scent always reminded her of Tulpil.

"The world isn't passing before you, you know," said Kitty.

"It feels like it is." Rosie fiddled with the leaf and Kitty rested her head on Rosie's shoulder.

Kitty prodded Rosie in the rib. "I've missed you."

"I didn't miss you." Rosie prodded her back and winked. Their regular letters were never the same as heart-to-heart talks over cups of tea and Kitty's famous tea cake.

In the distance, Rosie could hear the workers chatting, while they took a break from the intense heat of the midday sun. Their laughter and myriad languages had formed the background music of her life. She'd missed it so much.

Kitty sat up and faced her. "So why don't your parents want you to stay?"

"They seem okay for me to stay for a while but that's all. I thought they would have jumped at the opportunity to have me back."

"They've found ways to work around you not being here, I guess, and now you're offering to stay they probably don't know what to do with you."

"I've got plenty of suggestions." Rosie leant against the bench and stretched out her legs.

"So"—Kitty adjusted herself on the bench once more—"when are you going to tell me what else is going on?"

"What?" It came out with force and sounded suspiciously loaded.

"Wanting to come back because you miss family and you want to check up on them is understandable—for a short while—but you spent the best part of a year writing about how much you love Brisbane. Then you stopped."

"I was busy."

"Nu-uh, something is up and I'm not leaving this alone." Kitty held her hand on her lower back as she shifted position.

"Do you want to go inside and sit on something more comfortable?"

"I am perfectly fine and you're not getting out of it this easy. Rosie, we're best friends. If you can't tell me then who can you tell?"

Kitty stared at Rosie, who knew she'd lose this battle. There was no point in dragging it out.

Taking a deep breath, Rosie said, "I got fired."

"What? But you loved that job and you were doing so well!"

"I was…there's a whole story behind it." Rosie hadn't discussed this with a single soul, so airing her thoughts and fears for the first time—even with her best friend—cast shadows of regret and doubt in her abilities to assess people for who they really were.

Kitty placed her hand on Rosie's. "Take your time."

"My boss was always generous with praise and he'd look people in the eye and say hello as he walked past. Most of the bosses barely knew their secretary's names so him acknowledging us was welcomed. What took me a while to realize, though, is that more and more women in the secretarial pool would keep their heads down whenever he was around. I thought it was because they were busy, then I realized that maybe something wasn't right."

"Oh no."

"Because I wanted this promotion so badly, I worked really long hours. It was fine for a little while, then he started coming over and making suggestive comments about what I was wearing or my perfume or hair— basically any chance he got to talk about my appearance, he did. I felt so uncomfortable, and told him so, but he didn't care. Then he…" A sharp pain stabbed Rosie's throat.

Kitty squeezed Rosie's hand. "Go on."

"I swear, I did nothing to encourage him. He…" Her chest constricted like it did every time she recalled the event. "He cornered me and began groping me, kissing me…" Hot tears welled up even though she'd promised herself not to let the emotions get to her.

"Oh, Rosie." Kitty wrapped her arms around her. "I'm so sorry."

"It's not your fault."

"So, what happened?"

"I slapped him. Hard."

Kitty's laugh rang out across the backyard. Birds squawked in response. "I know it's not funny, though it's nice to hear he got what he deserved."

"He deserved more than that. When I threatened to tell his wife, he laughed, then said it would look like sour grapes because I was fired."

"He's the one who fired you?"

Rosie nodded. "I went to the director about it and he just said that it was my word against my boss's."

"And?"

"And my word held no weight. There were no witnesses and no one else would say anything because they'd lose their job. Plus, I'm replaceable, right?"

Kitty squeezed Rosie's hand. "You absolutely are not replaceable."

"In the business world, secretaries are dispensable because there's always someone else willing to take your job and put up with horrendous behavior from the boss."

"It sounds like you had a lucky escape. What are you going to do about it?"

Rosie moved her head from side to side, trying to stretch the stiff muscles in her neck. "I want to do something but I don't know what. It all seems so insurmountable. Me against the influential boss who's been there for twenty years…. Life was so much easier in AWAS. We just got on with the work and no one cared what we looked like or made unwanted advances." Rosie paused. "Although, when the war ended we got thrown back into our old roles. Do you think things will ever change?"

"I hope so." Kitty placed her hand on her belly and looked at it lovingly. "Especially if this little one is a girl."

"Wouldn't it be nice for her to grow up as an equal to men and not a second-class citizen?"

"It would, indeed. You need to get your mind off that idiot from Brisbane." A cheeky smile crept across Kitty's face. "Come to the dance with me on Saturday."

"No thanks, I'd rather stick near home."

"Just come for an hour or so. William would love to see you. It's been forever since you've seen each other."

"I have missed William's terrible sense of humor." Rosie laughed, recalling the first day they'd met. He'd been assigned the desk behind her at school and he'd dipped her plaits in the inkwell. Not to be outdone, she'd hidden a small tree snake in his desk, and from that moment on, they'd become steadfast friends. When William and Kitty had started courting after his return from the war, nothing had made Rosie happier than seeing two of her dearest friends fall in love.

"Please come with us." Kitty batted her long lashes.

"I don't think so."

She gave a self-satisfied smile. "So, we'll pick you up at seven?"

* * * *

William's ute rolled to a stop on the gravel and Rosie got out, offering her hand to Kitty as she exited. Rosie strained to hear music from the dance hall, but all she could detect were excited voices talking over the top of each other. She smoothed down her mint-green dress and adjusted the white belt.

"Why are you so nervous?" Kitty asked.

"What?"

"You've been fidgeting since we left Tulpil."

"I'm not nervous. I just…I don't know how I'm feeling, really. I haven't been to a dance here for such a long time and people will have changed—"

"Nothing changes around here," said William. "You look fine, Rosie."

"Fine?" She arched an eyebrow at this dangerous word.

"Lovely. You look lov-er-ly. Now let's go. My beautiful wife needs a cold drink and a place to sit."

"I'm pregnant, not poorly!" Kitty moaned as she stomped up the steps and into the hall.

Rosie skipped up the stairs but halted in the doorway when she was assailed by a wall of heat and cigarette smoke. The band were in the midst of setting up the stage and men were grouped together, having traded their dirty workwear for pressed shirts, ties and fancy trousers. Clusters of women laughed and patted their hair while smiling flirtatiously at possible suitors. Rosie resisted rolling her eyes.

She followed William and Kitty to a table at the end of the hall, far away from the preening peacocks. After pulling out a seat for his wife, then Rosie, William went over to the drinks station to chat to some colleagues.

Kitty used a serviette to dry the thin layer of perspiration from her brow. "The band is from Brisbane, you know."

"What on earth are they doing here?"

Kitty shrugged. "Perhaps they needed a change of scenery, just like some other people I know?"

"Hmmm..." Rosie cast her gaze around and noticed there still weren't a lot of immigrant workers present, even though more were now living in Piri River.

The band finished tuning their instruments and the room filled with the familiar notes of Tommy Dorsey's "Sunny Side of the Street." Within moments, the dance floor grew crowded with couples laughing and smiling at the upbeat music.

William arrived with three large glasses of ginger beer and placed them in the center of the table. "Care to dance, my sweet wife?"

Kitty looked at her ankles and grimaced. "If they're like this now, how will they be when I'm bigger?"

"Maybe you need to get as much dancing in as you can now," he said.

"I came here to watch." She closed her eyes and sipped the ginger beer. "Ahhh, delightful."

"So why are we here if you're not dancing?" asked Rosie.

"To listen to good music and be social." Feigning surprise, she said, "Oh look. Isn't that Rodney Johnson over there? He's always had a soft spot for you, Rosie, and I've heard he's an excellent dancer."

"I'm not interested in being courted."

"You say that now..."

Rosie shot William a look of exasperation.

He grinned and cocked his head in the direction of the dance floor. "As my wife isn't quite capable of dancing—"

"I'm totally capable! I am just choosing not to!" she shouted.

"Like I said"—he raised an eyebrow—"as my wife is not dancing, would you like to join me for a spin across the boards?"

"Thank you, that would be lovely." Rosie took his hand, grateful for a break from Kitty's scheming.

Rosie and William found a small space on the dance floor and she let her body move to the music, caught up in the moment.

William said quietly, "Kitty told me about why you left Brisbane."

Rosie stopped dancing and let go of William's hands. "Oh."

"But you knew she'd tell me."

Rosie nodded.

"Are you okay?" he asked.

"I'll be fine, I'm just...disappointed, I guess. I had so many hopes for my job in Brisbane."

"I'm really sorry it didn't work out." William's lips kicked into a wry smile. "Want me to go and sort out your old boss?"

"Ha! No, I'll figure it out. Or I won't."

"You shouldn't let him get away with it."

"I know," she said. "I'm thirsty."

"Okay, end of discussion, I get it," said William. "Maybe I should check on Kitty."

They crossed the dance floor and dodged the spinning couples only to find Kitty deep in conversation with a man with dark hair. He had his back to the dance floor and when he laughed, it was with his whole body.

"You better get over there, quick smart." Rosie laughed.

"Tomas? He's harmless."

"Tomas Conti?" She took a better look and her heart beat faster. With a dry mouth, she asked, "How do you know him?"

"I met him through Randall." William tilted his head to the side. "How do *you* know him?"

"We met last week on the bus from Brisbane." She studied the familiar way Kitty and Tomas spoke. "So, Kitty knows him?"

"We ran into him at the post office yesterday." William grinned. "Why the twenty questions?"

"Nothing." She feigned nonchalance. "You're not jealous that a handsome man is chatting with your wife?"

"Handsome, eh?"

She punched him in the arm. "Stop it! You should go and rescue your wife before the *handsome* man woos her away from you."

William laughed. "Kitty's married to *me* and I know she loves *me*. She's also having my baby. It will take a lot more than a handsome—as you tell me he is—man to rip her away from my clutches." Once more, he gave her a sly smile. "Tomas seems like a nice bloke. Maybe you should spend more time with him."

"Oh no!" She held up her hands defensively. "Don't you start with this matchmaking rubbish."

William put his hand under her elbow and steered her toward the table. Not that she minded too much. A new face in town, and one as attractive as Tomas's—with his large brown eyes and thick lashes—meant the evening might not be so bad after all. Then she remembered her stance on men: *not interested*. So why did Tomas Conti grab her attention?

"Tomas!" said William, a little too enthusiastically.

Tomas turned to face them and, once more, Rosie found herself in awe of his beautiful skin. He shook hands with William while Rosie stood out of Tomas's view.

"Your lovely wife has been telling me about the renovations on your house."

"Ah, yes, we are under a deadline of sorts." William nodded toward Kitty's ever-expanding belly. William draped his arm across Rosie's shoulders and pulled her close. "I believe you have met my very good friend Rosie."

"Ah, Rosalie. It is lovely to see you again."

Rosie returned his smile as she tried to cobble together a sentence.

Tomas studied her as the music slowed into a waltz. "Would you like to accompany me on the dance floor?"

Suddenly shy about being in his company, Rosie looked at the empty chair. Kitty pulled it next to her and rested her swollen legs on top. Her grin would have made the Cheshire Cat proud.

"All right, thank you," Rosie said.

Tomas held out his hand and she took it, refusing to look back at her best friend. Fine, Kitty and William could play their little matchmaking game but they wouldn't win.

Tomas placed his hand lightly on her waist and held her hand in the customary waltzing position. He exuded the confidence of a man who knew his way around a dance floor and, despite her mind protesting, she found her body relaxing. With a slight movement to the left, they began their journey across the boards.

"The band is good, yes?" he asked.

"Very good." A slight hint of spicy cologne hung in the air.

Turn. Sway.

Gosh he really is an excellent dancer.

"So…" Spin. Twirl. "How are you settling in, Tomas?"

"The weather, it is hot. The work, it is hard. The sky, it is a beautiful blue. The rain, it smells of magic. And the scenery…" His eyes connected with hers. "The scenery gets better with every minute that I am here."

Her face burned, as did her neck. *Please, please, don't let it show.* "I bet you say that to all the girls."

They spun to the other side of the dance floor. When he stretched out his arm so she could spin under it, she felt an underlying strength mixed with gentleness in Tomas.

"I wish you to know, Rosalie Stanton, you are the first woman I have danced with in a very long time."

A small laugh left her lips. "Oh, please."

"You do not believe me?" His tone sounded slightly offended.

"You're serious?"

"Of course. I am not one to lie."

Whether it was the earnest look in his eyes or her own desire for it to be true, Rosie chose to believe him.

The music picked up tempo and Tomas seemed keen to keep dancing but the balls of her feet had reached a point of unbearable agony from her new shoes.

"I'm really sorry, but do you mind if we have a break?" she asked.

Tomas escorted her to where Kitty sat, fanning herself while William looked at her adoringly.

"Would you all care for another cold drink?" asked Tomas.

"I'll come with you." William stood and accompanied his new friend.

Rosie watched the two men saunter over to the bar. When she turned around Kitty was rubbing her belly and not making any effort to hide her glee.

"He's lovely, isn't he?"

"Yes." Rosie avoided eye contact because it would only encourage this discussion.

"And it looks like you two had a nice time," Kitty persisted.

"Don't even think about it," Rosie said sternly, tapping her fingers on the table. "I'm heading to the ladies'. You coming?"

Kitty shook her head. "Surprisingly, I don't need to."

"Back in a moment." Rosie scooped up her purse, scooted past the dancers, and headed toward the exit at the side of the hall. Taking the steps down, she looked up to find a reedy figure with slicked-back sandy hair. He casually leant against the toilet wall while he smoked and laughed with a small group of men.

She balled her fists.

Damn.

Rosie should have known Ken Ridley and his mates would be hanging around here.

"Well, well, well." He threw the cigarette on the ground. "A sight for sore eyes, indeed."

Holding her chin high, she said, "Gee, Ken, I wish I could stop and talk but I...have somewhere to be." She turned on her heels to enter the safety of the hall but was stopped when Ken's fingers dug into her arm. She wrenched it away. "Stop it!"

"Why don't we take a little walk?" A wall of alcohol moved in on her as his face came closer to hers.

"No, thanks." She kept her tone polite, careful not to anger Ken, who had always been unpredictable.

"Come on, Rosie."

He went to grab her again and memories of her recent run-in with her boss overtook her. With as much force as she could muster, Rosie shoved Ken in the chest and it was followed by laughter and "ooohs" from Ken's cronies. Rosie rushed up the stairs only to slam into Tomas, who stood like a sentinel at the entrance of the hall.

"How may I assist?" His kind tone made hot tears well in her eyes.

"No assistance needed, truly." Her voice shook as much as her hands.

Tomas peered down at Ken who stood at the base of the stairs surrounded by his drunken mates.

"Leave her alone, dago!" Ken shouted, a slight sway in his stance.

"Don't listen to him." She put her hands on Tomas's arm and tried to steer him away. Rosie had no idea what temper Tomas had, but if Ken and his gang decided to start a fight—which they were likely to do—she didn't want Tomas injured because of her. "Please, let's go back into the hall."

Tomas stood his ground. "If this person is doing the wrong thing by you—"

"No, he just… Really, I am fine. No damage." Except for her confidence.

"Perhaps if I—"

"Please, Tomas, let's just go back inside and forget about them."

He looked reluctant but did as she asked. They returned to the table where William and Kitty sat, totally oblivious to the goings on outside the hall.

Rosie collapsed in the chair and Tomas sat beside her, his companionable silence reassuring.

Kitty leant forward, concern in her eyes. "You look like you've seen a ghost."

She took her time sipping from the glass. "Just Ken Ridley up to his usual tricks."

William was on his feet, pushing up his sleeves. "Where is he?"

"I'm all right, really." Rosie sat up straight.

"You don't look all right," said Kitty.

"You don't have to worry about me." She sipped the drink again, trying to appear calm but her shaking hands made the liquid quiver. Placing it on the table, she turned to Tomas. "Thanks for being there."

"I am glad to be of assistance." He frowned and ran his hand through his thick, dark hair. "This Ken Ridley does not appear to be a person of gentle personality."

"You're right. He is not of gentle personality at all. I'm sorry about what he called you."

"Dago?" Tomas laughed. "It does not upset me. I have been called much worse. There are racists in every corner of the world."

"Unfortunately, you'll find a cluster of them here." She paused, then said, "My father included."

"Does he not have workers of ethnic origin?"

"He has a big problem with Italians and refuses to employ them," she said, wishing she hadn't brought up the subject.

"I am Sicilian."

"He groups everyone together. My family are immigrants also, so he shouldn't behave this way toward anyone."

"But you are white," Tomas said, his tone without malice.

"I know that makes it easier, especially as we've been here for a few generations, but the government's White Australia Policy was the dumbest idea ever invented. Fancy choosing which people to admit to your country based on their race and not what they're like as individuals."

"What about these 'beautiful Balts' who arrived last year? Did they not open the doors for people of other nationalities?"

"They only let them in because they couldn't get enough Ten Pound Poms to come out here. Then the Baltic beauties arrived, but Australia needed more people. So, the Displaced Persons Scheme started and people from your country, Greece and Yugoslavia were allowed entry. But you probably know that, right?"

"Yes, I know of many people who have made Australia home now. But of course, there are many who were here from before the war, yes?"

"True." She ran her finger along the edge of the table. "The Italians who weren't naturalized Australians were put in internment camps because the government was petrified Italians would join with the Japanese and take over Australia."

"But we changed to the side of the Allies."

"Yes." Perhaps getting involved in a political discussion was too much. After all, she had no idea what had gone on in Tomas's world and it would be so easy for her to accidentally say something wrong and offend him.

"It is all right," Tomas said.

"Pardon?"

"You have a frown." His gentle smile relaxed her. "You do not need to worry, I am enjoying your company."

Relieved, and slightly flustered by his compliment, she took a moment to compose herself. "The Italians who were held in internment camps during the war, when Italy was still on Germany's side, worked very hard and helped Australia cultivate enough food to keep us from starving. Their tireless work was invaluable, so when Italy switched to supporting the Allies, Australians finally started looking at Italians in a much better light."

"But we are still called dago."

"Some people are just small-minded." *Like Ken-bloody-Ridley.*

"I am afraid this is very common. The world should be a place of peace, not anger." Tomas closed his lips and stared at the dancers spinning and laughing.

Rosie couldn't take her eyes off her companion.

Tomas Conti was handsome. Yes.

Intriguing. Yes.

Someone who could mess with her heart? Hell, yes.

Chapter 5

Rosie put the last of the vegetables into the pot, happy tomorrow's lunch was already organized. She quickly put on the lid then arched her back and stretched. It had been a particularly difficult day in the kitchen, as the low cloud cover had kept in the heat. And now, with the sun starting its slow descent, the temperature had dropped slightly.

Although the work in the kitchen was hot, it wasn't as bad as in the fields. The constant cutting, gathering and heavy lifting of sugarcane strained even the fittest of men's bodies. She marveled at how they could endure the laborious work, day in, day out.

Her father's men had increased their hours due to the shortage of workers because of his refusal to hire Italians. Sometimes, Rosie couldn't understand her father. If it was a war-related issue, then wouldn't he would spout vitriol about the Japanese and Germans? Yet he happily sat on the verandah and drank beer with Klaus from down the road, and he often stopped and chatted with Mrs. Himura at the grocery store. So, what was it about Italians that he despised with such fervor?

Since the dance a few days ago, her thoughts constantly returned to Tomas. He'd been so kind and chivalrous and, of course, charming. And rather than swoop in like some knight in shining armor, he'd silently stood by, ready to assist her if need be. Most men she knew would have attacked Ken with fists flying without any consideration that a woman could look after herself. The fact that he didn't endeared him to her.

Rosie threw the rest of the vegetable peels into the container for the chickens. In Brisbane, she'd missed their cluck-clucking and the way they followed her around when she collected their eggs.

She went to the icebox and pulled out the water she'd put inside to chill. Running the cold glass across her forehead, she contemplated what to do next. Her mother's novel sat on the edge of the kitchen table—how lovely it would be to sit on the verandah and take a moment to be in total peace while dusk crept across the land. The need for a frank conversation about her staying at Tulpil had permeated every corner of the house, and no one was willing to fully address it—yet. This evening's effort of avoidance had seen her father take off for the pub to drink, despite him being exhausted from incredibly long work days. Her mother had settled in for brandy and bridge at a friend's house, and Rosie now had the opportunity to relax. She considered the book again. It would be so wonderful to lose herself in a story. To immerse herself in a foreign land far, far away. What would it be like to travel to a different country? To learn a new language? To try new and interesting foods? To learn new customs?

A sigh escaped her lips.

A knock at the door drew her attention back to the stuffy kitchen. Guzzling the last of the water, she placed the glass down and made her way up the dark hallway to the front door. Through the mesh of the thick fly screen she could make out the silhouette of small, thin man with hunched shoulders.

"May I help you?" She squinted, trying to make out the visitor's features.

He removed his hat. "Please, I look work."

Rosie opened the door a fraction so she could see his face clearly. The gentleman's ruddy complexion and gray temples gave the impression he was in his late sixties—an age difficult to find employment in the tough sugarcane industry.

"The work, I do hard..." He scratched his head as if willing the English words to form on his tongue. He wiped his brow, which seemed unusually sweaty for someone who worked in the fields and was used to enduring the heat.

She felt for this poor man and even though she'd have loved to say he should talk to her father, it would be a waste of time.

"I'm really sorry but—"

The man's eyes rolled in the back of his head as he swayed to the left, his thin hand reaching for the wooden doorframe. He missed, and collapsed headfirst in a heap on the boards, the impact sending dust clouds into the air.

"Oh!" Rosie knelt down and tried to turn him on his side, but he weighed more than he looked.

He let out a low moan and gingerly rubbed his head.

"Don't move, please." She rushed into the kitchen at the back of the house and grabbed ice cubes and a cloth. Running along the hallway again, she flung the door open and found the man attempting to sit up, but he kept listing to the side. She put her hands under his sweaty armpits, willed her strength to double, and helped guide him so his back was against the wall of the house. Blood oozed from a deep gash in his forehead and she gently placed the ice pack on the large lump. He winced, then looked up at her, a flurry of Italian words tumbling out of his mouth. A singular tear trickled down his face, leaving a clear trail through the dirt coating his skin. He grabbed her free hand with both of his as his pleading eyes searched hers.

She mimed drinking from a glass. "I'll fetch you some water. Did you feel dizzy before you fell?"

He stopped talking.

"Dizzy?" she asked again, this time holding her hands to her head and moving it around in slow motion.

"*Si.*"

"It could be the heat."

Again, he looked at her with questioning eyes.

"Hot." She fanned herself.

"*Si.*" He launched into another lengthy monologue, his voice rising and eyes widening. His face crumpled in pain. Concerned with his distress, she wished she could understand him and offer the help he needed.

However, she knew one person who could.

"Wait, please." She held up her hand and hoped he understood.

Rosie ran inside and picked up the phone. It took a while before Lorraine on the exchange finally picked up. Rosie begged for her call to be placed urgently and waited for it to be connected. She stared at the clock on the wall and prayed he was back from the fields by now.

The phone rang out and she asked Lorraine to try again. Rosie's shoulders tensed as she watched the hand on the clock tick by with each agonizing second.

"Hello?" Came the heavily accented voice.

Rosie let out her breath.

"You are now connected," said Lorraine.

The phone clicked, signaling the operator had done her work.

"It's me, Rosie."

"Rosalie Stanton of Tulpil?"

She smiled at him making it sound like she was a lady on an English estate in the Jane Austen era.

"Tomas, I need your help."

* * * *

After calling Tomas, Rosie stayed with the man on the verandah as he dozed. Occasionally he would moan, wake with a start, and clutch his stomach. Maybe she should call Dr. Wilkinson and get him to come? If her father hadn't taken the ute she could have driven to the surgery. Then again, without someone who spoke Italian it would be impossible to find out what the man was saying and get the right information to make a diagnosis.

"Come on, Tomas."

As if on cue, she spotted a set of lights moving quickly up the driveway. The engine revved as the car dipped in and out of potholes. It gained speed up the hill and quickly came to a halt. The headlights flicked off and a figure emerged, his heavy footsteps thudding across the ground. He raced up the stairs and knelt next to Rosie.

"How are you?" Tomas squeezed her shoulder. His reassuring touch calmed her.

"I'm feeling a little helpless."

She moved back so Tomas could see the older gentleman who was dozing once more. Tomas inspected the gash and gently placed his hand on the man's arm. He spoke quietly, rousing him from his slumber and instead of the petrified look in his eyes, the older man's expression was one of relief. He spoke to Tomas and pointed at his head and stomach, then he clasped Tomas's hand.

Tomas looked over at Rosie. "The name of this man is Luka Abrami. He is of the region Marche. He is looking for work."

"Yes, I gathered he needed work, but I'm so sorry I can't help him." Oh, how she wished she could. "What's wrong with him?"

Tomas's expression was serious. "He has an ulcer in the stomach but must work to survive."

"Could we help him into the house?" Surely her father wouldn't object to a sick, elderly man crossing his threshold.

"I have offered for him to stay with my family." Tomas stood and gently lifted the man. "Rosalie, please open my car door."

She hurried down the steps and opened the passenger side door. In the distance, she saw a pair of lights moving toward the house. *Damn. They'd come home earlier than expected.*

Tomas guided Luka to the edge of the verandah while Rosie came back and took Luka's bony hand. Together they helped him down the stairs, his frail body shaking as they went.

The lights in the distance drew closer.

Rosie and Tomas worked as a team as they maneuvered Luka into the passenger seat of the ute, but his weakness made it slow-going and difficult.

"*Grazie*." Luka wrapped his fingers tightly around Rosie's arm.

"It is a pleasure to help. I hope you feel better soon." She hoped he heard the sincerity in her words even if he didn't understand them. She looked at Tomas. "Maybe you should take him to the doctor."

Tomas rubbed the back of his neck. "Yes, yes, I should."

Gravel crunching under tires drew their attention to the car moving up the driveway. The lights disappeared for a moment as the car dipped behind a hill but soon reappeared, silently growing closer with each second.

"It may be best if Luka and I…" Tomas tilted his head in the direction of her parents' vehicle.

"Yes, it probably is. I'm sorry."

"There is nothing of which to be sorry."

"I'm still sorry, though." She shrugged and gave a half-smile. "Thank you so much for coming to Luka's rescue. Will you let me know how he is?"

"Of course, of course." He went around to the driver's side of the car, opened the door then stopped and rested his elbow on the top of the roof. "Do you think…" He shook his head. "It does not matter."

Rosie eyed off the car coming perilously close. "Can we talk more? Later?"

Tomas nodded, slid behind the driver's wheel. The engine sputtered into action as he ground the gears, reversed and took off. He waved his hand out the window and she watched the red tail lights move closer to the bright white beams of her parents' ute. She sucked air between her teeth and held her breath.

Please, please, drive past each other.

Tomas's rear lights brightened as he braked and her father's ute pulled up beside him. Two dark figures got out of the cars and a pain rushed through Rosie's hand as her grip tightened around the verandah pole.

All she could make out in the distance were the outlines of her father and Tomas facing each other, their backs straight, their arm movements jerky. It seemed to take forever before the men got in their respective cars and left in a cloud of dust.

Rosie sat on the top step. A light breeze danced across her skin, giving some relief from the stifling heat. Her father's ute halted and it felt like an agonizingly long time before he got out and walked around to open her mother's door. When she exited, her wavy hair was still in a stylish updo, her skin glowing but not perspiring. There was a slight sway as she crossed the dirt in her high heels and climbed the steps. She placed her hand on Rosie's shoulder and gave it a squeeze. Her mother then went into the house, a small cloud of alcohol fumes trailing behind her.

Rosie's father took off his hat and rubbed his forehead with the back of his hand. He leant against the car, his legs crossed at the ankles, arms crossed against his chest. The physical distance between them felt less than the emotional gap that had developed over the years.

"I met our neighbor," he finally said, his tone noncommittal.

"Tomas."

Her father grew silent again and she wished she could read his mind.

"Would you like a cold drink?" she asked, hoping this might be an escape route to avoid conversation.

"Why was he here?" Her father's voice remained steady.

She drew her shoulders back, refusing to feel guilty for doing what any decent human should. "Signor Abrami came looking for work but he collapsed on the verandah. I couldn't understand him so—"

"You called the neighbor who speaks Italian."

"Yes." This was going surprisingly well. Had she misjudged her father after all?

"Do not call him ever again."

"I will if someone needs help!" She balled her hands at her side.

"Stay away from the Contis. Those wogs cannot be trusted."

"Dad!"

"How do you know him?"

"I met him on the bus from Brisbane." She put her hands on her hips.

"And?"

"And why are you so worried?"

"Stay away from that Conti. I'm serious." He walked up the steps, his large frame moving past hers.

"That's it?"

Her father paused then turned to face her. "What are you expecting me to do? Yell and scream?"

She chewed her lip.

"Do you think I'm an ogre?"

Her silence gave him the answer.

"I am extremely disappointed," he said.

Summoning courage, she said, "Well, I'm also disappointed."

"I have to get up early." He turned on his heels, quickly opened the screen door and let it slam shut behind him.

Making her way down the stairs, Rosie walked away from the house and over to the ancient swing set, red more from rust than red paint. She slowly lowered herself onto the half-tire swing her father had made when she was seven. The hard rubber dug into the back of her thighs, but she ignored the discomfort as she pressed her toes into the ground to gain forward momentum. The swing moved back and forward, the creaking rope strangely comforting, taking her back to the days when she'd spend hours hanging upside down from the bars or getting her brothers to push her sky-high on the swing. Her family had been so close back then. Her father had been kind, not volatile. Her mother had been engaged, not removed. Her brothers funny and loveable, not taken by war.

As she swung her legs, Rosie leant back and gazed at the stars twinkling in the inky sky. What she wouldn't give to go back to the world she once knew.

Chapter 6

The next day, Rosie leant against the railing of the verandah, staring at the vast expanse of Tulpil in the midafternoon light. Cane fields stretched as far as the eye could see, the lush mountainous backdrop an artist's dream. When Rosie had been away and moments of homesickness had threatened to swamp her, she'd closed her eyes and been transported from the concrete of Brisbane to the beauty of Tulpil. She'd imagined herself walking through the fields, cane towering above, gently swaying in the cool breeze, frogs croaking and birds singing in the distance, the scent of damp soil around her.

"Rosie!"

She looked up to find Sefa, one of her father's workers, who'd been with them for countless seasons.

"What's wrong?" Sefa rarely came up to the house.

"Where's Mr. Stanton?" he asked.

"I thought he was… What's happened?" She left the shade to go down the stairs and into the bright sunlight.

"There's been an injury."

"Oh no." She followed Sefa, whose large feet pounded the earth, taking them along the slope and toward the large tin shed. A group of workers had gathered in a circle and Rosie pushed through the jostling and noisy throng. A multitude of languages flew around as she broke free then skidded to a halt.

At the center of the circle was Jeks from Latvia, a recent arrival on the farm. He towered above Loto, from Fiji, who had worked tirelessly for her family for years. Loto clutched his side and glowered up at Jeks, who stood over him while the crowd around them grew rowdier. The second

Jeks saw Rosie he flicked something above the head of the crowd and it landed off to the side. Another Latvian raced over and retrieved the object. He bolted out of view.

"What's going on?" she demanded as her gaze travelled from one man to the next.

"It was an accident," said Loto, who wouldn't meet her eyes. He tried to stand but winced and collapsed on the dirt. That's when she noticed the blood oozing between his fingers.

"Get me clean cloths, now!"

The crowd fell silent and a couple of young men scampered off to the small room at the side of the shed where they kept emergency medical supplies. Her helpers were back in seconds and she quickly grabbed the cloths, drowned them in antiseptic and applied pressure. Loto winced.

Heavy footfalls pounded across the ground and she looked up to find her father and Bartel sprinting toward her, Sefa in tow. Her father knelt beside her, then moved her hand away so he could apply pressure on Loto's wound. "I've got this now."

"But—"

"Call the doctor. Tell him we're on the way," her father said forcefully.

She ran up to the house, glancing over her shoulder at the group of men quickly slipping away. Jeks was in a corner, standing with crossed arms as he spoke to Bartel. Jeks's expression was one of nonchalance. If it was an accident, surely he would show more remorse. And what had he thrown away when she first got there? A weapon?

"Rosie! The doctor!"

Blinking rapidly, she grabbed the screen door and raced down the hallway to the phone. Lorraine on the exchange picked up and quickly connected her with Dr. Wilkinson. Within minutes, she and her father were speeding into town with Loto slumped against Rosie, his body covered in sweat as he muttered in his native language. She pressed the blood-soaked cloths firmly against his wound and, as the tires sped along dusty roads, she prayed they weren't too late.

* * * *

Rosie stirred the vegetable soup then dipped a spoon in to give it a taste test. "Perfect."

She dished out a large serving into a bowl on the tray ready to take to Loto, who was now stitched up and recovering in the worker's barracks. She picked up the tray and turned to find her father standing in the doorway. Since arriving back at the house, he'd spent the best part of two hours interviewing the men about what had happened.

"Any luck?" she asked.

Her father took off his hat and shook his head. His face and arms were streaked in dirt and he looked as if he hadn't slept for a week.

"Do you want some soup?"

"Thank you, yes." Her father sat down heavily at the wooden table and she gave him the bowl meant for Loto. She'd give Loto more time to sleep off the painkillers and she'd serve up a fresh one for him shortly.

"That was some nasty business," her father said as he spooned in large chunks of vegetables and broth. He smiled. "This is your best to date."

"Thanks." Rosie sat opposite him.

"Listen, I'm sorry I yelled at you before."

"You were right to do so. Every minute counted and I didn't act as quickly as I should have."

"You shouldn't have been involved," he said.

"Sefa came looking for me when he couldn't find you or Bartel." She sat back. What did he expect her to do? Nothing? "Where were you?"

"Sorting out a matter and I needed Bartel with me." His spoon hit the bottom of the empty bowl. "This is why I don't want you involved with the business. Men will be men and no woman should be in a position to witness such outbursts. What if you'd been caught in the scuffle?"

"I would have found a way to protect myself. Besides, there are workers like Sefa who would look out for me. I'm not some pathetic little daisy that needs to be taken care of every minute of every day."

Her father rested his elbows on the table. His left arm shook, like he couldn't keep it still. "We're never going to agree on this, are we?"

Rosie shook her head sadly. "I don't think so."

"When are you returning to Brisbane?"

"Why are you so desperate to send me away from Tulpil?"

Her father looked at his shaking arm and moved it to rest on his leg.

"Look, Rosie, we love having you here. We've missed you. But we have a system here that works. And I don't need to tell you how hard farm life is. Brisbane is a chance for you to relieve yourself of the heartache of life on the land."

"So why have you stuck with it all these years?"

"It's all I know. Don't get me wrong, I love what I do, but I never had the opportunity to experience another kind of life. *You do* now."

When she looked at her father, she saw an unexpected depth of sadness. "What's wrong?"

"I just want you to be happy."

"Dad—"

"I do not want a repeat of what happened between me and Alex."

"What's that supposed to mean?"

"The argument." He looked away and concentrated on the trees outside.

After Alex had signed up with the RAAF, it had been a painful goodbye at the train station. Her father had been adamant that another son of his would not go to war, but Alex had been hell-bent on doing his duty for king and country. An ex-naval officer from the Great War, their father knew what atrocities his second son would face and no amount of pleading would change Alex's mind. The goodbye between her brother and father had been fraught with tension, angry words and regret. Rosie and her mother had tried to diffuse the situation but to no avail. Since then, her father had lived with the guilt.

"Let's try and find a compromise, Dad."

A knock at the kitchen door interrupted them and a ripple of relief went through her. She rushed over and found Sefa standing on the steps, his expression one of apprehension.

"Is everything all right?" she asked.

"Yes, yes, but Loto, he…he is awake and you asked me to tell you."

"Is he hungry?"

Sefa nodded.

She broke into a wide smile. "Well, that is good news. Tell him I'll be down in a minute."

Sefa took off down the stairs and Rosie heard the kitchen chair scrape against the boards. Her father had a fresh bowl in his hands and walked over to the simmering pot of soup. "I will take it."

"I don't mind." She grabbed the tray and he placed the bowl on it but the contents spilt. Rosie grabbed a tea towel and mopped it up.

"I do not want a daughter of mine down at the worker's barracks."

"I walk past there every day!" It was nigh impossible to keep the frustration out of her voice. "You can't protect me forever. Besides, what do you think will happen?"

"I don't like the way some of the new men look at you."

Rosie had grown up on Tulpil surrounded by men and had never felt like the object of their fantasies. There was no way she would tell her father about what happened in Brisbane now. Rinsing the tea towel and hanging it on the rack, she said, "I am the boss's daughter and they wouldn't be game to say or do anything that would upset you. Besides, shouldn't you trust your workers?"

"They are men, and men are..." He frowned. "You're not going down there."

"John!"

The front screen door slammed as Bartel hurried down the hallway. He entered the kitchen, his face red, sweat pouring off him as his small round eyes darted around the room. "Oh, hello, Rosie."

"Hello, Bartel," she said, grateful for the interruption.

"You have news?" her father asked.

"Not what you want, I'm afraid."

"Bloody hell." His fist met the table. "Let's fix this for once and for all." Her father grabbed his hat and stormed down the hallway, Bartel in tow.

"What about Loto's soup?" she called out but her father and Bartel had already disappeared down the steps and into the car. They took off down the driveway at a cracking pace and Rosie stared at the steaming bowl.

She picked up the tray. "No point in it getting cold."

* * * *

Sefa pushed open the door to the room Loto shared with three other men. Loto's roommates were a few bungalows away, loudly playing cards and doing whatever the men did during the evening. He lay on the cot, his eyes closed. Rosie crept over to his bed and whispered, "I've brought you something to eat."

He blinked rapidly, as if taking a moment to realize where he was. "Miss Rosie, you should not be here."

"This is what I said," Sefa raised an eyebrow at her. "Mr. Stanton will not be happy."

"He doesn't need to know anything." She indicated that Sefa should help Loto to a sitting position. He did so and she gently placed the tray on Loto's lap, careful not to knock his freshly bandaged wound. "Do you need some help?"

Loto shook his head, his eyes fixed on the soup. "Thank you for your kindness. I do not deserve it."

"You are a good person and a devoted worker." She stepped back. "You've never got in to a fight before, so why now?"

"It was not a fight."

Rosie tilted her head to the side, a silent interrogation skill she'd learnt from her mother.

Loto concentrated on the soup, eating slowly.

Sefa cleared his throat. "Perhaps I should accompany you back to the house."

Rosie held up her finger. "Loto, I hope in time you'll tell me what happened. Or, if you don't feel comfortable discussing it with me, then please, tell my father or Bartel."

He looked up; his lips twisted awkwardly. "It was an accident."

Pushing aside his obvious lie, she asked, "Was this a hierarchy thing?"

Loto looked at Sefa and they both shook their heads. Sefa stepped forward. "Rosie, please—"

"No matter what it was, I will make sure your medical bills are paid for." She had no idea how, but she'd figure it out some way.

"Mr. Stanton said he would pay," said Loto, his expression one of humbleness.

"He did?" Rosie's view of her father warmed and she began to question if she'd been too harsh on him. Maybe...

"Rosie, it is best if you leave now." Sefa glanced at the doorway.

She listened for the arrival of a car but didn't hear anything other than laughter from the men in the distance. She had no idea where Jeks was, but she suspected he was with his fellow countrymen and steering clear of the rest of the workers.

"Loto, I realize neither of you want to cause any trouble, but could this have been a race issue?"

"There was no fight—"

"Loto, please." She resisted placing her hands on her hips for fear of coming across as a school ma'am.

"Yes." He bowed his head.

Sefa gave his friend a frosty look.

"I did wonder." Rosie took a deep breath.

Loto's large eyes held fear when he looked up at her. "Will you tell Mr. Stanton?"

"I need to, yes, but don't worry, this won't affect your position here." She hoped with all her heart it wouldn't, but she had a duty to her father to let him know what the issue had been. Her suspicions had been proven correct and it had to be nipped in the bud before it blew up and created havoc. Rosie walked toward the door then turned back and asked, "What was it about?"

"He called me a Kanaka and said I should have been shipped back with all the others."

It was beyond her how a recently arrived Baltic knew about the ridiculous law the Australian government had put in place forty-odd years ago.

Although it was before her time, Rosie had heard about the government's decision to deport indentured Pacific Islanders—known as Kanakas—so Australia could implement the White Australia Policy. She was horrified that anyone would think such a law was a good thing but, unfortunately, there were many who had agreed with this move. Loto's father, along with Sefa's, had been among the few Pacific Islanders who had escaped deportation and remained on Tulpil, thanks to Rosie's grandfather. For someone like Jeks to say something so insulting, it was no wonder the normally passive Loto had found himself in a fight. She just wished it hadn't been with a knife.

The sound of a car speeding along the gravel caught her attention and her heart raced. *Damn.*

"Loto, rest up and don't worry. It will all be fine," Rosie said.

If only she fully believed it.

* * * *

Rosie's father strode up and down the verandah, hands clasped tightly behind his back. He hadn't spoken a word in what felt like forever. The normal chatter of the men had ceased for the night as most had retired drunk or exhausted, or both. Off in the distance, the bright lights of the Conti residence shone through the darkness.

"Dad…"

He held up his hand and drew his brows together, continuing with his pacing. Eventually he stopped, rested his hands on the rail and stared into the distance, away from the direction of the Conti farm. Rosie hated feeling like a naughty schoolgirl waiting for the principal's verdict about her punishment.

Turning to face her, he let out a long, sad sigh. "I cannot begin to tell you how angry I am."

"But I found out what the fight was about. Now you can address the issue."

He gripped the railing. "That's not the point at all. You deliberately defied me after we had spoken about why I didn't want you down in the worker's barracks."

"I was only there for a few minutes. Nothing happened." What did he think would transpire? That some worker she'd known for years would suddenly fall in lust with her and want to have his way? How ridiculous.

His frown grew deeper. "You tell me you want to stay at Tulpil and work for me, yet you go against my wishes."

He had a valid point—and it hurt. "I'm sorry, Dad."

"Sorry is not good enough. If I had actually been thinking about saying yes to you staying and working here, I certainly would have changed my mind after today."

"But I got the answer..." She let the sentence fall away when she noticed her father sway and the thin film of sweat on his forehead. "Are you all right? You look pale."

"Yes, I am fine. Listen, Rosie, I know your heart is in the right place," he said slowly, "but you are dealing with men here. Men who work the land and who often have sordid or tragic histories. The fields are no place for a woman." He pushed himself away from the rail. "I'm checking on Loto."

"Perhaps if you let him sleep a bit longer then..." She took in his intense stare and closed her mouth.

"I'm not going to question him right now. I just want to check on his wound and make sure he's comfortable." Her father shook his head. "I do have a heart."

"I know." Rosie studied her dusty boots. Looking up, she asked, "Where were you and Bartel?"

Her father's back stiffened. "It's all sorted now. Nothing you need to worry about."

Her father turned and walked down the steps. Rosie rested her elbows on the rails, her gaze fixed on the Conti's house in the distance. She wished she had the courage to go and visit Tomas.

A moan followed by a heavy thump on the gravel drew her attention to where her father was.

He lay crumpled in the dark.

"Dad!" She ran down the stairs and dropped on her knees where he lay face-down. With all her strength, she rolled him onto his side, her heart racing, adrenalin pumping.

She shook his shoulder but no response. "Dad!"

Placing her hand under his nose, she checked for any sign of breathing. A faint breath touched her skin.

She shook his shoulder again. "Open your eyes. Please!"

A low groan left his lips but his eyelids remained closed.

"Dad." She leant in close and stroked his forehead.

No reaction.

"Help!"

Silence.

"Help!" Her throat burnt from screaming and she prayed her voice would carry in the still evening.

A moment later, a door squeaked open and footsteps pounded up the path toward her.

Chapter 7

Tomas's nerves were set on edge as he traipsed up the last hill to their destination. Images of the terrified young soldier haunted him, even though he tried to cancel them out by conjuring up happy visions of prewar family vacations on the coast in Cefalù. Those carefree and peaceful holidays felt like a lifetime away and far, far removed from the war-torn country he still loved with all his heart. He missed his family. He missed his old life. He missed the country he'd grown up in.

Abato motioned for Tomas to walk with him at the front of the line.

"Why didn't you shoot that soldier, Conti? If you see one, you shoot, because rest assured they wouldn't think twice about shooting one of us."

"But—"

"How can I trust you'll protect my sister if you won't kill a German or one of Mussolini's bastards?"

Tomas mulled over Abato's question. He had a damn good point. Would Tomas trust someone to protect his family if they weren't willing to shoot the enemy?

"You can trust me. You have my word," Tomas meant it.

"The *only* reason I'm handing her over to you is because you never failed me or Rachel when we were kids. You defended us like we were of your own blood. Plus"—he fixed his gaze on Tomas—"she can stay with your family while she recovers."

"We're not on speaking terms."

Abato reached up and grabbed Tomas's shoulder so hard it felt like he was being pierced by knives. "Then fix it."

Abato held his gun at the ready, the hushed conversation apparently over. Tomas clutched his weapon and quietly followed Abato as they edged their way closer to the small hut. The rest of the men stood some distance away, their eyes peeled for any sudden movements.

The moon pushed through the clouds, leaving the ramshackle house in hazy shadows. Half the roof was missing, the windows were boarded and an eerie silence permeated the cool night. Stepping lightly across the gravel, Tomas reached the side of the door and placed his back against the wall, his heart pounding, his body drenched in sweat.

Abato stood on the other side of the door and quietly rapped out an intricate series of knocks. A second later a female voice asked, "Who is it?"

"Who do you think?" Abato said, a smile in his voice—the first time Tomas had heard that since they were teenagers.

The door clicked open and a small hand beckoned them. By the time they'd entered, Rachel was in a corner, hand resting on her belly. Her large eyes travelled from one man to the other.

She jutted her chin toward Tomas. "Who is this?"

"It's me, Tomas Conti." He stepped forward but stopped when Rachel reached under her shawl and pulled out a gun and aimed it at the middle of his forehead.

"Who?" Her voice was steady and firm.

"Don't you remember?" He willed his voice to remain calm. "I lived on the next street over. In Palermo."

Rachel kept the gun pointed at Tomas as she glanced at Abato. "What the hell is he doing here?"

"Rachel, put the gun away. Why would I bring someone here to hurt you?" Abato glanced at Tomas then back at his sister. "Conti is here to help get you to—"

"I am perfectly capable of getting to Palermo myself. Stefano shouldn't have told you about what happened." Her large eyes and small oval face gave her the appearance of a frightened woodland creature.

"I'm glad he did and I'm happy you waited for me to get here." The softness in Abato's tone surprised Tomas.

"It's only because I have information you need now. Then I'll be on my way to Palermo, and"—she glared at Tomas—"I will be going alone."

Abato handed a folded piece of paper to Tomas. "Take her here. This doctor is a sympathizer with our cause. Do not leave her side. I will be in contact when I can."

"Abato, a word, please." Tomas motioned for Abato to join him in the far corner of the room.

"What?" Abato growled.

"Is she stable enough for the journey?"

"You think I'd deliberately put my sister in danger?"

"I know you wouldn't," said Tomas, not entirely convinced this statement was true. "It's just that she seems to be in pain."

Abato reached into his pocket and pulled out a small flask. "This will help."

"Shouldn't we check her wound?"

"When did you get your medical degree?" Abato glanced over at his sister, who sat with her back against the wall, eyes closed, lips pursed.

"I'm not trying to be difficult, I just need to know what we're dealing with here."

"What we are dealing with is my sister needing to get to Palermo and receive medical help."

Tomas studied the green shawl on the ground, a small, dark red stain ruining the soft wool. The gun Rachel had clutched now lay at her side and next to her was a small battered notebook he hadn't noticed before.

Not caring about Abato's potential wrath, Tomas went over to Rachel and knelt beside her. He gently touched her shoulder. "May I check your wound?"

She turned away but winced and held her hand on her stomach.

"Please, Rachel, I'll be gentle. I promise."

She mumbled and nodded, the feistiness having faded.

Tomas reached into his pack, pulled out his medical kit and lay it on top of the canvas. He unhooked the lantern from his pack and deftly lit a match, then the wick.

"I'm just going to lift your shirt to look." He did so and found a bandage caked in dried blood. "This dressing needs redoing and I'm going to need your brother to keep the light close so I can see what I'm doing."

Tomas looked over at Abato who willingly came over and cast the light near his sister's side.

Rinsing his hands in rubbing alcohol, Tomas asked, "Were you stabbed?"

Silence.

"Rachel, I need to know."

"Yes, but he came off worse than me." Anger fueled her words.

Rachel kept still while Tomas quickly set to work cleaning the wound and padding it with thick, sterile bandages. He felt her forehead. It was hot and clammy.

"You need medicine for fever." Tomas cocked his head in the direction of a bottle of liquid in his kit. Abato reached for it and passed it over. How quickly the roles had reversed.

"Rachel…" Tomas offered her the capful of medicine.

"I need to get to Palermo."

"You will," Abato said, kindness in his tone. "Tomas will take you and keep you safe. Besides—" Abato continued whispering in her ear. Rachel's grimaced and she nodded, her ashen face solemn.

Whatever Abato said, had a marked effect on his sister. She got up gingerly and Abato grabbed the gun and book and stashed it in her pack.

He whispered in her ear once more. She narrowed her eyes at Tomas. Enveloping her in a gentle hug, Abato kissed her on the cheeks then turned to Tomas.

"I expect you to maim, destroy or kill anyone who tries to get in the way of my sister." Abato held her hand and squeezed it. "And you, my dear sister, deliver that book the second you get to Palermo."

"Medical help first, of course?" Tomas asked, deliberately ignoring the reference to the book. If he was supposed to know what was in it, he'd be told.

"Book then medical. Rachel agrees."

Abato handed Rachel's rucksack to Tomas, who swung it over his shoulder.

"One more thing, Conti." Abato waved his pistol in Tomas's direction. "If anything happens to my sister, I will hold you fully responsible." He took a deep breath and puffed out his chest. "I will hunt you down. And I will kill you."

* * * *

Tomas's senses remained on high alert as he and Rachel traipsed through the predawn darkness up and down the valleys, slowly making their way to Palermo. The option of using a vehicle or animal was too risky as they needed to stay away from roads and remain undetected. They had started out at a reasonable pace, but as the miles unraveled behind them, Rachel's breathing grew more labored. Up until now he hadn't doubted she was strong enough, but as the hours slid by, so did her strength. The short distance left to Palermo felt as far away as London or New York.

Rachel stumbled on small rocks and Tomas grabbed her before she toppled into the ravine.

"We should rest for a minute." He motioned for her to sit on a large rock at the end of a valley. That way he could keep a close eye on the paths in and out, in case company they'd rather not keep happened along.

"No," she said. "We need to keep going."

"Rest," Tomas said firmly and steered her to the rock. He pulled out his canteen, undid the lid and handed it to her. "Drink."

"Walk." The word sounded strangled.

"Rachel, you will not make it if you don't take a moment to eat and drink." He stood above her, his hands on his hips. If being an ogre meant she'd listen, then so be it. "It is my job to get you to safety and I am not going to fail."

"Because my brother will kill you?" A small laugh escaped her lips and her breathing seemed more steady. "He's changed, hasn't he?"

"We all have," Tomas said.

"Not you." Rachel took a swig from the canteen then handed it back to him. She winced and her hand covered her abdomen.

"You should drink some more."

"I've drunk enough. Ow!" She doubled over, clutching her stomach.

Tomas pulled the pack off his shoulders and looked for the medical kit.

"No." Rachel shook her head vehemently. "Let's just go."

Tomas placed his hand on her forehead. "You're burning up again."

"I'm fine." Her face scrunched up.

"You are far from fine. Now lie on this." He took off his jacket and spread it on part of the rock that formed a natural bench. Tomas lit the lantern, uneasy about it broadcasting their presence.

"No, Tomas. Let's just go."

"Not until I check your wound." He pointed to where his jacket lay.

Rachel glared at him but did as he asked. He handed her the canteen so she had something to grip as he did his work. Cleaning his hands, Tomas ever-so-slowly lifted the bandage, the lantern's light casting a yellow glow.

Rachel's normally pale skin looked red raw around the wound and a viscous, yellow fluid leaked from the site. Tomas quickly set to work and cleaned what he could, aware that every second the wound was exposed meant it could get worse. What was he to do, though? Leave it to fester and have her die in the mountains? Abato's threats came rushing back but they were unnecessary. Of course, Tomas would do everything in his power to help Rachel and he certainly didn't need the added pressure of Abato's threats hanging over his head. Though Tomas wasn't so naïve as to think the threats were empty.

This situation only brought home how very unprepared he was for life out in the field. Even though many groups like Abato's existed and were fighting for the same cause—freedom from fascists—they didn't work together, leaving gaps in the network, gaps that could be ripped apart by the more experienced German and Italian soldiers.

After he cleaned and dressed the wound, Tomas quickly set about packing up. Rachel remained on the rock, her eyes closed while she tried to catch her breath. He went to shove the bottle of rubbing alcohol in the side pocket of Rachel's pack but it wouldn't go in. His fingers felt around inside the pocket and he found the book. Pulling it out, he glanced over at Rachel who lay still, her eyes firmly shut.

Tomas quickly turned his back to her. He should leave well enough alone but if he were risking his life getting Rachel and this all-important book to Palermo, surely he should be privy to its contents. He flicked open a page. In neat, cursive writing were names, dates and coordinates. None of it made sense.

Rachel stirred and he quickly shut the book and thrust it into the pocket.

A solitary tear slid from the corner of Rachel's eye and Tomas moved to wipe it away, but changed his mind, unsure if she'd misconstrue his action.

"An hour more and we'll be there," he said quietly.

Rachel opened her eyes and nodded, her bottom lip trembling. Giving in to the desire to comfort her, he moved toward her, but stopped when she jutted out her chin, a slight spark in her eyes. "Don't even think about it."

* * * *

Despite the festering wound weakening Rachel's whole body, she pushed through the pain. As they moved through the deserted streets of Palermo, a sense of foreboding overwhelmed Tomas, but he swatted it away, refusing to spend time worrying about what-ifs.

The rising sun cast an orange glow on the cobblestoned streets as they turned the last corner. Rachel leant heavily on Tomas as he tried to keep her going, her legs barely able to support her weight. Thankfully, the street remained quiet. Tomas scanned the houses, trying to find the right one. He spotted it a few doors up and he turned to Rachel, whose face was ashen, her lips without color.

He helped her to sit on the nearest doorstep. Bending down, he whispered, "Just wait here. I'll go and check we've got the right place."

She leant against the railing as he hurried to the house and climbed the steps. Tomas rapped on the door with the same series of knocks he'd learnt from Abato and a moment later the sound of shoes rapidly crossing floorboards echoed down the hallway behind the door.

"Who is it?" asked a gruff voice in a half-whisper.

"Dr. Bianchi, I'm a friend of Bruno Abato's. I have a package."

A second later the door clicked open. A short, round man in his seventies peered over thick glasses. The creases in the doctor's forehead were deep, like he'd spent all his days scowling. His pallid complexion made him look sickly, and the red rims of his eyes gave the impression he and sleep were not acquaintances.

"Where is it?" the doctor asked.

"Down the road."

He stuck his head out the doorway and spotted Rachel slumped over. "Get her inside!"

Tomas ran to Rachel and scooped her in his arms. Her head rolled back and her eyes fluttered as she drifted in and out of consciousness. Tomas hurried into the doctor's residence and quickly followed him to the back of the house, his arms aching from Rachel's dead weight. They turned a sharp left and Tomas found himself standing in a sterile room that reeked of ammonia.

"On the table!" barked the doctor and Tomas gently lay down Rachel.

"Owww," she moaned and clutched her side. Her eyes flew open, full of panic.

"It's all right. Dr. Bianchi will look after you." Tomas looked over to where the doctor was busy scrubbing his hands.

"The book…" Her voice sounded so small in the large room.

"It can wait."

"No. We need to…" She rolled over and dry-retched. All that came up was foul smelling bile that left a trail down the side of her face. Tomas grabbed the nearest cloth and wiped it away. She whimpered and clutched his arm so hard her fingernails dug in and broke his skin. He stood steadfast, stroking her clammy forehead.

Tomas was thankful Rachel couldn't see the look on the doctor's face as he stood behind her and filled a syringe with clear liquid. His solemn expression did nothing to allay Tomas's fears that this could be too little too late. Had Tomas pushed her too far? Should they have risked travelling by road?

Abato's words came smashing in to his consciousness and repeated on an endless spool: *If anything happens to my sister, I will hold you fully responsible. I will hunt you down. And I will kill you.*

Rachel's groans grew more intense and Tomas held her cold, sweaty fingers as he muttered, "You will be up and about before you know it."

"Promise?" she rasped.

He studied her dark, sad eyes so full of trust. "I..."

The doctor shoved the thick needle into her arm and injected the fluid. Rachel's screams filled the room.

Chapter 8

Rosie sliced the custard apple in half with so much force the knife wedged in the chopping board. Pulling the fruit apart, she jabbed the spoon into the soft pale flesh and scooped it into a glass bowl. Tension raced across her shoulders, and her temples throbbed. She forced herself to take a moment and rested her hands on the counter top, her head lowered. This anger was ridiculous. She was very relieved that Dr. Wilkinson had managed to see her father so quickly after he collapsed, but hadn't her family suffered enough with losing Geoffrey and Alex? Why would God put them through more grief by her father suffering a stroke?

Forcing her anger to a simmer, she sliced the lemon and drizzled the juice over the custard apple, just how her father liked it. Once again, hot tears welled up in Rosie's eyes with the realization of how close they'd come to losing him. For all his bluster and stubbornness, she loved him dearly and couldn't imagine a world without him.

Rosie took a deep breath and poured ice-cold water into a glass and placed it on the tray. She finished off the presentation by adding her father's favorite hibiscus to a small vase. The violet with pink around the edges represented happiness and she liked to think it had that effect on her father, even if only for a moment.

"Helloooooo!" The screen door creaked open and Rosie went down the hallway to meet Kitty, whose belly was rounder than a beach ball. In her hands, she balanced a small wooden box filled with jars of pickles, tomatoes, and bottles of…something.

Rosie grabbed the load from her friend as they both made their way to the kitchen. Whispering, she said, "Thank you, but you didn't have to."

Kitty whispered back. "Is your dad asleep?"

"Yes."

"How's he doing?" Her voice was back at its normal volume. If this was Kitty's attempt at a whisper she pitied her poor baby. This child would never sleep.

"Fair to middling," Rosie said.

"How are you?" Kitty touched Rosie's arm lightly.

Rosie shrugged. "I'm all right. I'm just doing what needs to be done."

"You better call me if you need help." Kitty gave Rosie a knowing stare.

"I will." Although she and Kitty both knew Rosie would tough it out alone for as long as possible.

They entered the kitchen and Rosie indicated for Kitty to close the door that led to the hallway.

"By the way, I didn't bring these." Kitty nodded toward the collection of jars.

"Huh?" Rosie placed the box on the kitchen table and picked up a bottle: *oliu d'olivi.*

"I found it on the verandah." Kitty helped herself to the jug of water from the ice chest. She waved it in the air and Rosie nodded that yes, she'd like some.

Rosie started sifting through the contents and placed them on the bench. She lifted the bottles out, examining the contents. They were filled to the brim with preserved fruit and vegetables, the labels neatly written in what she suspected was Sicilian. Placing her hands on her hips, she looked at the collection then noticed a slip of folded paper. She opened it and in neat swirly writing, it read:

Thinking of you.

T

Kitty sat at the table and sipped the water. "Who's it from? A certain neighbor from Italy?"

"There are lots of people from Italy in this town." Rosie folded the paper and stuffed it in her apron.

"There's only one who makes you go bright red like a kid caught with her hand in the cookie jar."

Rosie grabbed a loaf of freshly baked bread and concentrated on cutting it into thick slices. She put them on a plate and carried it over to the table, along with a jar of lemon butter she'd made a few days earlier.

"How are you really doing, Kitty? You're looking rather...flushed."

"I'm feeling rather cranky, bloated, tired, and more done than a Sunday roast. I'm not even at my due date."

"So, pregnancy is agreeing with you then."

Kitty lifted her feet onto the chair and gulped the rest of her water. "My ankles are fatter than my thighs."

Rosie grabbed the jug from the ice chest and filled up Kitty's glass. She sat down and took a sip out of her own.

"Now, let's get back to the very handsome Tomas Conti who likes to deliver homemade goodies. He seemed quite taken with you at the dance."

"Stop it!" Rosie threw a nearby tea towel in Kitty's direction. Her friend ducked then poked out her tongue. "I'm not interested."

"Your nose is growing."

"And your luck is running out."

Kitty shrugged, her expression one of nonchalance. "I'm pregnant so you can't pick on me."

"Playing that card, are we?" Rosie got up and started placing the bottles back in the box.

"What are you doing?"

Rosie continued until the box was full. "I'm just putting them away for now."

"So, your father doesn't see them? I love your father, but he is racist."

Sitting heavily on the chair, Rosie stretched her legs. "It's a bit more complicated than that."

"Than singling out one nationality and accepting everybody else?"

Rosie paused. "Mum told me there was some dispute or other going on with the Contis. He's been too sick for me to ask, but if it's an ongoing thing then someone in this family has to deal with it."

"Oh."

She eyed off the basket of homemade goodies. "Do you think that's a bribe?"

Kitty held out her hands in a questioning manner.

"No, he wouldn't," Rosie said, hoping Tomas wouldn't resort to such tactics. "Maybe I should pay a visit to Mr. Conti."

"Shouldn't you find out what the problem is first?"

"I don't want to bother Dad."

"Hmmm," Kitty said. "So...how are things going around here? Is Bartel helping?"

A lump formed in her throat as the muscles in her neck tensed. "There's only so much Bartel can help us with."

"The workers need a proper boss. Someone who is vested in this business," said Kitty.

"I know."

"They need you. Your father needs you."

Rosie let Kitty's words hang in the air. They echoed the exact same thoughts that had spun like a merry-go-round since her father had become incapacitated.

"They're going to have to let me stay. Bartel's been doing it alone for the last couple of weeks, but he needs help."

"I don't get why they were against you staying in the first place," said Kitty.

"They expect me to build a life in Brisbane, not have a tough life on the farm, blah, blah. I'm not buying it entirely, though."

"Why not?"

"Why would they not want their only surviving child at home with them?" Rosie shook her head. "Mum hasn't been…doing that great and we know what's happened with Dad."

"Then it makes sense for you to be here."

"Yeah, I just wish it was under different circumstances." Rosie picked up a jar of olives and studied it. The weird little things in juice didn't look particularly appetizing. "Maybe things worked out the way they're supposed to."

"Maybe."

Kitty finished the water and Rosie poured her another. She let out a sigh.

"Stop it," Kitty said.

"What?"

"Your father's stroke was not your fault."

"How did you…?"

Kitty tapped her head. "I moonlight as a mind reader. Didn't you know?"

Rosie burst out laughing but quickly stopped when she heard her father's raspy voice call from the living room down the hall.

"I'll be back." She retrieved the tray then hastened to her father.

"How are you feeling?" Rosie entered the room, forcing herself to sound cheery, even though her heart broke every time she saw his feeble state. He looked like he'd lost two stone and aged twenty years.

He mumbled something and she strained to hear him.

"Pardon, Dad?"

Since the stroke her father had needed to adjust to the changes in his body, including his speech. Although it had only been a short time, Rosie had discovered that by studying his lips and watching his eyes, she could usually figure out what he was saying. Her mother, however, found it extremely difficult.

Her father attempted one more time, his words rolling into each other, but she finally got it.

"Tired. So very, very tired," he said.

"Perhaps if you close your eyes again—"

"No." Spit flew out and landed on his crippled hand. "Too much sleep."

She hadn't yet mastered how to deal with her father's elevated crankiness. Perhaps she never would. Although, it had only been a short time and everyone still needed to adjust. Everything was a waiting game right now—a waiting game with no end date.

She stabbed the fruit on the tray with a fork and held it in the air. "Custard apple?"

Her father shook his head like a petulant three-year-old.

"Please, Dad, you need to eat."

He drew his lips together and he refused to look at her.

"Kitty's here. I'm sure she'd love to see you."

"Baby?"

"Not yet, she still has some time to go." At least her father showed interest in something. "Shall I go get her?"

He shook his head. "I'm tired."

"I understand everything's topsy-turvy right now, Dad, but—"

"You cannot understand." His speech sounded more slurred.

"You're right, I can't *fully* understand. What I do know is there are a whole lot of people worried about you and praying—"

"Praying is useless."

"It's not just praying, Dad. Your workers are going the extra mile to keep this place running. Bartel has gone above and beyond, but neither he nor the other workers can do it forever."

Her father grunted and continued staring into the dark corner.

"Something has to change, just for the short term." She refused to believe the doctors when they said recovery was nigh impossible and everyone just had to adapt to her father's new world.

"Dad…"

Silence.

"Please, Dad…"

More silence.

She slammed the fork and fruit onto the tray. "You have to eat. And you have to make a decision about what we're going to do about Tulpil because we can't keep going on the way we are." Her father's reticence only fueled her determination. It was now or never. "Given the circumstances, it should be me who takes over. It only makes sense because I have a duty and a vested interest in ensuring things run smoothly."

He didn't flinch. Didn't blink. All her father did was keep goddamned silent. "No."

Rosie bit her lip, not trusting herself to not run off at the mouth. In the distance, she could hear Kitty running water and the clink of dishes being washed. She should be resting, but of course Kitty refused to be waited on hand and foot. If Rosie were in the same position she wouldn't allow it, either. A small smile formed on her lips.

"There is nothing to smile about." Her father grumbled.

"No, there isn't. I'm not offering to do this so I can stay at Tulpil. I'm offering because you need a family member overseeing the operation. What's that saying? Blood is thicker than water?"

"Bartel has been with me for a long time. He's been doing the tallies for the men and payment for suppliers. He's also collecting payments for deliveries."

"But—"

"Rosie…" Her father closed his eyes for a moment, his lips drawn into a thin line. "Just leave it be. Bartel will manage the farm. He knows the men and how everything works. We need to keep this place going. So many men and their families depend on it. Maybe—" Her father shifted position and his movements were jerky and appeared painful. "Maybe you could do the books *in the office*. That would free up Bartel to be with the men more. However, you step over the line, you lose the position."

"All right," she said.

"There is one more condition."

She shouldn't have been surprised. "Yes?"

"You tell me why you don't want to return to Brisbane."

"We've been through this—"

"Rosie…"

She couldn't. It was too painful.

"Rosie?"

"I was fired." The words tumbled out with embarrassment, hurt and fear rolled together. She tried to keep her voice calm as she recounted the events leading up to her rapid departure. All the while, she averted her gaze. Finally, she summoned the courage to look directly at him.

He had been staring at the dark corner, and when he finally looked at her, her fears melted away. "I am so sorry, sweetheart."

"It's all right, Dad. I've come to terms with it." It was better for him to hear this than to know the wound remained raw.

"You shouldn't have to come to terms with it." His voice was loud, way louder than he'd spoken since the stroke. "He needs to be hung, drawn and quartered. I want to wring his neck."

"Dad, please, the last thing you need is to get upset."

"And I was concerned about the men here," he said quietly.

"I feel safer at Tulpil than anywhere else, Dad."

His fingers twitched and she reached for his hand. It shook beneath her grasp.

"Sweetheart, I do not want you to use Tulpil as a place to hide."

"I'm not doing that, I promise. Dad?"

"Hmmm?"

"I have a question and I really need to know the answer. Mum mentioned something about a dispute between us and the Contis." There, it was out in the open, floating above their heads.

"What did she say?"

Small beads of sweat broke out on his forehead and she feared this question may have been too soon. "She just said there was an issue."

"Land."

"Huh?" she asked then remembered who she was speaking to. "Pardon?"

"Land. They said the title is wrong and some of our land is theirs."

"Is that true?"

Once more, her father concentrated on the dark corner of the room.

"Is it, Dad?"

"Yes." It came out like a hiss.

"So, did you make things right?"

"Yes." The rising anger within was palpable.

"How much did we lose?"

"That patch on the river bend," he said, annoyance pushing out his words.

"Will it have a big effect on us?" she asked.

He feebly shook his head. "No, but that's beside the point. That land has been in our family for years then these people come in and start checking titles and what-not—"

"So, it wasn't legally ours?" She shifted forward but the strong sunlight hit her eyes. Leaning to the side, she said, "We did the right thing giving it back."

Her father grumbled.

"I don't understand what the problem is," she said.

"Flaming Italians."

Rosie stood. "We were in the wrong and they were in the right. Why are you always so angry with Italians? Would you feel this way if our neighbors were French?"

"No."

"Spanish?"

"No."

"Lithuanian?"

He looked away and she was annoyed with herself for pressing so hard when he was unwell. If the issue had been resolved, then that was all she needed to worry about.

His eyes finally connected with hers. "You will never understand."

"I could try." Her voice sounded calmer and she hoped it would encourage him to finally open up.

"It's the past. Water under the bridge."

"This water seems to be gushing like a river in wet season."

"Leave it alone, Rosie."

Rosie let commonsense take over and she sat quietly. Her father looked ready for another nap and she needed to be careful how far she pushed him. He'd just agreed to give her a chance to do the books so she should be grateful for small victories.

"I'm sorry if I've upset you." She meant every word.

It took quite some time before her father turned to face her again. The anger had left his eyes and in its place, a deep sadness had taken up residence. "Thank you."

"For?"

"Just…thank you."

"Are you thankful enough to eat some fruit?" She gave a cheeky smile.

His small nod encouraged her to pick up the food and hold it in front of him. He took a minuscule bite and spent a minute chewing.

"Thank you for trying, Dad."

He swallowed hard. "Small steps. No leaping."

But Rosie felt she was about to take the biggest leap of her life.

Chapter 9

1943—Palermo, Sicily

Tomas stood at the base of the steps to his family home, hat in hand, heart beating rapidly. It had only been two weeks since he'd seen them but it felt like a lifetime. When he'd last crossed this threshold he'd stormed out the door and onto the street, frustrated with his parents' inability to understand why he would ditch his engineering career in favor of fighting for the rights of his countrymen. Maybe now they would be willing to hear him out.

He knocked on the door, the early morning sun shining on his back. Every second seemed to drag. Rachel's operation had gone surprisingly well and she'd spent the past week in a spare room at Dr. Bianchi's house but their time was up. Rachel needed a new place to recover and Tomas had racked his brains for a solution. As promised, Tomas stayed by Rachel's side as she moved in and out of consciousness, continually muttering about a man named Paolo. Tomas tried quizzing her, but the conversation had been one-sided. Why hadn't Abato mentioned this Paolo before? Was he a contact? Is that who the notebook should go to? Rachel hadn't been in any state to hold a conversation so, for now, Paolo remained a mystery and just a name that haunted her lips.

Tomas raised his hand to knock again but hesitated, unsure whether he should be relieved or anxious if no one was home. With all the confusion about Abato and the young Italian soldier, as well as the exhaustion of getting Rachel to safety, Tomas wasn't sure he had the energy to deal with his family. For Rachel's sake, though, he needed to give her shelter and his family was the best option.

Tomas knocked hard and this time heels clacked along the floorboards as they hurried toward the door. It creaked open, leaving a small gap and a pair of dark brown eyes peering at him.

"Nonna, it's—"

The door flew open and arms enveloped him. "My boy! My boy has returned! Come! Come in!" She placed her small hands on his back and ushered him into the foyer and into the kitchen.

Her warm greeting left him dumbfounded.

"What are you waiting for? An invitation?" Nonna laughed. Tomas shook his head.

"I—"

"You think I would be mad at you forever? A lot has changed since we last saw each other."

"It's only been two weeks," he said.

"Well, a lot can change in twenty-four hours." She gazed up at him, the light catching the deep wrinkles etched on her face. When he was a kid, he'd loved running his fingers over those lines and asking what each one represented. Nonna had a story for every single line: *This one is for the worry for our country's future. This one is for the happiness and laughter you bring me. This one is for the smiles your nonno gave me every day.*

Nonna gently pushed him onto a kitchen chair. "You have heard?"

Tomas leant forward. "Heard what?"

Nonna let out a sigh and sat down heavily on the chair opposite. "And you call yourself a soldier."

"I don't, I'm a—"

"The Allied troops have arrived."

"What? When did that happen?"

"Overnight."

No wonder he'd missed it. He'd been asleep on the chair next to Rachel's bed at the surgery. And because he'd snuck out early to see his family, he hadn't been around when the household woke to the news.

"What happened?" he asked.

"The American and British troops parachuted in near Syracuse. Rumors are they'll move north."

Tomas let this news sink in, surprised, stunned, and overjoyed that finally, the underground groups would have world-class armies to support them in getting rid of the fascists. Although more lives would be lost—

many innocent—and countless others would be traumatized by the bloody battles that would be fought.

"Perhaps you should go further north," Tomas said. "We've got cousins in Milano who would take you in. Mumma and Papá could go, too."

"Don't be ridiculous," said Nonna. "No one will ever come between me and my home."

"It would only be temporary," he said, realizing this could be the start of a massive lie, "just to ensure you're safe."

"Nowhere is safe, is it?" She angled a finger at Tomas. "Your nonno thought you and he would be safe at that political meeting but he was wrong, wasn't he?"

The familiar wave of sadness mixed with pure terror took hold of Tomas once more, like a blanket of fear and regret he could never fully discard.

A renowned journalist, his nonno had planned to meet with a group of Jewish people who were discussing their rights after Mussolini published the Manifesto of Race ahead of changing racial laws in Italy. The Jewish Italians were to be stripped of their Italian citizenship and forbidden to hold influential jobs, including with the government. They'd lose rights to their properties and marriages to non-Jews would be abolished. Tomas's nonno, a well-respected man and passionate humanitarian, had been invited to the meeting with the hope he could help the Jewish Italians by using his contacts. Although his nonno was initially against the idea of Tomas accompanying him, he'd finally relented, figuring his twenty-year-old grandson should keep abreast of politics because it infiltrated everyone's lives and it was better to be informed rather than remain in a state of ignorant bliss.

What no one had expected was Mussolini's Blackshirts to arrive brandishing guns and batons and killing needlessly at their peaceful—and secret—gathering. People ducked for cover under chairs, tables, in corners. Bullets flew. Shouts deafened. Panic reigned. Caught in the fray, the streets running red with blood, Tomas and his nonno escaped, but a bullet hit his nonno in the heart. He'd collapsed in Tomas's arms, not breathing, blood soaking his shirt.

That night, Tomas's world—and his family's—changed forever.

Nonna sniffed as she dabbed her eyes with the apron. "The past is the past."

Tomas struggled to hold his composure, thrown into traumatic memories he'd tried so hard to forget. "You don't need to be brave, Nonna."

"I do. You do. Everyone does. These are trying times, my boy, and they will only become more difficult as time goes by. Who knows what will happen with the arrival of the Allies." A long sigh left her lips. "Sometimes

I wonder if we'd be better off living elsewhere. Don't get me wrong, Palermo is my home and it will always be, but I can't help wonder what it would be like to live in a place where people can walk the streets without fear of getting arrested for looking at someone the wrong way." She drummed her fingers on the table, a distant look in her eyes. "What about Canada? New Zealand? Or that place with those weird creatures that bounce like rabbits but are as big as a small horse?"

"Kangaroos?"

"That's it! Australia, land of the kangaroos. Do you think they have olive trees there, Tomas?"

"You just said no one would ever come between you and your home." He cocked an eyebrow.

"Maybe home is where you make it. I would be just as happy living in the mountains as I would by the ocean. As long as I have my family with me." She wrapped her fingers around his. Her skin felt drier, her bones more prominent. Tomas looked at Nonna—really looked at her—and noticed how gaunt and pale she'd become since he last saw her. This war had taken its toll on everyone and it broke his heart to see his grandmother suffering this way.

Nonna withdrew her hand. "Sometimes I imagine being able to sleep soundly without worrying about what's going on beyond these walls. But don't mind me, these are just the dreams of a foolish old woman. Besides, your parents would never agree to such an outlandish idea."

"Probably not." Tomas looked around and asked, "Where are they?"

"Your father has gone down to the factory to sort out some issue with the machinery and your mother left early for something-or-other."

"How are they?" he asked cautiously.

"If you're asking if they're still angry with you, then yes, they are. None of us wanted you to deliberately put yourself in danger. They'll forgive you when they see you are safe and sound."

Tomas's gaze rested on Nonna. Although he'd loved his nonno dearly and they had been like peas in a pod, Nonna had been the only person he'd ever confided in. She'd been his advocate. She'd never let him down. She'd always kept her word. So, Tomas opened his mouth and the whole sad, sordid story of his time with Abato and his men poured out. He deliberately left out any mention of Rachel as he didn't want to bombard Nonna with too much information at once. Besides, he needed to ease into it and mentioning Rachel off the back of everything he'd just said may not be the best idea.

Nonna listened intently and took in every word. When he'd finished, she gave his arm a squeeze. "You have so much love—your love for our country. Love for our people. Maybe you need to rethink how you see your role in all this. Killing is not in your heart, my boy."

"It just feels…wrong. But I have to do something. I can't sit around and—"

"You are an intelligent young man. You have a degree. You *know* people." She raised an eyebrow, giving him the same knowing look he'd received all his life.

"Politics?" Tomas drew his brows together. "No. No way."

"Of course, not politics! Do you think I would be insane enough to suggest that?" She slapped her hands on the table. "You have a brain. You have a heart. You don't need weapons. Words can often be more powerful. Find a way to use them."

"Like Nonno?" he asked, slightly confused.

"The last thing I want is for you to put yourself in a position like him. I loved that man," she sighed, "but he always trusted the wrong people. Whereas you, my dear boy, seem to do better in this regard."

Tomas clasped his hands in his lap and studied them. "There were times out there when I doubted my choices *and* the people I was with."

"But you never doubted whose side you were on," Nonna said.

"Of course not."

"So, put the gun down and find a way to help that won't have you shot."

"Anything to do with these people could have me shot," said Tomas.

"I know"—she smoothed down her apron—"and as much as I wish you wouldn't get involved I understand why you can't watch this country fall apart. Even recently I've gotten…" Nonna sat back and pursed her lips.

"Even recently you've gotten, what?"

"It doesn't matter. You need to find a way to use your voice and intelligence and fight this war without weapons."

Tomas tilted his head to the side. Nonna was not usually one for being cryptic.

"Why the change of heart, Nonna?"

"I can't deny What's going on around us any longer. No one can. It's on our doorsteps and can barge in here at any minute. The arrival of the Allies has given me hope, but hope alone doesn't win wars."

"Speaking of hope…" It wasn't the neatest transition but it would have to do.

"Yes?"

"I have a friend—you know her from a long time ago—and I'm hoping you'll find it in your heart to help." Layer by layer, Tomas revealed the story about Rachel, all the while carefully studying Nonna, who remained quiet. By the time he'd brought her up to date, Nonna was leaning forward, slowly nodding, concern in her eyes.

"Do you trust her?" Nonna asked.

Tomas didn't hesitate. "Yes."

"Then we must help," she said.

"You need to realize there's danger in doing so, and I wouldn't ask if we weren't desperate. And then there's a small matter of Mumma and Papá…"

"Leave that with me. You go ahead and tell Rachel she is welcome here."

Tomas's shoulders dropped with relief and that's when he realized how much tension he'd been carrying. He felt terrible putting his family in this position but, given Rachel's mental strength, Tomas figured her physical recovery would be swift. If she managed to stay resting…. He had a feeling Nonna would make sure she did.

Nonna placed both palms, down on the table and locked eyes on him. "Now we have your friend sorted, you need to think about what you're going to do. The only way to stop this country, and the rest of the world, from imploding is for people like you to find a way to make things right."

Tomas lowered his head. "It's such a big task."

"You're the first person in our family to get a degree. You had your doubts that you could do it, but you pushed through." Nonna got up, went to the cupboard and returned with an orange.

"Where did you get this?"

"You're not the only one with connections. It's yours. You've worked hard for it." She pointed at the fruit in his hands. "Could you shove a whole orange in your mouth?"

"No." He brought the orange to his nose, closed his eyes momentarily and inhaled the aromatic citrus.

"What if you peel away the layers, break the orange into sections and deal with it one piece at a time? You'd get through it, no? You'd achieve your goal."

"You do love your analogies, don't you?" Tomas smiled, the first time he'd done in days. Hell, it had been weeks. Maybe Nonna was right. Maybe he could bring together the elements needed to invoke change. Tomas broke off a piece of orange and shoved it in his mouth. His taste buds delighted in the zesty, fresh flavor, reminding him of his auntie and uncle's orange groves outside of Palermo where he and the family used to go for day trips. Life in those villages had been so easygoing, a peaceful, rustic existence.

Peeling off another section, Tomas said, "All right. I'll look into it."

* * * *

The conversation with Nonna swirled inside Tomas's head as he strode toward Dr. Bianchi's house. His people could use an engineer who understood the designs of bridges and buildings that could help in attacks… but those attacks could still lead to the loss of life of innocent people.

Tomas dodged the scrawny stray dogs and winked at the young kids, many malnourished and draped in ragged clothes. War had destroyed any hope in this country. He could see it in his people's eyes. There was no spark, only fear of the unknown. What kind of life was this? One his people didn't deserve, that's for sure.

Tomas climbed the steps to the doctor's house and was let in by the wife. Dr. Bianchi stuck his head out from one of the far rooms and gave a nod. Still no evidence that he was capable of a smile. But why would he? This doctor spent most of his time stitching up those wounded in this bloody war.

Tomas made his way to the end of the hall and entered Rachel's room. She was already dressed and sitting on the edge of the bed. Smoothing down her hair, she gave a wide smile. The difference between a woman on the brink of death almost a week ago and this ray of sunshine was incredible.

"I have a solution," she said.

"To?"

"To where I'll stay." Rachel adjusted a black shawl around her thin shoulders.

"You're staying with my family, remember?" She hadn't been high on drugs when they'd had this discussion, so why the change of plans? "Besides, your brother has charged me with looking after you."

"I'm going to stay…" Her eyes didn't meet his. "With a…my…friend."

"What kind of friend?"

"One I've known a very long time." The words came out fast.

"I'm sorry, Rachel, but your brother—"

"I'm going and you can't stop me." She stood and looked up at him, her expression defiant. Rachel swayed a little and put her hand on the bed. She narrowed her eyes, as if challenging him to say anything.

"I can stop you and I will."

"You can't and you won't." She tugged angrily at the shawl.

"Please, come to my family's home. There's a spare room and you're welcome."

"I've made arrangements and there's no arguing," Rachel said. "It's only for a short while, anyway. I plan to be back out doing my job as soon as I can."

"Almost dying hasn't scared you?"

She snorted. "No. Why would it?"

"It's a dangerous job."

"Everything's dangerous when there's a war in your country. My goal is to end the rule of these tyrants. Isn't yours?"

"Of course, it is."

The hardness in her eyes melted and the squareness of her shoulders softened. "Listen, Tomas, I'm sorry for being abrasive. You went through so much to get me back to Palermo and I haven't shown my appreciation for what you've done."

"You haven't lost that stubbornness you had as a kid." Tomas smiled and so did Rachel. "You need to do more of that."

"What?" Her smile instantly fell away.

"Smiling becomes you."

"Please, don't." She cleared her throat. "Bianchi told me the Allies have arrived, but they won't help us on our terms. It will be theirs."

"You don't know that. I want to see the bloodshed stop, but I think there are other ways to do this without more killing."

"Are you a pacifist?" Her tone sounded incredulous, slightly horrified. "Do you think you can march up to Hitler and ask him to put the guns down? What about Mussolini? Do you think the Blackshirts will stop torturing people and go on a holiday? Do you really think that would work?" She placed her hands on her hips and raised her eyebrows.

"That is ridiculous and I am certainly no fool. Look, my job is to look after you and that's what I'm going to do. Please, let's go."

"No." She folded her arms across her chest. For a woman who displayed elements of strength beyond her years she contradicted it neatly with moments of complete immaturity.

"Listen—"

"I'm not changing my mind."

"Then you need to tell me who this person is and where you'll be. I will be keeping a close eye on you." What did Abato want him to do? Manhandle Rachel by dragging her to his house and tying her to the bed? Surely Abato trusted his sister enough to choose decent company.

"I'm going to stay with my husband." She jutted out her chin, daring Tomas to argue.

"Husband?"

"Yes," she said, as if he should have known.

"Your brother never mentioned you were married."

"Well, we're not married. We're just…sort of…. we were together. He's like a husband." Once more her eyes didn't meet his.

"But you're not with him now?"

"I will be."

A shimmer of disappointment fell on him and he needed a moment to take stock.

"Listen," she said, yanking him into the present, "you better not be judging me because of my choices."

"I am not the morals police," Tomas said, "and I am not judging you." Although he wondered what on earth Nonna would say if he told her the unmarried Rachel had run off to be with a man.

"I love him and he loves me. He will make sure my recovery is swift." She lifted her pack and that same notebook Tomas had discovered fell on the bed. "Oh shit."

"What?"

Rachel stared at the book lying innocently in front of her. "It should have been delivered the second we got to Palermo. God, my brother's going to kill me."

"You were delirious and almost died, what the hell did he expect? Give it to me." Tomas held out his hand. "I'll deliver it for you."

"No." She picked up the book and clutched it tightly against her chest.

"Then let me take you to where you need to go. You are still under my care."

She stalked over to the door and yanked it open. "Like hell I am."

Chapter 10

Rosie stood in the garden, clutching a cup of tea as she soaked up the warmth of the early morning sun. Today was her first day on the job and she had every intention of making it an excellent one.

In the nearby fields, the sugarcane stood to attention, waiting for the men to arrive and set to work—stoop to cut the base of the cane, straighten their backs, cut the top of the cane, drop for collection—over and over again until the heat of the day became unbearable. As the men were paid by how much cane was cut, they only stopped for a swig of water to prevent themselves collapsing from dehydration.

A heavy footfall drew her attention to the left of the house. Bartel rounded the corner, the large Akubra hat shielding his face as he walked over to her.

"Are you ready for your big day?" Bartel's smile appeared to be more of a grimace.

"I am."

"Your father says you are to remain in the office." His statement sounded more like a command and it irritated her. But she had to keep Bartel on her side because if she put one foot wrong he'd be sure to report it to her father.

Rosie forced a smile. She'd never warmed to her father's foreman, but they didn't have to be best friends, all they had to do was get along—somehow.

"There may be instances when I need to find you to clarify something," she said. Surely he didn't expect her to be chained to the desk all day, every day.

Bartel adjusted his hat. "I am sure it could wait until I return for the day."

"Maybe…" There was no point in going in circles with this man. Rosie just needed to get on with her job and prove to her father she was more than capable. "So, are you up to date with the supplier accounts?"

"Of course." He shook his head, as if it was impossible that he wouldn't be.

"Bartel, I didn't mean to offend. It's just with everything going on some things may have fallen by the wayside."

"I can assure you that everything is up to date." His surly tone didn't help matters, but she let it slide.

"Great." She finished off the last of the tea, even though it was now cold. "I'd better get to it."

Bartel turned on his heels and pounded down the steps.

Rosie watched him stride across the gravel toward the shed, dust flying behind him. No wonder he hadn't married. With a personality like that he'd be hard-pressed to find a woman who'd put up with his surliness.

Trying not to let his mood crowd in on her day, Rosie went to her father's office and stood in the doorway. Piles of papers lay on every conceivable surface—the spare chair, the desk, the floor, and the walnut cabinet that had belonged to her grandfather. Letting out a deep, long breath, Rosie sat on the dark green leather chair. Her grandfather had been an interesting man who had scared the living daylights out of her. He was gruff, sported a constant scowl, but he looked after the cane gangs who worked for him, while neighbors ruled with an iron fist. And no matter how busy her grandfather was, he'd always find a moment to let young Rosie sit on his knee and tell him about her day—the frogs she'd caught and let go, the tree she'd made friends with, the nest of baby birds she'd discovered. Rosie missed her grandfather dearly. What would he make of the goings on at Tulpil these days?

Rosie checked the calendar. Thursday. The day to check the cane gang's tallies and make payments. She needed to get organized quick-smart so the men received their money on time. Rosie stood and rummaged around the piles and it took a few minutes before she located the ledger and hoisted the heavy book onto the desk. Leaning forward, she scanned through the pages, checking what each cane gang was owed and if they had accrued any loans with her father that needed to be paid.

As she worked her way through the figures, things didn't add up— literally. She tried two, three times and even a fourth, but the cash she had in the safe didn't match and the figures for the men didn't balance, either. And there'd been a few payments missed to suppliers. Surely there'd been a mistake. Maybe Bartel could explain how he'd worked it out.

Putting on her hat, Rosie went in search of Bartel. It was now lunchtime and she suspected he wouldn't have strayed too far from the shed.

Rosie rounded the corner and spied Loto in the distance. She asked, "How are you feeling?"

His hand instinctively went to his side, though he forced a smile. "Much better, thank you, boss."

"Boss?" Where did that come from? She laughed lightly. "I'm just plain old Rosie."

"Miss Rosie." He grinned. "But you are the boss now."

"My father is still the boss and Bartel and I are assisting him. Speaking of which"—she glanced around and saw Sefa walking toward them—"have you seen Bartel?"

"No." Sefa took a swig of water out of the canvas bag hanging off the pole.

"He's supposed to be out with the men. Is he in the eastern corner?"

A look passed between Loto and Sefa.

"What's wrong?" she asked, a ripple of apprehension in her belly.

"Miss Rosie, the men haven't—"

Sefa shook his head. Loto shuffled his feet and looked down at them.

"The men haven't, what, Loto?" she asked.

"It is nothing, I am sure it is a misunderstanding," said Sefa, scowling at Loto.

Rosie's gaze travelled from one to the other. Neither man looked at her directly. "If there is something I should know—or my father should—I need to hear it. Now, please."

"The men have not been fully paid for weeks," Sefa finally said. He shoved his hands in his pockets.

"Since my father got sick?"

"No, before then," Sefa said. "At first I thought it was strange but Bartel…"

Rosie said, "As soon as you see Bartel, please ask him to come up to the office. I need to speak to him right away."

* * * *

Rosie sat at the desk and stared out the window, while the sunlight fought its way through the half-open shutters. She'd tried to concentrate on other accounts, but her mind, and eyes, kept returning to the payment records for the workers. The phone rang in the hall and she jumped up and went to get it before the ringing woke her father.

Picking up the receiver, she said quietly, "Hello?"

"Is that you, Rosie?" Came a familiar gravelly voice.

"Yes. How are you, Mr. O'Reilly?"

"I am fine, fine," he said. "How's your father?"

"He's doing all right but…"

"Yes, I heard he's been through quite a lot, which is why I'm calling to say not to worry about the overdue fuel accounts. He can fix me up when he's able. The last thing I want to do is put stress on him and the family."

Rosie drew her brows together. "I'd found some overdue accounts but I am pretty sure Bartel fixed most of them up last week."

She heard a rustle of papers. "No. They're still not paid."

"Can you wait a second, please?" She balanced the receiver on the top of the box and went to the office. There she scrounged through the paperwork and found a couple of bills from O'Reilly's Service Station. Taking them with her, she picked up the phone and said, "Bartel's written down that it's been paid."

"Then he must be mistaken. The last payment I received was six weeks ago."

"Oh." She stared at the yellow paper in her hand. The Stantons had known the O'Reilly family for years, the friendship between her father and Mr. O'Reilly stretching back as far as their school days. So, there was no reason for Mr. O'Reilly to lie about accounts not being paid. Especially as there had never been a problem before…

If this had been an isolated case she could give Bartel the benefit of the doubt, but this, coupled with Loto and Sefa mentioning about the men not receiving their money…

"I'm sorry for the delay in paying you, Mr. O'Reilly. I'll get the money to you as soon as possible." She stared at the front door, itching to get out there and find her father's foreman.

"Don't worry, Rosie. Just whenever you can. Please send your father my regards."

"I will. Thank you. Goodbye." Rosie hung up so quickly Mr. O'Reilly didn't have a chance to bid farewell. Gripping the paper tightly in her hand, she ran down the stairs, across the yard and to the shed where she found Sefa.

"Where's Bartel?" It hurt to get the words out as she gasped for breath.

"He went up to the house an hour ago." Sefa looked genuinely puzzled. "I did as you asked and told him to see you urgently."

She glanced around then noticed Bartel's car was missing. *Oh no.*

Returning her attention to Sefa, she said, "I need to find Bartel. While I'm away, you are in charge."

"Me?" Sefa pointed at his chest, his eyebrows nearly hitting his hairline.

"Yes. I won't be long." *Hopefully.*

"Is this…" He studied his dusty shoes. "Is this about our pay?"

"I'll be back soon." She couldn't voice her concerns.

Rosie went back to the house and quietly opened the screen door before grabbing the keys off the hook. A small gust of wind caught the door and slammed it shut.

Shit!

"Rosie?" her father croaked.

"Yes, Dad?" She moved to the doorway and plastered on a smile.

"How is it all going?" He maneuvered himself up the pillow.

"I'm working my way through it all." At least it wasn't a lie.

"What about Bartel? Is he leaving you to do your job?"

"He's...not kicking up a stink."

There. Not a lie. How could Bartel cause trouble if he wasn't around? Quite easily, apparently...

"Right, well, I must get back to it," she said, trying to figure out how she could drive the ute away without her father's suspicions being raised.

He nodded then a small, lopsided smile formed on his pale lips. "Thank you."

Rosie waved her hands in a dismissive manner. "It's nothing. Thank you for having faith I could do this."

If only current events didn't make her question her abilities.

* * * *

Dust flew through the open windows of the ute as she sped toward town. Her knuckles had turned white, her fingers ached from gripping the wheel, and the muscles across her shoulders ached from tension. Tulpil had been in her family for generations, her ancestors weathering drought, flood, fire, famine, war. There was no hope in hell that she would let a hot-fingered foreman put a dent in the already-dwindling coffers of her family's livelihood.

Pulling up in front of Reg's Pub, she turned off the engine and stared at the second story, where Bartel rented a room. Even though he'd been offered board at Tulpil, he'd declined, saying he liked to separate work from his personal life.

Staring up at the open windows on the second floor, she could make out the faded floral curtains billowing in the light breeze. Taking a deep breath, she exited the ute and looked around for Bartel's vehicle. There were a handful of cars she recognized—Robert Henderson's, Stuart Dover's and Bertie Sherrington's—but no sign of Bartel's battered beast. Rosie walked over to the front doors on the corner of the building and hesitated.

The Public Bar—a ridiculous misnomer—was only for men, with women being forced into the Ladies' Lounge. And even then they couldn't buy their own drinks. She really shouldn't enter, but right now Rosie didn't care for archaic rules. Besides, the publican, Reg, was yet another old school friend of her father's. Surely Reg would make an exception this time. It wasn't like she was going to demand a brandy, lime and soda.

Rosie glanced up the street and saw the trio of Mrs. Daw, Mrs. Marriott, and Mrs. Aylwin gathered out the front of Mitchell's Bakery. Ranging from short and rotund to reed thin and lofty, the devout church women turned all eyes on Rosie. She gave them a quick wave, well aware she would be the subject of gossip until the next victim surfaced.

Grabbing the handle with both hands, she yanked open the door. It was heavier than expected and as she stood in the doorway, she peered into the darkness. Cigarette smoke and stale beer assailed her nostrils as she allowed a moment for her eyes to adjust. Her ears filled with men's deep voices as they chatted, apparently unaware of her presence. Just as she stepped forward she noticed a figure striding toward her.

"Hello, Reg." She kept her tone light.

He gently grasped her elbow and steered her through the door and onto the street. The sun glinted off his red hair and fair skin. "You can't be coming in here like that, Rosie. Do you want to cause trouble?"

"You still enforcing that ridiculous rule?" She shook her arm free.

He cocked an eyebrow. "What do you want?"

"I'm looking for Bartel."

"He's not here," Reg said quickly.

"Come on, Reg. If he's here, I need to know."

"Why?" Reg looked past her shoulders and down the street behind her. She turned around but no one was to be found.

She narrowed her eyes. "You haven't asked me why he isn't at Tulpil working."

Reg's face turned as red as the tomatoes she'd picked from the garden the day before.

"Reg…"

"Fine. He swung past about an hour ago. In a mad rush, like a rabid dog was after him. He went to his room, grabbed his bag, came downstairs and threw money across the bar at me."

"What for?"

"Rent for the room. He owed me a few weeks."

"But we pay him regularly. Surely he had enough to pay you board."

Reg looked at her as if she'd just crawled out from under a rock. "You don't know, do you?" He shook his head. "No, of course you don't. How could you?"

"What?"

Reg paused, as if deciding if he should say any more.

"Please, tell me what you know." If she had to beg, she would.

"He gambles," said Reg.

Her shoulders dropped. "Badly?"

"If he'd saved the money he spent on the gee-gees he'd have a palace by now."

She had desperately wanted to be wrong... Bartel needed to be found. Maybe she could talk some sense into him. Get the money back somehow... Then reality hit hard. "He's skipped town, hasn't he?"

"More than likely." Reg looked toward the bar. "I've got to go."

She nodded. "I understand."

He took a few steps then turned and faced her. "If I get wind of anything about Bartel, I'll be sure to let you know."

"Thanks, Reg."

"How's your father?"

"He's..." An image of the frail man at odds with the world flashed before her. "He's finding things difficult at the moment, but we'll work through it. We always do."

Reg gave a knowing nod. "He's a lucky man."

"How so?"

"He has you looking out for him. And for Tulpil. The boys were telling me about your new role there. I always knew you had potential, Rosie. I'm sorry your father is so ill, but I'm glad to see you have the chance to shine."

She smiled at his kind words but inside her stomach churned.

* * * *

After dashing from shop to shop and the occasional house asking if anyone had seen Bartel, Rosie had come to the sobering conclusion that he had most definitely skipped town. With a heavy heart, she drove back to Tulpil, her mind a mess of distressing thoughts. Was leaving Sefa in charge a mistake? Had the men loaded all the cane to go to the mill? If they hadn't, they'd be behind schedule and this would cause her current headache to turn into a migraine. Then there was the whole question about informing her father about the latest developments. She could keep it from him, but this was his business, he should know, although Rosie was petrified about what this could do to him. Learning of the betrayal by the one man he trusted and discovering the farm was now in financial risk... Rosie doubted his heart would cope with such news.

With one hand on the wheel and the other rubbing her throbbing temple, she flicked on the headlights as dusk settled in. The sky had turned a magnificent red and blazes of pink and purple stretched across the horizon. Any other day she would have pulled over to take in the sight, her heart swelling with pride in the land she called home. But today was no ordinary day.

Turning the ute off the bitumen and onto the dirt road, she grasped the wheel with two hands, trying to keep it out of the large potholes scattered along the road. Darkness descended quickly and she raced along. Although she hadn't organized it with Sefa, she hoped he'd stayed behind to fill her in with the events since she'd left him in charge.

In the distance, she could see the lights of Il Sunnu. The Queenslander house overlooked the farm like a king lording over his land. No doubt Tomas would have finished work, his smooth hands getting more beat up with each passing day. Had he known about the dispute between his family and hers? Surely he would have mentioned it if he did.

Pushing out a sigh, she continued toward her house. Since her father had taken ill she hadn't had a chance to catch up with Tomas. She missed his smile. His gentle laugh. She missed the warm, happy feeling she had whenever they were together.

For now, though, Rosie had to deal with a whole lot of unexpected headaches.

Chapter 11

By the time Rosie arrived at Tulpil, the workers had packed up for the day and were back at their dwellings. As she'd hoped, Sefa and Loto were waiting for her return. They stood out the front of the shed, heavy in conversation when she pulled up. Turning off the engine, she got out of the ute and gently closed the door.

"How did the men go this afternoon?" she asked.

"Good, good." Sefa nodded. "Very good."

Loto backed this up with a nod.

"Thank you for filling in. I really do appreciate it," she said. "Please, go and enjoy your evening. I'll see you tomorrow."

With that she hurried along the path and up to the house. The harsh verandah light bit through the darkness and as she climbed the stairs, her confidence waned. This would not be an easy conversation.

Entering the living room, she found her father sitting in the reading chair, his hair neatly combed, his reading glasses on. His cheeks were rosy and he sat straighter, like he'd found some of the strength he'd lost since the stroke.

Looking up from the newspaper, he asked, "How was the first day?"

Sinking onto a chair, Rosie took a moment to compose herself; the more she willed the brewing tears away, the more they wanted to break free.

Empathy shone in her father's eyes—she hadn't seen this look in years. She gulped down a sob.

"What's wrong?"

She shook her head, fearing her voice would crack. Her father's frown didn't help matters as surely he was thinking a woman who cried after the first day of work wasn't up to the job.

"Was it Bartel? Because if he's gotten cranky about you taking over the books—"

"He's gone, Dad." She looked at him through bleary eyes.

"What do you mean he's gone?"

"I checked at the hotel, but Reg said he'd left in a hurry."

"What?" With his good hand, he lay the newspaper across his lap and took off his reading glasses.

"The men told me they hadn't received full pay and then Mr. O'Reilly called to say your accounts were overdue. I went through the books and found Bartel has been skimming from our accounts."

Her father stared with wide eyes. She checked for any changes in his skin color, in case there was any trembling or shortness of breath.

"You must be mistaken." His tone remained even.

"I wish I was, Dad, but after speaking with Reg and finding out he has a gambling debt…" She really did not want to continue.

"He told me he'd kicked that habit." Her father's voice held a steely edge, despite his slurring.

"You knew about his gambling problem yet you let him look after the books?" She threw her arms wide. "Why would you do that when I was begging you to let me help?"

"Because you're—"

"Don't bother finishing that sentence. And I stupidly thought you had started to believe in me."

"That's not what I meant."

"What did you mean then?" she countered, her hands on her hips.

"Letting you get involved was a risk and now look what's happened."

"Are you serious?" Incredulity swept through her. "This is not my fault. You should be grateful I found out when I did." Her father stared at the newspaper. "I think the fact that the men trusted me enough to tell me about their shortfall in pay speaks volumes for the respect they have for me. What a shame you don't have the same for your own daughter."

She stormed out of the room and down the steps. Jumping into the ute, she fumbled for the key, cursing like her brothers might have.

The tires spun in the gravel as she took off down the hill and toward Kitty's place in town. At least she'd get a sympathetic ear from her best friend.

The bright headlights cut through the darkness and just as she rounded a bend, a large kangaroo bounded in front of her. She slammed on the brakes and as the ute skidded in the dirt. She heard a pop and the vehicle lurched to the left.

"Damn!"

The roo hopped merrily into the distance as the ute listed to the side. Grabbing the torch out of the glove box, Rosie got out to inspect the damage.

A blown tire.

Great.

She pulled out the toolkit from the tray and rested the torch on the road so she could get started. Any other time, Rosie's anger would have risen as a result of the damaged tire but, in a way, she was thankful she could take out her frustrations on the stupid vehicle. Working with her hands had always been a great stress reliever and took her back to the happy days when she'd worked for the Australian Women's Army Service. Before too long the wheel was off the car and she had the spare ready to put on.

"May I be of assistance?"

Rosie jolted and dropped the spanner. She held the torch and shone the light directly into the speaker's eyes.

Big, brown, beautiful Italian eyes.

Tomas used his hands to shield himself from the harsh light. "You could shine this somewhere else, yes?"

"Oh! Sorry!" Rosie rested the torch on the bonnet. "What are you doing out here?"

"I could ask the same of you." He nodded toward the decimated tire laying on the road. "May I help?"

"No, no, I'm totally fine." Her words sounded a little forceful, so she added gently, "But thank you for the offer."

"I would like to keep you company." He followed this with a smile that she happily returned.

"Sure. Thanks."

"So…" they said in unison. Their laughter swirling through the darkness.

"You first," she said, grappling with a sudden bout of coyness.

"I have not seen you around much," he said.

"I've been so very busy." Why couldn't she look him in the eye? "I should have thanked you much earlier for the lovely box of food you sent over."

"I understand, I have been busy, too. And it is our pleasure. It was the idea of my nonna and my mother."

"Well, please thank them for me."

"I will."

This polite and formal conversation drove her crazy because right now she felt like a schoolgirl with her first crush. After spending time with Tomas at the dance she'd got the distinct impression he was interested in her, yet here they stood in the dark, acting like almost-strangers. It was all so…odd.

Not sure what to say next, Rosie returned to wrestling with the stupid nut that wouldn't go on straight. Her sweaty hands slipped and she grazed her knuckles on the metal rim. "Ow!"

Tomas knelt next and took her hand. His skin was a little rougher, but his touch just as gentle. Her body temperature soared.

He used the torch to examine her knuckles. "You need a bandage."

"I'll be fine, honest." Their eyes locked and she quickly turned away, concentrating on the stubborn bolt again. "Do you mind holding the torch for me, please?" she rasped.

He let out a laugh. "I am more than happy to."

"What's so funny?"

"You."

"What?" She looked up to find deep smile lines around his eyes.

"You are very independent."

"You better not think that's a bad thing."

"No! Not at all!" He held up a hand in defense. "I like this. It is refreshing. The only females I have met here in Australia are traditional. And you, Rosalie Stanton, are not of the traditional variety."

"Hmmm…." She narrowed her eyes as she let his words sink in. "So that's a compliment?"

"But of course! You remind me of my nonna. My grandmother."

"Your…grandmother?" Any chance that there was romantic interest from Tomas exploded like a firework into the expansive black sky. No one wants to court their grandmother.

"*Si*! She is strong. Independent. She does not do what society thinks she should. My nonna, she believes that we are all equal."

"Do you think the same as her?"

"Of course!"

Her liking for this man just increased tenfold. "I have a feeling I would like your nonna a lot."

"And my nonna would very much like you." He paused for a fraction of a second. "Perhaps as much as I like you."

The butterflies that had been flapping in her stomach took full flight.

"I…" Words! She needed words! Good words! "Thank you?" This was all she could come up with? *Good grief…*"So…uh…I better get this fixed."

Rosie knelt down to wrestle with the tire again. She frowned at the wheel, shyness crashing in on her.

"Rosalie, please…"

"Just…one…twist…" With a forceful turn the last bolt was on and the job was done. "There!"

She stood and wiped her greasy hands on the towel from the toolkit.
Tomas shook his head and smiled. "You are strong."

"I'm not really." Her arms ached, her knuckles smarted, and she
suspected tomorrow her back would be feeling the aftermath of lifting
the heavy tire.

"I mean mostly in here." He pointed at his heart, then his head. "And here."

Unsure how to respond, Rosie placed the tools back in the suede pouch
resting on the bonnet, then put them in the back of the ute.

"I…" She stared at her feet shuffling in the dirt. Appalled by her shyness,
she forced herself to look up at him. "I like how you find it so easy to say
what you think."

Tomas drew his brows together. "Why would I not?"

"Because the culture here, especially between men and women, is
to remain understated. Not to talk in depth about what you're thinking
or feeling. Sure, a husband may tell his wife that he loves her, but for
strangers like us—"

"We have met a few times, so I consider us good friends." He winked
and she laughed. His happy-go-lucky manner bolstered her confidence.

"I can very easily imagine us being good friends." Though a nagging
voice in her head told her there was one subject that needed to be broached
and now was the time, whether she liked it or not. "There is one thing we
should really talk about."

"And this is?"

She hesitated, wishing she could ignore it but knew there was no way she
could. "My father said there was a dispute between your family and mine."

"Ah," Tomas said. "Yes, there was a problem. I only discovered it after
I arrived here."

"You didn't mention it at the dance. Wouldn't it have been a good idea
to say something?"

"Why? I did not want to spoil the moment with the business of family.
I was enjoying the time with you."

Rosie let his last sentence sink in. He did have a very good point. "I
did enjoy dancing with you that night."

"I had much fun myself."

"The land problem was resolved, right?" She hated harping on about
it, especially when there were much more pleasant topics.

"Yes, it was. Your father understood the title was wrong. He was not
happy, but he did the thing of honor and gave that piece of land back."

"That's him, honorable to a fault."

"You and I are all right, yes?" Tomas looked at her with expectant eyes.

"About the land thing? If my father was happy to settle, then yes, I am sure we are all right."

"So, good friend Rosalie, why are you out here alone and driving like you are in a racing car?"

"I had to deal with an issue today and my father wasn't exactly happy with the way I handled it."

"Oh?"

Rosie shoved her hands in her dress pockets. "He doesn't have faith that I can help run the farm because...because I'm female. And it hurts that he thinks like this."

"Speak to any woman from any country and you will find the same problem: They are judged by who they are born as, not what they can do." Tomas stepped closer, his eyes earnest. "I am very sorry you are experiencing this."

Rosie shrugged. "I don't know how to change it."

"If anyone can make a difference, I imagine it could be you."

The moonlight reflected in his eyes and Rosie found herself surreptitiously taking a step closer.

Tomas leant forward, just a fraction.

He was so close.

If she moved in just a bit more—

Tomas gave a nervous cough. "Is this why you drive like a crazy person? Because you are angry with your father? Where were you going?"

And just like that, the moment fell away. She couldn't have imagined it, could she?

"Kitty's house," she said quietly.

"Would you like me to escort you to her house, to make sure there are no more flat tires? Or if the tire becomes flat again I can hold the torch for you?" His suggestion gave her hope that he wasn't quite ready to say goodbye. Neither was she.

"I'm all right but thank you all the same." What on earth was she saying?

"If this is your wish." He clasped his hands behind his back.

"Tomas?"

"*Si*?" His large eyes looked hopeful.

"What were you doing out here? I would have thought you'd be eating dinner with your family or...something." She swatted away the idea of him taking a girl to the pictures.

"At the end of the workday I like to walk alone and take in the beauty of this land."

Rosie rested her gaze on the shadow of eucalypts and wattle behind him. "So, you like the landscape here?"

"Of course! How could I not? It is beautiful, no? Look at this—" He walked over with the torch to the silver wattle and reached out and gently touched the yellow flowers. "Mother Nature is an artist. Here—" He broke off a flower and handed it to her. "Two years ago, in Italy the women started to receive this flower as part of *La Festa della Donna*, International Women's Day. We do this to celebrate women and show we value what you do. We want women to know they are not alone in the struggle to be considered equal."

"Wow." She held the flower like it was her most treasured possession. "I didn't even know there were wattles in Italy. I thought they were only in Australia."

"I believe we imported them a long time ago. We call them Mimosa."

"Hmmm…" Rosie inhaled the flower's scent. It seemed sweeter than it normally did. "So, this plant is significant for both of our countries."

"Yes, it is."

"Do you miss Italy?"

Tomas drew his brows together. "Sometimes yes, sometimes no. I miss my people, the culture, history, the language. It's a part of who I am and always will be."

She nodded, relaxing in his company, his alluring accent, his warm personality.

"But Italy is a country that has been through much. So very much. War. Political problems. The people struggle every day, but the rich do not care. The ones in power laugh from their comfortable chairs with their bellies full of good food and wine." His tone held an edge and he stared off into the distance. He turned to her and said quietly, "But no matter how much I wish for things to change, they will not. Maybe now that I…" He shook his head. "I am sorry, I must bore you with talk of a country that you do not care about."

"Tomas"—she went to reach for his hand then quickly pulled away, surprised at how familiar she'd become—"I care about a lot of things and I feel for the people in Italy. In fact, I care deeply for all the people in war-affected countries. I can't possibly know what your people have gone through, but from what I have read and heard, it hasn't been easy."

"No, it has not. At times, I feel like I have deserted my people but…" he ran his hand along the back of his neck. "Adjusting to a new culture can be difficult. People are not always understanding."

"Many have a hard time seeing outside their own sheltered worlds," she said. "We're all humans and no matter where we are born we should respect each other regardless of nationality and culture."

Tomas leant against the car and crossed one leg over the other. "I like the way you think."

"And I..." There was no way she could finish this sentence.

"You?"

"I like having these conversations with you." Apparently that sentence could be finished.

"Then we should have more. Perhaps you will join me for an evening walk some time. We can do a walk and talk."

Before she had a chance to think it through, her heart answered: "I'd like that very much."

Chapter 12

By the time Rosie left Kitty's she'd had enough time to think things through. Kitty's level-headedness, despite her raging hormones, had helped Rosie put everything into perspective. She hadn't yet figured out how to recover the missing money, but she at least had a plan of how to talk to her father calmly.

Rosie quietly entered the house, ensuring the screen door didn't slam behind her. The aroma of freshly baked pie wafted from the kitchen.

"Rosie?" her father croaked.

"Yes?" She entered the bedroom where he lay on his side, propped up by her grandmother's crocheted pillows. "Where's Mum?"

"Kitchen."

"Right." She leant against the doorframe, not sure if she wanted to enter or keep her distance.

"Listen, I'm sorry if what I said angered you." He paused and she waited for more but nothing was forthcoming.

"And?"

"And that's it."

She studied his sallow skin, the dark rings under his eyes, his thin frame. Was all this arguing over something they would never agree on worth it? Why was it so important that he see her point of view?

Tension gripped her shoulders once more. "What are we going to do now Bartel has gone?"

"Maybe you're wrong about the accounts. Maybe…" His voice trailed off and his shoulders dropped. "Maybe you are right." His head hung forward and he covered his eyes with his good hand. "How could he do this?"

"I'm sorry I didn't tell you straightaway but…"

"But?"

"I was scared." There. Now it was out in the open.

Her father looked up, puzzlement in his eyes. "Why?"

"Because I thought it might set off another stroke," she said, not enjoying this conversation but at the same time relishing this moment of open communication. It had been so long…

Her father pushed himself up a fraction more. It was a struggle, but his expression remained determined.

"I am stronger than you think," he said.

"So am I, Dad."

Her father studied her with intensity, his blue eyes unblinking, his lips not moving. When he reached for a glass of water she resisted helping him, as the doctor had suggested he attempt everyday tasks. The nurturer in Rosie wanted to rescue him, but she let him be, as painful as it was to witness his shaky hand spilling water on his shirt. He took a sip, placed it down and sponged off his top with a nearby tea towel.

"Dad, I should call Sergeant—"

"No." His words came out with force. "No police involvement."

"Why not?"

"Bartel is a good man. He is just confused. Give him a day to realize what he's done and he'll return."

Rosie took a moment before voicing the opinion that would do her no favors. "Bartel is not returning, Dad. He's skipped town with the money. And anyway, if he did come back, he probably wouldn't have much—if any—left because he would have used it to pay back his debts." *Or gambled it away.*

"It just can't be…" He didn't look up as he slowly shook his head.

"What if we make an agreement? If Bartel isn't back within forty-eight hours, I go and talk to the police. This has to be filed, Dad. What if he does it to someone else?"

"He was with me for over ten years," he mumbled, "working by my side."

Rosie's heart went out to her father. She couldn't begin to imagine what it would be like to implicitly trust someone only to discover a betrayal that cut so very deep.

Her father took a deep breath and lifted his head, as if shaken out of the well of despair he was poised to tumble into. "I will need all the accounts."

"But—"

"I'm feeling better." He forced a lopsided smile. "I can stay here on bed rest and go through the figures."

"That's not resting," she said.

"I'm just double-checking, that's all. If it is what you say it is, then we need to find a way out of this." Her father lifted his good hand to his heart, made a strange sound, and sucked in air. Rosie went to him.

"What is it? Should I call the doctor?" She was up and on her way to the telephone.

"No, just a flutter. It happens every so often."

"How often?" she asked, her voice firm.

"Not often enough for anyone to worry."

Rosie sat back down and reached for her father's hand. The roughness of his hands against her soft skin reminded her of the days when just the two of them would walk along the riverbank after he'd finished work for the day, and they would chat about the latest book she'd read or they'd sit and study the star constellations. She missed those days almost as much as she missed her brothers.

"You need to let Dr. Wilkinson know about this. And," she added, "doing the books is too much pressure. I will collate everything; then we can talk and you can make some decisions about how we're going to pay back the men."

"Bartel needs to be replaced immediately."

"Sefa could be my right-hand man. He knows the ins and outs and I trust him." She worried that the word "trust" didn't hold as much weight as it once did at Tulpil.

"I trusted Bartel." Her father lowered his eyes.

"You trust me, though, right?" Her father didn't look up. "Right, Dad?"

He gave a curt nod. "Yes, yes, of course I do, but there is no way I want you dealing with those men."

"They're not animals."

"They're *men*. And you're a *woman*." He shook his head, a wry smile on his lips. "Why are you so pigheaded?"

"I learnt from the best." She followed this with a grin. The building tension dissolved a fraction.

"What about Brisbane?" He sounded apprehensive.

"That was totally different."

"How?"

"Because here I'm the boss's daughter."

"Men are men."

"What I experienced in Brisbane was an imbalance of power. I was at the mercy of a man who felt he could do and say whatever he wanted. But you and I both know not all men are like that. We can't tar everyone with the same brush just because of their gender. Just like we can't make assumptions about people because of their nationality." She paused, but he didn't bite. "There is a whole different order at Tulpil than in Brisbane."

He lowered his head, deep in thought. Eventually he looked up. "I'm not getting into the nationality debate, but you do have a point about the workers. You can do Bartel's job until more suitable arrangements can be made."

Rosie bounced on the chair, unable to contain her excitement. "You won't regret this, I promise you."

Her father didn't answer, a deep frown creasing his brow once more. "We're in a mess, Rosie."

"I know, but you have me here to help—whatever it takes," she said. Without thinking, she kissed him on the forehead, then stepped back, surprised. Her father looked at her, his expression one of shock.

"Rosie, I really don't like us arguing."

"I don't, either. We'll figure this mess out. Somehow."

"I have to hand it to you," he said, his tone reminiscent of when she was younger.

"Hand me what?"

"You always find the silver lining." He paused for a moment then lowered his voice, "There is one more thing we should discuss. It's about your mother…"

"I've noticed it, too." They exchanged knowing looks, but the conversation halted when her mother's footsteps echoed down the hall and she appeared in the doorway.

Wiping her hands on the apron, she said, "Dinner is warming in the oven for you, sweetheart."

"Thank you, Mum." Rosie tried not to notice her mother's shaking hands or the way her left eye had started to droop. This only ever happened if she'd had too many nips of brandy. "Why don't you put your feet up? I'll clean the kitchen."

"You do enough around here, Rosie."

"I'm not taking no for an answer." With that, Rosie headed for the kitchen, but before she left the room she spied her mother collapse heavily on the armchair next to her father.

Rosie sat down to her meal and allowed herself to replay the conversation she'd had with Tomas earlier that evening. *You are very independent*, he'd said. Just like his nonna.

Hmm…

She loved that Tomas had so much respect for his grandmother and obviously valued women's strength. She'd never met a man who seemed to support and appreciate strong women before. Yet another string in Signor Conti's bow.

* * * *

The next day, Rosie rounded the corner of the shed then stopped in her tracks. The workers were already clustered together, talking in low voices as some took long drags on their cigarettes and others played cards. Her heart raced and perspiration pooled at the base of her spine. Why on earth did she think she could possibly be in charge of men who knew much more about cutting cane than her? The last time she'd tried to cut sugarcane she'd nearly taken off Bartel's head. *What a shame she'd missed.*

Fear clawed at her insides as she drew closer. The men turned to face her and even though Rosie wanted to spin around and run for the house, she pushed forward.

"Good morning." Rosie was relieved her voice didn't crack. Her gaze travelled around the crowd and she identified the nationality of each person and used their language to greet them individually. *Bongu* in Maltese. *Sveiki* in Latvian. *Hallo* in Afrikaans. *Kamusta* in Filipino. *Bula* in Fijian. *Zdravo* in Yugoslavian. And so it went. The men answered back, most with a smile, and this small gesture seemed to create a more convivial atmosphere. She just hoped it lasted.

Bracing herself, she said, "On behalf of my father, I want to thank each and every one of you for the extra time and effort you have put in while he's been ill. We truly appreciate all your support and all that you have done."

A few of the men nodded, but no one looked directly at her.

She continued, trying not to let it unnerve her. "I realize we all need some time to adjust to the changes but it shouldn't affect our output. We have the potential to make this the most productive season we have ever seen. And please know that I am here to listen and help in any way I can."

The men looked around at each other, as if sending telepathic messages. There were a few surreptitious shakes of the head while others stared at their dusty boots.

Eventually, Loto stepped forward, his face riddled with guilt. "The men want to know when they'll get the money they're owed."

Sefa cleared his throat. "Rosie is aware of this, as is Mr. Stanton. They are fixing the problem as we speak." His dark eyes met hers and she hope he sensed her appreciation for his assistance.

"We need our money," said Jeks. He moved closer, his large frame towering over hers. After the incident with the knife and Loto, he'd morphed into the background and not caused any trouble, which made Rosie all the more suspicious.

"You will get your money," she said firmly, then took her time looking at every worker gathered in the circle. "It will just take a little time. However, each of you will be rewarded for your patience."

"How?" asked Jeks.

"You heard Miss Stanton," said Sefa. He made a show of looking at his watch.

"I promise you, Jeks, you will not be disappointed. No one will." As soon as she said it, Rosie realized she may have just dug a very deep hole.

Chapter 13

Rosie sat on the couch of Kitty's living room and cradled the newborn as Kitty made a pot of tea.

"Please let me do that," Rosie said.

Kitty set about organizing the teacups and fruitcake on the tray. "No. You have enough going on at the farm."

"You only gave birth two days ago and she was early!"

"I'm not an invalid!" came the catch-cry Kitty had used all throughout her pregnancy.

Rosie had been running Tulpil less than a week and her bones now ached to the core and her muscles screamed for mercy. Now that she had the books in order, she had taken to being out in the fields with the men. She didn't cut the cane—that was their domain, and how much they cut dictated their earnings—but she helped check loads, which required occasional lifting. It was damn hard work and she had a newfound admiration for the men who did this year in, year out. Surprisingly, no one had voiced their concern or distaste in her being amongst them. As long as she did her job and didn't interfere with theirs, things moved along nicely.

Rosie looked up from admiring Kitty's blue-eyed cherub and studied her friend. "How are you really doing?"

Kitty brought over the tray and placed it on the footstool in front of them. She collapsed in the armchair. "I feel like death warmed up. And I thought pregnancy was the hard part!"

Rosie looked at baby Isabelle's smooth, pale skin and her tiny fingers and toes. "She's perfection."

"She is, isn't she?" Kitty held her finger against Isabelle's and the baby wrapped her tiny hand around it. "I hope she has a good life."

"You're her mother, of course she will!"

"That's not what I mean. What if she's like you—intelligent and determined? If she is then I want my girl to have opportunities that I never had. She needs someone to start this ball rolling. Someone like her godmother."

"Me?" Rosie pointed at herself. "You want me to be Isabelle's godmother?"

"Of course! Who else would be a better role model?" Kitty's blonde locks fell in her eyes and she pushed out a breath to blow them away. "My daughter and all the girls in her generation need someone to pave a better future for them."

"And you think I'm the one to do it? Why on earth would you say that?"

"You're the strongest woman I know."

Rosie tried to stop her lips twitching into a smile.

"What's so funny?"

"Someone else said something similar recently."

Kitty motioned for Rosie to hand over the sweet bundle and she did so reluctantly. Rosie's arms and torso felt cold now that Isabelle's warmth had left her. The little delight nestled against Kitty and a minute later Isabelle fell asleep.

Kitty noticed Rosie watching. "She doesn't always do that, I promise you." In a quiet voice, she said, "Let's not get off topic. So, was it someone who is new to the district who said you are a strong woman?"

"Stop it." Rosie returned her attention to Isabelle. The baby's long lashes rested gently against her chubby cheeks. A tweak of longing snuck up on her, but Rosie quickly pushed it away.

"Do you ever think you'll have children?"

How did Kitty do that?

"I don't know," Rosie said. "According to my mother, I'm on the shelf."

"She's a tad melodramatic."

"That's Cecile for you."

Kitty's gentle laugh filled the room. "Seriously, though, have you ever thought about it?"

"Of course I have, but that doesn't mean it will happen for me." Rosie picked up the pot of tea and poured some into each cup while Kitty carefully stood and placed Isabelle in the bassinet a few feet away. Kitty fussed over the baby and Rosie smiled, unable to fully comprehend that her best friend was now the mother of a little human.

"So, you're saying yes?" Kitty grabbed a cup of tea and sat down. She took a sip and studied Rosie over the rim.

"Yes to babies?" she drew this out, unsure how to answer. "Look, if it happens then yes, I'd be happy. And if it doesn't then…" She shrugged. "Being a woman is not all about having babies."

Kitty looked down at her hands for a moment. "Sorry, I guess I'm all caught up in this motherhood business."

"It's totally fine. This is your world now. Maybe it will be mine, maybe it won't, but if it ever is, I would like to think I could continue doing the work I want as well as raising my children."

"An interesting thought." Kitty sat back against the cushions and crossed one leg over the other. "So what did Sergeant Gavin say when you told him about Bartel?"

"He was shocked, just like we all are. He said if Bartel's left the district, which we know he has, then it's going to be hard to find him."

"I'm so sorry, Rosie."

"Thanks. I'll do what I can, but it's like trying to find a needle in a haystack. So I guess we just have to live in hope but…" She shrugged.

"As if you and your dad don't have enough to deal with. It's so unfair."

"That, it is." Rosie sighed.

"Sooooo…" Kitty's transition to a new subject was, at best, clumsy. "I heard a rumor about the Conti family."

"You know I don't get involved with rumors."

"All right then." Kitty acted nonchalant by turning her attention to her sleeping daughter.

Rosie bit her lip, trying to ignore the question that was burning to get out. The clock ticked on the mantelpiece while Rosie fiddled with the crocheted rug beside her.

"I like the greens you used in the rug," she said.

"Thank you." Kitty's lips twitched.

"Fine!" Rosie threw her arms in the air. "What did you hear?"

Kitty let the smirk break free then her expression turned serious. "Rumor has it there's a connection to Mussolini."

"What?" She shook her head. "Absolutely not possible."

"How would you know?"

"Because…well…Tomas and I have met a few times." She leant forward and quickly said, "Quite by accident."

"And?"

"And that's all. He spoke a little about Italy and how much he misses it, but he also said that he feels at home here."

"Hmm…" Kitty said. "So, could it be true?"

"That the Contis are fascists? Why would people think that?"

"Well, for starters, his family waltzed in here and paid for the property—in full and in cash. They keep to themselves."

"Tomas socializes quite happily."

"Yes, well, he's the exception."

"I know he has a nonna." Now it was Rosie's turn to act all nonchalant by tucking a stray chunk of hair behind her ears.

"He has a nonna here?"

"Apparently." She smiled, remembering Tomas comparing her to his nonna.

"What's so funny?"

"Nothing!" Rosie stood and straightened her skirt. "I need to get going."

"This doesn't interest you at all? Aren't you curious?"

Rosie sat on the edge arm of the couch. "It's not our business, though."

"But it's got you thinking, right?" Kitty looked like she was a detective about to crack a case.

"No." It came out a little strongly. "Well, I guess…"

"Aha!" Kitty waggled her finger.

"Right, that's it, I'm going home now." Rosie bent over and kissed Isabelle on the forehead then walked past Kitty and gave her shoulder a squeeze. "Try and get some sleep."

"That's like asking for it to snow." Kitty fanned herself with her hand. "Is it just me or has the humidity been awfully stifling today?"

"It's not just you." Rosie picked up her purse and car keys. "I'll see you on Saturday?"

Kitty nodded, but had already focused on the sleeping Isabelle. Rosie closed the front screen door quietly and made her way to the ute. A restlessness stirred within and the idea of going home and spending a night reading on the couch didn't appeal. She could go to the pictures, but there was nothing on that took her fancy. Perhaps she just needed to stretch her legs on a walk through town. After all, it had been quite some time since she'd visited Piri River without having to rush in and rush out. Perhaps Mrs. Daw's prize-winning bougainvillea had started to bloom, or Mr. Freeman had finished renovating his Queenslander and she could go and find out what color he'd chosen for the weatherboards.

Rosie left the ute parked out the front of Kitty's and sauntered the three blocks to the main street. Although the sun had already set, the heat of the day had been trapped in the bitumen. The cicadas accompanied her as she stretched her aching legs and breathed in the aromas of evening meals in the houses she passed. Her stomach grumbled as she rounded the corner and neared Reg's Pub, where the sound of laughter and men's deep voices floated through the open windows.

No matter which way the picture was painted, not allowing women into a Public Bar spoke volumes about the lack of respect for women in this country. Not that she wanted to prop herself up against a bar and drink herself senseless, but Rosie wanted the freedom to have a shandy if she chose, and she didn't need a man buying it for her.

The door to Reg's Pub flew open and banged against the red-brick wall. Ken Ridley staggered out the door, his shirt crumpled, hat askew.

"Rosheee…" He tried to tip his hat but lost balance and his shoulder hit the wall. A couple of Ken's cronies lurched forward to hold him up, but they were as drunk as him and they all toppled onto the footpath. Ken got up, straightened himself and tentatively walked toward her while she took a step back. He moved into her space again and an alcoholic haze settled around them. "Give me a kishhhhh."

"You need to go home, Ken." She subtly stepped back again, but he lunged forward. Rosie glanced around for the nearest escape route. Why did the streets have to be so deserted tonight?

"Come on, Rosheee. You and me, letsh go for a walk." His fingers grasped her elbow and she yanked it away. She looked to Ken's friends for assistance, but they were too busy ogling.

"Leave me alone!" she yelled. Ken grabbed her elbow again, his fingers digging deep into her skin. Anger roiled within and she fought to free herself. "Stop it!"

"Come with me." Although he slurred, his tone held menace.

Indignant and scared, Rosie ripped her arm free and bolted across the road. She fully expected Ken and his louts to follow but they took off in the opposite direction. Relief swept through her as she gave up on the idea of Mrs. Daw's bougainvillea's and concentrated on getting back to Kitty's. Fury fueled her steps. Why do men think it's perfectly fine to harass a woman, especially when she's alone? What kind of world was this?

She strode a couple of blocks, her anger growing with every step. Damn these men who think a woman is fair game. If Ken Ridley ever touched her again…

The sound of arguing made her stop and she looked over to find Ken and his mates shoving an old man. How did Ken get ahead of her so fast? The bastard must have doubled back.

"Go home, dago. No one wants you here," said Ken's mate, who was the size of a gorilla.

As Rosie drew closer, her heart banged against her chest. *Oh no.*

Ken had Luka Abrami by the collar and was leering in his face.

She could race back to Kitty's, but there was no guarantee William would be home yet. Besides, if something wasn't done now, this could escalate very quickly.

"Ken."

He turned and faced her, his thin frame swaying slightly. "What?"

She forced her tone to remain even. "Please, leave Luka be."

He gulped the rest of the beer then threw the empty bottle in the gutter. Glass shattered everywhere. Luka flinched.

"You an I-tai lover now? Whose bloody side are you on?" He threw his arms outward and Luka quickly stepped away, his eyes wide. Oblivious, Ken continued his diatribe. "They are coming to *our* country with their wog food and wog ways and trying to turn us into them."

Rosie clenched her fists. It would be so easy to lose her temper right now, but she didn't need to add fuel to Ken's already out of control fire. *Damn it.* "Italians have been in Australia for decades. You would know this if you took your head out of your arse long enough to look around."

Ken's mates chimed in with "oooh" and scattered snorts of laughter.

"Luka is not bothering you and he has just as much right to be on the street as we do. Now leave him be." She placed her hand under Luka's elbow and noticed his whole body was shaking.

"Well, he's in *my* country and his business is *my* business."

"He's not harming anyone. Just let him go."

"No." He glanced at his mates who rolled up their sleeves.

"What would your mother say?" she asked quickly.

"She…" Ken's steely glare also held a flicker of hurt.

Rosie felt terrible for bringing his deceased mother into this, but he had to be stopped in his tracks.

Luka took a tentative step toward Rosie.

The gorilla moved forward, but Ken held up his hand. "Leave it." He turned and faced Rosie. "For now."

Ken walked past Luka and slammed into him with his shoulder. Luka kept balance and straightened his back, holding his chin high. Just as it looked like the crisis had been averted, Ken spun on his heels. A large wad of spit left his mouth and landed at Lukas feet.

"Have a bath, wog." Ken sneered, then took off with his mates behind him.

"I am so sorry," Rosie said to Luka, who had his eyes trained on Ken and his mates as they staggered down the street. "Are you all right?"

"I am all right." The slight shake in Luka's voice didn't instill any confidence.

Rosie watched Ken and his posse until they rounded the corner.

"He pig," said Luka, his expression a mixture of anger and hurt.

"Pigs have better manners than him," she said. "Let me take you back to the Conti's."

Luka nodded then winced and pressed his hand on his belly.

"Should I get the doctor? Are you hurt?"

"No. Need rest."

"Are you sure? The doctor should be at home."

Luka held up his other hand as he sucked in a sharp breath. "Conti home. *Grazie*."

She helped Luka to the ute, every nerve alert in case Ken and his mates showed up again—although she suspected he was now passed out somewhere in a gutter. Hopefully one of the stray dogs used him as a pissing post.

Rosie couldn't contain her laugh.

Luka looked at her questioningly and she said, "One day, Ken Ridley will get exactly what he deserves."

Chapter 14

The next evening Rosie sat on the couch in the living room, trying to read but she couldn't concentrate. The incident in town with Ken and Luka had played on her mind for days. Tomas had been surprised when she'd turned up at his place unannounced, but when he saw Luka and she'd explained what happened, Tomas had thanked her profusely and whisked Luka into the house. Since then she'd heard nothing, but she hadn't expected anything different—after all, this was a busy time of year.

Oh, Tomas.

She missed his smile. Missed that twinkle in his eye when he laughed. Maybe she should take him up on his offer for a walk and talk. Maybe…

Tossing the book on the table, Rosie stood and made her way to the screen door. "I'm heading out for a bit."

"Tell Kitty we send our love." Her mother's voice echoed down the hallway.

Not wanting to correct her mother, Rosie grabbed the keys off the rack just inside the doorway. Scooting down the steps, she jumped in the ute, turned on the engine and sped down the driveway before she changed her mind. If she got her timing right, he'd be heading out for his walk about now.

Reaching the hill crest, she pulled over to the side of the road and stared at the Conti's lights. What if he didn't mean what he'd said about taking an evening stroll together? What if he was just being polite? *Pfft.* Her life was full of too many what-ifs.

"Only one way to find out." She put her foot down on the peddle but quickly braked when a dark figure appeared from the shadows. "Jesus!"

The tall man approached her open window.

"You are very serious about this new career as a racing car driver, no?" Even in the darkness she could see the smile lines around his eyes.

"Very funny. I thought you would have been farther down the road."

"You are looking for me?"

She nodded, slightly embarrassed.

"I am so very pleased." He opened the driver's-side door and held out his hand to help her. Sure, she was more than capable of getting out of a vehicle herself, but this demonstration of chivalry made her heart flutter. Did this make her a hypocrite? Wanting independence and respect from men but basking in the moments when they treated her like a lady? Was the line as fine as she suspected?

"So…" Tomas's eyes connected with hers.

"So?"

"Do you always come here?"

A small laugh left her lips. "Is that a line?"

"Uh…no…" He removed his hat and scratched his head. "You found me. I…uh…"

"It's been a while since we last spoke, so I thought…" She finished it with a shrug.

He cocked an eyebrow.

"I miss your company, all right?" she said in haste.

He furrowed his brows and a small smile graced his lips. "You miss my company but you are angry with me?"

This was going as well as her short-lived career as an altar girl. "Sorry. I just have a lot on my mind. I was wanting to find out how Luka was."

Using Luka as an excuse didn't sit well, but what other choice did she have? Tell the truth?

"Oh." Tomas looked away for a moment then back at her. "I am sorry. It is remiss of me not to inform you."

"He's all right, isn't he?"

"Yes, yes, of course. A little shocked from the event. He does not want to go into the town again."

"I'm so sorry he feels that way." She didn't blame him, though. "Ken Ridley is mean and nasty and just horrible."

"I do not share love for him, either." Tomas shrugged. "But let us not waste time talking about this person. Tell me, what else is on this mind of yours?"

Rosie breathed in deeply and tried to get her thoughts in order. Would telling him the truth be so bad? Only one way to find out…"I thought your company might cheer me up."

Tomas's large eyes held concern. "You are sad?"

"Not sad. Just...I don't really know what I feel right now. There's so much going on that my head is spinning."

"I think you need a walk and talk." Tomas gestured at the moonlit road in front of them.

"I think you're right."

He formed a D with his arm and she slid hers through his. He matched his step with hers as they strolled along the dirt road that wound between the cane fields. Rosie was happy to be in the moment, to enjoy the inky sky above, take in the powder-spray of stars and revel in the balmy evening.

"For someone who said she wishes to talk, you are very quiet."

They continued along the road, small clouds of dust trailing behind them. With each footstep, the angst, the frustration, the unfairness of it all bubbled to the surface until she couldn't contain it any longer. "Life is bloody unfair."

Tomas gave a sage nod.

"Kitty thinks I'm a hypocrite."

"Because?"

"Because I lament about the double standards women suffer in this day and age yet I do nothing about it."

"But you are running Tulpil, no?"

"Exactly!"

They walked on. Rosie sensed Tomas's brain ticking over.

"Out with it." She nudged him gently with her elbow.

"What?"

"I can tell you have something to say."

He stopped, gently removed her arm from his and faced her. "You will not like it, I am afraid."

A sinking feeling washed over her. "Tell me."

"I wonder if your friend Kitty is right."

Rosie narrowed her eyes. "About me being a hypocrite?"

"I do not know if this is the correct word, but you talk a lot about how hard it is for women in Australia. This new position at Tulpil is a chance to prove females are capable of many great things. Will you use this experience to help other women?"

"How on earth can a farm girl from rural Queensland change the plight of women in this country?"

He ran his hand along the cane as they continued to walk. "You have already started."

"How?"

"You are running a cane farm!" He threw his arms wide. "How many women do you know who are doing this?"

She shrugged.

"Can you not see you are already making a difference?"

Rosie watched her feet make imprints in the dirt.

"You have a good heart, Rosalie Stanton. Look at the way you help Kitty."

"She's like a sister."

"And look at the way you helped Luka."

"I'm only being human." She stopped and faced him. "What has gone on in your life to have so little faith in the kindness of others?"

Tomas looked away.

"Tomas?"

"Life in Australia is just different." He kept his eyes trained on the cane growing tall and proud.

"And?"

"And that is all." Once again, talkative Tomas clammed up and she was left wondering why.

They continued walking, silence enveloping them. When they rounded the bend that led to Tomas's house, she halted and stared up at the lights shining through the windows. Although it was too dark to see, Rosie imagined the intricate latticework running along the verandah and the rose bushes that had been planted more than fifty years prior to Tomas's family arriving.

"Are the roses still growing well?" she asked, desperate to slice through the air of discomfort.

"You know the house?"

"Of course! I practically grew up there when the Ellis family owned it."

"Yes, I now remember you saying you played there when you were a child." Tomas appeared lost in thought. "My nonna is only ever at home in the garden."

"My grandmother was the same."

"She is not with you now?"

Rosie looked at her broken nails. "I'm afraid not."

"I am sorry for your loss."

She lifted one shoulder then let it drop. "I was very young when I lost both grandparents. I still miss them, though."

"A grandparent is special. I cannot even think about…when…" Tomas shook his head. "I do not want to think about such a thing."

"Of course not." She rested her hand on his arm and he relaxed under her touch. "Do you still have your grandfather?"

"No."

"I'm so sorry to hear that. What was he like?"

The muscles in his arm tensed. "I prefer not to talk about the details of my family."

"Why not? I'll tell you anything you want to know about mine."

A wall of reticence shot up between them. Cicadas in the nearby grassland serenaded them, yet the symphony that could have been so romantic was wasted.

"You know people think it's strange that you're the only one from your family who goes into town, right?"

"Where have you heard this?"

"People talk."

He coughed. "My family are very private people and they prefer to spend all their time at Il Sunnu. Plus, we have employees to run errands into Piri River when I am unable."

"All the workers are from your country, right?"

"Why does it matter?"

"It doesn't matter to me but it seems to matter a great deal to people in this town. There's an air of mystery about your family and people like to speculate." Though, would the townsfolk do this if it were a family that had been in Australia for three generations?

Tomas stared at her, his expression not relaying a single emotion.

"Tomas?"

"What?"

"Don't you care that people are talking about your family?" She made sure her tone sounded caring.

He looked to the heavens for a moment. "Why should I care what people think? They do not know me and I am not here to impress them."

"So you don't care that they think you've got some strange connection to Mussolini?" She should have put the brakes on two minutes ago.

His body stiffened and he stepped back. The convivial bond between them fraying and flapping aimlessly in the breeze.

Panic clawed within. "Tomas, I'm only repeating what I've heard. I—"

"It is time for me to return to the house."

"Tomas—"

"I am going."

She stepped forward and blocked his path. He moved to the side and she got in his way again.

"Rosalie, let me pass."

"No."

"Rosalie." His tone held anger, but she didn't let it sway her.

"Tomas, I don't know you very well but I would hope that you have enough trust in me to talk about this."

"Why? So you can tell your Australian friends I am a fascist?" Hurt clouded his handsome face and a ball of regret mixed with frustration pushed against her rib cage.

"I don't know what your political allegiances are, Tomas. I don't know what you believe in. That's the whole point, isn't it? No one except your workers—who are all Italian—know your family."

"So?"

"So there are people who don't trust others who come from countries that were once part of the Axis Powers. Questions are going to be asked."

"We joined the Allies in the end," he said. "Besides, I do not have to answer the questions of anyone."

Tomas skillfully dodged her and took off toward Il Sunnu, his long legs carrying him a great distance in a short time.

"Tomas." She tried to keep up with him.

"I am done with talking, Rosalie. Go back to your *Australian* family— where you belong."

Chapter 15

Tomas walked up a street a few neighborhoods from his family home. This trek to the place where Rachel stayed had become part of his routine these past few days. The walk gave him plenty of thinking time to figure out his next move but, to date, none of his ideas had stuck.

Shoving his hand in the canvas bag hanging from his shoulder, Tomas extracted an orange and peeled the skin to reveal the juicy, orange flesh. He took a bite and memories of the discussion with Nonna came flooding back: *What if you peel away the layers, break the orange into sections and deal with it one piece at a time? You'd get through it, no? You'd achieve your goal.*

His goal, of course, was to see his Italy return to a state of peace and prosperity and for his people to thrive once more. Figuring out how to reach that goal was the issue. First, though, he needed to check on Rachel.

After her hasty exit from the doctor's the other day, he'd followed her to a nearby house and met this Paolo character—the man purportedly the love of Rachel's life. When Tomas had first shown up, Paolo had been wary and done a terrible job hiding his jealousy. But Rachel had smoothed things over, promising Paolo there had been no intimate moments with Tomas, who was "one of her brother's lackeys." The comment had hurt, though what did Tomas expect? Her illness and the stress of the situation in the mountains wasn't conducive to them really getting to know each other. Not that he was sure it would ever be a good idea, but that damn cat and curiosity...

It didn't sit well that he wasn't following Abato's instructions to the letter, but he couldn't hold Rachel against her will. So to offset the lack of the twenty-four-hour guard Abato wanted, Tomas had arranged to visit Rachel every day. She wasn't happy about it but she had no choice as far as Tomas was concerned.

He arrived at the small house with the black door and knocked. No answer. He'd not been impressed by the dump she was living in with Paolo, but what could he do? Newspapers were piled high, there was a pathetic excuse of a mattress shoved on the floor in the corner, and the place smelled musty. She'd insisted this was where she wanted to be and that it was a palace compared to the hellholes she'd lived in while out in the mountains fighting for the cause. Besides, considering how many places in Palermo were shells of bombed buildings, Paolo's abode was almost luxurious.

Tomas knocked again, figuring Rachel was napping—something she'd done regularly since the operation.

Nothing.

"Rachel!" he said in a loud whisper, not wanting to alert the neighbors to his presence. He had no idea who lived in this street and in his mind, no one could ever be fully trusted.

He banged louder. Still no answer.

Tomas twisted the doorknob and to his surprise, it opened. Stepping into the dimly lit room he waited a moment for his eyes to adjust. The door closed with a click behind him and he lowered his voice. "Rachel, it's me, Tomas. I've brought some medication for you."

"Go away," came a muffled voice from the far corner.

"Rachel?" Tomas walked over to where she sat, her back against the wall, knees drawn up to her chin. Kneeling next to her, he asked quietly, "Should I get the doctor? Is it your wound?"

"It's nothing. You need to go. Now." When she looked up her eyes were full of terror. Her hair was a matted mess and it was stuck to the sides of her face and caked with something dark red...

Oh no.

Gently placing his hand under her chin, he tried to turn her face to get a better look. She yanked her head away and stared at the wall.

"What did he do to you?" He tried to remain calm, even though his body surged with anger.

"Nothing." She went to bury her head, but Tomas placed his hand under her chin again and gently encouraged her to look at him. This time she didn't resist. The skin was so swollen her eye looked like a slit, her cheekbone bore a red and purple circle and her bottom lip and forehead had deep cuts.

"Paolo did this?"

She nodded and burst into tears. Collapsing into his arms, her thin body let out all the pain she had shoved into a deep emotional cavern.

Helping Rachel to her feet, he grabbed the ratty blanket and wrapped it around her. "I'm taking you home."

* * * *

Tomas paced up and down the hallway, fury fueling his footsteps, rage opening and close his fists.

The door to the bedroom clicked open and Nonna raised her finger to her lips. She stepped into the hallway, shut the door behind her and motioned for Tomas to follow her into the kitchen.

They sat at the table and Nonna smoothed down her apron. "She is in a bad way."

Tomas let out a long breath and lowered his head. "Why did I let her go with him?"

"For the reasons you gave me. You couldn't force her to do something against her will."

"But I was supposed to protect her."

"You did. You rescued her after a severe beating and..." Nonna's pained expression told him what he'd feared most.

"No."

"I'm afraid so."

He jumped to his feet, the chair scraping against the floor. "I am going to find him and—"

"And do what?" Nonna threw her hands wide. "Kill him?"

"He can't get away with this." For the first time ever, he felt capable of killing someone and it scared him. "I'm going to find him." Tomas grabbed his jacket and gripped it so hard his fingers ached.

"Don't. Please," said Rachel. She leant against the doorframe, her hair combed, one side of her face black and blue. When she moved into the kitchen, Rachel looked smaller, like a wounded bird. She sat gingerly. "I am begging you, Tomas, please leave this be."

"I can't." He bunched his jacket in his hands.

"Sit, please." Her large eyes implored him and he did as she asked. Towering above her like some angry giant would not help anyone. "You have done more than enough and I thank you from the bottom of my heart. However, you have to leave this alone. It's between Paolo and me."

"It's not the first time, is it?"

Rachel bit her lip. A large tear ran down her face.

His heart went out to her. "Your brother doesn't know about him, does he?"

Rachel studied her clasped hands in her lap. "No."

"I thought as much, because if your brother did know, Paolo would not be alive today, would he?"

She shook her head.

Tomas tried to keep calm when all he wanted to do was smash his fist through a wall. Or against Paolo's face. "We can't let him get away with it. He has to pay."

"Tomas..."

He looked over at Nonna, who shot him a warning look. He couldn't push this any further—Rachel would clam up or, worse, she'd hightail it out of Palermo and away from his watch.

"I'm going for a walk." Tomas stood and strode down the hall.

"Where are you going?" Rachel called behind him.

He didn't answer.

* * * *

Tomas had stalked the streets of Palermo until the sun dipped behind the horizon and a coolness descended upon the city. With every pounding footstep, the violent feelings grew, leaving him disturbed that someone could elicit such a strong reaction.

Rounding the corner, he arrived at Piazza Canzone. Now blanketed in darkness, the square remained quiet except for the fountain where water trickled down the worn stone and pooled in a green stench at the base. What had once been a place of beauty now had a sinister and dark feel—so unlike when he was a child and the residents would promenade of an evening, dressed in their finest as they stopped to chat with friends and family. That seemed like a lifetime ago. These memories needed to be nudged to the side as they served no purpose other than to dishearten his hope for a future that wasn't draped in destitution and war.

"We need hope," Tomas muttered as he looked down at the feet that had taken him across town and into his old neighborhood.

"I heard you were back in Palermo."

Tomas looked up to discover the owner of the voice was a man with sandy hair and toothy grin. Tomas couldn't contain his happiness. "Well if my eyes don't deceive me, I would say Donato Moretti is standing right in front of me!"

"Your eyes are correct!" Tomas's old school friend pulled him into an embrace, then slapped him on the back. "My god, it's been forever! What brings you here?"

"My legs needed a stretch."

"That's a hell of a long way to walk, my friend."

"I also needed the fresh air," said Tomas. "How did you hear I was back in town?"

"The good old grapevine." He raised an eyebrow, but it only confused Tomas.

"I don't understand."

Donato leant in close. "Abato."

"Ab... How?"

"We're all in this together."

"You're...?" Tomas looked around the empty square. "I never knew."

"There are many of us. In fact"—Donato slung his arm around Tomas's shoulder—"I'm off to a meeting now. Why don't you come along?"

The last place Tomas wanted to be was at a meeting that could attract the attention of Mussolini's men. Painful memories crashed in on Tomas of the last few moments he'd spent with his nonno at the Jewish meeting. Surely bloodshed like that couldn't happen again. It just couldn't... but it just...might.

"I don't think I should go," he said.

"Why not?" asked Donato.

"They don't know me."

"They know me very well. If I vouch for you, that's all they need."

Maybe if Tomas went to the meeting, it would help him figure out his next step. Fear gripped his insides.

"So is your silence a yes?" pushed Donato.

"It's..." He needed to find a way to extract himself from Abato, as slaughtering young, terrified Italian soldiers was inhumane. There had to be a better way. Perhaps the answer was at this meeting. "How did you hear from Abato? I've been waiting on a communication but haven't heard a thing."

"Networks, my friend, networks. Abato's a loose cannon—that we know—but he's valuable. His fearlessness gets the job done, though every so often we have to rein him in." Donato motioned for them to start walking. Tomas followed, his legs having already made the decision even though his head and heart weren't sure.

"No doubt you've heard about his sister," said Tomas.

"Only briefly. I heard you got her back here. Abato made sure he got that detail. He also heard the book was eventually delivered."

"Was the story on the front page of the newspaper?" He couldn't help the sarcasm and luckily his friend laughed.

"Look, I'm the first to admit there are massive communication leaks and gaps that need plugging, but what can we expect? We're not organized like an army and there are major egos getting in the way of us all working together. Yet every so often news travels like wildfire." Donato let out a short laugh. "Do not look so concerned. She's alive, right?"

"Yes." Tomas tried to block out the state he'd found her in only a few hours earlier.

"So all is good and you and she will return to her duties in no time. When do you head back out?"

"I don't really know." He had so many decisions to make and none of them appeared easy.

"Well, this evening you come to the meeting with me. You just never know what will happen, especially now the Allies have arrived. Tonight, the future may change right before our eyes."

Chapter 16

Rosie sat in the kitchen with her father and passed him the specially designed spoon. Through trial and error, she'd finally come up with a design that could make his life easier now that he had to adjust to being left-handed—if he'd give the spoon a proper try. Instead, he looked with suspicion at the specially designed utensil in his hand.

"It's just a matter of practice, Dad."

"I can't do it." His dejected tone broke her heart.

"Please, just try."

"I can't do it!" He dropped the spoon and it clattered against the table.

"Time is all we need."

"I don't have time. Neither do you." He tucked his left foot under his crippled right leg to move it into a more comfortable position. That small maneuver gave Rosie hope.

"You're doing great, Dad."

"Nonsense," he grumbled.

"Maybe I need to make some adjustments to the handle." She picked up a glass of water and sipped it slowly.

"What is it?" he asked.

Taking the time to put the glass down, Rosie sat back on the chair and fiddled with the hem of her shirt. "I've been trying to put this off…"

"Put what off?"

"I'm managing to pay the workers their wages but we should have paid them the extra they're owed by now." Recalling the last conversation with Sefa, she said, "There have been rumblings—"

"We don't have the money." Her father looked down at his crippled hand and shook his head. "I may be asset rich but I am cash poor. Bloody

Bartel took a sizeable chunk." Her father rubbed his chin. She wondered if he had realized he'd sworn.

"What are we going to do, then?"

"I don't know." With his good hand, he reached for the glass of water but he lost his grip and it fell and smashed to the floor. "Damn it!"

"It's all right." She knelt on the floor and used a towel to clean it up. "I'll get you another one."

"I don't want another one. I want to be out of this damn chair and running this damn farm!" He slammed his left fist against the armrest. A moment later his face scrunched and he covered it with his hand.

Rosie went to him. "I'm sorry, Dad. I wish I could change things."

He looked up, his eyes glassy but no tears had been shed. Not that she expected to see them as she'd never seen her father cry, not even at Geoffrey's funeral.

"You can't change things, Rosie, but you have made them easier. What you have done...running this place and making sure the workers do their job, and trying to find ways for me to do everyday things...I'm ashamed to say I have not given you enough credit."

Tears welled up and she tried to force them back, but a solitary one slid down her cheek.

Her father looked at the offending droplet and said, "You are still way too emotional."

"It's who I am," she said, trying not to sound defensive. "So, is this a thank you?"

He nodded, then closed his eyes, and that was the end of the conversation.

* * * *

Rosie adjusted the basket on her elbow as she walked swiftly down the main street. Once again, she had to squeeze in a trip to town to collect essential supplies because her mother wasn't fit enough to drive. Her mother's not-so-secret boozing concerned Rosie immensely, but between looking after her father, running Tulpil, and trying to figure out how to bring in more money, she barely had a moment to scratch herself. Add the continual cycle of kicking herself over Tomas, and Rosie's days were chock full.

Tomas's words had hurt. And as much as she wanted to erase their last conversation from memory, she couldn't let it go. His easy manner and familiarity had led her to believe that she could be honest, though apparently honesty was not something Tomas could handle. She didn't know his countrymen well enough to gauge whether this was a cultural difference or just one of Tomas's idiosyncrasies. Either way, it had left a bitter taste in her mouth.

Rosie opened the car door, placed the basket on the passenger seat, and was walking around to the driver's side when she stopped, having spotted Luka Abrami. His cheeks were rosier, his back straighter, and his eyes held a cheeky glint when he approached her and tipped his hat.

"Rosie!" Luka clasped his rough hands around hers, his large eyes saying more than his limited English could.

"I'm glad to see you out and about and looking healthy. I'm sorry those brutes were so horrendous in their behavior."

He may not have grasped her every word but he seemed to get the gist. "*Famiglia di* Conti very nice."

"*Famiglia?* Family?"

He nodded and smiled.

"*Festa*, yes? Satiday?"

"Sorry?"

"*Festa casa di* Conti. Satiday. You come? For *grazie* help me? Two time?" His broad smile made her want to accept the invitation instantly, but she couldn't now that she'd managed to offend Tomas. Her heart sank. She needed to make things right between them. If only she knew how.

"I would love to go with you, Luka"—and she meant every word—"but I just can't. It's a very kind invitation, though. And please, you can stop thanking me. I'm glad I was able to help when you've needed it."

Luka nodded, but she had no idea if he fully understood even though she'd spoken slowly and enunciated properly. It would be so nice to have a few Italian words up her sleeve.

"*Grazie* help." He grinned, tipped his hat and took off at a pace much quicker than most men his age could handle.

A laugh escaped her lips at Luka getting the last word in. Rosie adjusted the basket on her arm. A shiver ran up her spine, as if an unwelcome presence was in her midst. She turned around.

Bloody hell.

"You can't babysit that dago forever." Ken towered above her. She resisted the urge to step away.

"Leave him alone." Her calm voice didn't reflect the turmoil surging within.

"I don't like you talking to those I-tai's."

"And I don't like you talking to me in this manner." She glanced around for Ken's cronies but it was only him. Clutching the keys to the ute, she said, "I have to go."

"What's the hurry?" He moved in front, blocking her path. She stepped to the side and he did the same.

"For god's sake, Ken! Let me pass!"

"Or?" His breath reeked of rum. He'd already been drinking? The pub had only opened an hour ago.

"Or I won't get my work finished." Ken moved in on her and she pushed him in the chest with her one free hand. "Stop!"

A loud, throaty laugh tumbled through the air. "*Your* work?"

Rosie jutted out her chin. "Yes."

"Your old man must have lost his mind when he had that stroke. Women have no place being in charge."

She clenched her fist. It would be so easy to punch Ken in the nose. She'd experienced enough punch-ups between her brothers to know exactly where to hit and at what angle to cause damage. But she was better than that.

Squeezing the keys in her hand, she opened the vehicle door. "You have your opinions and I have mine."

"But it's not just my opinion, is it? People are talking. Doing a man's job. Getting in with those wogs—"

"Enough!" She really shouldn't let him get to her.

He leant on the bonnet of her ute and she contemplated pushing his filthy hands off her vehicle but decided against it. The less physical contact with him, the better.

When he spoke, it was accompanied by a sneer. "You should think more about the company you keep, especially with that wog who hung around you at the dance like a bad smell. That's all I'm sayin'."

She grit her teeth and yanked open the door. Sliding into the driver's seat, she started the engine and wound up the window, despite the heat of the day.

Ken's scrawny frame sprawled farther across the bonnet. With his face right in front of her, he yelled through the windscreen, "You've made a massive mistake!"

She revved the engine and Ken got off the bonnet and stood to the side, arms crossed on his torso. His glower would intimidate most people—but not Rosie. She put the ute into gear and pushed the pedal to the floor. Dirt flew behind and as she drove away. She glanced in the rearview mirror. Ken remained motionless, his legs wide apart, glaring eyes fixed on her vehicle. He stared her down until she turned the corner and lost sight of him.

She shouldn't be so unnerved by Ken's hostility. He'd always had that element to him, especially as he'd never forgiven her for rejecting his advances in the past. The dig about Tomas and her working at Tulpil really got to her. It shouldn't have, but it did.

Before long Rosie was back amongst the cane and an overwhelming sense of peace washed over her. Keen to get home and finish up the rest of the day's work, she pushed the peddle down hard and zoomed up the hill, only to find a ragged figure staggering in front of her.

"Shit!" She slammed on the brakes and the ute shuddered, skidding across the gravel, out of control. Gripping the wheel, she took her foot off the brake and jammed it down again, steering the vehicle back on course. The ute jerked forward and stopped, slamming her back against the seat. "Jesus, Mary and Joseph."

The figure continued sauntering down the road, oblivious to the accident he'd almost caused. Indignant, Rosie jumped out of the car and marched toward the vagabond.

"Hey!" she yelled, but the guy continued to ignore her. "Hey!"

Rosie's legs carried her swiftly past the unkempt man and she turned to face him to get his full attention. Maybe he was deaf? His bushy beard obscured his face, as did the tattered hat that covered his eyes. He clutched a rucksack that had been patched so many times it looked like a quilt. The boots he wore were scuffed and filthy, as were his pants that had holes in the knees.

"Hey! You nearly caused an..." Her words trailed off when the vagabond removed his hat and his eyes stared into hers. "Oh god," she rasped.

Rosie's legs buckled and she fell heavily to the ground, the sharp stones digging into the flesh on her knees. She didn't care. The pain couldn't outweigh the disbelief that suffocated, yet breathed life into her at the same time.

"Rosie?" Alex bent over, his big blue eyes full of concern. God, how she'd missed those eyes with that cheeky sparkle, although the shine and playfulness had gone and he seemed to have aged at least twenty years.

Alex was home.

Rosie placed her shaking hand in Alex's, her knees still wobbly from the shock. He hoisted her to a standing position.

"Alex...what...how..." Her brain refused to connect with her tongue and a thick fog descended upon her. This couldn't be. Alex was missing, presumed dead. Yet here he was, in flesh and blood. "I..."

Alex's gentle smile convinced her he was not a mirage.

"Oh, Alex!" Rosie squealed. "Oh my god! It's you! It's really you!"

Her brother wrapped his arms around her, pulling her close to his chest. The strength that she remembered wasn't there anymore. Or maybe it was...hesitation?

"I've missed you so much, my Rosie." Alex's voice sounded strained, as if words didn't come easily.

"You have no idea how I've missed you, little brother." She snuggled in closer. Although he looked like he hadn't showered for weeks, he actually smelt fresh. "Where have you been? Why didn't you tell us you were alive?"

Alex let go of her and stepped back, like she'd just punched him in the gut.

Instantly, she wanted to protect him, but at the same time, she desperately wanted to know what had kept her brother away for so long.

"Alex?" She reached for his hand but he stepped away even further, his eyes not meeting hers. Rosie moved closer. "Alex?"

He shut his eyes. "I'm not ready to talk about it."

"All right." She picked up his bag and went to the ute. She'd just have to wait until he was ready. Rosie loaded the bag in the back then turned and asked, "Shall we go?"

Alex's mind looked like it was anywhere but in Piri River. "Yes."

He walked over then reached for her hands, taking a moment to study her. "When did you grow up? You look like Mum, you know."

"So I've been told." She loved hearing that she looked like Cecile even though Rosie couldn't see it. Her mother had a finer bone structure, was more petite, her hair less chaotic and it was a beautiful blonde, not fiery red like Rosie's. Her poor father never got a look in when it came to Rosie, but she had definitely inherited his stubbornness.

Rosie gestured for Alex to get in the passenger seat. He did so, but grimaced when he bent his left knee.

"What's wrong?"

"Nothing," he snapped then rested his rough hand on hers. "I'm sorry. This is all a bit overwhelming."

"You can say that again."

"This is all a bit overwhelming," he said.

Rosie burst out laughing, reveling in the silly childhood game they used to play. When her laughter stopped, she studied her brother. A smile had barely registered on his lips.

Rosie went around to the driver's side and got in, started the engine and took off down the road, this time at a less frantic speed.

Alex is back!

Alex is alive!

"Just wait until Mum and Dad see what I've brought back from my shopping expedition."

Chapter 17

The screen door creaked open and Alex stepped out to join Rosie on the verandah. Red and orange streaked across the endless sky, casting a warm glow across the fields. Alex grimaced and gripped the arms of the chair as he maneuvered onto it. Given the last time she mentioned his knee, Rosie decided to leave that topic alone.

"You look a bit different," she said.

Alex ran a hand over his clean-shaven face. He looked down at the clothes Cecile had kept in his bedroom for all these years, unable to part with her son's belongings. "I guess I looked a fright."

"Just a bit."

"I've been travelling…roaming…whatever you want to call it. I had no one to impress. My appearance was just one less thing to worry about."

"You have lots of worries?" she asked.

"Don't, Rosie."

"Fine." Although it was far from fine. However, for now she had to keep the pace slow, let Alex get used to being back at Tulpil. And let Rosie, her dad and mum get used to having Alex once more. For how long was anybody's guess.

"How's Dad doing?" she asked.

"Better than we thought. He seems to have taken my sudden appearance rather well."

On the drive back to Tulpil, Rosie had filled Alex in about their parents— the stroke, and Rosie's fear that their mother's drinking had increased dramatically. Alex had taken it all very well. A little too well. Surely, his reactions should be more heartfelt?

Stop judging, Rosie. You can't possibly know what he's been through.

While Rosie and Alex sipped iced tea, frustration snuck up on her. She couldn't think of one subject to talk to about. Actually, she had plenty, but was too afraid to bring anything up for fear of being snapped at again.

"It's exactly as I remember." Alex fixed his gaze on the farm as his hand clutched the glass, covered in condensation.

"Not a lot has changed," she said, happy to hear his voice.

She glanced sideways at her younger brother. The fading daylight highlighted the deep lines etched on his weathered complexion. Gone was the baby face that once had girls swooning at his feet, and in place was a much harder, older, strained version of the brother she once knew.

Alex cleared his throat. "Dad says you've been running the show since he...has become unwell."

"Yes. I've enjoyed it more than I thought."

"Do you want to continue doing it?"

"Of course." The muscles in her neck tightened. Warily, she asked, "Why?"

"No reason." Alex focused on the fields once more.

* * * *

Rosie stood in front of the small tractor, trying to get a better grip on the spanner so she could tighten the bolt. The stupid machine had stopped working days before and, so far, no one had been able to figure out why. She refused to let a broken-down piece of machinery get the better of her. Although, if she were entirely honest, she needed to let out the frustration that had been building up since Alex had arrived home. She loved having her brother around, but it felt as if everyone had to tread on eggshells because no one was willing to confront the elephant in the room. How can anyone disappear, presumed dead, and come back without an explanation?

Rosie gave the spanner one more twist. It slipped and her recently healed knuckles grazed the metal, sending searing pain throughout her hand.

"Argh!" Rosie kicked a nearby wooden crate. A deep throbbing ran from her toe, up her foot and shot up her shin. She doubled over, cursing the ridiculousness of kicking an inanimate object.

"Do you always take your temper out on poor crates?"

She turned to find Alex's lanky frame standing nearby. His lips kicked into a smile.

"Do you always laugh at people when they're injured?" She gingerly placed her throbbing foot on the ground and shook her sore hand.

Once more his smile faded into seriousness.

"What's going on?" she asked. Good grief, the pain hadn't subsided yet.

"Dad's asked me to take over." Alex shoved his hands in his pockets and looked everywhere but at her.

"What?" She stopped shaking her hand. "Why?"

"Because…" He shrugged.

"Because only Stanton men should run the place?" Fury mixed with disappointment surged through her.

"Listen, Rosie, it's not my fault. I only—"

"Do you want this job?"

He shrugged again.

"Alex, I know I will never be able to comprehend what you've been through, I just want you to understand that it hasn't been all roses here. I've carried the burden of being the only sibling at Tulpil and I had to fight really hard for this position—you know what Dad's like—so please, excuse me, for being upset and hurt." She took a long, slow breath. "And I am not going to let this go without a fight."

As much as Rosie wanted to rant and carry on, she couldn't. It wouldn't be fair to Alex. Besides, her father's fingerprints were all over this.

"I get it, Rosie. You're right, I don't want this responsibility, but Dad railroads everyone into what he wants them to do."

"So what *do* you want?"

"I don't know."

A strangled sob filled the air. Her brother crumpled in a heap against the workbench. She went to him and wrapped a comforting arm around his shaking shoulders.

"He can't ask you to do something you don't want. It's clearly not the right time." Any concern about her own plight disappeared into the ether when she studied her brother's glassy eyes.

"It's not that I don't…I…" He pulled away and hammered the bench with his fist. Sunlight streaming through the open door highlighted the dust flying through the air.

"What is it?" She lowered her voice, taking the same caring tone she used when he was younger. His shoulders instantly relaxed.

"I don't know where to start," he mumbled.

"Start wherever you want."

Alex nodded and rested his head against hers. Silence shrouded them and in the distance, she could hear the men finishing up for the day, the myriad of accents and languages mixing together.

Whether conscious of it or not, his hand gently massaged the same knee he'd denied had hurt the other day.

Finally, he opened his mouth and she held her breath.

"It's just been...hard, you know?" He shook his head. "How could you possibly know? How could *anyone* know?"

"No one can, Alex. But we're here for you. Whatever you need."

"What I need you can't give me. No one can. No one understands. *No one*."

Outside the footfalls of the workers grew louder, their laughter emanating through the gaps in the shed.

"I...I need to go." Alex jumped up and ran out the far door.

* * * *

Rosie stood in the doorway of the lounge room after returning from three hours storming the walking tracks near Tulpil. Indignation had fueled her steps until she'd finally lost steam and returned to the house and taken a cold shower in readiness to face her father. She now observed him, totally oblivious to her presence as he studied the ledgers. He barely slept these days and spent a great deal of time mumbling to himself. Rosie didn't have it in her to offer to help now that Alex had delivered the news. What upset Rosie the most, though, was her father didn't even have the courage to tell her himself.

Calm, Rosie. Remain calm. No matter what her mind said, her pulse raced and her body remained in a tense grip.

From the safety of the doorway, she said, "Do you remember when I used to go into the shed with you when I was little and you'd let me pass you tools when you were fixing equipment?"

Her father peered over his glasses. "That was so long ago, Rosie."

"But you remember, right?"

He nodded then returned to the accounting ledger.

Even without his full attention, she had to get this out. "We'd spend hours in there and you'd happily guide me as to what tool did what." Her throat tightened. "You gave me an education in mechanics and a love for the land. That's why I joined the Australian Women's Army to work as a mechanic. You taught me so much. You inspired me, Dad."

Her father lowered the book and stared at her. He tilted his head back and concentrated on the ceiling. Looked at the floor. Finally, he locked eyes with her. "Why are you telling me this?"

"Because as soon as the boys came along, I faded into the background. You pushed me away. We..." All the years of hurt balled into a large lump in her throat. "We stopped spending time together in the shed."

Now the time had come to get everything out in the open and for her father to understand the impact of his actions. Instead of fearing a fallout, Rosie felt confident she could deal with whatever arose if he listened to her—really, listened to her.

"Dad—"

He looked up. "Do you really think that?"

"What?"

"Think that the boys were more important than you?"

Rosie hesitated, then forged ahead. "Yes."

A shot of hurt flashed in his eyes. "My dear girl, I never meant for that to happen."

"But it did, Dad. The minute they were old enough to walk, you had them pegged as your successors."

He paused for a moment. "Out of the three of you, you were always the one that had an affinity with this land."

"So why did you push me aside?"

His chest rose and fell and he moved his lips, as if willing the right words to come along.

"Dad?"

"You know the answer to this."

Rosie placed her hand over her belly as if protecting it from another emotional punch. Glancing at the door, she considered making a hasty exit but, whether she liked it or not, their relationship was out on the table, being slowly dissected.

Her father shifted on the chair. "Putting a woman in charge of a cane farm is not the done thing. I broke with tradition because I had to."

"So even though you *told* me I was doing a good job, I am cast aside when a man comes along to fill the role."

Her father didn't move a muscle. A moment later he motioned for her to come over to him. She did so reluctantly, and sat on the chair opposite.

"Rosie, I am so, so sorry." With his left hand, he reached out and wrapped his fingers around hers. "Going against tradition just isn't...easy."

"No, it isn't."

"Rosie, please, come here." He motioned for her to move closer. This time she didn't feel so reluctant. In a wave of nostalgia, she rested her head against his chest, the steady rhythm of his heartbeat bringing comfort. How long had it been since they'd shared an embrace? When was the last time they had actually sat down and spoken about their feelings? Her body jolted involuntarily. *Never.* So what had changed?

"Are you all right, sweetheart?"

"I'm fine, really." She moved back to the chair. "It's just that we haven't really…talked."

He nodded. "I'm a man of few words, I know, but that doesn't excuse the way I've treated you. I should have spoken to you first." He paused, as if gathering his thoughts. "Being stuck here has given me time to reflect on all the things I have done over the years." His eyes were earnest. "I know I've been unreasonable and far from fair, it's just that there are so many factors I have to take into consideration. However, you deserve better treatment from your own father."

"Where does this leave me?" she asked.

"Let me think some more, Rosie. Maybe we can find a way to make things work." The slight reluctance in his tone didn't instill any confidence.

The room fell silent and the tick-tock of the grandfather clock echoed from the hallway.

"Alex needs something to help him get up in the mornings because otherwise he'll be wandering aimlessly," her father said, as if the conversation had never stopped.

"I know." It was good to hear someone else voicing their concern for Alex. "Is that why you asked him to take over? To give him something to focus on?"

"Yes." Her father scratched his crippled arm and even that proved a difficult task. "I didn't think of the impact it would have on you and for that, I am sorry."

"But you won't change your mind about who runs Tulpil."

"No."

She drew her lips into a thin line, then decided if they were going to be entirely honest she had to let it all out. "I don't think he's capable."

"I don't agree."

"He won't even tell us about where he's been all this time. It's obvious he's been traumatized and I do understand it would be hard to talk about it but—"

"You've never been to war, you could never understand." His tone held an edge once more.

"I'm not doubting you have a better understanding than me, but how can you let Alex run Tulpil when he's clearly not ready? It could affect everyone. Please, don't get me wrong, I love Alex, but I don't know if lumping him with all this responsibility is the right thing. Maybe if he and I shared the role then—"

"No. He needs to step up and embrace responsibility like a man."

"He needs time to heal from whatever it is that's troubling him."

"The best way to heal is with good honest work."

How quickly the tables had turned. Her father had started to sound reasonable, then, like a flash of lightning, he changed again.

She stood, her heart heavier than it had been when she'd first walked into the room. Without a word, Rosie headed out the front door. Just when she'd thought she'd made progress, she ended up even further behind.

* * * *

Hours later Rosie stood in the kitchen, broke off a piece of freshly baked bread and shoved it into her mouth. The warm, fluffy delight melted on her tongue as she reached for the bread knife to help herself to a thick slice. The knife broke the crust and steam escaped, filling the room with an aroma that made her stomach grumble. In theory, she should have no appetite after the conversation with her father, but her mother's cooking had always been irresistible.

The sound of smashing glass came from the laundry below and Rosie raced down the back steps and flung open the door. On the floor were the remains of a brandy bottle with large shards scattered across the ground. In the corner, her mother was curled up in a fetal position, her forehead smeared in blood.

"Mum!" Rosie went over and inspected her mother's hands. A piece of glass was embedded in her mother's palm but she seemed oblivious to the pain.

"Oh, Mum." She tried to hoist up her mother's shaking body but to no avail. Rosie stroked her mother's hair and contemplated how to get her out of the stifling heat of the laundry and upstairs to the bedroom to lie down. "How did this happen?"

Her mother's blank stare relayed nothing. It smelt as if she'd bathed in brandy.

"Please, Mum. Talk to me."

Her mother's gaze fixed on the chunk of glass in her hand.

"Ohhh!" Her eyes widened as she wailed and started waving her hand around, as if trying to shake the glass loose. Blood oozed across her pale skin and Rosie grabbed her mother's arm.

"Mum! Please! I'll fix it, but we need to get you out of here first."

Rosie stood and used the toes of her shoes to make a pathway through the debris. Returning to her mother, who cowered in the corner, Rosie placed her hands under her mother's armpits and used all her might to lift her. For such a fine-boned woman, Cecile was quite heavy.

"Mum, use your legs and I'll guide you."

"He's gone…" she slurred.

"Who? Alex? No, he's here. He's returned to us, remember?" Rosie's back ached with the weight of her mother but she persevered, guiding her through the laundry door and toward the base of the stairs that led up to the kitchen.

"No." Cecile shook her head. The bright sun caught a sheen of sweat across her pale skin. "*He* has gone. Oh god, he's gone!"

She buried her head in her uninjured hand and gut-wrenching sobs shook her shoulders.

"Is it Dad? Dad's here and he's doing fine." That wasn't quite a lie.

"No!"

"Geoffrey?"

Her mother waved her wounded hand in a dismissive manner, as if the pain didn't register anymore. Rosie grabbed her mother's wrist.

"Please, Mum, we need to fix this up. Then you can talk to me about What's bothering you."

The sobs intensified.

"Mum…let's just tend to your hand and get you a cool drink." *Of water*.

"No one can know," her mother slurred then wiped a blood-streaked hand across her face.

"Know what? That you've sliced your hand? I can't hide that." Perhaps when her mother had sobered up and her hand was stitched she'd make more sense.

"No one can know!" shouted her mother before she passed out.

Chapter 18

Rosie's mother remained tucked up in bed with a stitched and bandaged hand, sleeping off the booze while Rosie's father slept on the couch, accounting ledgers on his lap. Alex was nowhere to be seen and as the sun dipped beyond the horizon, the heat of the day wrapped around Rosie as she paced the verandah. Kitty was in the next town over, staying with her parents for the weekend and Tulpil—the one place that brought Rosie such joy—closed in on her, like her lifeblood was slowly being sucked out, leaving her body weak and her chest hollow.

Rosie walked down the long gravel drive and to the road that led to town. The scent of the ylang-ylang flowers sweetened the air and the trill of the kingfishers melded perfectly with the rhythm of her shoes crunching along the stones. A cool breeze grazed her skin as the heat fell away and became more bearable. In the distance, she heard music but couldn't distinguish what genre. It didn't sound like the usual tunes she heard in these parts. It was more rhythmic, like the music she'd heard Italians play when in town.

The Conti party.

Of course, she should have remembered. Although she'd set out to spend time alone to clear her head, the enticing music made her want to wander up to the Conti house. But it was a ridiculous idea. She had no business forcing her way into the party after Tomas had made it abundantly clear he didn't want to see her.

Rosie stopped to watch the lanterns in the distance. They swayed in the gentle breeze while a bonfire burned brightly in a cleared paddock. She couldn't make out any of the dark figures, but it seemed that every Italian within fifty miles had congregated for this celebration—of what, she didn't know.

Then it struck her: Why would the Contis throw a party when they were renowned for keeping to themselves? She should have known better than to listen to town gossip. If she'd ignored it, then she wouldn't have had that ridiculous argument with Tomas.

Sighing, Rosie continued down the road, leaving the Conti house behind. Laughter floated from the party as she hastened away, her heart growing heavy.

She kicked a stone that went flying into the darkness and landed with a thud against a tree stump.

"What did that poor stone do to you?" A deep voice asked from the darkness.

Her heart skipped a beat as she spun around. "What are you doing here? Do you always sneak up on people like that?"

"Which question would you like me to answer first?"

"Either. Both. I don't know..." She drew her brows together.

Tomas stepped out from the darkness and once again, her heart picked up speed.

"I am here because I saw a shadow," he said.

"And?"

"And I did not know it was you until I got closer."

"And?" What was wrong with her brain? Who was the one who spoke English as a second language?

"First, I thought the figure was a person invited to the party. You stood looking at the house for a long time. I thought this person must be shy. So when I saw the person walk away I thought I should go and tell them to come and join the party."

"Then you realized it was me. The *Australian*."

"Ah. I see you are still angry." He drew close and she caught the scent of his spicy cologne. "I must apologize for my bad behavior."

"Are you saying this because you accidently saw me now?"

Tomas jerked back, like he'd been slapped in the face. "Rosalie, I have been spending much time figuring out how I could ask your forgiveness. My manners were very bad."

"Yes, they were."

He lowered his head. "I was wrong. I was shooting the messenger."

"Yes, you were." Silence snuck between them. Rosie dragged the toe of her sensible shoes through the gravel, grappling for the right words. Quietly, she said, "I shouldn't have mentioned the Mussolini thing. I know it divides people."

"It does. Rosie, we should be able to talk about most things, yes?"

"But some subjects are out of bounds?"

"Yes."

"Which subjects?"

Tomas waved his hand in a dismissive manner. "Let us not worry about this now. Perhaps you would like to join me?" He motioned for Rosie to thread her arm through his.

"Thanks all the same, but I don't think so." Only minutes ago she'd lamented about not being up at that party on the hill. Where was her nerve?

"Please, I insist. It is my way of an apology."

She could continue on her way and envelop herself in the darkness and quiet of her own solitude. Or she could head to the bright lights and music of a party with people she didn't know but who fascinated her all the same.

"Rosie?" Tomas's expectant eyes drew her back into the moment.

To hell with it. "Sure. Let's go."

* * * *

The aroma of tomatoes, onions and a few unidentified foods wafted through the air as Rosie stood off to the side of the main gathering. Tomas had ducked off to fetch her a drink, which gave Rosie a chance to lurk in the shadows and view the lively crowd. She reveled in the anonymity while she tried to gather courage to join the throng.

"Rosie! You come!" Luka greeted her with a large smile as he walked up and planted a kiss on both cheeks. "Good?"

"Yes, yes, I am very good, thank you. And you?"

The light from the lanterns made his eyes twinkle as he gave an affirmative nod.

He patted her hand affectionately. "I happy you here."

"So am I." She took in the front garden where twenty or so kids darted through the crowds of women in flowing dresses and men in smart shirts and trousers. She looked down at her casual dress and shoes, feeling very self-conscious. Everyone laughed and smiled, they ate and drank, and they greeted each other with warmth. Now, witnessing the friendliness of the gathering, she felt more alone than ever.

"Ah, I see you have found Luka." Tomas passed her a glass filled to the brim with red wine. "This is from the vineyard of my cousin in New South Wales."

"He sends it up to you?"

Tomas's gentle laugh sent a shimmer of happiness through her.

"No, my cousin is here. He brings many bottles!" Tomas pointed at a pile of crates stacked near the steps leading up to the verandah.

Rosie politely sipped the deep red wine and tried not to pull a face when it burned the back of her throat. The only time she'd tasted wine was at a dance a few years ago when she and Kitty had taken a few swigs from a bottle William had swiped from his auntie. They'd gotten so drunk that they'd fallen into a ditch and laughed about things that weren't even remotely funny when sober. A smile formed on Rosie's lips.

"You like it, I see?"

"Pardon?"

"The wine." Tomas pointed at her glass. "You like it because you are smiling?"

"Oh! Yes, yes. It's lovely." To prove the point, she took another sip and was surprised when it didn't burn at all. Instead, the rich liquid slid down her throat and left a taste of cherries mixed with black currents. A strange combination but it somehow worked.

"I am happy you like it."

Rosie took another swig from the glass.

"And I am glad you are here."

She nearly choked. "Thank you. I'm glad I am, also."

Although shyness made her want to look away she held his gaze, determined not to be a wilting flower.

Tomas cleared his throat. "I hope you do not feel strange to be the only...uh..."

"Australian?"

"Yes."

"No, I don't mind. In fact"—she glanced around—"I feel very honored to have been asked." Although Luka had initially invited her, it didn't count as it wasn't his party. And the only reason she was here now was because Tomas had mistaken her shadow for someone else.

"You will find we are friendly and not just to our own kind." He raised an eyebrow and she knew exactly what he was getting at.

"All right, perhaps I was wrong to listen to gossip—"

"Perhaps?"

"I was wrong to listen to gossip."

"You will not find a fascist among us. And yes, my family does not socialize with those who are not from our country because of this reason— others think we are all fascists."

"And you're not," Rosie said.

"Exactly. We are not. We get tired of explaining ourselves so sometimes it is easier to be with our own kind."

"Isn't that kind of...racist?" *Oh. That may be a bit too far.* And just when she was getting back in Tomas's good books...

Tomas rubbed his chin, as if giving her question much thought. Eventually, he said, "I do not think of it that way. We have the same celebrations, the same traditions, the same food. We stay together because we understand each other."

Rosie contemplated Tomas's answer, now happy she'd asked. "I guess Australians do the same. We tend to stick together. And come to think of it, even the different nationalities on Tulpil stay close for the exact same reasons you said. Though at other times they socialize with everyone, no matter where they come from."

"Like this evening," Tomas said. "You are the representative of Australia."

"No pressure." She laughed and Tomas joined in.

The distinctive notes of a violin quieted the partygoers. Rosie turned to see a man in his sixties with a gray beard and salt-and-pepper hair, holding a violin and bow. He gently teased out notes of a mournful melody which floated along the light breeze. Enraptured, Rosie didn't dare move for fear the spell would break.

A few loud, sharp notes changed the tempo and the violinist's eyes opened as a grin spread across his face. The same grin she'd witnessed on Tomas.

"Is he...?"

"My father? Yes. His name is Cosimo. And over there"—he pointed at a tall, slender woman in a stunning red dress—"is my mother, Beatrice."

"She's beautiful. And your father is so talented."

Tomas nodded and Rosie's gaze returned to Tomas's father playing the violin with fervor as a group of guitarists joined in. Young teenagers rhythmically tapped sticks against *bottles* of varying sizes. Men, women and children created a dance floor in the dirt as they spun each other around, laughing and dancing with pure delight.

"He's very good," she said.

"His grandmother—my great-grandmother—was an opera singer."

"Really?"

"Musical talent runs in my family. Except me. I am afraid I was not born so musical."

"I didn't inherit that gene, either."

"Although"—Tomas held out his hand—"I may not play music or sing, I can dance."

Rosie glanced at the couples who moved joyously to the upbeat music that was so foreign to her. "I don't know how."

He leant in, his voice low, his warm breath against her ear. "Then let me show you."

Tomas wrapped his fingers around hers and she tried to calm the shaking that threatened to overtake her body. It wasn't like she hadn't held hands with a male before, but this was…different. The males she'd stepped out with in the past were immature, whereas Tomas was a man.

He gently held her hand and led her through the moving crowd. Dust clouds danced around people's feet, laughter filled her ears and the delicious aroma of crusty bread floated into her nostrils.

"You are ready for fun?" He grabbed both her hands.

"Yes?"

"Just follow me."

The band were now in full flight. Tomas held her close and guided her through the throng. She let her body relax, allowing him to set the pace and the course, and as she did so, all the stress about her family and Tulpil floated skyward.

Tomas hadn't lied when he said he could dance, and she loved being in his capable hands. The music filled her heart, her body instinctively responding to Tomas's.

She moved closer.

He held her tighter.

Their lips only inches apart.

"Please?" Luka tapped Tomas on the shoulder.

Tomas jolted and Rosie stepped back, her face burning.

"It would be impolite for me to keep Rosie all to myself, no?" Tomas looked at her apologetically.

"Yes! Of course I will dance with you, Luka," Rosie said, a little too enthusiastically. She needed a moment for her temperature to lower, to catch her breath, let her head and heart meet up.

Tomas gave her a salute as he walked into the shadows. Luka smiled and spun her around, his ancient body more capable than she'd originally thought. Although not fluent in each other's language, the music and dancing became their method of communication. She couldn't help but wonder why Luka had chosen Australia. Did he have family and if so, were they still in Italy? Was he working to bring them out here? Or had he lost them in the war, like so many others who had made it to Australian shores? She looked around at the faces of people who didn't appear to have a care in the world. Was that the case now or were they still battling demons? What were their stories?

Now was not the time to delve into such things. Instead, she concentrated on basking in the glory of dancing freely and living in the moment. Every so often she caught a glimpse of Tomas, who kept glancing at her, even though he was in deep conversation with an older lady.

The band finished their set with a flourish and Luka brought Rosie over to a table piled high with fresh produce. Tomatoes, olives, cheeses, dried meats, freshly sliced fruit...

"Eat." Luka gestured for her to try a green olive.

She popped it in her mouth and let it rest on her tongue. A bitter, acidic flavor attacked her taste buds and she tried not to screw up her nose. Luka's amused expression showed he'd expected such a reaction. *Cheeky fellow.*

He pointed to the cheese. "Good."

Keen to get the acrid taste out of her mouth, Rosie picked up a small square of cheese and bit into it. Creamy deliciousness danced across her taste buds. It didn't cancel out the taste of the olive, in fact, it complemented it. She spied a few jars of the green and dark purply-black olives that looked like the ones that had been delivered to their house when her father was first ill. If the contents of those jars were as interesting as what she'd experienced here, she would need to open the jars sooner rather than later.

Rosie looked over to where Tomas had been standing but he'd disappeared, as had the older lady he'd been speaking with.

Luka carved off a large chunk of bread and slapped on cheese, salami, tomato and an assortment of pickled vegetables. He handed it to her and she held it with both hands as she tried to figure out how to attack it. Luka busied himself with making one for himself and her stomach grumbled. Opening her mouth, she took a massive bite and tried to chew, but it was a feat nigh impossible. The mixture of flavors appealed to every taste bud. Feeling awkward, Rosie turned away so no one could see her overstuffed mouth, but then she saw Tomas. Right. In. Front. Of. Her.

"You like it?"

She nodded, still unable to swallow the chunk of food that had formed a wad in her mouth.

A painful gulp got rid of it and she forced a smile, praying she didn't have any remnants on her face.

"Yes," she rasped. "It's delicious."

His lips twitched as if trying to contain a laugh. "You are welcome to come here and enjoy our food anytime."

"Thank you."

Tomas shoved his hands in his pockets and glanced over her shoulder. He frowned and gave a short shake of the head at whoever was behind her. Curious, Rosie turned around and noticed the old woman he'd been talking to earlier. Her gray hair was in a high bun and she wore a simple black dress that skirted her curvy frame. She couldn't have been much more than five feet four.

The lady raised her eyebrows and pointed at Tomas, who let out a long sigh. "My nonna wishes to speak with you."

"Is that a bad thing?"

"She's just…she is one for very strong opinions."

"And she has an opinion about me?" Rosie wasn't so sure she wanted to speak to Nonna now. "Is her English as good as you've been telling me?"

"It is almost better than mine."

Tomas's nonna's large brown eyes appeared friendly enough. She certainly didn't seem to be the unwelcoming Italian grandmother cliché she'd heard about.

"Come on"—Rosie tugged at his hand—"I want to meet her."

"Wait, please." Tomas withdrew his hand from hers. "Her opinion is strong about the Australian women."

"Because we're not all good Catholics?"

"Are you Catholic?" he asked.

"Does it matter? I thought I was going to meet her to say hello, not ask for her blessing so we can get married." The second the words came out she instantly cringed. She hoped the sarcasm wasn't lost on Tomas. "Not that we…uh…I didn't mean…"

He gave a gentle laugh and relief swept over her.

"I understand you are joking, Rosalie."

"I'm hilarious, huh?"

"So much hilarious. Besides, we would need to court before we got married. Or maybe my nonna will arrange a wedding with your father."

"Huh?"

"Do not look so scared, Rosalie. It is my turn to joke."

"Oh? Oh!"

"Please, do not get upset if she speaks her thoughts. She is like the wind—her mood can change and we never know which direction it will go."

"So why am I meeting her?" She threw her arms wide, her palms facing skyward.

"Because you are the only Australian at this party and she wishes to know why."

"You asked me here." Rosie waggled a finger under his nose. "Didn't you tell her that? Or does she think I make a habit of turning up at parties uninvited?"

"No, no, I have already explained, but she is as curious as the cat." He cupped his hand to the side of his mouth and said in a stage whisper, "No one says no to my nonna."

"Hmmm…"

"I will limit the length of the torture." Tomas held out his hand and she shook it.

"Fine, but you owe me."

"I believe I do."

Chapter 19

Rosie walked in step with Tomas, who shortened his stride to match hers. They skirted around the dancers who were back in full force now the band had started again, and within moments she was standing in front of the infamous Nonna.

"Nonna, please meet my good friend—"

"Rosalie Stanton." The way Rosalie Stanton rolled off Nonna's tongue sounded exotic. "It is good to meet you."

"It's lovely to meet you." Rosie slowed her speech, then wasn't sure if Nonna would think it patronizing.

A silence encircled the trio and a ball of uneasiness grew in Rosie's belly. Nonna had wanted to meet her, so wouldn't she have questions? Was she expecting Rosie to start talking? Was this some weird power tussle? Or was it a cultural thing where the youngest person had to initiate the conversation?

"You have a lovely place," Rosie finally said.

"*Grazie.*"

"This is such a wonderful party. I am honored to be here. It's so nice to hear the music from your homeland and—"

"Enough with this small talk. Tomas, help Zia Silvana."

"I am happy to stay here, in case you or Rosalie need help with translation."

"I have taught you English since you were a baby." She cocked an eyebrow. "Zia Silvana is the one who needs help, not me."

Nonna pointed in the direction of a woman who could easily pass as Nonna's sister. She struggled with a tray of glasses and Tomas went over to grab them. He glanced at Rosie, proffered an "I'm sorry" smile, then quickly returned to rescuing Zia Silvana.

"You, me, we talk. Come." Nonna motioned for Rosie to follow and, despite the elderly woman's short legs, Rosie had a hard time keeping up. They moved away from the party and toward the rose garden at the side of the house where row upon row of healthy, green bushes boasted an array of flowers. A rich floral scent hung in the air.

"These roses are magnificent. I'd heard you were a very good gardener."

Nonna concentrated on inspecting the leaves even though it was too dark to find any telltale spots of disease on the plants. "You like my boy."

Rosie bit her lip then realized she'd have to answer the question—truthfully—because Nonna didn't seem like the kind of person who would appreciate a barefaced lie. "He's a very lovely person."

"You want to kiss him, yes?"

Rosie's legs felt as if they were cemented to the ground. Was Tomas's grandmother always so forthright?

"I...uh..."

"I watch you dance with him. You have the stars in your eyes." Her expression didn't relay disapproval or approval and this line of questioning made Rosie curious about Nonna's motives.

"I..."

"Do not be embarrassed. He is handsome, I know this. It is from my side of the family." She grinned then her expression turned serious. "But he is not for you."

"Pardon?" Never in her life had she had such a candid conversation. And she didn't like this one bit. "We're just good friends."

"Pfft." She waved her hand. "Good friends mean nothing. You like him, he likes you. But whatever you have planned will not happen."

"I don't have any plans. I—"

"I am no fool."

Indignation pulled Rosie's shoulders back and drew her to full height. "Thank you for your concern..." *Of which it is none of your business...*"but the friendship Tomas and I have is just between us."

Nonna shook her head. The small laugh that escaped her lips irritated Rosie and a sharp pain in her gut told her that this Nonna lady was way more intuitive than Rosie had given her credit for.

"Is it because of who my parents are?" Rosie asked.

"No."

"Because I'm not Sicilian? Not Catholic?"

"No and no."

"Then why?"

"It is not my place to give a reason. You must not fall in love with him."

"I don't—"

Nonna tilted her head to the side.

"Love him…" Rosie said quietly.

Lively music filtered from the party as she stood in the semidarkness with Tomas's grandmother. Unease clawed at Rosie. This time Nonna had to be the one to break the silence.

"He is no good for any girl," Nonna eventually said. "He will only break your heart."

"But he's your grandson!" Rosie looked over Nonna's shoulder in case Tomas was nearby, but the garden remained empty.

"For this reason I say it is not a good idea to fall in love with him. No good for you. No good for him."

"I'm sorry, but unless you can give me a solid reason as to why I shouldn't *be friends* with him then I can't honor your wishes."

"If you do not follow my advice you are a silly girl."

"I'm far from silly." Rosie couldn't see why Tomas held so much affection for this woman. "Well, it's been…interesting meeting you. Thank you for showing me your roses."

Nonna nodded and turned her attention to the plants again. Rosie took a couple of steps then felt a small hand around her wrist. Twisting around, she stared into Nonna's brown eyes.

"My grandson is broken and cannot be fixed."

"He doesn't seem so broken to me."

"You do not know him like I do." Her eyes penetrated Rosie's.

"I know him well enough to know he is a good person." She hated that her voice had lost confidence.

"Good person—yes. Good for a husband—no. I understand you do not know me but please, have trust in me. I am trying to help you."

The sincerity in Nonna's expression disconcerted Rosie. Why would this woman speak against her grandson?

Nonna loosened her grip and Rosie pulled her hand away.

"Rosalie, I mean no harm. You are nice person and for this, you should not be hurt."

"Tomas has been nothing but kind to me."

"He is kind. He is just…" Nonna shook her head. "Complicated."

What Rosie had thought would be an innocent conversation now left her confused.

"Ah, I should have known you two would be here," came a deep voice.

Rosie looked up and she instantly felt relieved to see Tomas walking toward them. His dark wavy hair was slicked back, like he'd just dunked it in water.

"Yes, your nonna was showing me her roses."

She glanced at Nonna, who had moved away and was now heavily involved in examining her precious plants.

"This is all? She did not interrogate you?" Tomas smiled but it sagged when he caught sight of Rosie's expression. He faced his grandmother. "What did you say?"

"You are my grandson. I love you. Rosalie, she is nice. You have a nice *friend*."

Tomas drew his brows together.

"I must go now." Nonna put on a chirpy voice. "The guests need more food." Nonna disappeared around the corner, leaving Rosie and Tomas alone. Music from the band sparked up again but any desire to dance had left Rosie.

"I am sorry if my nonna is bossy."

"She's not bossy, she's just…good at saying how she feels."

Tomas slapped his palm against his forehead. "She said she wanted to ask about life as an Australian woman. Did she upset you?"

Rosie hesitated. Certainly Tomas had a right to know if someone had tried to drive a wedge between them. "I don't know if 'upset' is the right word. It was just more candid than I had expected."

Tomas looked around the empty garden. "Perhaps it is time I take you home."

"That's probably a good idea." The music now seemed too loud. The dancers laughed too much and a ripple of nausea rose in her belly from the rich food she'd consumed. "I'd rather walk by myself, though."

"Rosalie, please." He gently held her hand.

She instantly searched for Nonna in case she was lurking in the shadows, ready to disapprove. *How ridiculous. You're a grown woman, Rosie.*

"Let us do the walk and talk," he said.

"I'm tired—"

"This is why I should accompany you—to make sure you do not fall asleep in the bushes before you get home." His uneven smile eased the welling angst.

She had no idea why she'd let Nonna alter her mood. Nothing had actually changed between her and Tomas, so why did she feel so anxious now? Could Nonna be right? Was Tomas really a broken man? After all, he'd suffered through war, just like her brother Alex. Did he also have moments of terror or breakdowns that rendered him incapacitated? Should she actually listen to the woman who knew Tomas best and get out now, before her heart got more involved?

Rosie glanced at Tomas, who waited patiently for her reply. Perhaps a little more time with him might help her figure things out. "All right, we can walk and talk."

Tomas didn't contain his grin and motioned for them to take a shortcut down the side of the house so they could avoid the rest of the partygoers. They walked down the gravel road leading away from the bright lights and music, the moonlight struggling to shine through the clouds above. In the distance, thunder rumbled and lightning streaked across the sky.

She studied his kind face, and the butterflies inside her stomach went crazy. Once again she was mesmerized by his dark eyes and hair, his beautiful straight nose, strong chin...hell, she even loved that scar under his eye.

"Thoughts for pennies?" he asked.

"Huh? Oh!" She turned away, embarrassed. "Nothing."

"The look in your eyes tells me it is not nothing. Come with me."

He took her hand and they moved off the road to a grassy patch nearby. Both scouted for wayward wildlife of the poisonous variety and, discovering it was clear, Tomas took off his jacket and lay it on the ground for her. They sat and she liked his nearness.

"Please, tell me why the face of worry." Tomas studied her so intensely that trying to hold it in would be futile.

"Even though we're just *good friends*"—she used his language to emphasize the point—"your nonna insisted on telling me to...uh..." Why did it seem like a good idea half a second ago to blurt it all out? Now fear paralyzed her.

"To?" Tomas's expression didn't relay any emotion. If she could just read his thoughts...

"To...uh..." *Say it! Just say it!* "To not fall for you."

There. Done. So why didn't she feel any better? Probably because now she was totally exposed, vulnerable.

Tomas stared into the darkness, his fingers gripping his trousers.

"She is right." Tomas's words were mumbled but the message was clear. Rosie had not expected this. "Why?"

"There are many reasons."

"So tell me."

He turned to face her. "There is no point in having this conversation unless...unless you think we are more than the good friends."

"I honestly don't know what we are. All I know is I like your company. I want to get to know you better." The ease with which the words came surprised her. Never had she felt more relaxed in telling someone how she felt. What was this magic spell Tomas Conti had cast on her?

"Rosalie, you make me smile. You make my heart happy. But…" He took a deep breath.

"But?"

"But things, they are complicated."

"That's what your nonna said. Who cares if things aren't always straightforward? Life is messy. That shouldn't stop us from being with people who make us feel good."

"I make you feel good?" His genuine surprise only endeared him to her even more.

"Of course you do! You're easy to be with. I like that you're so different to other men I've courted…not that we're courting…but…" God, she was making such a mess of this. "I mean…"

Tomas reached out and ran his hand down the side of her face. His fingers left a trail of electricity and she tried to steady her breathing. He was so close yet so far away. She wanted to feel the sensation of his warm lips, his hands running through her hair, his hard body against hers, his breath on her skin…

Tomas moved near, his eyes not leaving hers. She leant in, her face tantalizingly close to his. Every inch of her being wanted him.

His warm lips met hers.

The world slowed and every worry she'd ever had disappeared into the stormy sky above.

Chapter 20

1943—Palermo, Sicily

Tomas sat on a rickety wooden chair next to his old school friend Donato Moretti. Tomas's every nerve felt on edge as he glanced around the hall, assailed by memories of the last political meeting he'd attended with his nonno—the metallic scent of blood, deafening sound of guns firing, people screaming, and the air thick with panic and hatred. These feelings and images he'd quashed for so long now threatened to overwhelm Tomas, but he held steadfast. This was not the same place. Not the same meeting. Not the same people. Yet the threat of being attacked was here, regardless.

"Are you all right?" Donato asked.

"Fine. I'm fine, thank you." Tomas had to close down these images before they overwhelmed him.

A low murmur between attendees grew while they waited. A beefy gent climbed up the steps and walked on to the stage. A hush fell across the room. Everyone's attention turned to the man in simple black trousers, light blue shirt. He shuffled papers, cleared his throat, then proceeded to methodically make eye contact with everyone in the room.

Donato whispered, "That's Vittorio Spina. He's one of the most important men in our district. If it's worth knowing, he knows it."

"He couldn't possibly know everything."

"Oh, he does, believe me."

"Shhhhh." A young woman turned around and scowled.

Spina addressed the crowd for over twenty minutes, everyone remaining motionless. No one coughed. No one sneezed. No one appeared to breathe.

Rather than the riffraff Abato had thrown together, this relatively large group of partisans in this small, poor neighborhood appeared better prepared.

"To sum up"—Spina raised his index finger above his head for emphasis—"the landing of the Allied forces here in Sicily is a godsend, but they need help. And what they need most is people on the ground—ears, eyes, contacts—who can give the Allied troops the information they need to make it as far north as possible. Of course, it's not all up to them." He puffed out his chest. "This is our country, our people. No one cares about our countrymen more than us."

"This is all well and good, but there is a problem." All eyes turned on Tomas and he wished he'd kept quiet. He wasn't even supposed to be at this meeting, let alone draw attention to himself.

Donato shot him a "for the love of God, keep your mouth shut" look, but it was too late. Tomas was already on his feet and any chance of anonymity had been shot to pieces.

"Who are you?" Spina demanded.

"I am Tomas Conti."

"I've not seen you here before." Spina gripped the sides of the podium.

"It is true, but I've been in the mountains with Bruno Abato—"

He held up his hand. "That's enough for me to know what kind of man you are."

"With all due respect, I don't think you do." A low murmur grew around him as people exchanged surreptitious looks.

"I am well aware of the type of man Abato associates with and I do not think anything you have to say will be new or will help our cause. We may be dissidents, but there are rules. There is decency. There is respect for other partisans."

It felt like a brick wall had just shot up, but it was too late to back down now. Tomas glanced at Donato, who sat on the edge of his chair, looking ready to flee should things get too heated. Tomas felt bad for his friend and hoped his standing up and voicing his opinion did not reflect upon Donato's relationship with these people.

Drawing himself up to full height, Tomas said, "It's true, Abato is a man of questionable behavior but he does get the job done. Anyone who has met him would not be surprised by my observation. What worries me, though, is that even though every partisan has the same goal, the groups are splintered. The networks are not as effective as they could be." Tomas paused, realizing speaking out about Abato meant it would likely get back to him. The floodgates were now open and it was too late for Tomas to slam them shut.

"What's your point?" Spina asked.

"My point is there needs to be some unity. There's power in organization. Look at the way Mussolini's men are working with the Germans. Yes, there are many groups of partisans willing to assist the Allied troops and free our country, but there's no consistency between the groups."

"And what do you propose to do about it?" Spina's grip on the podium relaxed slightly.

Donato looked up at Tomas, his expression one of concern mixed with admiration.

Tomas willed his brain to latch on to an immediate solution.

He got nothing.

"I will ask again: What are you going to do about it?" Spina locked eyes on Tomas. The gaze from audience members travelled from Tomas to Spina and back again, the tension in the hall palpable.

Spina inhaled deeply and angled a finger at Tomas. "You and me— we need to talk."

* * * *

Tomas sat in the courtyard of the family home, peeling an orange and breaking off sections and chewing them slowly. In this quiet space he found it easy to understand how his family could ignore the world outside these walls. In here, he could pretend the Allied and Axis Powers didn't exist. That Italians didn't fight against each other. And that his country wasn't in turmoil and being ripped apart by an array of political allegiances.

However, the moment he walked out the front door, reality hit—hard. Children still roamed the streets in rags, begging for food. Buildings remained in ruins with young families and the elderly doing what they could to find shelter amongst the debris. Neighbors turned on each other. Friends didn't trust one another. Mussolini continued to divide the people and even though Tomas wanted to grasp on to hope, it continued to be as elusive as the peace he craved.

The arrival of the Allies in Sicily was the only topic of conversation in Palermo, but everyone was wary about how they approached it. No one knew if the Allies could gain a strong foothold, and it was a matter of wait and see. In the meantime, partisan groups were preparing to offer their help with whatever the British and Americans needed.

Tomas looked at the blue sky, unable to fathom how quickly things changed these days. He finished the orange and strolled back into the kitchen. Rachel was hunched over the sink, her hands immersed in water as she washed the dishes and hummed a tune he didn't recognize.

"I can do those," he said quietly, trying not to spook her.

Her body jerked. "I'm fine. Honestly, I don't mind. It's the least I can do around here." She wiped her forehead with the back of her hand and left a trail of soapsuds above her brow.

Tomas smiled and moved toward her. He reached out and she took a step back.

"Tomas…"

"I'm just getting rid of the suds so it doesn't run into your eyes." His fingers brushed her forehead. Beneath his touch, her body trembled. "Rachel—"

"No." She shook her head.

"You don't know what I'm going to say." He moved away, conscious of not making her feel like a caged bird.

"You're a man, of course I know what you're going to say." She angrily grabbed a towel, dried her hands and threw it on the kitchen table. "You're all the same. You just want one thing."

This is what she really thought? What kind of traumas had she endured to believe that all men were animals?

"Rachel, I don't want anything from you."

"I'm sorry." She dropped her head forward and covered her face with her hands. Removing them again, she looked up, her eyes full of sadness. "You've gone above and beyond for me and you've never made an overture."

"Of course not."

Rachel sank onto the kitchen chair and Tomas sat down opposite her. She fell silent, the large bags under her eyes making her look years older than she was.

"You're safe with me, Rachel."

"I know." She ran her hand along the polished table, her fingers tracing the intricate and random patterns of the grain. "It's just…" she started, then drew her lips together in a tight line.

"It's just?"

"It doesn't matter," she mumbled.

"Everything matters. You matter. Please, talk to me."

Her fingers stopped tracing the lines. Tomas waited for her to continue, willing his patience to kick in—it paid off when she gave a slight nod of the head, as if giving herself permission to speak. "It's not easy, you know? As a kid, I lacked confidence. I always felt I was in the shadows. I was never noticed. I didn't exist."

"I knew you were there."

"But I was the annoying kid sister," she said matter-of-factly.

"You did your job well." Tomas tried to lighten the mood, but the stern look he received told him he'd been way off the mark. "Sorry."

"You don't need to be sorry. None of this is your fault. It's just life. Some people are in the limelight and others…aren't."

"Well, I, for one, think you have a lot to offer." From what he understood, Rachel's intelligence-gathering expeditions had been incredibly successful. "You know how to relate to people and they trust you. That's why they tell you things—important things that help our cause."

Her pale complexion took on a pink tinge. She looked away.

"You don't need to be embarrassed. It's a great thing you're doing. Your ability to get information is inspirational."

Rachel frowned. "That's because I'm a chameleon and I gain their trust by being the person they expect or want me to be. It's all a game, really. In reality, I'm no one of consequence."

"If you could see what I see—"

"Please, don't Tomas." She held up her hand.

"Why not? If you don't believe in yourself then you need to know others do." Tomas leant back against the chair and folded his arms. "If you have no confidence in your abilities why on earth would you go out in the field undertaking some of the most dangerous work possible? And doing it alone?"

Rachel stared at her clasped hands in her lap. "If I died then no one would miss me."

Incredulity swept through him. "I don't understand this at all."

"I don't expect you to." She turned her face away once more.

"Why do you place so little value on yourself?"

Rachel shrugged.

Tomas leant forwards. "Come to the meeting with me tonight."

"Why?"

"Because they need someone with your insight. I was only out in the field for a short time. I don't have the experience or knowledge like you have."

"I haven't been out there for nearly three weeks. Everything would have changed since the Allies arrived."

"But you were there for months on end before that. Perhaps giving some history might help them figure out how to move forward. No one who is based in Palermo has any decent idea as to what's going on outside the city. They have no clue what it's really like on the ground."

Rachel looked at him and, for a fleeting moment, he felt a flicker of…
something. He tried not to dwell on the word "attraction" but it was the
first—and only—word that came to mind.

There was no way he could entertain such a thought. Ever.

Chapter 21

Rosie stood under the banyan tree on the side of the road, reveling in a moment of peace. She never tired of witnessing the rolling storm clouds gathering, promising relief from the stifling heat. There was something special about rain-soaked soil, the tantalizingly aroma of fresh water nourishing the parched land. As she studied the moving cloud formations, Rosie's heart filled with love for this country.

Heavy footfalls caught her attention and a second later Tomas appeared.

"I am sorry I am late." Tomas's deep voice sent shivers up her spine. The twenty-four hours since they'd seen each other had felt like a week. He gently ran his hand down the side of her face then lightly touched her lips. She closed her eyes, wishing this would never end.

"Now, Rosalie Stanton," he said, jolting her out of her dream state, "do you feel like a walk and talk?"

"Sure."

They started down the road and, although she'd initially been shy seeing Tomas this evening, Rosie found herself relaxing in his presence, soaking in every aspect of this glorious man.

"Rosalie, where are your thoughts?"

Oh!

"Actually"—she scrambled for a topic—"my dad is making progress. I've been working on a design for cutlery for him and it's taken a bit of trial and error, but we've finally got there."

"This is very good news. It is hard to lose one's independence."

"I don't know if it's ever possible to fully adapt once there's a loss of independence. Although, maybe it's a matter of finding the silver lining."

"There isn't always one," said Tomas.

"Surely there's a thread, no matter how thin?"

Tomas clasped his hands behind his back, his brows furrowed. "There are too many instances of gray clouds and no silver linings."

She looked at the thunderclouds above. "You truly believe that?"

"Yes." Tomas concentrated on his boots making indentations on the gravel.

"I'm sorry you see it that way," she said.

Tomas stopped and faced her, "I do not say this to make you change your mind. It is just that"—he looked away—"we have different experiences in life."

"I know." She reached for his hand and was relieved when his fingers wrapped around hers.

"Rosalie, I like how you try to find the positive, even in situations that are very difficult."

She shrugged. "It's just who I am."

"Do not ever change this."

"And you shouldn't change you." *Ah, to hell with it.* Life was too short to mess around with matters of the heart. "I like you, Tomas. I like you a lot. I like how you make me laugh. I like the way your smile goes all the way to your eyes. I like that you care about your family. I like that scar under your eye. I like—"

Tomas touched his scar. "You like this?"

"Of course I do! It's part of you and as much as I would like to know how it happened, I won't ask. I'll let you decide when to tell me—if you choose to. I like that you're not perfect. None of us are. I just like you—very much—imperfections and all."

Tomas's wide eyes stared into hers. Panic set in as a pool of sweat developed in her lower back and her chest constricted. What the hell had she just done?

"I...I like you, too." He gently squeezed her hands. "I like you more than a lot."

His words held her in a warm embrace and she committed this moment to memory.

Tomas stepped toward her.

Rosie sucked in her breath.

Wrapping an arm around her lower back, he pulled her close, her body going willingly. When their lips met, the world spun slowly. Rosie tilted her head back, basking in his warmth, his strong body against hers.

Never in her life had she contemplated giving herself completely.

Never in her life had she felt more alive.

Time slowed, passion grew.

She could stay like this forever.

Tomas pulled out of their embrace, his dark eyes searching hers.

"What?" she whispered.

"This is not good."

"It's very good, Tomas." She reached up and ran her hand through his thick, dark waves.

"Yes, this is very good but…my nonna is right. You should not get involved with me."

"It's too late for that." She stepped forward but he moved to the side, the distance feeling a lot further than the inches separating them. She kept her voice low, trying not to be alarmed. "What could be so terrible that would warrant you *and* your grandmother telling me to stay away from you?"

"I can't protect you."

"I don't need protecting!" Her voice travelled down the valley.

The sigh that came from Tomas was long and sad. "I'm sorry. Of course, you can look after yourself. That's why…"

"Why?"

"Why nothing. My story is too long."

"Then tell me."

"No, it is better if you do not know."

"I'll be the judge of that." Her tone held an edge. She wasn't proud of it but the stakes had changed.

Tomas looked away, his face creased, as if he were dealing with a battle raging deep within. She waited—impatiently—and made a promise to herself that she wouldn't leave here without an explanation.

Eventually, he said, "If we are to talk then we will do so in a nicer place. Come." He held out his hand and she took it willingly.

They cut across the base of Il Sunnu and down a narrow path that led to the river that flowed past the Conti and Stanton properties. They climbed a steep embankment and travelled up another path that snaked through a cluster of eucalypts and, a moment later, Rosie found herself standing high on a hill, overlooking the valley she'd grown up in.

"Wow." The river below sparkled as the moonlight fought through the clouds, casting an eerie haze. Off in the distance she could make out her house set back from the road. It looked so peaceful and quiet, yet, inside, every member of that household was going through their own inner turmoil. Up here, though, she felt she could touch the moon and stars—everything was possible.

"This is the place where I do my thinking." He sat on a large rock and gestured for her to do the same.

She leant back on her hands and kicked her legs forward, crossing them at the ankles. "I can see why you like it so much."

He reached over and tucked a few strands of hair behind her ears.

"So..." she said.

"So...I said I would talk, I know. But my problem is that I do not know where to start. It is all so difficult."

"Maybe talking will make it less difficult."

He took a deep breath. "This...thing...is something that has haunted me every day for a long time. I do not wish you to think I am a bad person."

"It would take a lot for me to change my opinion of you." She smiled encouragement while she wondered what on earth could be so bad.

"There was death and it was my fault."

Chapter 22

Rosie concentrated on the valley and river beneath them. Only moments ago, she'd been immersed in the beauty and romance of being with Tomas. Now it felt like a suffocating shroud had landed on them.

"What happened?" she asked, her mouth dry.

"The situations were hard to control, they happened so fast." He shifted around to face her. "It was when I was in Italy."

"During the war? Because if that's the case then I can understand. My brother had to do things—horrid things—that haunt him every single day."

"Only part of it was because of the war."

She steadied herself. After all, Tomas had never given her a reason to question his ethics—not even after Nonna had that strange conversation with her. The way he'd said "there was death" could mean one. Or two. Or... Oh god, what had he done?

"I should not have said anything." He bowed his head, as if the weight was too much to bear. "My betrayal led to death. That is all you need to know."

Betrayal?

Thunder grumbled.

Raindrops fell on her skin.

Tomas shook his head. "I've said too much. It should be left in my head"—he rested his hand over his heart—"and here. It is my cross to bear and I should not burden you. For this, I am sorry."

Now she really wanted...*needed*...to know. "You can't say something as big as this then not tell me."

"Yet another mistake of mine. You do not need to make this your problem," he said gruffly.

"Did you think I wouldn't care? That something as big as this wouldn't have an effect on me? On us?"

Heavier raindrops.

A flash of lightning.

Rosie got up and stood on the path. Tomas did the same.

"I think it's best if I go," she said.

"I should not have been honest."

"I'm not sure what you've been honest about," she said. "You've thrown this mystery in front of me yet you won't follow through and tell me the truth. Is it because you've decided you can't trust me?"

He remained silent for so long she wondered if he was ever going to reply. Eventually, he looked up and said, "I wanted to tell you because you deserve to know the person I truly am but…I just can't."

"Can it really be that bad?" she asked, knowing it could be absolutely horrendous. She'd been around enough returned servicemen to see the torment in their souls and daily struggles. Hell, she saw it every time she was with Alex. Maybe she should give Tomas the benefit of the doubt. After all, he did *try* to tell her. It appeared that her brother and Tomas were grappling with similar demons. She reached out for Tomas's hand. "If you're not ready to tell me, I won't force you. And I do appreciate you trying. I am here anytime you want."

Tomas moved his hand away. He shook his head. "Rosalie, this is crazy. I'm afraid of you getting hurt and already, it may be too late for that. No good can ever come of this."

"Tomas…"

"I will walk you back to your house, but please, let us not talk about this again. I am stupid for ever thinking we could have this conversation."

Thunder clapped overhead.

The rain intensified. Clothes stuck to her skin.

Commonsense told her she was probably better off not knowing what events were haunting Tomas. Everyone had secrets, and it was the ones that bled into the conscience that destroyed the soul. Those were the secrets that wrecked families. Wrecked friendships. Wrecked blossoming relationships.

As she stood facing Tomas in the torrential downpour, Rosie felt the wall shoot up between them. And she had no idea if those bricks would ever come crashing down.

* * * *

Rosie glared at the offending tractor motor, determined it would not get the better of her. She'd barely slept all week and, despite the sane side of herself telling her to take it easy, she'd made a beeline for the shed as soon as she'd woken up, determined to fix this stupid engine once and for all. Gripping the spanner, she positioned it and held her tongue to the side, willing the nut to loosen from its rusty position. With care, she maneuvered it. All she had to do was one more twist and—

"Rosie!"

The spanner slid off and landed in the dirt. "Damn it!" She turned around to find Sefa standing in the doorway. "I'm sorry."

"It is all right." He stepped forward, and looked around the shed as if making sure the coast was clear. "I must discuss something with you."

"Is it about the workers? If it is, then you need to talk to Alex." She'd all but given up hope of ever getting her job back.

"This is the problem. He is impossible to talk to. We have asked about the money we are owed—"

"You haven't got it yet? I thought that had been sorted." What had her father been doing all this time?

"No and…" He drew a breath and took his time exhaling. "The men will leave if we are not paid very soon."

"You're getting some money, right?"

"Not enough." Sefa ran his dirty hands down the side of his trousers. "They are very unhappy. Some are already looking for work elsewhere. You could lose all of them, you could—"

"I told you I would bloody fix it!" Alex stormed into the shed, his face a furious red.

"Mr. Stanton—"

"Bugger off Sefa and stop annoying Rosie. She's not in charge anymore. I am!" He pointed to the entrance. Sefa hesitantly walked to the door then turned around to look at her. She mouthed "Leave it with me" and motioned for him to go. He did so, all the while looking over his shoulder at Alex, who paced the shed like a caged lion.

"Those bloody workers! What the hell are they good for? The lazy bastards. Wanting this and that. They should be grateful we take them on."

Alex's boots formed a trough in the dirt of the shed floor. She couldn't let this outburst pass as he'd had way too many recently.

"Alex, if it would lighten your workload, I could talk to Dad about the workers." Rosie kept her voice even and firm. If he sensed any hesitation she would likely bear his full wrath.

"No! This is my job now!"

"Then do it!" she yelled back, her virtuous intentions shot to smithereens. "For god's sake, Alex, you didn't even want this job!"

"Shut up! Shut up!" Alex dropped to his knees, his hands over his ears, his eyes squeezed tight.

Rosie rushed toward him.

"Shut up, shut up, shut up." He mumbled over and over again.

She put her hand on his. He yanked his away, his eyes wide with fear.

"What's wrong?" she asked, alarm running through her.

He shook his head and crawled backwards into the corner, and wedged himself between two stacks of long-handled tools. He buried his head in his hands, his body shaking from head to toe.

"Alex…" Rosie sat beside him, close enough to offer physical comfort but far enough to move if he lashed out.

Her brother's sobs echoed in the shed and she waited quietly, staring through the doors at the yellow and orange tinged sky. The men would return shortly and the last thing she, or Alex, would want is for them to witness him in this state. Yet it wouldn't be wise to ask him to move up to the house. Lord knows what her father would say if Alex wasn't being the man he was expected to be.

"I'm here," she said quietly.

He looked up, his dirty face streaked with tears, a deep fire burning in his eyes. "Where were you, Rosie? Huh? Where were you when we bombed the villages of innocent people? Where were you when our plane crashed and the Krauts were on our tail? Where were you when we had to go into that orphanage and sift through broken children to find ones we could save? Where were you? *Where were you?*"

Rosie scooted back, fear urging her to flee but love making her stay.

Her brother froze. "Oh god, Rosie, I'm sorry. I'm so sorry. I…" He fell forward. She reached for him and he collapsed against her.

"Shhh." Rosie stroked Alex's hair, her heart feeling his burden. She couldn't possibly know what he'd been through, but she could feel it in the way his body trembled, in his gasping breaths. She could see the sadness that had taken up residence within his soul.

Alex remained still for quite some time while Rosie fretted.

"I was in France," he mumbled.

"Pardon?" Just as Rosie leant in closer Alex sat up. He rubbed his eyes with the palms of his hands and sniffed.

"I lived in France after the war."

"Why didn't you tell us you were alive?" she asked.

Alex shifted on his buttocks, his eyes trained on the ground. "I needed a fresh start. I needed..." He closed his eyes briefly and mumbled, "I'm married."

"What? Where is your wife?"

"At home with the children."

"Children? Oh!" She couldn't contain herself. "How many?"

"Twins—boys." His lips kicked up at the corners. "They are almost two." He returned to staring into the corner of the shed.

"She left me." He paused. "Actually, she kicked me out."

"Why?" Rosie asked.

"For the same reasons you just witnessed." His shoulders slumped and he didn't look up. "I'm a mess, Rosie. This rage is like a freight train I can't stop. I thought returning to Tulpil...returning to something familiar... might help but, if anything, it's made it worse."

"How?"

"The images don't go away. The noise of the bombs. The bodies...it never leaves. Day and night it bombards me and it's making me insane. I thought Tulpil would be my sanctuary, you know, because it is so far removed from Europe, but I'm haunted no matter where I go."

Rosie's heart went out to her brother.

"What can I do to help?" She inclined her head so she could see Alex's eyes.

"I don't know." He sat back and let out a long breath.

In the distance, she could hear the workers returning.

"Come on." Rosie held out her hand.

Alex took it reluctantly and she helped him up.

"What are we doing?" he asked.

"Something we haven't done in years."

* * * *

The waters of Piri River shimmered as Rosie stood on the riverbank with Alex. He concentrated on the gentle flow while Rosie sat on the dirt and peeled off her boots and socks.

"You coming in?" She stood up and moved to the area she'd just checked to make sure it was safe to jump.

"No," Alex scowled. "I'm not in the mood."

"So you're chicken?" Rosie followed this with a grin and challenged him by raising her eyebrows.

"You're the chicken." Alex removed his boots and socks and took his time placing them neatly under the tree.

"Ready?" She got in the sprinting position. "One. Two. Three!"

Rosie made like she was about to jump but she let her brother take flight and splash into the river's cool waters. He disappeared for a moment, a cluster of bubbles making their way to the surface. She waited for Alex to bob up. It didn't happen. Rosie peered into the water, but it was too murky to make out anything. A few seconds went by.

"Alex?" She cupped her hands over her mouth. "Alex!"

Nothing.

"Alex!"

Not a single bubble.

Oh god.

"Alex!" Rosie raced upstream and jumped in. The waters sucked her down and spat her straight up again. Her hands and legs stretched out in the water, moving frantically as she tried to find her brother. A moment later a *whoosh* raced past her body and Alex appeared.

"Gotcha!" he yelled and let out a laugh that came all the way from his belly.

Annoyed but relieved, Rosie tread water and used the palm of her hands to splash him. A water fight broke out and they screamed and laughed and splashed like they didn't have a care in the world. After a while the craziness faded and they floated on their backs, staring up at the day fading into night.

"Do you love her?" she asked, her voice soft.

"More than anything in the world." There was no hesitation.

Rosie smiled, happy an old childhood pastime had given him some peace and joy.

"Will you go back?" Frogs croaked in the reeds while she waited for his reply.

He finally cleared his throat and said, "Not until I can put the pieces of me back together. She said she needs a whole man, not a broken one."

Memories of the conversation with Nonna flooded back.

She'd always thought war was a senseless act and now, having experienced the aftermath amongst family and friends, Rosie questioned the sanity of this world she lived in.

Swimming to the riverbank, she got out and sat on the edge. Alex did the same and he nudged her with his elbow. "Thank you."

"For?"

"For this." His hand swept over the scene before them. "I forgot how beautiful it was here."

"It's not bad, I s'pose." Rosie wiggled her toes and tried not to worry about the discomfort of sitting in soaking clothes. As much as she'd enjoyed this brief trip back to their childhood, they had to return to reality, no matter how difficult it was. "I need to ask you something and I don't want you to get mad."

"I'll try not to." Alex sounded like he meant it.

"Why didn't you contact us? We thought you were dead."

Her brother drew his knees up to his chin and stared at the river. "I was ashamed."

"What do you mean?"

Alex rested his head on his arms as he gently rocked back and forth. "I killed people, Rosie." When he looked up, his eyes were glassy. "I killed hundreds, maybe thousands of people. Innocent people. What kind of man does that make me?"

The uncomfortable conversation she'd had with Tomas a week ago muscled in on her.

Taking a moment before speaking, she finally said, "People do horrible things in war. Maybe you should talk to Dad, he was in the Great War and—"

"He was on a ship and hardly saw action. He wasn't in thick of it like me." Alex shook his head slowly. "What I did was murder."

"It was war." Her mind could not shake Tomas from this conversation.

Rosie wrapped her fingers around his and squeezed his cold hand. Minutes slid by.

She eventually let go. "We thought you were *dead*, Alex."

"I died on the inside," he mumbled.

"And Geoffrey died in real life." Frustration pushed out her words. "God, Alex, do you have any idea the torment you've put us through?"

He grabbed his boots and rose to his feet. She did the same.

"I'm done with this conversation," he said between gritted teeth. Once more, he appeared ready to fly into a fit of rage.

"Well, I'm not. Our hearts were broken—we mourned—while you've been in France leading another life. And now you've left that as well. What's to become of you? Do you think all those people died in the war so you could roam the globe being miserable and leaving a trail of broken hearts?"

"You'll never understand." He towered above, but she refused to let him intimidate her.

"You're right, Alex. I can't even begin to imagine what you've gone through and I am so very sorry that you have suffered…do suffer…the way you do. It's hard to watch you go through this, though you have a chance to make things right." She paused and puffed out her cheeks. "I can't believe I'm saying this, but Dad may actually have been right when he said good honest work is the best way to heal."

"I don't know, Rosie…"

"What else have you got in your life right now? Do you want a chance to be with your wife and children again?"

Alex concentrated on the boots in his hand. "Of course I do."

"Then bloody well fight for them, because you're the only one who can change things for the better."

Chapter 23

Rosie stood on the verandah and studied her father, who sat in the white wicker chair as he took in the expanse of Tulpil. Color had returned to his cheeks and an air of serenity had settled around him. It had initially taken some convincing to get him outside, but once he breathed in the fresh air and lay his eyes on the land to which his heart belonged, the deep creases in his face seemed to smooth out a just a little.

Rosie sat on the chair beside him. "I think we need to get you out here more often."

When he smiled, it was crooked, the right side of his face permanently showing the hell his body had been through. "Thank you for being so stubborn and forcing me to get out here." His eyes travelled the vista before them. Sugarcane swayed in the light breeze, the blue haze of the mountains in the distance, the bougainvillea in full bloom. "I've missed her."

"She's missed you."

"It shouldn't have taken me so long to get out here, but I just couldn't do it. I wasn't ready. I thought…" He closed his eyes briefly. "I thought it would break my heart not to be out there amongst it all."

Rosie placed her hands on her father's, surprised with his candor. "How do you feel now?"

"I feel like I've been reunited with an old friend." He turned to her. "How do you do it?"

"Do what?"

"How do you anticipate what someone needs? Even when they don't know it themselves?"

Rosie shrugged. "Intuition?"

Her father gave her hand a quick pat then rested it on his knee. "That was a smart move, Rosie."

"What was?"

"Taking your brother to the river. He told me what happened. You helped him connect with his roots. His memories from childhood. You gave him the courage to tell us what we needed to know."

Someone must have put something in the tank water because all of a sudden the men in her family were *talking*. Miracles did happen.

"So you're not angry with him for keeping us in the dark all this time? Has he told Mum yet?"

"She hasn't a clue and I think we should wait for the right time to tell her. Alex agrees. As for being angry"—he scratched behind his ear—"what's the point? He's explained his reasons and, believe it or not, I understand. I don't agree with what he did, but it's his life."

Rosie listened to her father and as she did so, a kernel of annoyance grew within. Alex could disappear for years and come home like the prodigal son, yet when she wanted something... Gah! She'd been over this a million times already.

"As soon as he feels better," her father said, "then he'll send for his wife and children."

"They'll come here?" That aspect hadn't entered her mind. *Oooh. Nephews!*

"That's his hope."

"Well, it would be nice to see it happen. Tulpil is the perfect place for kids to grow up."

"It is, it is." Her father couldn't take his eyes off the view before him.

Uneasiness grew within. The subject had to be broached. "Dad?"

"Yes?"

"I hear the workers haven't received their money." There it was. Out there now, waiting for a response.

Her father raised his eyes to the ceiling. His gaze dropped and he looked directly at her. "We don't have it."

"What are we going to do?"

"We have to sell off some land." Although his voice remained steady the pain in his eyes was apparent.

A lump formed in her throat. "We've already lost some land to the Contis. Surely there's a way around it?"

"No, there isn't."

"How much do we have to sell?" she asked.

"Enough to reduce Tulpil from the largest cane farm in the district to one of the smallest."

"No." She gripped the edges of her shirt. "We can't owe that much."

"It's not just the workers, Rosie. We still owe money to suppliers. And"—he rubbed his brow—"the bank."

"The bank?" Her voice came out an octave higher. Why had her father withheld this information for so long? To protect her supposed delicate sensibilities? "How could all this have gone unnoticed?"

"I have no idea," her father said. "A desperate man will find a way."

"How much money did Bartel take?"

"Enough to potentially destroy us."

* * * *

Rosie drove the dusty roads back from town after her meeting with Sergeant Gavin. He'd tried his best to be accommodating while she went through a laundry list of why the police should have found Bartel by now. He'd nodded and "hmmm'd" where appropriate, but Rosie hadn't felt like she'd made any headway. She made a mental note to follow up with the owners of other farms to whom she'd written to in case Bartel crossed their paths. William had reached out to his network of workers around the state, so there was still hope Bartel would be caught. Rosie clung to that belief like it was a life raft in a vast, stormy ocean.

Her fingers grasped the steering wheel so hard they turned white, but the color came back when she loosened her grip as thoughts of Kitty and Isabelle floated in. Rosie had called in on Kitty after going to the police station, and although the visit had been short and sweet, it had been enough time for her friend to bathe in peace and for Rosie to squeeze in some quality godmother time. The little cherub had grown considerably in such a short period and it reminded Rosie that time stood still for no one—that there's only one chance to make the most of this life and wallowing in pity did nothing but create barriers in making dreams reality.

She rounded the bend and slowed the car down as Il Sunnu came into view. A figure moved near the entrance of Tomas's place and Rosie squinted to try and get a better look. She should have put the pedal to metal when she realized it was Nonna but it was too late—Tomas's grandmother had spotted Rosie and was signaling for her to come over.

"Damn it," Rosie muttered as she pulled over, turned off the engine, and got out of the ute. She put on her best smile as she went to Nonna, who held a bunch of weeds in her gloved hand. "Good afternoon, Signora Conti."

The old lady waved her spare hand. "Please, call me Nonna."

"But—"

"Everyone calls me Nonna. It makes my family very big. We do not need to be related to be family, no?"

"I guess not." Rosie couldn't see why Nonna would even consider her as a remote family member given the last conversation they'd had.

"You look very pale. You need more sun." She reached over and pinched Rosie's arm. "You need to eat. Come." Nonna started toward the house and panic shot through Rosie. What if Tomas was there?

"Thank you for the invitation but…" Why did her voice sound so shaky? "I really need to get back home."

"It is obvious you do not eat there. Come with me, I fix you something special."

Rosie followed Nonna, well aware she would not win this argument. This is what Rosie got for slowing down and gawking at Tomas's house rather than heading home and getting on with life.

Rosie fell into step with Nonna, who traipsed up the driveway, stopping every so often to check the leaves of a plant or flower. The closer they got to the house, the harder Rosie's heart beat against her chest.

Nonna climbed the steps and entered the house and Rosie did the same, casting furtive glances around in case Tomas materialized.

"You are looking for Tomas?" Nonna asked in an innocent tone.

"No, I'm not looking for Tomas," she said, trying to sound cool, calm and collected.

Nonna's friendly laugh accompanied them down the hallway. "He makes you nervous?"

"No." This time Rosie sounded more confident. She should be struck down by lightning for lying to a grandmother.

"You did not listen to me." They entered the kitchen and Nonna gestured for Rosie to take a seat at the table.

"About?" Now it was Rosie's turn to act innocent.

Nonna's sigh was long and loud. She set about opening cupboards and the icebox and arranging various ingredients on a platter. Nonna set it down in front of Rosie and gestured for her to start eating. Her stomach grumbled. After leaving home so early this morning she'd forgotten to eat.

Rosie placed sliced cheese on a piece of bread then added a couple of olives. She put the bread down.

"You do not like?" Nonna sat opposite.

"I do, I just…" Rosie concentrated on the plate of olives. "Did you know about this?"

"What?"

"About him…you know…the betrayal that led to death."

Nonna's shoulders dropped and she rested an intense gaze on Rosie. "He told you about this?"

"Yes."

Nonna took a tall silver pot from the stove and poured black coffee into two small cups. She passed one to Rosie, who took it tentatively, never having tasted coffee before. Her family were staunch tea supporters and thrived on their ritual of tea preparation. Nonna appeared to have her own method when it came to coffee. She passed a sugar bowl with a tiny spoon. Rosie put in one. "You will need more," Nonna said.

"But I don't have sugar in my tea."

Nonna laughed. "One sugar is not enough."

Rosie did as she was told and kept adding until Nonna held up her hand. Rosie lifted the cup, inhaled the rich aroma of the dark liquid and took a tentative sip.

She nearly choked on the bitterness.

"The taste is acquired." Nonna reached over and patted Rosie's hand. "But I like that you try."

"Thanks." Rosie put the cup down and wondered whether Nonna had forgotten they'd left a conversation unfinished. Rosie had already been gone from Tulpil for too long and she needed to check on her father to make sure he'd taken his tablets. "Is this why you asked me in? To talk about Tomas?"

At least Nonna had the sense to appear surprised by the question. "Oh no. You looked hungry."

"I was in the ute on the way to my house."

"You were so slow I thought you might not arrive at your house before Christmas. I thought maybe you didn't have the energy to drive."

Touché, Nonna.

Nonna tapped her index finger on the table. "I told you to stay away from my grandson because you are a nice person, Rosie Stanton. My Tomas is a nice person also, but, he has done…things…that make him difficult to be in love with."

"Surely you can't expect him to never fall in love or marry?" She couldn't imagine Tomas becoming a priest and taking a vow of chastity.

"I am afraid love could break him."

Rosie got up and placed the coffee cups in the sink. "Love can heal."

"It does not heal everything."

"Besides," Rosie said, "it's not possible for people to break." No sooner had the words tumbled from her mouth than her vision blurred and Alex

---

182   *Alli Sinclair*

came to mind. She willed herself to remain calm, but the second Nonna reached for her hand, Rosie dissolved into a sobbing mess.

Nonna pulled her close. It had been years since her own grandmother had passed and, until now, Rosie hadn't realized how much she missed the loving and secure hugs of a grandparent. Despite efforts to hold back the tears, they came out thick and fast. Nonna stroked Rosie's hair and spoke quietly in Sicilian. Rosie instantly relaxed and the tears slowly dried up.

Nonna placed her hands on Rosie's shoulders and gently moved her away so she could look up at her. "This is not all about my grandson?"

Rosie shook her head and sniffled.

"Please, come with me." Nonna guided Rosie to a small dark room at the front of the house. She gestured for Rosie to sit on a large, red brocaded reading chair while Nonna closed the shuttered door and sat on the lounge. "I think you are in need of talking, yes?"

Rosie nodded, still not trusting herself to speak.

"I get us water." Nonna disappeared and Rosie used the time to catch her breath. No matter what Tomas had or hadn't done, his grandmother still loved him and, bless Nonna, her heart was big enough to look out for the girl next door who had fallen for her grandson. Nonna returned with a jug of iced water with a few slices of lime. She set about pouring and handed a glass to Rosie. "When you are ready, we do the talking."

The cool, clear liquid soothed Rosie's throat and the zesty lime flavor had a lovely calming effect. Setting the glass down on the tray in front of her, Rosie took a deep breath and said, "My brother has been so very mixed up and even though he's shown signs of improvement, I worry he won't have the strength to fight his demons."

Nonna nodded slowly but didn't speak for a while, as if allowing the words to sink in. "Sometimes, the demons will win."

"I know." Rosie sniffled again.

Nonna shifted on the chair and leant forward. "I tell you this: love does not conquer all. Whether love for the family or a man who captures your heart. Love can help, yes, but the answer can only be in the heart of the person who is suffering."

"I worry for my brother, my father. Even my mother."

"Your family has much hurt?"

Rosie nodded, slightly embarrassed by the state of her family. "Although there are so many people hurting in this world."

Nonna made a steeple with her fingers and slowly tapped them against her chin. "Sometimes it is very hard to find the good."

"It's there, I know it is, but it can get buried. Although, at times, I just feel so…helpless. It's like every time there's a step forward, there's two back." Rosie shook her head. "It's like what happened after the war when the men came back and women were thrown out of the jobs they'd come to love and be really good at. I understand why things had to change—so the men could adjust to their lives postwar and have a sense of purpose—but what about the women? We've experienced independence, new skills. How are we supposed to go back to the ways of old? And then there's…" She let the sentence fall away, not sure she should go down that road.

"There is?"

Nonna's kind expression encouraged Rosie to take the leap. "Then there is the whole issue of men who think they can treat women like objects, like we don't matter. Where's the fairness in it all? What would they do if women banded together and said 'no more'? What would happen, do you think? I would love nothing more than to find a way to help women find their voices."

Sparks shone in Nonna's dark eyes.

"You and I, we are of kindred spirits. And, there are many ways we can change the world, sometimes it is in a way you do not expect." Nonna looked at the doorway. Quietly, she said, "When I was in Sicily, I worked very hard to help other women." She sat back and closed her eyes, perhaps recalling memories she'd hidden for years. "Back when I lived in my home country, Mussolini and his men saw women as servants of the state—they think we live only to give birth, cook, clean, keep men happy and healthy—but"—she dipped her chin and looked up at Rosie—"you and I know we are so much more than this."

"We absolutely are."

"So for this, some of the women in my neighborhood would get together and help the *partigiani*—the partisans. We provided food and shelter. Sometimes, we passed on secret messages through the vendors in the markets and other times we would do it through the baker or the seamstress."

"There was a whole network?"

"Of course!" Nonna squared her shoulders. "We women are very smart, we know how to read people by watching and listening, seeing the small things that tell us more than words. The women of my country, they deserve so much better and it was my duty to do what I could to change this but it was all done in secret. No one ever knew."

"But you told your family, right?"

Nonna shook her head slowly. "My son would never approve, and Tomas, he had enough of his own problems."

Rosie didn't reply, unsure what to say. Why would Nonna trust her with this information?

Nonna filled Rosie's glass with water again. "This desire for women to find their strength and their voice is very good. I also believe it is possible to make change if we work together. Please, I would like to help."

"You would?"

"Do not sound so surprised, *bella*. I may be old, but my mind is sharp and my heart is full."

"I'm sorry, I didn't mean it like that it's just…"

"Just?"

"No one's seen you outside of Il Sunnu."

I have not had a good reason to leave, though now"—she smiled—"I have a very good reason. We women, we must work together. We may not be *partigiani*, but we can make much difference. Rosalie, the fire in your belly will serve you well."

Chapter 24

Tomas shifted on the hard wooden chair in a small room off the main hall, his nerves on edge as Spina leant on the table, drumming his fingers. Donato sat across from Tomas, who was unusually quiet. Rachel studied her clasped hands in her lap, her breathing shallow.

It had been a risk getting Rachel involved, but after a long discussion with Spina, Tomas didn't see he had any other choice. Besides, Rachel wasn't one to sit and watch the world go by. Once she'd put her mind to something, the task would be done. When she'd prepared her speech at the house, she'd sounded confident and Tomas had been impressed by her strength, yet when they walked through the doors of the hall, she'd turned into a quivering wreck, falling over her words, trembling like a deer.

After Rachel had finished her speech, Spina said, "I'm not so sure this idea is a good one."

"Why not?" Rachel's voice was barely above a whisper.

"Things have changed since the Allies arrived in Sicily." Spina leant against his chair and rested his arms behind his head. "They're losing ground as much as they are gaining it."

"Yes, I know. But my contacts...my contacts can..." Rachel's voice sounded an octave higher than usual. She glanced at Tomas. He gave her a nod.

"Look." Spina smacked his hands on the table. "I don't have all day so unless you can convince me this will serve a purpose, this meeting is over." Spina pushed his chair back, as if readying himself to make a hasty exit.

"But..." stumbled Rachel.

Tomas reached for her trembling hands and squeezed them gently.

She took a deep breath. "But my insider contacts at the Italian army's munitions stores, as well as relationships with informants such as teachers and priests, are invaluable. Especially in the regions where the Allies are struggling to gain hold. Those ears are on the ground and they will tell me everything I need to know. Everything *you* need to know."

"The Allies have their own men—ones who have spent *years* honing skills. Your contacts are good, but I am not so sure they hold much weight. Everything has changed."

"They don't know the mountains like we do." She crossed her arms and tilted her head to the side.

"They're not going to listen to us," Spina countered.

"Isn't it worth a try? We all want the same thing." Rachel's speech had now morphed from hesitant to self-assured.

"Let me think about it and I'll get back to you." Spina looked from Rachel to Tomas. "And you and I have to discuss your new role. Meet me here tomorrow. Same time." He raised his eyebrows and that gesture alone made Tomas nervous. Spina's new plans meant Tomas would have to sever ties with his own world, even though he'd just returned home and smoothed things over with his family.

Spina stood, and Donato, Rachel and Tomas followed suit. They said their farewells, and Tomas and Rachel left the building, stepped onto the dimly lit street and took off toward Tomas's house.

He didn't need to look over at Rachel to know she was beaming from ear to ear.

"You did well," he said.

"I couldn't have done it without you."

A cold gust of wind blew past, flaring out Rachel's skirt. Tomas tried not to look at her legs, but it was very hard not to notice the perfect curve of her calves.

"Tomas?" she asked.

"Pardon?" He chastised himself for getting so distracted.

"I asked what Spina meant about a new role for you."

A layer of dread formed around him. "It doesn't matter."

"Obviously it does if someone like Spina is having a one-on-one." She looked at him, her eyes wide. "What's he making you do?"

"He's not making me do anything," he said. Why did she have to ask so many questions? "It's right for the cause and that's what I have to remember."

"What is?" she asked.

"Let's just leave this alone. I can't tell you. I can't tell anyone."

"Fine," she mumbled. "I'm not happy about you not telling me but I understand the need for secrecy. I don't have to like it, though," she said. "Just as well you're still in my good books."

"I am?" He smiled, happier than he probably should be.

"You've been nothing but caring, even when I'm being difficult. You take it all in your stride. Not many men will do that."

A cold breeze stirred and Rachel shivered. Tomas took off his jacket and placed it on her shoulders. Her hand gripped his. A shot of electricity zapped up his spine.

"Rachel…"

She stopped, looked up, her face hidden by the shadows. "Don't spoil this."

"With all that's happened to you, I just don't think—"

"Don't think. Feel." She wrapped her arms around his waist and pulled herself close. Her hair smelt of fresh apples and her soft, warm body sent his senses into overdrive.

"I want to, I do, but it's not a good idea."

She stepped back and glared at him. "Why not?"

Where did he start? "First of all, your brother—"

"He's got nothing to do with it."

"I doubt he would see it that way. Then there's the…uh…your—"

"He's not a threat anymore. I should have known better than to keep going back to him." Rachel moved closer. "Tomas…"

God, he wanted her, but he couldn't. She needed time to heal. And getting involved with Rachel would only cause angst with Abato and no one needed that. Besides, with Tomas's possible new position and the Allied troops making ground, no one knew what the next day would bring. The next week. The next month.

"I…can't," he finally said. It nearly killed him.

"See? This is what I mean. I'm of no consequence."

Memories of their conversation in Nonna's kitchen crowded in on him. *I lacked confidence. I always felt I was in the shadows. I was never noticed. I didn't exist.*

"You're just like everyone else!" She yanked his jacket off her shoulders and threw it at him.

Rachel took off across the piazza and ran down the main road. For someone so small, she set a cracking pace and it took all his effort to keep her in sight. His legs ached and chest burned as he rounded a corner and ground to a halt. She sat in the gutter, rubbing her head. Raised voices and music came from the bar a few doors down.

Rushing over, Tomas knelt and helped her stand. "What happened?"

"I...I...tripped." Her breathing steadied and the shaking stopped. She let out a long, hearty laugh. "I think I may have knocked some sense into myself." This time when she looked at him, the fear and anger had left her eyes. A newfound strength had surfaced instead. "You are right."

"I am?" Now it was his turn to doubt himself. "About?"

"About so many things. But you are wrong about one." She leant toward him, her lips so deliciously close.

He could have her.

Now.

But...

"You dirty whore! This is who you've been fucking?" The shadows hid the face of a mountain of a man who lunged at Rachel. Tomas instinctively blocked the blow. His arm smarting from the brute's punch, though better for Tomas cop the pain than Rachel, who now stood by, screaming for help. Not one light in the neighboring houses switched on.

A beefy arm wrapped around Tomas's neck as Rachel yelled, "Get off him, Paolo! Leave him be!"

Punches hit Tomas's torso, his kidneys taking the brunt. Pain came with every blow, but Tomas would not give in. He couldn't. He knew these types. If he gave even the slightest hint of weakness, he'd be done for.

A painful blow in the gut sent Tomas over the edge. He gasped for air then grabbed the swine in a headlock while trying to avoid Paolo's fists, which flew in all directions. In a split second, Tomas lost his grip and Paolo ducked and freed himself. They stood eye to eye, chests heaving, fury raging.

With lightning speed, Paolo reached behind and pulled out a knife that glinted in the low streetlight. He brandished it menacingly as he and Tomas circled each other. In the background, Rachel pleaded with them to stop.

"How do you like her, huh? The dirty little whore will do anything," Paolo snarled.

Tomas glanced at Rachel, willing her to run. Out of the corner of his eye, he saw her bend over and pick up a broken bottle.

"You're coming with me, *puttana*." Paolo sneered at Rachel, who clutched the broken bottle behind her skirt.

"I am nobody's." Her voice sounded alarmingly calm.

Paolo spun and lunged for Rachel, but she moved to the side. He crashed toward the pavement and as he did so, he grabbed her skirt and pulled her down. The broken bottle rolled into the gutter. Tomas ran toward Rachel, intent on pulling her from Paolo's grasp, but the thug already had her pinned to the ground, knife against her neck, a thin line of blood on her pale skin.

"Let her go," growled Tomas.

"You've got to be fucking joking." Paolo grabbed her hair, yanking her up. Tomas moved forward, his fists clenched.

"Leave it, Tomas," she said, her eyes wide.

"No." He stood his ground, his body tense, ready to lunge at any moment.

"Please," she gasped.

"You're coming with me." Paolo yanked Rachel's hair again and tried to drag her away.

Rage roared through Tomas as he lunged and knocked the knife out of Paolo's hand. Tomas pushed him to the ground, but Paolo still had a firm grip on Rachel. Her arms and legs flailed in all directions. She fell headfirst, a sickening thud as her skull crashed into the steps of a neighboring house.

Tomas and Paolo wrestled on the hard pavement, both reaching for the knife, though Paolo was a fraction faster.

At first, the pain didn't register. All Tomas remembered was the flash of light then the cold, hard steel plunging into his skin, just missing his eye. Then hot pokers burning his flesh. He grabbed his face in agony, blood oozing between his fingers.

Paolo scrambled to his feet. He glanced at Rachel, who lay unconscious and a moment later, Paolo took off, disappearing into the darkness.

Tomas crawled over to where Rachel lay, unmoving. He lifted her limp body and held her close, searing pain rushing along his cheek. "Rachel, please. Wake up."

She remained motionless.

"Rachel…" A thick, hot liquid spread across his hand. "Oh god."

Tomas gently rolled her over to inspect the source of the blood. His chest hollowed. A steady trail of red viscous fluid ran from her ear and down her neck. When he checked her breathing, there was nothing.

"Jesus, no." Tomas laid her flat on the ground, checked for a pulse, but couldn't feel anything. Hot, salty tears stung the gash beneath his eye, though it was nothing compared to the pain in his heart.

Chapter 25

Rosie helped her father toward the back of the house, her hand under his elbow while his pale wrinkled hand clutched the walking stick. Since taking him outside a couple of days ago, he'd been keen to get out daily to spend time on the verandah so he could view his beloved Tulpil. She prayed he wasn't worrying that this view may not be his for much longer.

With help, her father eased into the large chair in the corner where he could enjoy the last rays of the day. In the distance, the voices of the men working the fields drifted toward the house, an array of languages and heavily accented English. The chatter of the workers always soothed Rosie, reminding her that family didn't need to be blood related. In her eyes, Sefa and his men were family, as well as Kitty. She imagined the Contis could become part of that close circle, but a few obstacles needed to be conquered before that could ever happen.

Damn. She missed Tomas like crazy and it irritated her that she couldn't shake him from her mind.

"Ow!" Her mother's cry echoed down the hallway. Rosie rushed to the kitchen and found her mother trying to wrap a tea towel around her hand.

"What happened?"

"I cut my finger. I'll be fine." A steady flow of blood spread across the white fabric.

"Sit down." Rosie guided her to a chair then pressed the tea towel against the wound and raised her mother's hand above her head. She glanced over to where a pile of sliced potatoes lay splattered in blood. "Here, let me take a look."

She gently peeled the tea towel away, all the while watching her mother out of the corner of her eye. Her face had gone pale, and the rims around her eyes were red, as if she'd been crying. Yet again, a blanket of alcohol hung around her mother.

Rosie took a look at the cut but it didn't need stitches. She dashed to the pantry and retrieved the kit with bandages and antiseptic and set to work on her mother's finger while Cecile observed quietly.

"There," Rosie said, happy with her handiwork. "Try not to get it wet for twenty-four hours or so. I'll do the dishes tonight."

"You're very good to me," her mother said quietly.

Rosie occupied herself with tidying up the medical kit. "It's all right, Mum."

"No, it isn't. Lord knows I'm not much of a help these days." Guilt clouded her petite features. "I'm sorry."

"For?"

"I'm sorry you have so much going on. With your dad, with Alex, with…" She gulped. "With me. I know I'm not the best mother in the world."

"I'm a grown woman, I can look after myself."

"I know you can, darling, but a girl should always be able to turn to her mother when she needs support." Cecile's smile looked so sad. "I miss my mum every day."

This topic always left Rosie sad because it reminded her that one day she may not have Cecile in her life. Her health was getting worse and it concerned Rosie immensely.

"What's wrong?" her mother asked.

"What?"

"You look worried."

"Actually, I am concerned about you," said Rosie.

"Why?"

Rosie groaned inwardly. How could her mum not get it?

"Mum, I think you should talk to someone."

"Who, darling?" Her bright response broke Rosie's heart. Her mother constantly flitted in and out of the real world, not fully registering conversations or happenings.

Taking a deep breath, Rosie said, "I think you should talk to a doctor… or with the minister of your church."

"I talk with Minister Robertson every Sunday!" Her mother's laughter sounded hollow, as if all the happiness had permanently fled. "It would do you well to go back to church."

Rosie ignored the barbed comment. "I mean really talk to him about…" This was harder than she'd imagined. "About your…problem."

"What problem?"

"Alcohol."

"I do not have any problem and I do not appreciate the insinuation that I do." Her mother arched a brow, then rose and went over to the bench to scrape the blood-spattered potatoes into the compost bowl.

"Mum…"

"Gosh darn it, Rosie! Stop sticking your nose into everybody's business! Why don't you work on your own problems instead of inventing bigger ones for others?"

A tidal wave of hurt washed over her and she stared at the woman who had changed so much in recent years. What had happened to the fun-loving mother who sang all the time and danced with her husband in the kitchen?

War.

Bloody war.

The bloody war that stole Geoffrey and took Alex away for so many years, only to return him as a shell of his former self.

And in the process it had changed her mother into a skittish, fragile human who couldn't see the real world thanks to a self-induced haze. When Geoffrey had first died, she'd sat in a dark room for hours then come out all sunshine and smiles, only to retreat to the darkness once more. Rosie and her dad had tried to ignore the alcohol fumes following Cecile wherever she went, hoping it was her way of coping in the short term. How wrong they'd been…

"Mum, I—"

A loud knock at the front door drew her attention. Perhaps it was best she left this conversation where it was for now. The hurt surging through Rosie would only cause more grief if she further expressed her thoughts.

Moving quickly along the hallway, she saw a familiar silhouette through the screen door.

"Hello," she said, her tone even. Rosie reached the door but didn't open it.

"Please, can we talk?" His thick accent melted her heart despite her wish to remain cautious.

"I'm busy."

"Please." Through the fly wire screen she could see his beautiful eyes and any resolve to remain aloof melted away.

"We can talk for one minute," she said firmly as she exited the house and led him to the far end of the verandah so they'd remain well out of earshot. Rosie crossed her arms, aware this caused a barrier between them.

"I owe you an explanation."

"You don't owe me anything." She should take the edge from her tone but found it impossible.

"I can see you are still mad."

"I'm not mad, I'm just...I don't know what I am." Her arms fell to her sides. "I'm annoyed at myself for getting upset when you wouldn't share more details. I should have understood that sometimes we change our mind about saying something because we lose courage." How many times had she done that recently? "I wanted to know what happened even though it's none of my business."

Her mother's harsh words echoed in her ears. Maybe Rosie did spend too much time getting involved in other people's problems.

A slight breeze shook the branches of the eucalypts. The heady scent, mixed with Tomas's cologne, danced through the air.

"Rosalie, I came here to explain because I like you very much and wish for us to continue as friends."

There was that word again. *Friends.*

"But," he said, "I must find the strength to tell you what is very difficult to say."

"Go on." She gave a nod, still scared about what the truth may hold.

Tomas inhaled deeply as he rested his hands on the rails and looked at Il Sunnu in the distance. "It all happened so fast."

His grip tightened on the railing and his body stiffened, as if memories he'd rather forget swamped him. She moved to squeeze his hand, but stopped.

Tomas stared at the fields, uncertainty in his eyes. The late afternoon sun beat down on her skin, and although she was accustomed to this climate, it felt like her body was cooking.

"Let's go sit in the shade, it's more private," she said quietly and motioned for them to head over to a corner of the garden that was protected from the sun and prying eyes. Tomas followed. She sat on the wooden bench while he paced the lawn, hands clasped behind his back, eyes concentrating on his moving feet.

He eventually stopped and stood still. "I will tell you all and when I am done, I pray you can forgive me."

Tomas started pacing once more and Rosie leant forward. As the words tumbled from his mouth, the light breeze turned cool and sent a shiver down her spine. Gray clouds swirled above. Tomas strode, threw his arms out as the story unfolded about Rachel. His gestures emphasized the trauma he had suffered—continued to suffer.

Rosie remained seated, trying to take in everything that had been laid before her. The way he agonized over something that didn't appear to be his fault broke her heart. Her emotions ran wild—shock, sadness, love... Love? How could love fall into this turmoil? Glancing at Tomas with his head down, his back hunched, and his face expressing the pain within, she knew that love was a feeling that sat so incredibly right.

"Tomas." She rose and stood by his side. "Tomas?"

He stared at her blankly, as if he hadn't registered her presence. She gently rubbed his back and beneath her hand his body trembled, all the hurt and grief and self-blame about to explode.

Tomas held his hands over his face and whispered in Sicilian.

"What did you say?" she asked quietly.

He looked up, the frown lines deep on his face. "Why are you so nice, Rosalie Stanton?"

"I'm not always nice."

"I believe this is a lie." This wasn't followed by the usual smile that conveyed he was joking.

Rosie removed her hand from his back. "You don't think I'm sincere?"

Tomas stared at her for so long she wondered if he'd lost the power of speech. Rosie moved away, not liking this strange turn he'd taken. It actually scared her.

"I am sorry," he finally said, his voice genuine. "I should not take my anger out on you. I admire your ability to accept people for who they are, but I am afraid that this will ruin our friendship."

"Tomas!" She threw her hands wide with exasperation. "Do you really think this is just a friendship?"

The last of the evening sun caught the gold flecks in his brown eyes and bathed him in a magnificent golden glow.

"I know exactly what this is." Tomas moved closer and gently caressed her face.

Her breathing grew shallow.

"My *bella*," he whispered before he placed his lips on hers. The world slowed, tilted on its axis, and sent her off-balance.

And she didn't mind at all.

Chapter 26

Rosie stood on the steps of the Rural Community Bank, waiting for the doors to open. The walk into town had done her good. It had given her a chance to stretch her legs and get her thoughts in line.

Rosie smoothed down her floral dress and glanced up and down the street. Mrs. Marriott and Mrs. Daw stood out the front of Lofty's Grocers yabbering about who knows what. Every so often they glanced at Rosie. Rather than torment herself with speculating what the topic of conversation was, she let her mind drift back to the events of the night before.

Tomas had bared his soul and she'd glimpsed a side of him she'd never expected. His pain was deep, his torment strong, and his honesty refreshing. Finally admitting her feelings for him had been a risk, but it was one she didn't regret. Although now, in the cold light of day, she wondered how their relationship would fare with so much going on around them. Perhaps today she could relieve one burden from her family.

The bolt on the other side of the door jiggled and a moment later Sheila Dobson appeared in the doorway.

"Rosie, hello!" Beamed the petite curly brunette. "I haven't seen you for ages!" Her eyes travelled the length of Rosie as she leant against the doorframe. "My, don't you look lovely! Doing something special?"

"No, I…" She'd gone around in circles all morning, thinking it was a bad idea one minute then a stroke of genius the next. When it came down to it, her father would have a pink fit if he knew what she planned to do right now. Though she couldn't sit and do nothing. Surely Mr. Channing would be sympathetic to their plight. "I don't have an appointment but I was hoping Mr. Channing would be available."

Sheila moved away from the doorframe. "Sorry, Rosie, but he has influenza and I can't see him returning for a few more days."

"Oh." This was not the news she'd been hoping for. "Please send him my best wishes and that I hope he recovers soon."

"Will do. Do you want me to make an appointment?"

Sheila went to walk inside, but Rosie quickly said, "No, I was just hoping to pop in for five minutes. Get some advice."

"All right. Well, try again later this week." Sheila tilted her head to the side. "How's your dad?"

"Improving," Rosie replied. It wasn't quite a lie, but she didn't want Sheila to know that her father's progress had been slow. The last thing Rosie wanted was their financial status jeopardized even further if Mr. Channing didn't see her father or brother as fit enough to continue running the farm. "Well, I best be off. Nice seeing you, Sheila."

"You too." She headed inside to the cool darkness of the bank.

Rosie remained on the steps and turned to face the street. The two town gossips had disappeared and a handful of young mothers strolled up the street, ducking in and out of shops or standing around and chatting with friends. *Didn't people have better things to do?*

The bank manager's absence had thrown Rosie but she had to hold it together to tackle the next job on her list.

* * * *

Pushing the door of the church open, she entered the darkness and walked to the front. Her legs gave way and she sat heavily on the pew. Although her intentions for being here were good, Rosie was swamped with guilt and memories of her mother berating her for sticking her nose in other people's business. But how could it be a bad thing when she was trying to help her mother?

The door to the vestry opened and in walked Minister Robertson carrying a large bouquet of flowers. Although very new to Piri River, he'd quickly settled in and become a staunch favorite with the townsfolk. Not much older than Rosie, his youth could have been an issue but the congregation embraced it.

Not quite ready to broach the reason for her sudden appearance at the church, Rosie observed him arranging the flowers in vases, his concentration impressive. A few minutes later he straightened his back and he turned around.

"I thought I felt a presence!" He laughed.

"Sorry. I didn't want to disturb you."

"Oh, it's fine. In fact, the church ladies would be more than happy about the interruption. They don't hold back on their disapproval."

"Because you're doing the flowers?"

He nodded. "It's a passion and I am not ready to give it up."

"I can understand." She leant against the backrest. The hardwood dug into her back and she shuffled forward.

"I haven't seen you here lately," Minister Robertson said.

"I've been...busy?"

He shrugged. "Contrary to popular belief, you will not burn in hell if you don't attend church every week. I must say, though, it is nice to see you here, Rosie."

"Thank you." She pursed her lips.

"Here." He picked up a bright yellow rose and walked over to her. "A little piece of sunshine."

"Thank you." Rosie accepted it and inhaled the sweet perfume.

"So, do you have time for a cuppa?"

"I'd love to." Nerves fluttered in her belly. Just because she had a cup of tea with the minister didn't mean she had to follow through on her plan...

The minister motioned for her to follow him through to the vestry, out the door and toward the small cottage that served as the minister's home. They walked along the stepping stones and as they passed a rainbow of flowers, Minister Robertson gently touched each bush and tree. He stopped and smiled at her, his face a light shade of red. "You probably think I'm crazy."

"No," Rosie said. "Although I would like to know what you're doing."

"I'm giving thanks for these beautiful specimens of nature. It's important to stop every so often and appreciate what we have, don't you think?" He continued walking and Rosie did the same.

"I never thought of it that way." Overhead, a few wispy clouds danced across the bright blue sky, and the towering eucalypts gave off a heady scent that swirled through the warm air. This was Piri River at its finest.

The minister entered the house and she followed him into the living room. Doilies were on every conceivable surface—on tables, on chair arms, on the back of the couch...

"I'm figuring the church ladies had a hand in decorating this place."

"You are figuring right. They take it in turns to tidy and drop around meals—as if I'm not capable of doing it myself. Don't get me wrong, I appreciate what they do." He left the room to go to the kitchen.

She heard crockery being moved around while the kettle came to a steady boil. "Can I help?"

"No, no, I'm happy to do this. Take a seat and I'll be with you in a minute. I hope you like lamingtons."

"I love them!" Happy memories of lamington-making parties with her brothers danced in her mind. When they were young, Rosie, Alex, Geoffrey and Mum would have an afternoon of lamington baking, where one sibling would do the cake, the other do the icing and the other dipped the cakes in the shredded coconut. A wave of sad nostalgia washed over her and she sat heavily on the settee. Her bottom hit the hard cushions and she adjusted her position.

On the small table in front, she spotted a pile of leather-bound books, entitled *Births, Deaths and Marriages*. With her family history reaching back a few generations, she'd never thought to look at the entries but now, with them right in front of her, curiosity got the better of her.

"Minister Robertson, do you mind if I look at these books?"

"Sure, sure!" He walked in carrying a tray. "And you can call me Jack."

"Okay...Jack."

"Feel free to look through them. They're quite interesting and it's helped me learn more about the families in the area. I've barely started, though."

"Ah, yes, there's some interesting marriages of convenience that have happened in this town—mostly to do with land ownership and protecting reputations," she said.

Rosie put down the yellow rose and picked up the book on the top and opened the front page. She started sifting through, looking for the entry of her parents' marriage, which was a year before she was born. She scanned the entries for July 1920 and noticed a few familiar names of townsfolk still in the area. Her fingers travelled lightly across the heavy parchment as she admired the beautiful penmanship of the person who had taken care in recording the history of parishioners in Piri River and surrounds.

Her fingers moved slowly so it took a while to locate the entry for her parents. When she found it, she had to bring the book closer to read it properly: *Cecile Louise Beauchamp and John Rodney Stanton—21 December 1921.*

The book slipped off Rosie's lap and landed with a thud. Jack picked it up and turned to the page she'd just had open. He passed it back to her but she shook her head.

"What's wrong?"

"Read out the date of marriage for my parents, please." Her mouth felt like someone had shoved a wad of cotton wool in it.

"Cecile Louise Beauchamp and John Rodney Stanton—21 December 1921."

Rosie froze while her mind whirled in a crazy fashion. "According to this, my parents married when I was six months old."

"Surely it's a clerical error," Jack said.

"My parents always told me they were married in 1920." Rosie's voice came out sounding oddly high, and a sharp pain stabbed her throat. Standing, she said, "I need to go."

"Perhaps finish your tea, give yourself a moment," he suggested.

Rosie tried to remain calm, though the effort felt futile. "Sorry, I'm just upset. I don't know how..." Her voice trailed off.

"Please, let me drive you to wherever you want to go."

"I'll be fine. I need to walk."

"If you insist." Jack went to the front door and opened it for her. "Rosie, if you need anything, anything at all, please call or come and see me. Promise?"

She nodded, unable to speak as confusion clouded her mind.

* * * *

What would normally have been a one-hour walk took almost two. Rosie was torn between going back to the house to demand an explanation or putting the confrontation off for as long as possible. Although she'd travelled this dirt road many, many times over the years both on foot and in vehicles, everything appeared so different now. The cane that whispered in the wind, now felt like it was mocking her. The heady scent of the farms made her stomach a swirling mess of nausea. And the happy blue of the clear sky might as well have been the thunderous black sky of wet season.

As she passed Il Sunnu, she debated about whether to go in and talk with Nonna or, even better, Tomas. But this was her problem to solve—if there even was a problem. Could she have been reading too much into that entry? Surely there was a logical explanation.

Rosie took off as fast as her legs would allow. Her calves burned and her lungs screamed for air. She reached the top of the driveway and slowed her pace, her body tired from the exertion. Although, what she really needed was a chance to catch her breath and figure out how to approach this.

She stopped at the base of the stairs and looked around the house she'd grown up in. To the left was the rusting frame her father had constructed from metal offcuts that he'd turned into a swing set with ropes and old tires. Further down the hill sat the cubby house where Rosie had spent her childhood with her brothers. They'd allowed her to dress them up in their mother's old slips while the trio had tea parties with Rosie's dolls. Bless them, her brothers never questioned Rosie's demands, happily going along with her wishes.

Rosie collapsed onto the step at the base of the stairs and focused on the mountains in the distance. They'd been a constant in her life, always there, just as her parents had been. However, the discovery of this lie had shifted something inside Rosie. What else had they hidden from her?

The screen door creaked open and Rosie turned to find her mother standing in the doorway. Her hair was plastered to the side of her face and her complexion redder than usual.

"Are you all right, Mum?" Rosie asked, trying to force some normalcy before she found the courage to question.

"Yes, yes, just scrubbing the pantry, that's all. I heard a thump and came out to see what it was. You look hot, darling. Let me fix you a cool drink."

Rosie got up and followed her mother, all the while wondering how she would broach such a subject. Should she ask her mother when they were alone? Or would it be better to have both parents in the room?

She entered the kitchen and found her father propped up in a chair, sipping tea, his cheeks flushed pink. He greeted her with the lopsided smile she'd grown used to since the stroke. Her heart sank. This was the best he'd looked in a long time—did she really want to be the cause of a setback?

"Where have you been, Rosie?" Her father pushed over a plate of biscuits. She picked one up and nibbled it but quickly put it down; the usually delicious treat now tasted like cardboard.

"Rosie?" her mother said. "Your father asked where you've been."

"I...uh..." She just couldn't pretend all was fine in her world any longer.

Her mother sat on a chair, her eyes full of worry. "What's wrong, sweetheart?"

"I..." *Find courage. Say what you need to.* "I was at the vicarage having a cup of tea with Jack—"

"Does he really approve of you calling him that?" her mother asked.

"He asked me to but that's not the point." Her words came out harsh, and she wished she could tone down the attitude, however she'd already worked herself into a state. "I was waiting for Jack to make tea and he had some books on a table."

"What sort of books? Why were you at the vicarage?" asked her mother.

"Mum, please, just let me say what I need to without interruptions."

"Fine." She sat back and crossed her arms.

"I was looking in the *Birth, Deaths and Marriages* register."

Her mother and father exchanged glances. He coughed, looked down and her mother's face flushed an even brighter red.

"Why did you lie to me about your wedding date?" There. It was out.

Her father reached for his cane and struggled out of the chair. Normally, Rosie would try to help, then have her offer rejected. This time, though, she didn't offer. She didn't appreciate her father taking leave after she'd asked such an important question. He glared at Cecile. "I always thought this was a bad idea."

He hobbled toward the hallway.

"Where are you going, John?" Her mother sounded panicked.

"You should have told her years ago." He disappeared, his shuffles echoing down the hallway.

With the departure of her father, the air in the room grew heavy. Her throat felt like she'd swallowed razor blades. "Why didn't you tell me? Were you worried that I would think less of you?"

Her mother hung her head and placed her hands over her face. When she looked up, tears streamed down her cheeks. She sniffed. "I don't even know where to start."

"I just need to know the truth." Rosie kept her voice soft.

"Oh, Rosie," her mother sobbed. "You don't know the half of it."

"Then tell me." Rosie hated that her father had left her mother to do all the explaining, but that was so typical—if a situation required emotion, he'd disappear.

Her mother dabbed her eyes with the apron and said nothing. Rosie waited some more, then her patience wore thin.

"Mum, I need you to talk."

She slowly shook her head. "I had hoped this day wouldn't come."

"What do you mean?" An ominous feeling settled around her. She tried to shake it free but it wouldn't budge.

Her mother fiddled with the lid on the sugar bowl. "Your father and I lied about our marriage date because…because…" Once more, her mother gulped and fell into silence.

Rosie reached for her mother's shaking hand. "Tell me, please."

"We lied about our marriage date because John is not your natural father." The words came out fast, like her mother was afraid she'd lose her nerve. And as the impact of her statement hit Rosie, a sharp pain stabbed her in the chest. The wind felt like it had been knocked out of her.

"I don't understand." Her tongue seemed swollen. Her mouth dry.

"I hadn't planned on keeping it from you forever, I was just trying to pick the right time."

"Dad is my father," Rosie managed to get out.

"He's not your *real* father." More sniffing from her mother.

Rosie pushed the chair back from the table. The wooden legs scraped against the boards and made a horrendous sound. She didn't care.

"What...How..." Rosie's body tensed. "When did you plan on telling me? When I was fifty?"

"Rosie—"

"You're only telling me now because you're backed into a corner and even your own husband won't bail you out." The anger that overtook the shock increased twofold.

"Rosie—"

"No, Mum, it's obvious that Dad..." He was still her father, wasn't he? He'd brought her up as his own, although, at times, he'd been cold toward her. She'd always put it down to his generation of men not showing their feelings—what if it was because he regretted passing Rosie off as his daughter? She squeezed her eyes shut. *Oh please, no.* She opened her eyes and focused on her mother. "It's obvious that Dad never agreed with you keeping this a secret."

"I did it to stop you from being hurt, sweetheart. I was worried you wouldn't accept your father...John...and—"

"You're kidding, right? He's my *only* father." Rosie narrowed her eyes. "Who was it?"

"Who?"

"Who fathered me?" God, did she have to ask everything twice?

Her mother got up and stood on her tippy-toes to open the cupboard door above the stove. She grabbed a teacup and lifted the lid off the ceramic jar on the bench. Out came a small bottle of brandy.

"You don't need that, Mum."

"I do."

"No, you don't." Rosie got up and gently pried the bottle from her mother's hands. Cecile collapsed on the nearby chair.

"His name is Vincenzo Pasquale."

"An Italian?" She sucked in her breath. "Is this why my father...John... my father...hates Italians?"

"It's not as simple as that, sweetheart." The look of fear on her mother's face caused Rosie to stop for a moment. This couldn't be easy for her. Then again, it wasn't exactly a walk in the sunshine for Rosie.

"I need you to tell me everything," Rosie said evenly. "Don't leave out a single detail."

"I'm sorry." Sob. "I'm so very, very sorry you had to find out this way."

Rosie felt hollow, like all the emotion had been drained out of her. "Who is this Vincenzo person?"

Her mother concentrated on the trees outside the window. The wind had picked up and the dark sky promised rain. Wherever her mother's mind had taken her, it left a smile on her lips which only irritated Rosie more.

"Who is he?" she asked, this time with more force.

Her mother didn't look at her. "He was my first husband."

"What?" Rosie gripped the edges of the chair, hearing, but not fully registering, the weight of her mother's words. "But Dad was your first..." She didn't even know how to finish the sentence.

Cecile placed her hands flat on the kitchen table—the same kitchen table that had served as a gathering spot for the entire family. Just in front of Rosie she could see the dents from when Geoffrey had dared Alex to lay his hand flat while Geoffrey stabbed the knife between Alex's fingers, getting faster and faster. Their father had blown his stack when he'd discovered the damage and the idiocy of his sons, but now, Rosie looked at the dents with affection, missing those crazy days.

"Vincenzo worked here at Tulpil when my father—your grandfather— was running it. He'd arrived from Italy when he was seventeen and he worked so very hard to make a good life for himself. He missed his family, so we used to go for walks and I'd teach him English and he'd teach me Italian."

Just like the walk and talk I do with Tomas.

Pushing this thought aside, Rosie asked, "How old were you?"

"Seventeen, but we were friends for three years before anything romantic happened," she said, her tone defensive. "We married when I was twenty, so I was not that young."

"What did your parents say?" As the story unfolded, Rosie could sense how hard it must have been for her mother. A tiny feeling of empathy crept in then anger caused a band of pain to race around her head.

"My parents didn't approve, of course. I was the farmer's daughter and shouldn't have been cavorting with the hired help. But love is love, no matter the social standing or nationality. If a couple want to be together, then they should."

All the pieces of the jigsaw she hadn't known existed started falling into place—her father despising Italians, his strong stance against Rosie spending too much time with the workers... Was he afraid she would fall in love with one of his men and get pregnant, just like Cecile? This explained so much about his over-protectiveness.

Her mother speaking about loving another man made Rosie extremely uneasy, however she had to quash the brewing anger and get the full story to make sense of it all. She really had no choice.

"So, my grandfather objected?" Rosie pictured Pop, with his bushy gray eyebrows, balding head, and beefy arms. Growing up, he'd put the fear of God into Rosie and she could only imagine his reaction once he discovered the clandestine affair her mother had embarked upon.

"Of course, he objected. In his eyes, Vincenzo was a no-good scoundrel who barely had a penny to his name. He was so very different to the Australian men and my father had no hope in ever understanding what I saw in Vincenzo. To me, he was everything." Once again, her mother's eyes held that faraway look but she shook her head, like she was forcing herself into the present. "I'm sorry, this must be extremely difficult to hear."

"It is." Rosie shifted on the chair. "But I need to know."

Her mother pursed her lips and blinked slowly. "After we suffered the wrath of my father, I decided I couldn't take his overbearing ways anymore."

"So you got pregnant?"

"No! Of course not! I was a virgin when I got married."

"Sorry, I—"

Her mother reached for Rosie's hand. "You have nothing to be sorry about." She let go and returned to fiddling with the sugar bowl. "We eloped."

Up until now, all Rosie had seen was a woman who was deeply troubled because she couldn't get over the death of Geoffrey and she'd spent years believing the worst about Alex. *Oh god.* Rosie did a quick calculation of dates. That meant Geoffrey and Alex were her half-brothers. *Half. Brothers.* A growing feeling of illness formed at the back of her throat.

"We got married out of town, not too far from Piri River, but far enough that it took some time before my father found us."

"What happened when he did?"

Rosie imagined her mother and Vincenzo enduring Pop's rage. It wouldn't have been pretty.

"My family disowned me." She hung her head. "We moved far away and Vincenzo found work on another farm. He was so clever, Rosie. Such a wonderful mind for numbers and engineering. He could take the simplest thing and make it functional and—" She looked at Rosie. "Just like you."

Rosie stood and walked over to the bench to pour a glass of water. She didn't care that it was warm, she needed something to loosen the grip of anxiety.

"I'm sorry, sweetheart, all this is difficult to take in, I'm sure."

"It's not easy," Rosie mumbled as she took a long gulp. Vincenzo was good at numbers, just like Rosie. Was that yet another reason why her father…John…struggled to let her do the books? Because Rosie reminded him of Vincenzo and his mathematical ability?

"I realize now it's something you should have known about a long time ago, but with the war and losing Geoffrey and then thinking we'd lost Alex…" She shrugged. "Time passed and it never felt like the right moment."

"I was old enough to know about this when Geoffrey went away."

"We were all so worried about him. The world was changing. No one knew what the future held. We—"

"They're all excuses!" Rosie slammed the glass on the counter so hard that water sloshed out the sides. "This is my life we're talking about! *My life!* You can't sit there and tell me how hard it is for you when you've known this all along and led me to believe I was a Stanton."

"Of course you're a—"

"I'm not! My entire life has been a lie. What am I supposed to do with this information now?"

Rosie looked at the door that led out to the back verandah. It would be so easy to run, to get away from this horrible mess, though what good would it do? Running would not give a different outcome. She was not a Stanton. She was the daughter of an Italian immigrant.

"When did you get pregnant?"

"Not long after we were married."

Rosie needed to get the facts then find some solitude to process it all. "When did you tell Pop about me?"

Her mother picked at an imaginary piece of fluff on her skirt. "I had no backbone then. Your grandfather, bless him, was a force to be reckoned with and frankly, I was scared. Although I managed to swallow that fear and wrote a letter to let him know he had a grandchild on the way. I posted it just before…" Her eyes welled up and she blew her nose on the edge of her apron. "As expected, I heard nothing."

"Do you regret it?"

"Regret marrying Vincenzo?" She raised her eyebrows. "Absolutely not. Otherwise I wouldn't have my beautiful girl."

The sincerity in her mother's eyes told Rosie's heart this was the truth. A small wave of empathy rippled through her. For her mother to give up her family because she loved a man so deeply…

"What happened to him?" Rosie asked, her voice cracking.

Her mother took some time before answering. "He died in an accident."

A heavy, sad feeling weighed on Rosie. Had she hoped he was still alive? That they could meet? So many emotions surged through her that she could barely hold on to a thought long enough to make sense of it. In a raspy voice, she asked, "How?"

"It was such a stupid, stupid accident. The roof of the shed was falling apart and something had to be done. Vincenzo naïvely volunteered to do the work—he'd done repairs like this elsewhere without incident—yet..." She dabbed her eyes. "The owners of that farm had no sense of safety for their men and Vincenzo bore the brunt of their idiocy. They're not entirely to blame, though. My grandfather had made sure Vincenzo was blacklisted from as many farms as possible. The only ones that would take him on were ones with dubious work conditions."

Rosie remained silent, trying to take it all in. Only a short time ago she'd gone from someone with one father to two, then back to one. Irritation about the cover-up disappeared as a new ache in her heart formed—an ache to know her natural father, to hear his voice, look into his eyes, to study the shape of his face, the curve of his nose...But those would forever be wishes that could never be granted. She'd have to live the rest of her life wondering about what could have been.

"I was a widow with no money. No one would employ me, not even cleaning houses, and I was destitute. The landlord let me stay on for as long as he could, but the time came for me to leave as he couldn't give me free rent any longer." Now that the floodgates had been opened, her mother appeared desperate to get it all out.

It occurred to Rosie that her mother had suffered exactly the same circumstances as countless other women who were widowed or deserted.

"So, you returned to your family?" she asked.

"I had no choice."

"Pop accepted you?" If he'd been as furious as her mother had said, then surely it would have taken some serious convincing to let Cecile come back to Tulpil.

"Your grandfather didn't accept me at first, but your grandmother persuaded him to let me back into the family fold. I was pregnant, and honestly, I don't think he had much choice. The women in our family can be quite formidable. Well, most of them." Her mother's gaze travelled to the brandy bottle sitting on the bench.

"Fine, do it. But we will be talking about your relationship with alcohol later," said Rosie.

Cecile jumped up and quickly poured the brandy into the cup. She took a gulp, sat down at the table and cradled the cup between her hands.

She seemed to relax instantly. Her mother took one more sip then said, "I knew my parents loved me but didn't love my choices. Once your grandfather let me through the door of the family home, he and I never spoke of Vincenzo again."

"I don't understand why he objected so strongly."

"As with most elopements, it boils down to class or culture. I loved my father but he was a snob. His own family had been working class and had struck gold, literally, and had invested their riches in cane farms. These investments tripled their money and from there, their fortune increased with every season. I've always said that new money is the root of evil."

"That's a bit harsh lumping everyone together like that."

"I don't expect you to understand, but things were so different back then. And it would bring disgrace upon the family if outsiders found out that I'd run off with an Italian worker."

"How did Pop explain your absence?"

"The official word was I'd been spending time with relatives up north."

"Oh." She couldn't even fathom what it would have been like to be rejected by family. Even with all the arguments and trials that her family had been through, Rosie had never felt like she could lose them forever—until now.

"What about...me? How did they explain that?"

"There was no way I was getting out of this scot-free, so we just let people believe I was pregnant to your father before I was sent to stay with relatives. Then we married after you were born. As I'd kept the relationship with Vincenzo under wraps, it was easy to fool the sticky-noses."

"No one questioned you?"

"Not to our faces. I'm sure I was the subject of town gossip. You can't live in a place like this and not be a hot topic. People can't mind their own business. It was a small price to pay, though. At least this way you had a roof over your head, food in your belly, and a mother who wasn't on the verge of a nervous breakdown anymore. And, of course, the love of your father."

"John," Rosie said, still unsure what to call him.

"He's still your father, darling."

Although Rosie's heart wanted to reject these revelations, everything now fell into place—her love for numbers, maybe even the strange sensation she'd returned home whenever she visited the Contis. She looked out the window at the streaks of gold forcing their way through the gray clouds.

Rosie had no idea what home meant anymore.

Chapter 27

Rosie sat at the table in silence. Across from her was Cecile, deep lines etched in her forehead. Her skin appeared paler and rougher, her eyes black pools. What kind of hell had her mother gone through back then? And how did her father come into the picture?

Her mother traced Geoffrey's dents on the table and Rosie wondered if Cecile remembered how they'd got there. Releasing a deep breath, her mother said, "When I first moved back, your grandfather and John...your dad...came to an agreement."

"You had an arranged marriage?" Rosie had no idea how many more surprises she could handle. The headache that had been simmering now boiled over and she massaged her temples, willing the incessant pain to go away.

"Are you all right?" Cecile rested her hand on Rosie's arm.

She pulled away. "No, I'm not all right. Everything I know has been ripped away."

"Darling—"

She turned to face her mother. "How can you have lied all these years? You're my mother, I trusted you!"

"I never lied, I just omitted—"

"Why did Dad marry you when you were having Vincenzo's baby?" The name stuck on the edge of her tongue, like she couldn't shake it off. Would she ever get used to saying it?

"Your father and I have been friends since I was ten," continued Cecile. "We'd gone to school together, spent our holidays swimming in the river and riding bikes all over the countryside. We were good friends."

"Only friends?"

"More than friends, for a short while. Then I met Vincenzo. I fell in love with his charm and his exotic ways captivated me."

"I still don't understand why Da—John—would marry you."

Her mother placed her hands flat on the table. "Your father and I always had a special relationship—"

"Obviously not special enough because you married someone else first."

Hurt flashed in her mother's eyes. "I understand you're angry but please, let me explain."

"Fine," Rosie muttered.

"Thank you," said her mother. "I want you to know that I have always loved your father. Even more so after he married me."

Her father was a good man, but surely he had limits about marrying a pregnant woman who had rejected him.

"Your grandfather promised John he'd inherit Tulpil if we wed."

"A dowry? He was bribed to marry you and…to be…my father? Oh god." She hung her head. "I don't see how this could get any worse." Her father had always been independent so why would he accept such a proposal?

"Rosie, I promise you, it is nowhere near as bad as it sounds. Yes, my grandfather wrote John into the will, but it was to preserve my future. After all, I was their only child. Your grandfather was extremely ill at this stage—we believe it was cancer—and his time on this earth was limited. Your father had experience as a foreman and so it made sense that he take over when the time came."

"Why wouldn't he leave Tulpil to you?"

"Your grandfather was a traditionalist."

"I know someone else in this family who is like that," she said, sounding more bitter than intended. "Are you telling me you were married in return for Tulpil?"

"No, darling girl. He would have married me regardless." Her mother went to take another sip then hesitated. "I don't mean to sound conceited. I've always had a soft spot for John and I knew he loved me. And when you were born"—her lips formed a nostalgic smile—"he loved you as if you were his own."

The penny fell to the floor, spun then rolled away and fell between the crack in the floorboards.

Her body ached.

Her head wanted to explode from the relentless pounding.

Cecile's large eyes were full of concern. "Tell me what you're thinking."

Rosie stood. "I don't know what to think. I'm angry, sad, heartbroken… There are far too many emotions to name." She marched toward the back door then stopped and turned. "I should have been told this a long time ago. This is my life, my heritage, my identity. And you chose to keep it secret."

"But you've always been so happy and I didn't want to spoil it—"

"I haven't been happy for years!" Rosie tried to remain composed, though an urge to scream at the top of her lungs overcame her. "I lived in the shadow of my brothers—"

"Rosie, that is not the case."

"It is, Mum. After Geoffrey died you went downhill with alcohol and when we thought we'd lost Alex…you switched off from the world. You barely noticed me and I had to learn to live with the guilt of being the only surviving child—and a girl at that."

"Do you really think that?"

"I *know* that."

"Oh, Rosie, it wasn't like that at all!" Her mother stood and walked toward her but Rosie took a step out the door, one foot on the verandah. "I love that you're my girl. Your father does as well."

"So why did I always feel like I was never enough? How many times have I tried to get involved in the business only to get knocked back?"

"You ran the place—"

"For five minutes! Then Alex showed up." Opening the door a fraction wider, she stared at the hill where Tomas had taken her after his family's party. That little piece of land was a sanctuary. She felt a strong desire to climb up there and shut herself off for as long as it took to process everything.

She needed to breathe.

She needed to think.

She needed to adjust to her new reality.

* * * *

Rosie sat at Tomas's secret spot, hugging her knees, staring at the valley below. Up here, she had a clearer view of the valley she'd grown up in, believing she was the child of John and Cecile Stanton. She studied the river that snaked through the valley; bringing life to the sugarcane, to the people. Workers from an array of nationalities had flocked to these fields for generations, intent on earning enough money to bring out family or buy their own parcel of land and marry a local girl or an imported bride. As with all aspects of life, things rarely turned out as expected. How many shattered dreams and crushed hopes were scattered amongst the cane? How many secret love affairs, broken hearts, and betrayals littered the nourishing soil? How many friendships had been destroyed because of greed, ignorance, or addictions?

Leaning against the large rock, she closed her eyes and bathed in the orange of the setting sun. If only the land could talk. Perhaps then, she'd better understand why her grandfather behaved the way he did. If he hadn't been such a stick in the mud, maybe she'd have had a chance to meet Vincenzo because he wouldn't have died as a result of laboring for farmers with no respect for workers. Although, if all that had happened, then John wouldn't have become her father.

She got up and brushed the stones and dirt off her skirt. Rosie needed to seek out her dad and talk. Blame couldn't be thrown at him for leaving Cecile to deliver the truth, it was entirely appropriate that he'd made himself scarce as this story had to be told by her mother.

Rosie's legs gave way and she sat down with a thud. Dirt flew up around her.

Maybe she wasn't ready.

A familiar light laugh travelled up through the scrub and a moment later Tomas emerged. "Are you going or staying?"

He climbed the last few steps to where she sat and he eased down next to her. His smile dropped when he saw her face.

"You have been crying?" He placed his arm around her shoulders. She instantly relaxed against his chest, a sense of comfort and caring wrapped around her as she listened to his heart steadily beating. *Thump. Thump. Thump.* Tomas whispered into her hair, "Tell me what has made you so sad."

Rosie opened her mouth but a large, painful lump in her throat stopped her from talking.

"Take your time, dear Rosalie. I am here, waiting, when you are ready."

His compassion made her want to blurt out the whole sordid story but an array of emotions tugged her in countless directions. It left her flat, disheartened, confused. She took a deep breath and moved back slightly so she could see Tomas's beautiful face.

"Why do you care so much?" she asked.

Tomas gave a small laugh but his expression turned serious when he noticed she hadn't joined in. "You do not know why?"

She shook her head, any confidence having been ripped away.

"Ah, sweet, sweet Rosalie, I wish you knew the effect you have on people." He ran his hand lightly down the side of her face, leaving a trail of tingles across her skin. "You never stop caring and your heart is big enough for twenty people. You make me laugh. You care what I think. And"—his fingers gently brushed through her hair—"this beautiful red matches fire in your soul. Rosalie, there are so many ways you are beautiful. How could I not love you?"

"I…you…you love me?"

Tomas cupped his hand under her chin and gently tilted it upwards. "Of course I love you. I've loved you from the minute we met on that bus. Anyone can see that you're a special person, my lovely Rosalie. I would be a fool not to tell you how I feel."

She bit her lip. "You need to know something because I'm not who you think I am."

"I would say I know you very well."

"You don't know me at all, Tomas. I don't even know myself anymore."

Rosie launched into the events leading up to the confrontation with her mother, the sliding scale of emotions, the confusion that reigned. Tomas listened and asked questions while he held her hand, giving her strength to go on. She didn't leave out one detail, and as the tale unfolded Rosie came to a new realization. "No wonder I always felt like the black sheep."

"What do you mean?"

"I tried to fit in by forcing my way into the business—accounting, mechanics—but it never really gelled, even though I was good at those things. I always felt I was trying to prove myself, trying to justify my existence."

"I am sure your parents did not see it this way," Tomas said.

She lowered her head, the pain having returned to her temples. Looking up into Tomas's dark eyes, she said, "You don't seem the slightest bit surprised about what I've told you. Why is that?"

"I have not led a protected life, I—"

"I haven't been that protected." She shouldn't sound so defensive.

"I do not mean to say that you have been," he said gently. "What I want to say is that with all I have seen and done in my life it is almost impossible to surprise me. Things happen, we try to deal with it the best we can and then we move on."

Rosie raised an eyebrow. "I'm not so sure you practice what you preach."

Tomas's back stiffened and she instantly regretted her words. Her emotional turmoil was not Tomas's fault.

"I have spent much time thinking about this," he said quietly.

"And?" she encouraged.

"And you are right."

"I am?" Should she have been so shocked? She loved that their conversations may have given him a light to lead him out of the darkness.

"Yes, you are. I cannot change the past—even though I wish with all my heart that I could. I have made mistakes—so many mistakes—and I regret decisions that have caused suffering to others. I do not think I will ever lose the guilt but I need to find a way to live with it. I must remember that the decisions I made at the time were the best they could be and I never planned to hurt or damage someone. Never."

"You've come a long way. You should be proud of yourself."

"I could not have done it without you, Rosalie. You see the world in a refreshing way."

She moved toward him, her confidence returning. "I love you, too."

When their lips met, her unstable world gained a semblance of balance. She closed her eyes, lost in his warmth, his light stubble tickling her chin. His hand roamed her curves and she luxuriated in his sensuous touch, every fiber of her being alive. Without hesitation, she pulled his shirt out of his trousers and slid her hand across his chest, relishing the thrill of caressing the skin she'd yearned to touch for so long.

Tomas ran his hands along her arms; goosebumps sprouted on her skin. A feeling of overwhelming love washed over her as she pushed aside the painful revelations of the day in favor of being in the moment.

Tomas pulled away, his dark eyes staring intently in hers. "Are you sure?"

"Absolutely," she said and pulled him close. Tomas took off his jacket and lay it on the ground. A deep love shone in his eyes and she knew this was the moment to finally let herself go. To find out who she truly was. Rosie ran her hand through Tomas's hair, and whispered, "Love me. Love me now."

Chapter 28

A half-dressed Rosie nestled against Tomas, the full moon shining on their entwined bodies. Stars twinkled in the clear sky, reminding her of how large the world really was. Yet in this vast expanse, she'd somehow found the perfect man for her.

Rosie should be appalled she'd just lost her virginity, but the warm glow within told her it was absolutely the right thing. Their lovemaking had cemented their love, and their relationship had escalated to a whole new level. Unfortunately, though, the timing was atrocious.

"You think a lot." Tomas pulled her closer.

"What makes you say that?"

"I can hear the tick-tick-tick in your head." He playfully tapped her forehead. "It is very busy in there."

"I can't deny that." She sat up reluctantly and slipped on her brassiere then her blouse. Buttoning it up, she said, "I don't want to be one of those girls who cling—"

"You are not one of those girls." Tomas did up his trousers then sat and pulled on his boots. "I suspect you wish to talk about what all this means."

She nodded, a trifle embarrassed for launching into this conversation so quickly.

"It means that I have fallen for you even more, Rosalie Stanton." He left a lingering kiss on her cheek. "Why would you think any different?"

"My head is one mess of emotions right now."

"I hope this did not add to that confusion."

"Definitely not," she said. "You know…" Should she continue? "I have no idea where life is headed but the one thing I do know is that I want you by my side."

"And I will be." His lips brushed hers and once again, any sense of being off-balance righted itself.

"I probably should be getting back." She pulled on the rest of her clothes and laced her shoes.

"Stay." Tomas reached over and straightened her collar.

"I want to but I have a lot of things to deal with at home." She stopped. "Tulpil used to be the one place I felt safe and now it just…feels so foreign."

Tomas guided her hand upwards and rested it over her heart. He held it in place. "This is where home is. I have spent too long trying to figure out what home means to me and I have finally come to the realization that your home is wherever you feel love."

"Not Italy?"

"Not Italy. Not Australia. Not the moon. Here." He squeezed her hand that still lay over her heart. "This is home and I hope you have enough space for me."

"This is a very big home, you know."

"Good, because I would like to move in."

"You already have."

* * * *

Rosie sat on the steps of Il Sunnu. The fading sunlight kissed her skin and, for the first time in what felt like forever, a feeling of finally realizing who she truly was came over her. It had nothing to do with making peace with her Italian connection, although that certainly explained her pull toward Tomas and his family. It was more about her soul connecting with her past—a past she hadn't realized she possessed until a week ago. She'd been grateful Tomas had been so understanding and given her space when needed. Even Tomas's parents, Cosimo and Beatrice, had shown concern and empathy for her situation. Meeting Tomas's parents had only reinforced how wonderful his family was and highlighted the fractured mess of her own life.

When Rosie returned to Tulpil late in the evenings, her parents never quizzed her about where she'd been spending her time. Rosie hadn't deliberately set out to avoid her family, but time was what she needed and she protected it like a newborn.

The screen door creaked open and Tomas appeared, carrying a tray laden with olives, cheese, fresh crusty bread and a jug of water and ice. He set it down between them, then sat and kissed her on the forehead.

"How are you feeling?"

"Confused. Happy. Sad. Angry." She let out a small laugh. "Quite frankly, I am a mess. *Still.*"

"You are my mess and for this I am grateful." He cut a few slices of cheese then stopped to look at the knife. "This has been in my family for many generations."

"The knife?" She looked at the innocuous utensil with a weathered wooden handle and tarnished blade.

"Yes." Tomas studied the knife from different angles. "It has many stories to tell."

"How old is it?"

Tomas shrugged. "The age is not important, it's the history that means the most to me."

"That's lovely for you, Tomas." She paused. "I'm afraid for me, though, what I thought was my family history is not mine anymore."

"You are speaking of your father, John, yes?"

"Yes."

Tomas rested his hand gently on her shoulder. "Blood is not always thicker than water."

She gazed at the rolling hills in the distance, the magnificent blue-green of the trees now looked alight with the setting sun. Nature, like humans, had an amazing ability to create illusions that not only fooled the eye, but the heart.

Rosie stretched her legs in front of her. "I am actually over the moon that I have an Italian heritage. It certainly explains a lot."

Tomas stroked her hair and she closed her eyes, reveling in his tenderness.

"Thank you," she said.

"For?"

"For being here. For listening. For just..." She knelt on the step and turned to place her lips on his. Pure love rushed through her. "For just being you."

"I can only be me, just like you can only be you—and you, my sweet Rosalie, are everything I could ever hope for, and more. I..." The sound of whistling drew his attention to the entrance of Il Sunnu and she turned to find a man strolling up the driveway. His hat obscured his face and hands were shoved in his pocket, his manner giving the impression he didn't have a care in the world.

Tomas stood and placed his hands on his hips. He cursed under his breath and even though he couldn't decipher all of it, she picked up *porca miseria*, bloody hell. An expression she'd heard before. Tomas narrowed his eyes while he paced, tugging at the hair on his head.

"Tomas?"

"You need to go." He kept glancing in the direction of this person, his eyes wide, like he couldn't believe what he was seeing.

"Why?"

"You need to go. I will find you later but probably not until tomorrow."

"But—"

"I beg you, do not ask questions." His firm tone told her there was no point in arguing.

"Fine," she huffed.

Rosie's tired legs carried her down the slope toward the man.

"Good evening," he said as his short, thin frame carried him up the hill. Close up, this man had quite the interesting look: a beautifully tailored suit—not dirty working clothes—a skinny oval face, and extremely bushy eyebrows.

"*Buonasera,*" she said. The word ran off her tongue with more ease than she'd expected. Since learning about her heritage, Rosie had decided to embrace not only the culture, but the language. While Tomas was out in the fields working, Nonna had sat with Rosie and given her a crash course in the basics. Rosie was a quick study and before she knew it, she had a working knowledge of her father's native language.

Her father.

How should she refer to Vincenzo and John? One was her natural father and the other was the father who brought her up. Both had significant roles in her life and, as she traipsed down the driveway, it occurred to Rosie she was grateful to both of them. Without Vincenzo, she would never have been born, and without Cecile marrying John, her mother wouldn't have been welcomed back into the family and Cecile and Rosie could have been forced to live a life of destitution. Not everyone was as lucky as her mother, who had found a way out of single motherhood. What about all the other women who were doomed to live one day at a time, praying they could put food on the table for the children and have a roof over their head? What kind of life did those poor women and children lead?

Then it dawned on her: Rosie could help the women and children who needed safety, needed hope. No one should suffer alone. They needed to feel loved, that someone cared. *Yes.* As soon as things settled at Tulpil, she'd talk to Minister Jack. Whether it was helping these women find work or child-minding or accommodation or just an ear to listen…whatever they needed…

With a spring in her step, she reached the bottom of the hill and turned to look up at the house. Tomas and the man were deep in conversation and it was hard to tell from this distance the tone of the meeting. Although, by the way Tomas stood rigidly, hands on hips, and the man gesticulating wildly, Rosie suspected this was not going to end well. But Tomas was his own person and had his own things to deal with. Just like Rosie.

She left Il Sunnu behind and turned right, her pace picking up. Once more, her thoughts turned to Vincenzo Pasquale. Did he have a deep voice? Was it heavily accented? What was his laugh like? Did he have a good sense of humor or was he a serious soul? What was his favorite food? Did he play a musical instrument? Did he look anything like her?

People had often commented on how much Rosie looked like her mother and not one person had ever mentioned her resemblance to John. Now Rosie knew why. How hard would it have been for her father to stand by and witness other people noticing there was no visible genetic connection? He must have suffered horribly.

Her poor, poor father.

They needed to talk.

Now.

Chapter 29

Rosie found her father in his favorite outside chair. He sat in the darkness, staring over Tulpil and when he caught sight of her, a slow, sad crooked smile formed on his lips.

Climbing the stairs, she asked, "Why are you in the dark?"

"The lights attract the bugs." With great effort, he leant on the elbow of his good side and shifted to face her. "Besides, I get a better view of the stars without the glare of a man-made light."

"Fair enough." Rosie glanced at the chair beside him but opted to lean against the railing, her back to the vast expanse of the universe.

"You've been spending a lot of time away from Tulpil." His tone wasn't judgmental, just matter-of-fact.

"Yes."

"You don't want to be here?"

"It's not that I don't want…" She didn't finish the lie. "No, I don't want to be here, but I can't avoid this situation forever."

Rosie studied the scratches on the wooden boards of the verandah. How many times had her father told off Rosie and her brothers when they were kids for pushing the metal trucks along the boards? How could she have ever known back then she wasn't a proper Stanton?

"Where have you been?" he asked.

"You don't want to know."

"I can hazard a guess." His tone now held a slight edge, and she didn't appreciate it.

"Why do you hate Italians so much?" she asked, her annoyance rising. "I'm half-Italian! Do you hate me?"

"Of course, I don't—"

"It's ridiculous to hang on to hate all these years just because Mum ran off with an Italian—"

"Rosie." Her mother appeared at the screen door and she gave a small shake of her head.

"Seriously," Rosie continued, past the point of caring what her mother thought, "it's crazy to despise an entire nationality based on one event, hurtful as it was."

Her mother and father exchanged glances.

"What?" Rosie's chest constricted.

"There is something you need to know." Her father rubbed his forehead.

Surely there couldn't be more buried secrets?

The screen door banged shut as her mother stepped out and stood behind her husband. Cecile placed her hand on his shoulder and for the first time in years, Rosie witnessed affection and tenderness between her parents. He patted her hand, motioned for her to lean toward him and whispered in her ear.

"Are you sure?" Her mother stood upright.

He nodded and Cecile moved to go inside the house but paused and held the screen door open. "You know we both love you, don't you, Rosie?"

"I know." Of course she knew. If she'd had any doubt about that she wouldn't be here trying to make sense of it all.

Her mother went back inside and Rosie hoisted herself up on the railing. She hesitated for a moment, waiting for her father to tell her off yet again for balancing on the rails but this time he let it slide.

"You're right, Rosie, it is wrong to lump all Italians together, but my experience with them has been so bad that I cannot see past it."

"Because Mum went off with Vincenzo?" Rosie still couldn't get used to saying his name.

"Actually, no." Her father reached for the glass of water next to him and he managed to hold it without spilling it everywhere. He took a sip and placed it back on the side table. Despite all the drama and hurt of the past week, it was so good to see him reaching milestones, no matter how small. "After Vincenzo died and I married your mother, we had a visit from his sister."

"I have an auntie?" It hadn't even crossed her mind that she could have grandparents and uncles and aunties, even cousins. There could be a whole family out there waiting for her to get in contact with them. If they knew she existed...

"You have three Italian aunties, but this is getting us off track. One sister came out to Australia as a proxy bride just before Vincenzo died."

Even now, with the shortage of single Italian women in Australia, immigrants often married women from their village by proxy. A family member would stand in as the groom at the wedding in Italy then the bride would board a ship and arrive in Australia, sometimes meeting her husband in person for the first time. Rosie couldn't ever comprehend how scary that must have been for the proxy brides yet, sometimes, these marriages seemed to be the strongest and happiest.

"Did Mum know her?"

"They'd met. Vincenzo's sister—"

"What's her name?" asked Rosie, probably sounding too keen. But this was a whole new world opening up to her and although it had been painful, there was a sense of wonder about this other part of her life. "Did she know about me?"

"Her name is Gianna." He cleared his throat. "Rosie, it would be easier if you just let me say what I need then you can ask me all the questions you like and I'll answer them as best I can."

"All right," she said, feeling a tad guilty about her enthusiasm for the Pasquale family.

Her father rubbed his chin. "When Gianna came to visit, she was all smiles and sunshine, but she had every one of us fooled."

"You let her visit even though you were passing me off as your own child?"

A raised eyebrow reminded her to zip her lips. "She was having a hard time adjusting to her new life in Australia. Cecile felt sorry for her and let Gianna look after you every so often because you made her happy." He paused and a small smile crept on his lips. "You were such a pretty little thing. Never stopped laughing. But"—his expression turned serious once more—"it turns out we were wrong about Gianna—so very, very wrong."

The hot breeze lifted the back of Rosie's shirt and made her already overheated skin rise in temperature.

"She'd been with us a couple of weeks, telling us that her husband had gone farther north for work and she was lonely. The only other person she knew was your mother and, naturally, Cecile wanted to help out a woman who was doing it tough. Your grandfather didn't approve but by then he was too frail and had given up on ramming his opinions down everybody's throats. I guess he thought that if I didn't have a problem with Gianna staying there was no point in arguing."

Rosie nodded, conscious of not interrupting her father's flow.

"We didn't think much of it at first. Gianna was fond of taking you in the pram and being outside made you happy. Your little round face would stare up at the trees and sky even though you should have been sleeping.

All you wanted was to take in your new world." Her father said softly, "I may not have fathered you, but I have always loved you as my own."

"I know, Dad." Rosie sat on the chair beside him. She placed her hand in his. "I'm sorry I ever doubted it."

"And I'm sorry I've given you cause to question." He squeezed her fingers. "So, just like every other day, I worked while your mother rested and Gianna took you out in the pram. But one day"—his hand trembled—"you didn't return."

"What happened?" She leant forward, her hand tightly gripping his.

"We still don't know the details but I suspect she'd planned it all along. Wooed us into a false sense of security, made us trust her with you." He frowned. "I have never been so scared in my entire life. Your mother was distraught and every single person in Piri River and beyond dropped everything to find you."

"How long was I missing?"

"Five days, eighteen hours and twenty-three minutes."

"Oh." she sat back against the wicker chair.

"Turns out everything was a lie. Well, apart from being a proxy bride. When she'd arrived in Australia she was lonely but quickly had a network of Italian friends. The rest of her family, who were due to immigrate to Australia, told her that you belonged with them, that Cecile was not a fit mother and you deserved to be with a large family who would care for you."

"Gianna did as they asked?" Possibilities ran around Rosie's head of what her life could have been had Gianna successfully kidnapped her.

"She was young, heavily influenced by her family and hadn't had any luck in conceiving a child of her own," he said.

"But my name on the birth certificate would have given me away. Did they think you wouldn't come looking for me?"

"I don't know what they thought, but through Gianna's connections she managed to find helpers. I'm sure she would have figured out a way to cover your true identity."

"How did they find me?" The reality of the grave situation sank in and left a cold, hollow feeling in her stomach.

"As soon as we figured out what Gianna did, the bush telegraph went into full swing."

"Where was I?"

"Six hours north on a station outside a town so small it wouldn't even be a pinprick on a map. I'll never forget the dedication and help complete strangers gave us. They got our girl back."

She swallowed hard, trying to relieve the dryness in her mouth and throat. "I don't know what to say."

"You don't need to say a thing. You wanted to know why I despise Italians and now you do."

"They're not all the same."

"I know." He shifted on his chair. "But that family worked together so closely and they used their network—all Italians—to take you away from us."

"That could have happened regardless of nationality. It could have been an Australian family. Or Yugoslavs. Russians. Fijians. Latvians. Dad, I'm here now, there's no need to hate Italians anymore."

"I don't know, Rosie. The pain of losing you to a bunch of strangers has never left me and I will never forgive them. I just…" He rubbed his forehead. "I don't care if it makes me racist. I cannot trust Italians."

"Dad—"

"Look at the Contis taking back that land."

"It rightfully belonged to them," she said, exasperation creeping in.

"There was never any trouble when the Ellis family owned the property," he mumbled.

There was no point in dragging this out. He'd explained why and, to a point, she could see his reasoning, especially as he'd clung to this for over two decades. Maybe now the truth was out in the open, he'd eventually come around. Only time would tell.

Rosie braced herself when she asked, "What happened to the Pasquales?"

He shrugged. "I don't know. The police tried to press charges, but Gianna had run, as had her husband."

"And her parents who were supposed to come out here?"

"They never did. Your mother and I kept in contact with the detective running the case for years and he would check regularly with immigration officials."

"They could have gone under a different name."

"Possibly. I doubt we'll ever know."

Although the story about her abduction hadn't sunk in yet, Rosie couldn't help but wonder if, given the chance, she would want to meet with the family who had ripped her out of her mother's hands. A mixture of sadness, anger, longing and confusion swirled inside her.

Darkness descended once again as the half-moon rose in the sky. Low cloud cover obscured the stars while thunder rolled in the distance.

"Perhaps we should go inside." Her father reached for his walking stick and Rosie placed her hand under his elbow to help him stand.

"Thank you," she said.

"For?"

"For telling me everything and not protecting me."

"If I have learnt anything from this stroke, it's that you are not my little girl anymore, but a strong woman capable of taking on the world. I am so very grateful."

* * * *

The heat inside the metal shed was almost unbearable as Rosie worked on her arch nemesis—the tractor. She'd gotten up early to enjoy the coolest part of the day but the heat had quickly risen and her body was now covered in perspiration. Rosie didn't care, though, as today was the first time in over a week when she actually felt at peace.

Chewing on her lip, Rosie turned the spanner one more time. *Plop!* The nut that had been rusted so tightly now lay in the dust.

"Aha!" She picked it up and brought it to eye level. "I *knew* you wouldn't get the better of me!"

"Rosie..."

She turned to find Alex standing in the doorway. Sefa stood next to her brother, his head bowed.

"What's wrong?" she rasped.

"The men have walked." Alex's eyes wouldn't meet hers.

"What?" She put down the bolt and went to the shed door. Sticking her head out, she listened for the usual chatter and thump of knives hitting the thick cane.

Silence.

Spinning on her heels, she faced Alex and Sefa. "What's happened?"

Alex still didn't look at her. Sefa's eyes met hers. "They couldn't wait any longer for their money."

"So they left? Now? Right when we need them most?" The bulk of the cane had reached maturity and was ready to harvest. "We need to get them back."

"They won't return," Sefa said. "They would rather cut their losses than keep working with the possibility of never getting paid." Sefa scratched the back of his neck. "There is no shortage of work out there."

"We need to talk to Dad." Rosie started for the house. Alex called out but she couldn't decipher it because she'd broken into a run. Taking the stairs two at a time, she yanked open the screen door and clomped down the hallway toward the office. She didn't care her boots made a dusty trail, that was the least of her worries.

Rosie arrived at the office doorway and leant against it, her lungs burning. "The workers—"

"I know." He looked up from his desk.

"What are we doing about it?" Rosie willed her racing pulse to slow down but the stress only made it faster.

Her father placed his hand on a pile of papers as if he was protecting them. "I'm about to sign over a large piece of land to the Wilsons."

"What?"

"There's no choice," he said.

"I could track down the workers and talk to them. Alex isn't the best at diplomacy so maybe they'll listen to me. Sefa's still here and if I can get people like Loto back on board—"

"That's enough, Rosie." His voice was firm but gentle.

"What if Bartel shows up on another property somewhere?" She doubted it would be close to Piri River but with so many people travelling and picking up work at various farms, perhaps someone would come across Bartel.

"We cannot live in hope forever. Look, we have to face the reality that we are in a terrible mess. Nothing short of a miracle will help."

Rosie collapsed on the leather reading chair. Defeat fought to take over but she refused to let it. Something could be done, surely? "I can't believe Bartel did this to us."

Her father rested his head on his hand. He mumbled something but she couldn't make out a word of it.

She leant forward. "What did you say?"

He lifted his head and looked directly at her. "I said it was not all from the hands of Bartel. We were already on a downhill spiral, but you couldn't possibly have known from looking at the books."

"I don't understand. I went through those thoroughly. There were some gaps but you filled those in when I asked you." Rosie paused and let the conversation sink in. "Is this why you didn't want me to stay at Tulpil? Because there was a possibility you'd lose the farm and you didn't want me to get settled here?"

A single nod from her father confirmed it.

"And then you lied to me about our finances? How could I have ever worked anything out without knowing the full story?"

"I didn't lie, I just omitted the truth." He flinched when he saw her narrowed eyes. "I was embarrassed about how I'd handled the books and I should have listened to you much earlier. Now we're in a bind that could cost us our future. All because I was too pigheaded to believe I could be wrong."

Rosie could easily have fumed, instead she chose to take the path of empathy. He'd grown up in a world where women had their place and men had theirs and ne'er the twain should meet. Her parents were a product of their generation. As much as Rosie wanted to be angry and blame her father for his ridiculous beliefs, she couldn't. Just like he couldn't blame Rosie for hers.

None of this counted right now, though, because Tulpil was slipping from their grip.

Chapter 30

Rosie stood in the kitchen, staring out the windows. The bougainvillea had been trimmed and the fruit picked off the trees, but none of this made any difference to the ghostly atmosphere of Tulpil. The usual boisterous chatter of the workmen had dwindled to the odd conversation between Sefa and Alex. When she could, Rosie went into the field to help.

Rosie cut up the custard apple, wishing she wasn't part of a continuing lie—or omission as her father preferred to call it—though she could see the short-term benefit of keeping her mother in the dark. Confronting a past she'd buried for so long had taken its toll and Rosie worried that the slightest thing could send her deeper into the well of despair. Brandy fumes permanently wafted after her. And, despite their best efforts, Rosie and Alex, had been unable to find the hiding spots for alcohol.

Rosie glanced up at the clock. Two-fifteen. If she hurried, she would catch Minister Jack before he took Bible class. Last time she'd seen him, the discovery of her parents wedding dates had thrown her off her original trail: to speak to Jack about how to best help her mother through the darkness. This time, she wouldn't get waylaid. Plus, while she had Jack's attention, she could talk to him about her idea to help disadvantaged women and children. She had no doubt he'd say yes to using the church hall as a meeting place where women could share a cup of tea, make connections, and have the chance to build a village of like-minded souls.

The phone in the hallway rang and Rosie ran to answer it before it woke her mother.

"Hello?" she whispered.

"Connecting you now," said Lorraine.

"Rosie!" Kitty squealed down the line. "William's found out where Bartel is!"

"What?" The receiver almost dropped from her hand. "How? Where?"

"A few hours north of Cooktown."

Rosie slumped against the wall. "That's miles away. How did William track him down?"

"Remember Lachlan Boyd?"

"He worked with William for a while, right?" Could this truly be happening? At the eleventh hour they might finally find the man who pushed them toward financial ruin?

"That's him. Anyway, William cast the net wide, as we all did, and Lachlan called only a few minutes ago and said this man sounded very much like Bartel."

"I need to see him," she said.

"What? Are you crazy? Let the police do their work."

Her friend had good reason, but Rosie had an even better reason not to get the police involved. "If I find Bartel and, if by miracle, he has some of the money left, I can do a deal with him. We could take whatever money he has in exchange for letting him go."

"He's a criminal, Rosie…"

"He's a man with a gambling habit that drove him to do something incredibly stupid. What he did was wrong—on so many levels—but I would say the guilt he's suffered from double-crossing us has been eating away at him. He worked for us for almost a decade, for god's sake. I would like to think I have a good handle on what makes him tick."

"Leave it to the police." Kitty's firm tone felt like she'd reached down the phone and grabbed Rosie by the collar.

"I'm not leaving it to the police because if they arrest him and he still has some money, it will be tied up as evidence until he goes to trial, if it gets that far. Or he may have hidden it and won't tell the police where it is because it would incriminate him. If I find him, however, I can hold an arrest over his head if he doesn't hand back the money."

A small laugh escaped Kitty's lips. "You've come up with all this just now? You should be a detective."

"Ha! I don't know about that. Let's see how this goes."

"There's no point in begging you not to go, because I won't change your mind. Promise me you'll take someone with you? Maybe William—"

"No, he can't afford to take time off work. Besides, I don't want you left alone." Her father wouldn't cope with the trip and the emotional turmoil of seeing Bartel could set him back. And Alex needed to be around to try and figure out how they could get the workers back. "You know me, I'll figure it out."

* * * *

Rosie rapped on the door of Il Sunnu and waited for someone to answer. Short, light steps echoed down the hallway and out of the darkness arrived Nonna, her smile large, her eyes sparkling.

"Rosalie!" She opened the door and grabbed Rosie's hand, leading her straight to the kitchen and depositing Rosie on a chair. Nonna started preparing coffee. "Let me fix you something."

"*Grazie*, Nonna, but I need to find Tomas."

Nonna stopped what she was doing. "What is wrong?"

"I just need his help, but it may take him away for a day or two."

Nonna waggled her finger. "I hope you are not up to no good."

"It is entirely aboveboard." *Sort of.*

Nonna tilted her head to the side and crossed her arms. "He is finishing for the day. You will find him near the shed."

"*Grazie.*" She stood and walked toward the back door.

"Rosie." Nonna got up and clasped her hands around Rosie's. "Be careful with my boy. He is in a bad mood."

"Why?"

Nonna shrugged. "He tells me nothing."

"Thanks for the warning." She exited the house and headed straight toward the shed. Rosie took a little extra time walking through Nonna's rose garden, enjoying the rainbow of yellows, pinks, oranges and reds. The scents were divine and she wished she had enough time to stand amongst the blooms and take it all in. In the distance, she could hear the familiar thump of metal against cane and the occasional conversation of Tomas's men.

It only brought home how desperately quiet Tulpil was now.

Her boots crunched the gravel as she walked and tried to get everything straight in her head. The idea could easily sound preposterous if she didn't deliver it properly, especially if Tomas wasn't in a mood to deal with dramas outside his own family. Although in the week she'd spent at Il Sunnu, she and Tomas had grown even closer. Perhaps a visit from her might soothe his nerves.

Picking up pace, Rosie reached the shed where Tomas stood with a clipboard in hand as he took an inventory. Even from this distance, she could see his deep frown as he muttered to himself and scribbled furiously.

"Tomas," she said quietly. They had seen each other yesterday, yet it felt like a lifetime ago.

He remained focused on the clipboard, his pen digging into the paper.

"Tomas." This time a little louder.

"What?" He spun around, his expression one of annoyance.

"Hey! You don't need to bite my head off!" She should have paid more attention to Nonna's warning.

"Sorry," he mumbled then threw the clipboard onto the workbench. He walked toward her then stopped, leaving a considerable distance between them.

Taking a deep breath, she let it out slowly. "I was hoping you might be able to help me."

"Not now, Rosalie."

"But—"

"Please, not now."

"But—"

"Rosalie!" Tomas grabbed the hair at his temples. "It is not a good time to talk."

"When then?"

"I don't know." Tomas went over and picked up the clipboard, immersing himself in paperwork once more. It didn't escape Rosie that her father often did something similar.

Annoyance surged through her. Who was he to treat her like this? She deserved much better and he needed to know.

"I'm not going until you tell me what's going on."

"It's nothing." He remained hunched over the clipboard.

"It is definitely *not* nothing. I'll help in any way I can. However, I can't do that unless you talk to me." An idea struck her and she thought it was gold. "Why don't we do our walk and talk? We haven't done that this week. I miss it."

When he looked at her, his expression was apologetic, his tone soft. "Rosalie, this is not something you can help me with. No one can. It is best if you stay away from me. You have your own problems to work out and so do I."

"Does this have something to do with that man who was here?"

"It doesn't matter. None of it matters." He shook his head sadly.

"Who was he?"

"Rosalie, please. I cannot answer this."

"You can answer but you choose not to. Listen, the last two times we've seen each other you've spoken to me in a manner that is far from affectionate."

"Which is why it is best we do not see each other. I have many problems to fix and I am not nice to be around. For this, I am sorry."

"Talk to me, Tomas." She was on the verge of begging and had to stop herself.

"I have to go." Tomas hung his head and ran a hand across the back of his neck as his long strides took him toward the house.

Rosie stayed where she was, refusing to run after someone who had made it abundantly clear they were not going to talk.

Rosie went into the rose garden and inhaled deeply, hoping the sweet perfume of the roses would bring some calmness. It didn't work. She balled her fists. She didn't need the likes of Tomas Conti. She was her own person and could stand on her own two feet.

Although it would be nice to have Tomas by her side....

Nope. If Tomas chose to push her away she would go with her dignity intact and head held high.

If only the hurt would disappear.

* * * *

Unable to stand being at Tulpil and tormented by the clear view of Il Sunnu, Rosie had jumped in the ute and taken off into town to find Sergeant Gavin. It had been foolish to think she could confront Bartel and demand money, and it had been even more foolish to think Bartel would actually have anything left in the coffers. The sergeant had made a few calls and promised he'd get back to Rosie the second his people in Cooktown found Bartel. She just hoped they weren't too late.

Not ready to go home, Rosie drove toward Minister Jack's. Taking a right down the main street toward the church, Rosie noticed someone similar in stature to the man who had visited Tomas the day before.

"No way," she said under her breath as she pulled over and watched him from afar.

He stood in front of the Fitzpatrick's art deco cinema and tipped his hat at passersby, his smile wide, his dark eyes friendly. Women in pairs nodded as they passed him, then broke into laughter at whatever he said as they continued on their way.

Rosie exited the ute and shut the door. She studied him for a little longer before crossing the street and walking over to him. He tipped his hat, his smile broad. A moment later that smile faded and his eyes narrowed.

"You the girlfriend of Conti?"

How to answer that? After today's events, she had no idea.

"He's my neighbor," she finally said.

"You know he is fascist? He love the Mussolini. All his family love the Mussolini."

That was rather straight to the point.

"Mussolini died three years ago." Rosie didn't like this topic of conversation, especially given the reaction she'd received in the past when mentioning the rumors to Tomas. "Anyway, even if Tomas Conti was a Mussolini supporter—which I know he wasn't—what does this have to do with me?"

He stared at her, his eyes unblinking.

"Who are you?" she asked.

"I am someone from his past who has come to right the wrongs he has committed. He is a liar. He is a murderer and he will suffer."

Rosie's belly turned.

"He kill my sister."

"You're Rachel's brother?" Had he really tracked Tomas down all the way from Sicily? Or was he an immigrant who had managed to find Tomas through the grapevine?

"I am Bruno Abato. You know of me?"

"All I know is Rachel had a brother and Tomas has never forgiven himself for letting you down."

Bruno let out a laugh laced with cynicism. "He is of a cold heart. Tomas Conti is a traitor."

She heard his words but didn't give them any weight. "Why are you telling me this?"

"Because he ruined the life of my sister and also of me. The *famiglia* Conti are liars. Fascists. They take their money from the people of Sicily and they come here. Tomas Conti betray me. He take my future."

"Even if this were true, what am I supposed to do about it?"

"You tell the people of this town. I am new here, they not believe me but you are the daughter of a family who live here long time, no? The people, they have respect for you. They believe you. Then the Contis, they have no choice. They leave. They lose everything."

Rosie drew her lips together. "How would you know if I've been here a long time? I could have arrived last week."

"You are Rosie Stanton, no?"

"What? You've been spying on me?" The shock sent shivers down her arms. "I need to go."

Rosie spun on her heels and took a few steps, but he grabbed her arm.

"Let go!" Rosie shook free and ran. Abato was on her tail.

She picked up her pace and a moment later, she heard a set of feet gain on her. Spinning to face him, she said, "Seriously, leave me alone!"

Abato pulled a large piece of paper out of his jacket and shoved it in her face.

She should have kept running.

She should have run to Kitty's and locked herself away.

She should have done many things, but the one thing Rosie shouldn't have done was look at the photograph.

Chapter 31

Rosie's first reaction to the photo was one of disbelief. She stood on the footpath of the main street, gasping for air and staring at an image of Tomas standing with a bunch of men. They all wore black shirts—the uniform of Mussolini's militia.

The muscles across her shoulders and neck tensed. Her heart beat rapidly.

In the image, Tomas leant over a large table covered in paper as he looked directly into the camera. She couldn't work out what the insignias meant on the shirts of the men next to Tomas, but judging by how many stripes they had, they must have been ranked highly.

"I don't believe you," she said. "It has to be a fake."

"Oh no," said Bruno, "it is no falsehood."

She had to play this down because too much interest would only cause Bruno Abato to hassle her even more. "The past is the past. Australians are not interested in whether someone is a fascist."

As much as she wanted to believe her own words, she wasn't so sure how much truth was behind them. Even now, Italians suffered the barbs of people blaming them for Mussolini's actions, no matter the beliefs of the Italian in question. Ken Ridley was a classic example of someone who could not leave the past behind and preferred to create a future full of hate.

Pretending to Abato that she didn't care would at least buy her some time until she got to Tomas and asked for an explanation. Surely she should give him the benefit of the doubt. Although what the hell was Tomas doing with a bunch of Blackshirts? He didn't look under duress in the photo; in fact, he appeared relatively calm.

Turning, she made an attempt to go but halted when Bruno said, "He leave me for dead."

"Tomas would never do that."

"You think he is good man?" Bruno shoved the photo near her face. "Look! Look at Tomas Conti, a fascist with the men of Mussolini! He kill many people. Innocent people. The Tomas Conti you know is not the real man!" Bruno's voice carried down the street and the young mothers he'd been so friendly to now looked at him with displeasure. They quickly moved around the corner and out of view. "Look!"

Once again he shoved the photo in her face and, as much as she wanted to deny it, the image didn't lie.

Rosie's lungs couldn't fill with air. Tomas had told her he was a partisan. That he'd fought against a government that treated a majority of their people as second-class citizens. That he'd done what was needed in order to get the desired result. Not once did Tomas ever mention that he had swapped allegiances and sided with Mussolini. The photo, however, told an entirely different story.

* * * *

Rosie sped to Il Sunnu, her head a crazy mess. When the pristine Queenslander came into view, she slowed down and pulled to the side of the road. How on earth would she broach this subject?

There was only one way.

Turning the steering wheel, Rosie put her foot down as the ute climbed the hill leading to Il Sunnu. Inside a minute she'd parked and found herself at the front door, rapping on it anxiously.

"Rosalie!" came Nonna's voice from the darkness.

"Is Tomas here?" She shouldn't be so abrupt, but Rosie didn't have the patience for pleasantries right now.

Nonna pushed open the screen door, her large eyes staring up at Rosie. "He has gone to help the Clarks." Nonna motioned for her to come inside. "Do you want some coffee?"

"I'm sorry, I can't stay, but thank you all the same." She turned to go, then stopped and faced Nonna again. "I need to tell you something. It's about a man who visited here."

"That no good lout, Abato?" Nonna asked. Normally Rosie would have smiled at Nonna's excellent use of Australian slang but not today. Perhaps Rosie was rubbing off on Nonna as much as Nonna was rubbing off on her.

"You know him?"

"I know him, yes."

Rosie said, "This Bruno Abato is really unhappy with Tomas. He's making all kinds of threats—"

Nonna waved her hand dismissively. "Tomas will work it out. I am not worried."

"He plans to tell people, especially your workers, that you are all fascists and that Tomas was with the Blackshirts and—"

"Oh, no, no, no." A look of panic flashed across Nonna's face, but she quickly recovered and feigned nonchalance. "Abato is angry with my Tomas and he will do what he can to make his life very difficult. He will lie. He will cheat. He will do whatever it takes but we will not let him get to us. We will stand strong." Nonna's lips trembled.

"But there's a photo of Tomas with the Blackshirts—"

"Nonsense!"

Rosie jumped then regained composure. "It's true, Nonna, I saw it with my own eyes."

Nonna looked past Rosie's shoulder, as if making sure there were no extra ears nearby. Her face was stern. "When a difficulty arises, the Contis face it with boldness and courage. This Abato is like a sail—full of wind."

Rosie wasn't so convinced.

* * * *

Rosie and her father sat on the verandah, the black night marred by rolling clouds. Thunder roiled in the distance and flashes of lightning lit up the mountains. A warm breeze rustled the trees. The air felt damp, the scent metallic.

"Looks like a storm is imminent." Her father had his eyes fixed firmly on the brewing turmoil.

"It could still pass," she said, not holding out much hope. "So…"

"Bartel," he said. "Thank you for telling me. I know you had good intentions to find him but it was a crazy idea. No amount of money is worth jeopardizing your safety."

Rosie lowered her eyes, feeling like a schoolgirl being reprimanded by a teacher. "I thought…"

"I know what you thought and"—he patted her hand—"I admire your tenacity and your heart. I'm glad you let the police deal with it."

"But the money—"

"He's in custody now, so we just have to wait to find out what the full story is. Chances are he's spent every cent." Her father could easily have clung to bitterness or sadness, but instead his tone was one of resignation. "I have no idea how we are going to get all the cutting done."

"I can help."

"You have helped in so many ways, Rosie. You've taught me a lot. Your strength to take on every situation without collapsing is incredible. I am proud to call you my daughter." Hesitation ran across his face.

Warmth and affection flooded through her. "And I'm proud to call you my father."

He looked away briefly and Rosie detected he was forcing tears to stay at bay.

"You've always been my dad."

Her father rested his hand at the back of her head and he pulled her close. Rosie leant against his shoulder. "We'll get through this."

"I should have found Bartel earlier," she mumbled.

"It's not your fault. You have gone above and beyond for this family."

"It wasn't enough."

"Iced tea?" The door creaked open and her mother appeared with a large tray of glasses and jug of tea with ice and lemon. She placed it on the small table and Rosie stood to let her mother sit down. "It's all right, I'm happy to stand, darling."

"How are you feeling?" Rosie asked tentatively.

Her mother's lips managed to kick into a small smile. "I'm getting there."

For the past few days Rosie had noticed her mother seemed less dazed. Happier. Maybe…just maybe… Perhaps Rosie was being too hopeful, reading into things that possibly weren't there.

"Where's Alex?" Rosie asked.

Her mother poured tea into three glasses. "He's sound asleep on the couch—with his work clothes on."

Rosie looked at her father and they both raised their eyebrows, their lips twitching.

"Oh, you may think it's funny but I've just spent all day cleaning that living room." Her mother's tone only sounded half-annoyed. She handed a glass to Rosie, who stepped forward to take it.

"Thanks," she said.

The wind picked up dramatically and the rustle of the trees became more intense. Rosie leant against the railing and sipped tea while she gazed out at Tulpil stretching out before her. To subdivide it, even in a small way, would mean losing a piece of her family's history forever. How many years had family members toiled in these fields? How many babies had been born within these walls? How many dreams had been fulfilled and how many hopes had been dashed?

She sighed. There had to be some way to preserve Tulpil as it was. The way Tulpil should be.

"You know…" she started, but her voice trailed off when she noticed an orangey-yellow glow in the distance. The light appeared to be in the small gully that led to Il Sunnu. As she watched it, the light grew brighter and spread wider. "Oh no."

Her mother stood next to Rosie, her eyes fixed on the same light. "What is that?"

Her father coughed and Rosie helped him up. With his walking stick, he moved over to where Rosie's mother stood.

"Is that…" He narrowed his eyes. "A fire? What are those idiots doing? It's too bloody windy. And anyway, why would they start with that field?"

Her stomach churned. "Mum, call Sergeant Gavin!"

Rosie ran into the house, grabbed her keys and bolted to the ute. She could have called the Contis but by the time it took to raise the alarm by telephone she could be on their property and banging on their door. The tires spun in the gravel as she shoved the vehicle into gear and accelerated down the driveway and onto the main road. To her left, the dark fields glowed brightly as the wind pushed the flames toward the Conti's house.

Rosie sped down Tomas's driveway, arrived at the house and slammed on the brakes. She ran up the steps, yelling, "Fire! Fire!"

Tomas's father, Cosimo, was the first to answer the door. He scratched his belly, turned on the verandah light and squinted. A second later his eyes opened wide and he yelled at the top of his lungs while running toward the worker's barracks.

"What is this noise?" Nonna appeared in her nightgown, her gray hair in plaits.

"There's a fire down near the riverbank and it's spreading."

"What?" Nonna hastily donned her cardigan and boots. "You have seen Tomas?"

"Isn't he with the Clarks?"

Nonna shook her head. "No, he returned an hour ago then someone called him and he left. I thought it was you but…" Nonna clutched Rosie's arm. "What if it was Bruno Abato?"

"We'll worry about that later. Get Beatrice and go to Tulpil. The wind's blowing in the opposite direction so you'll be fine." Nonna hesitated and Rosie pointed at the car. "You need to leave. Now."

"But—"

"Just get yourselves to safety. My parents will look after you." Her father hadn't swayed in any way with his view on Italians but given the situation.... Nonna shouted into the house and a second later Tomas's mother, Beatrice, appeared.

"Please, you need to go," said Rosie.

"You come with us. This is dangerous." Nonna pleaded.

"They're going to need as many hands as possible. It's your job to get to safety."

Nonna grabbed Rosie's arm. "You must come."

"No." She stood firm. "Now please, leave."

Nonna glanced at the growing flames then hurried to the ute. Beatrice was frozen to the spot. Nonna said something and Beatrice shook her head, as if waking from a stupor. The women got in the ute and took off, the vehicle stopping and starting, the red lights of the brakes flashing on and off.

The air crackled as the smoke grew thick and the stench of burning cane and debris filled Rosie's nostrils. In the past, she'd loved that burnt caramel smell but now it brought nothing but fear. If they didn't control this fire, the Contis would lose their entire crop. There would be no way they could cut all that burnt cane and process it before the sugar disappeared. The cane would be useless and their livelihood for the season destroyed. Rosie glanced behind her. They could even lose their house.

Rosie pulled out a handkerchief and dunked it in the nearby water barrel. She placed it over her mouth and tied the corners in a knot at the back of her head. Picking up a hessian sack that had been hauled out of the shed by one of the workers, Rosie sprinted toward the fire, quick on the heels of Tomas's father and the other men. She joined them in a tight line, using the hessian sacks to contain the flames. The irrigation system pumped furiously but it couldn't contend with the raging heat.

Rosie's skin prickled and her lungs burned. She had to quell the panic that wanted to make her run. There was no way she'd leave now, no matter how dangerous it was to stay.

The dried leaves and grass only added fuel to the fire. Strong gusts lifted the burning debris and deposited it in other parts of the field, creating spot fires that meant the group had to break off and put them out before they took hold. The intense smoke stung her eyes and they watered relentlessly, but she pushed on, refusing to allow the blurred vision to stop progress. Pops and crackles surrounded them, the ground exploding in random spots. Foxes, toads, cane beetles, rabbits and snakes fled the cane, their homes destroyed by the flames. A fox brushed her leg as he bolted past, his tail singed.

The muscles in Rosie's arms ached, her chest felt like someone was sitting on it, and her skin, like it was suffocating. Her clothes clung to her body, making movement difficult. Sweat trickled into her eyes, mixing with the ashes and dust.

In the distance, a trail of headlights sped up the driveway then pulled over to the side of the road. Figures jumped out of the cars, dragging blankets, hessian bags, buckets…whatever they had handy to fight the blaze that was dangerously out of control. As the new arrivals took their place throughout the fields, Rosie recognized a few familiar faces: her brother Alex, Sefa, Loto, other workers who had left Tulpil in dispute, Sergeant Gavin, Minister Jack, Reg from the pub, Mr. O'Reilly from the service station, Stephen Channing from the bank. The townsfolk had turned up in droves and the determined look on everyone's faces told her Il Sunnu wasn't going down without a fight.

Alex drew up beside her.

"Where did all these people come from?" she shouted over the crackling and hissing.

"Dad." He smashed the hessian sack onto a spot fire.

"What?"

"He called Lorraine to get the word out. You know how fast the town grapevine is. And when he asks, people listen, right?"

"True enough." Rosie bashed the hessian against burning debris. "But why? He doesn't like the Contis."

"Doesn't matter." Alex wiped his forehead and left behind a black streak. "Dad said no farmer deserves to suffer something like this."

She managed a smile, despite the dire situation.

Alex moved away, concentrating on an area that had gotten further out of control.

A loud pop pierced her ears and sparks flew in front of her. Rosie instinctively threw her arms in front of her face and ducked. Strong hands pulled her to a standing position and she looked up to find Tomas staring down at her, one side of his face blackened.

"What are you doing here? It's not safe!" Tomas yelled over the growing inferno.

Rosie removed the handkerchief that had dried out and was now a useless barrier from the smoke.

"We are beating this bastard!" She swung her arm back then smacked the hessian hard on the ground, extinguishing the flames.

"Get out!" he boomed. "It's too dangerous!"

She looked up, about to stand her ground then noticed his left eye was swollen and completely closed. "What happened?"

"Never mind about that now." He pounded the flames with hessian.

Another pop followed by shouting made them turn around.

"Oh god." She covered her mouth with her sooty hand. "The fire's headed for the house!"

Chapter 32

1945—Salò, Italy

Tomas sat at the table in the small office and rubbed his biceps. The air had turned unusually cold for this time of the year and his thin uniform did little to combat the weather. He checked his watch again.

Forty-five minutes.

Forty-five minutes he'd been in this dank room with no windows, waiting for his contact to appear. It had taken months of stealthy maneuvering through the partisan networks, training, falsifying documents and learning codes to get to the point of finally working with Mussolini's army in the newly formed Italian Social Republic in northern Italy.

Things had moved swiftly after the Allied forces had arrived in Sicily. They'd fought the Germans valiantly, sometimes right beside the partisans, and with a country in turmoil and the Allies set to win, the monarchy had made the move to oust Mussolini. While the ink was drying on the newly decreed alliance of Italy with the Allies, the Germans helped Mussolini escape by setting him up in German-controlled northern Italy. The result: Tomas's beloved Italy was now in a civil war that had turned the streets to rivers of blood.

Tomas fiddled with the rolled-up paper containing details of the construction of half a dozen bridges further south. No amount of training had prepared him for this moment. What disturbed him most, though, was that this was only a meeting with the contact who had gotten him this position. Tomas wasn't even in the thick of it yet. How would he cope when he was amongst Mussolini's most loyal?

Soon after Rachel's death, Tomas had begun working with Spina in the noncombatant role they'd initially spoken about. Tomas's knowledge of construction was second to none, and after initially helping in Sicily, Tomas found himself moving north.

Up until going undercover, Tomas had tried to contact Abato to explain what had happened to Rachel but he'd failed every time. Abato hadn't attended his sister's funeral, which was a small, sad affair with only Tomas, his parents and Nonna present. Rachel's death had sent Abato deep into the mountains, leaving his group behind and cutting off all forms of communication. With every knock on Tomas's door and every letter that arrived, a sense of dread took over, but not once did Abato get in contact. In the darkness of the early hours when insomnia struck, Abato's last words rotated in Tomas's head on an endless, torturous spool: *If anything happens to my sister, I will hold you fully responsible. I will hunt you down. And I will kill you.*

The door creaked open and in walked a tall, thin man with a head of thick, gray hair. Tomas had only been given Valerio's name as a contact and now, while he studied this man who looked like a placid grandfather, Tomas wondered how Valerio could kill innocent people—the people he was fighting for—to keep his cover and get important information back to the partisans.

Valerio gave a curt nod. "Zini."

"Valerio," said Tomas, still not used to his new identity as Alberto Zini from Ragusa, Sicily.

"Come." He cocked his head in the direction of the door.

"I thought we were—"

"Lieutenant Bandiera wants to meet with you *now*. They're planning on moving south faster than expected. There's word the partisans are gathering more members and we need to strike before it gets out of control." Valerio peered over his glasses. "You have everything?"

Those three words meant so much more than anyone could ever know. All the training in obtaining messages and dispersing them through the networks had brought Tomas to this moment and he couldn't afford to disappoint. Once again, his past failures forced their way to the front of his mind but he pushed them into the dark recesses. He needed to be clear. Focused. Composed.

Tomas picked up the paperwork and followed Valerio down the hall and outside onto the piazza. Bright sunlight blinded Tomas for a moment and he held up his hand to shield his eyes.

"Come," Valerio said.

Tomas fell into step as they crossed the piazza and walked toward the building that had been commandeered for the republic. He put his head down, concentrating on his boots as they travelled the cobblestones. Tomas kept in step with Valerio, who held his head high. Every so often Tomas glanced up to see people going about their daily business—women with young children, old men talking with friends, shopkeepers arranging their wares—no one seemed concerned they were living in one of the most volatile regions of Italy. A German stronghold, Salò had become a prime target of the Allies. It was only a matter of time...

They rounded a corner and climbed the stairs. The Italian soldiers blocked their path and demanded Tomas's papers. Tomas handed them over, his hands steady while his insides were in turmoil. Valerio's eyes told Tomas to keep his trap shut and follow his lead. The soldier handed back the papers and cocked his head in the direction of the door. Tomas breathed a mental sigh of relief while he followed Valerio to a large room at the back of the building. When they entered, dread and regret pulled Tomas's muscles so taut a band of pain wrapped around his head. How the hell could he pull this meeting off?

* * * *

For the past week, Tomas had been working closely with the men assigned by Valerio. Nothing of note had happened so Tomas withheld sending messages because every time he did, he'd put himself, and others, at risk.

Another meeting had just finished and the men were talking amongst themselves while Tomas rolled up the maps. A moment later, a young man with a camera entered the room. The kid's wide eyes reminded him of the young Italian soldier that Abato had slaughtered. Even now, after so much time, that image would not shake itself free. That, along with memories of his grandfather's murder and Rachel's death, remained in the present, torturing Tomas in moments of silence.

"Ah!" Bandiera slapped the kid on the back. "Just in time." He turned to Valerio, Tomas and the other men. "For our leader."

"Pardon?" Tomas asked.

Valerio frowned and Tomas instantly regretted his faux pas.

Bandiera either didn't care or hadn't heard as he waved for the men to gather around the table.

"Roll out the maps," Bandiera ordered Tomas, who did as asked. The whole goal of this mission was to slip under the radar, not be part of

Mussolini's album of snapshots. Bandiera barked orders as to who would stand where and what pose they'd hold. Tomas hunched over the map, pointing, while Valerio, Bandiera and the other men took their places. Thankful he was looking down, Tomas held his pose and prayed this photo went no farther than Mussolini's office. He'd worked too hard to get to this point undetected. If a defector from the partisans identified him, Tomas might as well pull the trigger on himself.

"Up! Look up! All of you!" Bandiera demanded and Tomas had no choice.

The bulb flashed and the young photographer made a hasty exit. Shortly after, the men slowly filed out of the office. Valerio and Tomas split from the others and headed south. The cool day wrapped around him and he shivered. How long could he keep up this charade? He'd left a brokenhearted family who didn't fully understand his need to follow this path. It had hurt, keeping them in the dark, but he had to do it to protect them. All they knew was he had an important job and he'd be gone indefinitely. He missed them immensely. Missed his beloved Palermo. The Sicilian culture. The warmer climes. He missed a world that once existed in peace and he couldn't predict when peace would come again—if ever. Which is why he had to do what he was doing now—no matter the risk.

"You're doing well," Valerio said quietly as he kept his head up and looked confidently around the busy street.

"I have so many doubts. I—"

"Shhh." Valerio held out his arm, stopping Tomas's progress.

Across the street a noisy crowd chanted and waved their fists, the air thick with anger.

"What's happening?" Tomas whispered. A second later, his question was answered. A group of men in thin ragged shirts and ripped trousers were marched through the crowd by German soldiers. The onlookers jostled the prisoners and yelled abuse while the men, with hands tied behind their back, walked with their heads held high, as if they were in a parade for victors, not captives.

Tomas had heard about these lynching mobs. He'd managed to avoid them over the years but now, in a region where fascism ruled with an iron fist, he had no choice but to watch the event unfold before him. He closed his eyes briefly and said a silent prayer for the men who were walking toward certain torture that would likely end with death.

A prisoner who couldn't have been more than eighteen stumbled, almost losing balance. The soldier nearest whacked him with the butt of his gun and the prisoner collapsed on the ground. Another soldier barked orders at him to stand up but the boy was weak, barely able to lift his head.

The soldier swung his leg and landed a heavy boot into the partisan's rib cage.

Tomas forced himself to remain still, even though it tore him apart.

The prisoner didn't make a sound.

A gun was pointed at his head. With effort, the boy pushed himself to his knees, then held up his hands, his eyes wide, his body shaking.

The gunshot rang through the street.

The boy collapsed to the ground, a pool of blood staining the cobblestones.

The crowd's bloodthirsty cheer filled the freezing day. Tomas sucked in his breath.

"Oh no," he whispered.

"Shut up," Valerio said out the side of his mouth then coughed as he fiddled with the collar of his black shirt.

Clenching his fists in his pocket, Tomas took a good look at the partisans. Throughout the whole situation, none of the other men had shown a visible reaction. Was it out of necessity or because they had seen so much brutality that they'd been numbed?

The men were ordered to walk and as they grew closer, one particular captive caught Tomas's attention. He dragged his feet, as if every step was painful. His head hung low, the rip in his shirt exposing the red and purple welts on his dangerously thin rib cage. Tomas wouldn't have recognized him if it weren't for the bushy eyebrows that framed the eyes he knew so well.

Tomas dug his nails so hard into his palms, he could feel them bleed.

As if sensing Tomas's presence, the prisoner's head turned, his steps faltered. A soldier shoved him in the back and he stumbled forward.

Standing amongst a crowd of angry fascists with German and Italian Republic soldiers clutching guns at the ready, Tomas had to watch Bruno Abato march into hell and he couldn't do a thing about it.

Chapter 33

Rosie stood in one of Il Sunnu's fields, her gaze fixed on the mountains that had always felt like a custodian, protecting the residents of Piri River. The setting sun painted streaks of red and yellow across the sky and the smell of burnt cane and foliage hung in the air. Once the fires had been extinguished, everyone had set to work, not stopping until the cane had been cut and hauled away for processing before the sugar evaporated. It was long and arduous work, but it had been done quickly so the Contis stood a very good chance of making some money from the season.

From what she could gather, every able-bodied person in Piri River and surrounds had shown up to save the farm of people they didn't really know. She was thankful the townsfolk were so willing to put themselves in the face of danger to help. And, she suspected, they would do it all again if they had to.

"What are you thinking?" Tomas's lips grazed her ear.

She stepped back. "What are you doing?"

"I thought—"

"Nuh-uh. The last two times we saw each other you were rude and, quite frankly, nasty." Should she be pushing this issue right now, after all that had happened?

Tomas ran his fingers through his hair, leaving behind a trail of soot. "I should never have treated you like I did. I was just very confused and…it is no excuse. I was wrong and stupid and I am so sorry."

His sincerity shone through and her heart wanted to believe him.

"Your behavior the last time I saw you, it had to do with Abato?" she asked.

"You know about him?"

Nonna hadn't told him about Rosie's visit?

"He showed me a photo of you. In..."—her mouth felt dry, so very, very dry—"a black shirt."

Tomas squeezed his eyes shut and massaged his temples. "It is true. I was one of Mussolini's men."

She couldn't swallow and the adrenalin she'd been surviving on fell away, leaving her body an aching mess. Rosie stared at the ground, wanting to collapse in a heap, but at the same time she wished her legs were strong enough to carry her away; to remove her from a situation she couldn't fully comprehend. She didn't even know if she wanted to understand.

"Rosalie..." When Tomas touched her cheek she unwittingly flinched. "I want to explain."

She gave a short nod, her legs feeling like they were cemented into the ground. As Tomas told her the story of how he'd gotten involved and why, she studied his expression, listened intently to his tone, and watched the way he held his body. She looked for the slightest hint that lies fueled his words, but her head, and, more importantly, her heart, told her this man only spoke the truth.

When Tomas finished, he looked at her expectantly. She had no idea what to say as her mind tried to connect all the pieces together. A spy? Although she'd heard about spies during the war, she certainly never thought she'd meet—actually, fall in love with—a real one.

"In war, things...they get very complicated very quickly. Sometimes it is impossible to think things through. You must act in the moment and hope that what you do is right for your cause. For your people."

When Rosie had worked with the Australian Women's Army Service it had been in Australia, far removed from a war front. Of course, northern Queensland and the Northern Territory were under constant fear of bombings, but Australia had had it easy compared to other countries. Rosie had never lived with the dread of waking up in the middle of the night and being dragged out of the house by a group of unknown men. She'd never had to live with the fear of being thrown into prison for something as innocent as associating with, or being related to, enemies of the state.

"But why a spy? Surely that meant you would have to kill your own men."

"I didn't plan to be a spy. When I fought with the *partigiani* I could not kill. No matter how bad a war is, I could not take a life. Though there are many out there who would disagree with my view."

She needed to understand. Needed to make sense of this. She wanted so desperately to feel like she could trust Tomas with her heart once more.

"Rosalie, the photo you saw was taken when I was undercover. I did nothing directly that harmed a person, I promise you. My heart is torn by the things I saw—things I never knew humans were capable of. It still haunts me to this day."

Rosie sucked in a deep breath, her chest still hurting from the smoke and swinging the hessian sack. "Why didn't you tell me before?"

"Why bring up a past that is so very difficult to explain? Besides, since that moment I saw Abato in Salò, I have carried guilt around with me. I thought he was dead. I thought my silence had killed him."

"Did you tell Abato about it? Surely he would have understood you couldn't do anything."

"I did, but he chose not to believe me. It was easier for him to choose hate over reason," he said.

"I guess he wanted to blame someone for his sister's death. And he could cause trouble by telling everyone you were a fascist."

"With that photo, he would have done much damage, but it would have taken time. Maybe he was impatient and setting a fire gave him instant satisfaction." Tomas threw his arms wide.

"So it was deliberate?"

"Last night he called to say he wanted to talk. He apologized for his behavior and said he wanted to make things right."

"He would have been lying, you know that, don't you?"

"I wanted to believe him. We had been through so much...I thought after all this time..." Tomas let out a long breath. "My thinking was wrong. The shock of seeing him when I thought he was dead..." He shook his head. "I was relieved and surprised to see him but..."

"It's not a bad thing to try and see the good in people. Unfortunately, not everyone is capable of being a decent human being. What happened after he called you?"

"I went into Piri River but couldn't find him where he said he would be. I waited, then a young boy showed up with a note. Abato had paid him."

"What did the note say?"

"This is my translation: *To betray a friend is to betray God. Those who betray go to the fiery depths of Hell on earth.*"

"Jeez," she said. "He put a lot of thought into this. So getting you into town was a decoy?"

"Yes. To make me waste my time."

Rosie shook her head.

"When I discovered Abato's plan to delay me, I hurried home and saw the flames by the river."

"Abato was there?"

"I found him with petrol and matches, but it was too late. The fire spread very quickly."

"What did Abato do?" she asked.

He pointed at the swollen eye that had taken on various shades of black and purple. "He may be small but he is very strong."

Rosie cast her mind back to when Abato had her in a hold and the pain she'd experienced from his forcefulness.

"We fought with our fists and the flames grew bigger. He had a cane knife and used the handle to hit me on the head and I fell. When I woke up, he was gone."

Rosie grabbed his arm. "You could have died!"

The heat and smoke, let alone the flames, could easily have turned back on Tomas if the wind had changed direction. She dreaded thinking about what could have been.

"Perhaps yes, but I am still here. When I woke up there were so many people already helping." He smiled. "I hear your father organized this."

"I believe he did." She really did need to thank him later. "Do you honestly think the police will find Abato?"

"I think Bruno Abato is long gone from Piri River." Tomas gazed out at the burnt fields. "I thought I knew Abato once but I guess I never knew him at all. He was not always a bad or angry person. Circumstances in his life meant he made some terrible choices." Guilt mixed with remorse clouded Tomas's face. "I should have done something when I last saw him in Italy."

"How?" Rosie asked. "You had to keep everything secret?"

"Yes…" He breathed in slowly. When Tomas held her hand, a shiver ran up her arm. "I cannot change the past, I realize this now. I must look forward to the future. Our future."

Chapter 34

A week later Nonna stood in the dark at the edge of her rose garden, patting her red eyes with a lace handkerchief. The fire that had taken out three-quarters of the property, including half the house, had also destroyed most of Nonna's roses. A couple of bushes had miraculously escaped the licking flames and Nonna softly touched the surviving petals and leaves.

"I'll help you with a new garden." Rosie put her arm around Nonna, who leant her head against Rosie.

"*Grazie*." Nonna looked at her roses one more time, a sad smile on her lips. "They have suffered much distress but they will survive and they will grow strong."

"Just like us." Rosie squeezed Nonna's shoulder. "It's time."

"I am not ready."

"Why not?" *Oh no.* Tomas had warned Rosie this might happen.

"They do not know us. And there have been all these rumors. What if people believe them? I have spent all my time staying away, closing the door to their world. What if they do not like us?"

"They want to meet you and I promise that they will absolutely love you. Just like I do." Rosie planted an affectionate kiss on Nonna's forehead.

Rosie gestured that they go and this time Nonna moved forward, slightly hesitant. They left the half-destroyed house behind them and followed the path that led down to the shed. Strung between the trees were party lights, gently swaying in the light breeze while underneath them, Tomas's father and other musicians were setting up. A steady flow of cars snaked along the driveway and parked in a nearby field that had been cleared where the fire had ripped through. Those arriving brought platters and beer and wine, flowers and chocolates, baked goods and smiles and hugs. Every person stopped to greet Nonna, Tomas's father and mother, and Tomas, who couldn't stop beaming. He looked over at Rosie and gave her a cheeky wink.

The food was deposited on large tables just outside the shed, the Australian favorites mixing with delicacies from Italy, the Baltics, Africa, and the Pacific. The balmy night filled with friendly chatter and laughter—a stark contrast to the horrifying scenes played out on Il Sunnu not so long ago.

"This looks beautiful." Rosie's mother sidled up to her. "What a lovely idea of the Contis to thank everyone."

"They're really nice people, aren't they?" Rosie said.

Her father nodded and she placed a hand under his elbow to guide him. These days he seemed to be relying less on her strength to help him get around.

"Dad, thank you for making such a big effort to come here. I know it's taken a lot of your energy." *Physical and mental.*

"Ah, Rosie, it is my pleasure. I was wrong. Not all Italians are the same."

"Sometimes it's good to be wrong." She laughed and he did the same.

"They're actually very good eggs." Her father's gaze travelled over to where Tomas stood chatting with Alex. Every so often they broke into laughter and patted each other on the shoulder. "I'm looking forward to collaborating with the Contis. I must say"—he looked at the table groaning under the weight of booze bottles—"it was a wise choice not to start tomorrow."

Alex waved goodbye to Tomas and headed up to where Rosie stood with her parents. Alex still battled his anxiety when an innocent sound or event would bring him to his knees, but he was doing the best he could and maybe one day Alex would find the sunshine he so desperately sought.

He nudged her. "He's a nice bloke, Rosie. You've chosen well."

"Why yes, I am a lucky girl."

"Speaking of lucky…" Alex dug his hand into his back pocket and pulled out a light blue envelope with red-and-blue stripes around the edges. "I got some mail."

"From France?" Rosie grabbed it and sure enough, the missive was covered in French stamps. "What does this mean?"

She handed the letter back to her brother, who clutched it against his chest. "It means she is willing to talk about how we can reunite."

"What? What!" Rosie jumped up and down. "Are they coming here?"

Alex shrugged. "It really depends on what happens with Tulpil." He glanced at John.

"I can't make any promises," their father said, "but we are giving this our best shot. With the Contis and their men on board, we'll get this season sorted and once I pay them their share, we should be out of dire straits."

It had taken some swift negotiation on Rosie and Tomas's parts, but the deal their fathers had struck benefited everyone beautifully. With most of the men from Tulpil having already found work elsewhere, and the Conti's farm mostly harvested after the fire, it made total sense for the families to join forces. Of course, her father was reluctant at first, but with the Contis living at Tulpil while they sorted out new housing arrangements, John had gotten to know Tomas and Cosimo quite well over an incredibly short period of time. The barriers that her father had spent so many years building had toppled down brick by brick, helped greatly by Nonna's excellent cooking, especially her Sicilian apple cake.

With this change in circumstance, Stephen Channing had done some impressive string-pulling with management and given the Stantons the time they needed to get over this last hurdle and sort out their financial issues—with Rosie now firmly at the helm of the family's finances. Debts, finally, would be paid.

"Back later," said Alex as he moseyed across the way to speak to a couple of his old school friends. For the first time since arriving from France, Alex had made an effort to talk to people outside the family.

"Thank you," said her father.

"For?"

"For giving me more chances than I deserve. I know I'm an old stick in the mud who should listen to his daughter."

The ghost of Vincenzo Pasquale would always be a constant in Rosie's life and she didn't mind at all. She carried his genes, and, according to her mother, his eternal love. Rosie had enough love in her heart for two fathers and she felt so very lucky.

Her father looked over at Alex near the food table. "You bring out the best in him and he'll do well to have you working by his side."

"I'm glad he doesn't mind."

Her father shook his head. "Not in the slightest. If anything, he seems happy to have you there on the days when he's not coping so well."

"So, no luck with Bartel?" Rosie asked.

"Not two coins left to rub together. We just have to trust the legal system now."

Rosie sighed.

"We'll get through this, sweetheart." Her mother wrapped her arm around Rosie's waist and pulled her close. Rosie rested her head on her mother's and inhaled the divine scent of peppermint shampoo. It was a welcome change from brandy.

With the arrival of the Contis, Cecile had moved into hostess mode and spent all her days making sure their unexpected guests felt welcome. Nonna, Beatrice, and Cecile had taken to cooking together, teaching each other recipes from their respective homelands.

"Rosie! Rosie!" Kitty ran up, breathless. "You need to come quick!"

Kitty pushed Rosie gently in the back, urging her forward.

"Why?"

"Don't waste time with questions, just come!"

"What?" Rosie laughed.

"Look! Look!" She pointed at William, who balanced an empty bottle on his nose. On Kitty's mother's lap sat little Isabelle, her eyes wide as she threw her head back and let out a belly laugh that made her body jiggle. Her roly-poly arms and legs waved around as she took delight in her father's antics.

"It is the simple pleasures in life that we cherish the most," said Minister Jack, appearing beside Rosie.

"So very true." Rosie glanced around at the growing crowd who laughed and chatted as they mixed with each other, no matter the nationality, no matter the language. The entire population of Piri River and surrounds had turned up. With the exception of one Ken Ridley.

"Thanks to you, young Isabelle may live in a different world for women." Jack raised an eyebrow. "Are you ready?"

"Ready?"

"Your first meeting is next week. How are you feeling?"

"I'm feeling very good, as a matter of fact." She couldn't stop smiling. "Nearly all the women I spoke to this morning have said they will come along to our meeting. Nonna has been doing the same with the Italian community. Both of us have had women cry when they realized they don't need to be alone, that there are people—like me, like you, like Nonna— willing to give them the help and support they need."

Nonna handed Rosie and Jack a glass of wine each. "It is good. Medicinal. *Â saluti!*"

Rosie and Jack clinked glasses and once again, Rosie reveled in the delicious berry flavors.

"Between us," Rosie continued, "I'm pretty sure we can figure out how to start up a system so the women can take turns in child-minding while the others work or improve their maths and English skills." As soon as Rosie had put out feelers, she'd discovered one of the reasons so many women found it difficult to find work was their level of education. By teaching them the basics, they at least had a fighting chance in gaining work outside a kitchen, even in this rural community. She expected pushback from some of the males—but even though her group was small, together they were strong.

"It's a good thing you're doing," Jack said.

Rosie waved her hand, slightly embarrassed. "I only came up with the idea. Nonna's the one with the expertise."

Nonna linked arms with Rosie. "We make a good team, no?"

Despite the devastation at Il Sunnu, Nonna had insisted that she and Rosie get this new project underway. Nonna had said she needed to feel useful, and starting this support group for women was exactly what she needed. It also occurred to Rosie there was the possibility that, through the group, she might find a way to address what happened to her in Brisbane. Although she had no intention of ever returning to that office and dealing with that pig of a boss, she worried for the other women there who may suffer the same fate as her. There was no way he'd get away with doing more damage and Rosie vowed she would somehow find a way to fight it.

She looked over at the band that had just started up. Tomas walked toward Rosie, hands outstretched, his beautiful lips turned up into a very enticing smile.

"May I take this lovely lady away for a moment in time?" he asked.

Nonna gently pushed Rosie in the small of her back. "Yes, yes. We are done with talking. We should now dance. And eat! We should eat!" Nonna turned to Minister Jack. "Have you tried my famous Sicilian apple cake?"

"I do not believe I have." Minister Jack held out his arm and Nonna rested hers on his. They headed toward the tables and Nonna quickly busied herself with cutting a thick slice of cake. She placed it on a plate, along with a pile of other sweet treats while Jack laughed and happily tasted everything she offered.

"Are we standing here all of the night?" Tomas asked, the smile lines around his eyes deepening.

"No! Come on, let's go!" She grabbed his hand and pulled him toward the patch of dirt just in front of the band. The space was already crowded with couples and young children who danced to the easy rhythm of Cosimo's band.

Rosie and Tomas spun and dipped and laughed as dust swirled around their feet and music filled their ears. Out of the corner of her eye, Rosie spotted William dancing with Kitty, who had Isabelle in her arms. The sweet little bundle never stopped smiling, her eyes wide as she took in the wonder of the world around her.

"Rosie?" Tomas stopped and she realized she'd slowed down her dancing. "Is something wrong?"

"Oh no! Everything is absolutely right."

"You need a break?"

"Actually," she said, "I think I do."

They moved to the side and Tomas passed her a glass of water from the table. She took a long sip, enjoying the icy liquid.

"I have a question," she said.

Tomas raised an eyebrow.

"What did you do after…you know…the war ended. Why didn't you come to Australia with your family?"

He took a long gulp from his glass and slowly put it down on the table. "For years I fought for the freedom of my people. I sacrificed, witnessed bloodshed, lost those I loved…I gave my soul to my beloved Italy. But…" His voice cracked. "But in the end, I did not feel that she loved me back. I tried to stay. I tried to live a normal life. I worked as an engineer in Rome, but the country I knew, the people I knew, were so very different. I was different."

"You can't have war and expect things to be the same, though."

"Yes, yes, this is true. I do not know how to explain it…I just…" His frown was deep. "My heart was too broken. Maybe it was me that could not love her like I once did."

They held hands and walked past the half-burnt Queenslander. To see it close to ruins without much hope for repair saddened Rosie.

"What are you going to do about the house?" she asked.

Tomas gave a half shrug. "We are caught between restoring the past or building a new future."

They continued along the path toward the river, slowly making their way through the fire-ravaged fields. The three-quarter moon lit their path, and as they walked, she noticed something that made her stop.

She studied the tiny green leaves poking out of the blackened ground.

"Oh wow," she said, kneeling down.

Tomas joined her and studied the small plant pushing its way through the debris.

"It's a fighter," she said. "It's survived the burning fields."

"It's already won a tough battle."

She reached over and gently traced her finger along the scar under Tomas's eye. "Sometimes the biggest battles are the ones we have inside us."

He gently wrapped his fingers around hers then stood and helped her up. In the distance, music and laughter filled the air as the stars twinkled in the dark sky, framed by the ever-present mountains.

Rosie breathed in the balmy evening.

This was her land.

Where her soul belonged.

The country her heart loved.

Rosie looked up at Tomas, whose lips slowly turned up in that alluring, heart-stopping way. She had another love, and he was right in front of her.

Tomas pulled Rosie close and when he kissed her, all the jigsaw pieces of Rosie's life finally clicked together. Never again would she doubt her place amongst the burning fields.

Author's Note

The year 1948 was a period of dramatic social change all over the globe. World War II had ended in 1945, and afterward many people found adjusting to their new way of life a challenge. Women who had experienced independence working in nontraditional jobs while the men were away fighting now had to return to their traditional roles of wife or mother; newly arrived immigrants had to adapt to a country that was very foreign to them, while still coming to terms with events in their homelands, and; countless returned servicemen struggled with what we now call post-traumatic stress disorder, although it wasn't yet a known condition.

Writing *Burning Fields* gave me the opportunity to research this period of life and it is interesting to see how far, or how little in some instances, we have come. Equality, racism, and sexism are topics that are still very relevant today, and it is my hope that *Burning Fields* will spark discussion between you and your friends, book club members, work colleagues or family members...whoever has an interest in helping society find a fair and equal world for everyone.

Rosie and Nonna created their own organization to help others, and there are countless associations today that work very hard for respect, understanding and equal rights for all. For example: Amnesty International, UN Women, World Health Organization, White Ribbon, Ultraviolet, National Organisation for Women, American Civil Liberties Union, InterAction, Equality Now, ProMundo, CARE, Sonke Gender Justice, Centre for Health and Social Justice, The Gender and Development Network, Organization for Security and Co-operation in Europe, National Organization for Women (NOW), The Association of Women's Rights in Development, Object, Women's Environment and Development Organization, Fawcett Society, Outright Action International, The GREAT Initiative, Womankind, Families for Freedom, National Network for Immigrant and Refugee Rights, are some of the many wonderful organizations helping women, children and migrants. If Rosie and Tomas's story has inspired you, please get in contact with an association that appeals to you and offer your support. It will be greatly appreciated!

I hope you enjoyed reading *Burning Fields*. I love hearing from readers, so please feel free to contact me.

Thank you and happy reading!

—Alli

Website: www.allisinclair.com
Instagram: instagram.com/alli_sinclair/
Facebook: Alli Sinclair Author
Twitter: @allisinclair

Acknowledgments

Once again, I am so very blessed to work with a wonderful group of people who love stories as much as I do.

A huge thank you to the talented and magnificent team at Kensington Publishing. It's an absolute delight working with all of you. Extra special thanks to my wonderful editor, Esi Sogah, whose passion for the written word shines through in everything she does. Esi, your fabulous feedback and encouragement is always greatly appreciated and your eye for detail is amazing.

A super big thank you to the brilliant Lucienne Diver of The Knight Agency. I adore working with you and your insight, support and enthusiasm is fabulous. Thank you so much for all that you do.

A very special acknowledgment to the Yirrganydji people, especially Jeannette Singleton and Dr. George Skeene, for giving me permission to use words from their language to name Piri River and Tulpil.

Thank you so much to the Cairns Historical Society, Lisa Marcussen from the Australian Institute of Aboriginal and Torres Strait Islanders Studies, Terricita Salam from James Cook University, Cassandra L Shaw for flora and fauna expertise, Ashlyn Brady for educating me about life on a cane farm, and Nicki Edwards for her fabulous medical expertise. Thank you also to Auntie Suze and Brian for your amazing knowledge of the Cairns region and sugarcane farms, and a very big thank you to Dr Paolo Baracchi from Co.As.It and the Museo Italiano for your excellent and very helpful knowledge and access to immigration information.

Grazie to Silvana Inderberg, Paolo and Santina Valenti for your insights into Sicily and Italy and making sure my Sicilian and Italian translations were correct.

A huge thank you to Helen Boreham and her gorgeous daughter, Isabelle, who deals with anxiety and would like would people to know "you don't need to suffer in silence and the more it's talked about, the easier it becomes." Thank you, dear Isabelle, for being the inspiration behind Rosie's goddaughter and being the strong, vibrant young lady you are.

Thank you so much to all the booksellers, book bloggers, librarians, journalists and every reader who promotes authors and their books. On behalf of every author, I extend a huge thank you because without you, our stories would not be make it out in this world.

Of course, I need to thank my writing crew who think it is totally normal if I talk to myself or the characters in my head. Thank you to: Dave Sinclair, Di Curran, Nicki Edwards, Delwyn Jenkins, Heidi Noroozy, Juliet Madison, Kerri Lane, Louise Ousby, Natalie Hatch, Lisa Ireland, Rachael Johns, Supriya Savkoor, T.M. Clark, Tess Woods and Vanessa Carnevale for brainstorming and cracking the whip when needed.

A whole world of thank yous to my extended family and non-writing friends who don't mind when I'm a little distracted with my characters and plotting. This journey is so much sweeter with your unwavering support. Special thanks to Mum, Dave and my beloved Dad (missing you always) for encouraging me to follow my dreams.

Thank you to my partner Garry, my gorgeous kids Rebecca and Nicholas: you are the sunshine in my life and your laughter the sparkle. Love you so very much!

This book is dedicated to my beautiful mum, Judy. Thank you so much for your love, support and introducing me to the world of books. I wouldn't be where I am today without you.

And a special thank you to you, dear reader, for choosing to spend time with Rosie and Tomas amongst the Burning Fields.

A Reading Group Guide

Burning Fields
By Alli Sinclair

About This Guide
The suggested questions are included
to enhance your group's reading of
Alli Sinclair's *Burning Fields*.

1. The story is set in lush northern Queensland. Have you ever been there? If so, was it what you expected? If not, what do you imagine it would be like?

2. Rosie and Tomas's relationship was challenged on many levels, especially as they came from different cultures. Do you think it is easier today for couples from different cultures to be together? If so, in what way? If no, why not?

3. Although this story is set around seventy years ago, many topics covered are still relevant all over the world today. What do you think has or hasn't changed in terms of women's rights? The treatment of immigrants?

4. There are lots of organizations out there working for equality for women and immigrants. Are there any you are affiliated with or would like to know more about? Which ones?

5. Life on the land has always been a challenge. Many farms these days are struggling to keep afloat. Do you think it is much different to what Rosie and her family were experiencing? In what way?

6. Rosie's desire for equal rights for women and immigrants was ahead of its time. What moments in history can you recall where someone has challenged the "normal" way of doing things and tried to create equality for others?

Meet the Author

Alli Sinclair is a multi-award-winning author of books that combine travel, mystery, and romance. An adventurer at heart, she has climbed some of the world's highest mountains and immersed herself in an array of exotic destinations, cultures, and languages. Alli's stories capture the romance and thrill of exploring new destinations and cultures that also take readers on a journey of discovery. Alli volunteers as an author role model with Books in Homes, promoting literacy and reading amongst young Australians.

Visit her at www.allisinclair.com.

CPSIA information can be obtained
at www.ICGtesting.com
Printed in the USA
LVHW092229151120
671787LV00042B/613

9 781516 109173